BOULEVARD OF CONFUSION

SPIES OF THE CIVIL WAR ~ BOOK 2

SANDRA MERVILLE HART

WILD HEART
BOOKS

Cover design by: Carpe Librum Book Design

Author is represented by Hartline Literary Agency

ISBN-13: 978-1-942265-58-0

PRAISE FOR BOULEVARD OF CONFUSION

Civil War romances weren't on my list of books to read until I picked up Sandra Merville Hart's captivating debut novella, *A Stranger on my Land.* I read her entire first series and now look forward to each new release.

Boulevard of Confusion, the second book in Hart's Spies of the Civil War series, is a compelling read. In 1862, as the Union army closes in on Richmond, Washington City resident, Beatrice Swanson, struggles with her role in her father's covert mission and the pounding of her heart in the presence of Confederate businessman Jay Nickson. Would information she could glean from him to help the Union be worth jeopardizing the perfect union her heart had always longed for?

Hart's skillful and poignant portrayal of this tumultuous time in our nation will steal your emotions and renew your appreciation for the brave men who left their life's blood in the soil of American history and for the courageous women who risked their lives for them.

— STARR AYERS, AWARD-WINNING HISTORICAL ROMANCE AUTHOR OF *FOR THE LOVE OF EMMA* AND *EMMA'S QUEST*

Sandra Merville Hart's, *Boulevard of Confusion,* the second book in her Spies of the Civil War series, took me straight into the minds and hearts of ancestors who dealt with the same issues all those years ago. Set in the city where my great-grandfather breathed his last, this book had a personal appeal to me. From the parlors of the genteel South to the battlefields outside major cities; from a hospital filled with wounded Confederate soldiers tended to by ladies from the Union, this one was a page-turner. Historical accuracy is a hallmark of Sandra's work we've come to expect. Throw in spies from both sides of the war and a budding romance and this book has it all. Highly recommended.

— **DEBRA DUPREE WILLIAMS, AWARD-WINNING AUTHOR OF *GRAVE CONSEQUENCES*, A CHARLOTTE GRAVES MYSTERY**

Testing of friendships and family ties is authentically portrayed in Sandra Merville Hart's *Boulevard of Confusion,* where readers feel the strain of choosing loyalties during the Civil War. Told in a sweet and gentle style, the grim realities of wartime still come through, as readers are carried from parlor to riverside, and from the city streets of wartime Richmond to a field hospital on the fringes of battle. I greatly enjoyed this well-researched story where intrigue meets romance, and suspicion finds root in even the closest relationships—while love still abounds.

— **NAOMI MUSCH, AUTHOR OF *SEASON OF MY ENEMY* AND *SONG FOR THE HUNTER***

Lovingly dedicated to Donna and Barb,
The world's best sisters
Were God's gifts to me.

"Above all, love each other deeply, because love covers over a multitude of sins."

— 1 PETER 4:8 (NIV)

CHAPTER 1

WASHINGTON CITY
FEBRUARY 7, 1862

"My Aunt Trudy has invited us to make a prolonged stay with her." Beatrice Swanson held the letter closer to the gaslight lamp in the elegant parlor decorated in shades of mauve and blue. She scanned it again before glancing at her cousin, who sat on a cushioned chair adjacent to hers. "Meg, you remember her, don't you? Gertrude Weston?"

"I'm not likely to forget such a loving, gracious woman." Meg Brooks glanced up from her knitting. "Don't you remember when your mother and my mother took all of us girls to Richmond? We stayed at her home for the better part of the summer."

"That's right. I was nine." Memories of picnics, boat rides on the James River, and lazy days spent at Uncle Isaac's plantation increased Bea's nostalgia for carefree days. Nothing like these days, when one never escaped war news.

"I turned sixteen that summer." Pink tinged Meg's cheeks. "I was courted for the first time there. It's difficult to believe that ten years have passed."

"It wasn't Thomas?"

"Gracious, no." Meg's eyes brightened and then dimmed like the waning moon outside. "I didn't meet Thomas for another year. Mother always fretted that our six-month courtship wasn't long enough, yet time has proved otherwise. We were married almost seven years."

"He was a good man." Beatrice touched her cousin's shoulder, blinking back her own tears at the sadness in Meg's eyes. The widow had finally spoken of her beloved husband, gone nearly two years. Surely that was a good sign that healing had begun.

"The best." Meg straightened her shoulders, and Beatrice's hand fell away. "This isn't her first invitation to you and Annie."

"You are also included."

"That's very kind." Meg's fingers rubbed across the blue yarn soon to be a blanket.

A log crackled, shooting a spark onto the hearth. "Everyone receives a warm welcome at my aunt's home."

"I need a change of scenery, but do you think your father will agree to us traveling to Virginia while the war rages?"

"It's a short trip, only about a hundred miles." Bea gave her a playful grin. "Why would he hesitate?"

"The war."

Bea dropped the letter on the wood table beside the lamp. The Army of Potomac was in Virginia, with her own brother-in-law camped at Minor's Hill as part of General Morrell's Brigade. "I wish John and Annie had waited until we were all back in Washington City to marry last month."

"The uncertainty of when John will march South…they made the best of a tough situation." Setting her knitting on the chair beside her, Meg knotted her hands. "Especially since we were all in Boston for his father's funeral. Who knows when both sides of the family will be together again?"

"I suppose." Poor Annie hadn't even had her wedding dress. The seamstress had labored over the gown for three weeks, and it still hung upstairs. The pink dress Bea had planned to wear was equally unused, but she could wear it to a party, at least. Those disappointments had paled in comparison to her brother's absence. He was being held at Fort Warren as a prisoner of war. He hadn't been able to see his sister married to his best friend.

Meg weaved her fingers into the sweep of auburn curls gathered with combs. "At least Will has since been exchanged."

"That's another thing that bothers me." Beatrice ambled to the massive first-floor window and pushed aside the curtain to stare into the darkness. Blond ringlets brushing against her shoulders reflected in the glass against the night. "We barely spent three hours with Will at Fort Monroe before the Flag of Truce boat whisked him away."

With a long sigh, Meg joined her at the window. "Two days ago. Just think. He may be holding his daughter for the first time as we speak."

"A comforting thought." Bea's heart lightened at the possibility. "Hannah will be two months old tomorrow. I'm eager to meet my sweet niece. Father decided that North Carolina is too far away to travel until things settle. Our disappointment at this delay is one reason I believe Father will agree to our Richmond trip."

The door opened, and Annie slipped inside. "Are you discussing the invitation?" She joined them at the window.

Beatrice nodded.

"You've been out of sorts for weeks. Maybe a trip will do you good, but I don't know that Father..." Annie looked around the room. "He's not home from the bank yet?"

Bea glanced at the mantle clock. "No, and it's after eight.

Perhaps our trip to Fort Monroe this week left him behind on tasks."

"He works too hard." Annie sighed.

"He always has." Bea rested her forehead on the cold pane. "Meg will accompany us if Father gives his consent."

"You will?" Annie's face brightened. "That makes me happier in my decision to remain here. For now."

"Why?" Beatrice stepped back. She had depended on her sister's cooperation to insure their father's agreement.

"Because John may be able to visit a day or two before he marches out. I can't miss the opportunity to see him."

Meg inclined her head. "Any news?"

"Nothing official, though he expects they'll leave when the weather warms." She turned to the darkness of the window. "I miss him already."

"I agree it's best you stay." Meg touched her arm. "Those are difficult circumstances." She turned to Bea. "When do you want to go?"

"There's an Inauguration for Confederate President Jefferson Davis later this month. I'd like to be there. I attended President Lincoln's Inauguration last year."

Annie stared at her. Meg raised her eyebrows.

"Our brother fights for the Confederacy, Annie. No matter our loyalties, it seems like a historic event."

Meg placed another log on the fire. "Is that why you want to go to Virginia?"

"No." Beatrice scarcely understood her reasons. "I simply feel that I must go. Aunt Trudy's spirits are low. She needs the comfort of family."

Annie's shoulders drooped.

Bea gripped her sister's wrist. "She'll understand why you remain at home."

"We must obtain passes." Meg poked at the burning logs.

"Traveling won't be as easy as it was before the hostilities began."

"Father will help us." Bea's confidence in her father, a wealthy banker with many connections, was complete. First, she must convince him to allow her and Meg to travel to Richmond for an extended visit.

Meg and Annie had gone to bed when Beatrice heard a noise in the hall. "Father? Is that you?" She left the parlor and peered down the hall dimly lit with lanterns hung sporadically on the walls.

"Bea?" Hiram Swanson's slow stride brought him into view. "I thought you'd be asleep."

"I can't sleep." She reached up to kiss his cheek. "Have you eaten?"

"I had supper with a business acquaintance at the Willard Hotel." He peered behind him. "I came through the back door, wondering if Rebecca had any cookies or pie lying about."

"You and your sweet tooth." Beatrice laughed. "She left you a bowl of cherry cobbler. I'll fetch it. Do you want lemonade with it?"

"I suppose the coffee, if there is any left, is as cold as the night."

"Quite likely." Though Beatrice didn't share his love of the beverage, she wished she knew how to prepare it. "Water, then? Or milk?"

"Water, please."

"Sir, may I take your coat?"

Beatrice swung around. She should have known their gray-haired butler hadn't retired with his wife to their cottage in the woods behind the mansion. Irving Grant took pride in giving excellent service to her family. As long as her father was out, he'd watch for him.

"Yes, thank you, Irving." After shrugging off his coat, Hiram gave it and his hat to his butler. "Up rather late, aren't you?"

"Yes, sir. Is there anything you require tonight?"

Hiram waved him off. "Go on home. I'll see you in the morning."

"Very good, then, sir. Good night, Mr. Swanson, Miss Beatrice."

"I'll bring your cobbler into the parlor, where the fire's still going. I pushed two chairs closer to the fireplace to warm you."

"Ah. Was ever a man more blessed in his children than I?" A twinkle lit his weary eyes.

"Not likely." She laughed, teasing him. "I'll be right back." Despite his sleepy demeanor, she decided as she hurried down the shadowed hallway to make her request tonight. His exhaustion might incline him to agree.

He was lounging against the cushioned back of an armchair when Beatrice set the cobbler, linen napkin, spoon, and a tumbler of cold water on the round table beside him. "This smells delicious…and it tastes as good as it smells. You'd never know it's made using canned cherries."

"Except that it's February." His eyes gleamed at the first bite. "Tell me what's on your mind."

She traced an intricate leaf pattern carved into the chair arm. "Does anything have to be on my mind for me to wait up for you?"

He chuckled. "It's long been your custom to wait up for me when you're troubled about something rather than allow a matter to wait for the morrow."

"Perhaps you're right." She laughed a little at this tendency in herself. "A letter arrived from Aunt Trudy today."

"Did it now?" He shoveled in another bite as if starved.

"Yes, the fighting has upset her. She has invited Annie, Meg, and me to come for an extended visit. She thought President Jefferson's upcoming inauguration would sway us."

"She wants you so soon? That's only a couple of weeks away. What's the rush?"

"To be fair, all her recent letters have hinted at our coming. She wants to meet Annie's new husband, though she understands it's not possible." Beatrice clasped her hands together. "She's lonely since Uncle Parker passed."

"He's been gone twenty years." He set down his empty bowl on a side table. "You'll have to do better than that to convince me."

"She *is* lonely... and perhaps nervous about the fighting. But I guess I want to go as much for myself as for her." Blue flames engulfed the burning logs. "I'm restless. Longing for my Southern family. Will's captivity depressed my spirits to such an extent that only a prolonged visit with him would have eased it."

"Scarcely three hours." Hiram rubbed his hands over his face, rough whiskers making a sandpaper noise, his early morning clean-shaven skin a distant memory. "Not nearly enough for a father starved for his son's company either."

"I know." She spoke softly. Her father was a strong, confident man, yet Will's captivity weighed on him. Stripes of gray hair had thickened in his brown mane the past year. She breathed a silent prayer of gratitude that the heartache of Will's imprisonment was behind them. "Annie refuses to leave Washington City for fear she'll miss an unplanned visit from John."

He shook his head. "A vain hope, I'm afraid. After the extended leave last fall and the two weeks to bury his father, I'm afraid it'll be some time before the Union sets him loose for any length of time."

"At least they had enough time for a quick wedding."

"Not the grand affair I'd planned for my sweet daughter." His shoulders slumped. "But best under the circumstances."

"True." Neither had it been the day she'd dreamed for her

adored sister, yet Annie had been a radiant bride for her groom, who'd had eyes only for her. Would anyone ever feel that way about Bea? Of her many beaus, none touched her heart the way John had her sister's. Bea resolved to wait for such a love.

"As to traveling to Richmond"—Hiram shook his head—"I can't leave the bank for weeks."

"Are we still losing customers, Father?" She searched his wary expression. Annie had explained that some customers had withdrawn their money last year to move South.

"No. For months I feared the loss of great numbers of our customers, but that time seems to have passed." He raised open palms heavenward. "We weathered the storm."

"Good news." Tension eased from her back. Except for wedding preparations, the family had continued to be frugal. Perhaps it made a difference. "Please don't think you need accompany Meg and me to Virginia."

"Troops from both sides are camped in that state." Hiram contemplated the dying flames. "I fear more battles will be fought there."

"As the capital, surely Richmond is the safest place in the Confederacy."

"Agreed." He rubbed the back of his neck until it turned red. "Normally, I would not consider it."

"Meg will be with me." Bea caught her breath, sensing that he was wavering.

"A competent and reliable companion indeed." His fingers thudded against the wooden chair arm.

"Please, Father. I'd experience a special moment in history, especially if the South wins."

His head jerked toward her. "Do you feel that's possible?"

Bea's eyes widened. "I think it's unlikely." Will, her courageous brother, had fought for the Confederacy before his capture and planned to rejoin after seeing his family. Her daily prayers always included a plea for his safety. "Yet certainly, it's possible. I cannot wish defeat upon Will. Nor do I desire the Union to lose."

"That was my dilemma." His fingertips pressed together until they turned white.

"*Was* your dilemma?" Her body tensed. "What do you mean?"

"Will's captivity in a Northern prison altered my thinking. I can't, in good conscience, stand in opposition to my only son."

Her heart skipped a beat. Did he mean…?

"I was born and raised near Richmond. I love Virginia. Still consider it my home. Thanks to your mother's compassionate nature, I cannot abide slavery." Hiram shook his head. "Will agrees. He isn't fighting to preserve it. No, your brother fights to protect his home from an invading army. I can't fault him for that."

Beatrice gasped. "I thought…I—" Her heroic father teetered on the pedestal that she'd placed him on as a child.

"That I was for the Union?"

She managed a nod beyond the chaos in her heart.

"I was, though I did my best to help your mother's old friend, Widow Greenhow, when she asked for it. Nothing much. Information about troops, fortifications, weaponry, and the like, information that seemed public knowledge. Certainly, I considered everything I told her as already known to Confederate generals. I gave it for a time and then stopped, fearing repercussions on the bank and my daughters."

Which mattered most, the bank or his family? Ice formed in her stomach. Her father had provided information to Rose Greenhow before she was arrested as a Confederate spy? Did that make *him* a spy? She covered her mouth with both hands to keep from gasping.

"Never fear. You ascertained my loyalty correctly last summer."

"What about all those late meetings? Times when you left and didn't explain where you were going?"

"Ah, yes." A sheen of sweat dotted his forehead. "I walked a fine line with my customers who support the Confederacy. When they came to me for reassurance, I had to provide it or risk losing their deposits in our bank."

The room spun. "You mean—"

"I allowed them to believe my loyalty is with our Southern neighbors." Hiram lifted his chin. "Just as I allowed my staunch support for the Union to shine when speaking with Northern loyalists."

She stared at a rose pattern on the rug. "That's why you gave the appearance of helping Mrs. Greenhow."

"Just so. She was a former bank customer. And your mother's friend." He ran a finger under his collar. "It was a dangerous undertaking, one that threatened to embroil our family in scandal. In my estimation, the only thing that saved us was that I never wrote any information down for Rose. All was given in a quick, hushed conversation. I left no evidence."

Little things took on new meaning. Father had often seen the widow to the door when she left. Fear gripped Bea. Might her father be arrested if his help became public knowledge, especially since the widow was still in prison?

"As I said," Father continued, "back then I supported the Union. Recent circumstances altered my thinking." He leaned forward. "You told me earlier that Will's capture and exchange left you feeling restless, unsettled. Did you expect a protective father to feel differently?"

Shock silenced her. They lived in the North. Had done so all her life. What did this change? "Does Annie know?"

"No." Hiram straightened his shoulders. "Your sister is loyal to the Union. Her husband was recently promoted to second lieutenant in the Union army. As much as she loves him, I doubt she'd have married him if he supported the South."

"Annie's loyalty has never wavered," she whispered.

"I respect her devotion but can no longer share it." He placed a firm hand on Bea's arm. "She must never know."

Beatrice covered her face to block out his agonized expression.

"Keep my secret so that we'll remain close after the fighting ends." Hiram's hand fell away. "War has a way of dividing family. Friends. I'm determined it won't separate my family by anything more than miles."

"Annie felt betrayed that Will fought for the Confederacy." Her hands bunched the folds of her wool dress into tight fists. She forced her fingers to relax in her lap. "I never did."

"Nor did I." Standing, he propped his arm on the fireplace mantle next to the clock.

After eleven already. Her chaotic thoughts caused her head to ache.

"Will you keep my secret? From Annie, John, Meg. Everyone up here?"

Bea wished he had never burdened her with knowledge in the first place. It must weigh on him as well. "I will." To cause further division in the family was out of the question. "Rely on it."

"Excellent." He pressed his palm to his forehead. "About Richmond. You still want to go?"

"Of course." Her father's revelations had so jolted her that she'd almost forgotten her original request.

"I can obtain the necessary passes. No need to worry on that account." Low flames swayed as he paced in front of the fireplace. "I'm giving my consent on two conditions."

"Yes?" Hope swelled like a bubble.

"First, Meg goes with you. When she returns to Washington City, you are to come with her."

"I will." She couldn't restrain her smile. "And the second?"

Father halted in front of the fire. "Your Uncle Isaac has written me. We haven't been close for many years." His back stiffened. "Your mother explained to you children how crushed I felt not to inherit a portion of the plantation as my father told me to expect. I'd always wondered why he…" He shook his head. "As I started to explain, Isaac has written of conditions in Richmond. He's asked for my aid." He turned on his heel to face her. "I've decided to comply with his request. You'll help."

The brothers hadn't been close for years. Mystified, she inclined her head.

"I'm sending money for the Confederate government. You'll hide it among your clothing and smuggle it to Richmond in my place."

CHAPTER 2

"Jay, Trudy Weston has invited us to dine with her after church services tomorrow." Mary Nickson glanced up from her needlepoint in the comfortable parlor. Lamps perched on end tables on either side of her armchair cast adequate light on the white linen fabric.

"Glad I'm off tomorrow." Jay Nickson set his newspaper aside to talk with his mother. After a full day at Tredegar Works and then drilling in late afternoon for its battalion, he wasn't certain he wanted to know the latest war news anyway. "A visit with Aunt Trudy will be like a tonic for me."

"You work too hard."

"No more than anyone else at the ironworks." He laid his head back against the high-backed cushioned chair. Pink—his mother's choice, purchased after his father's untimely death. "Our foundries are running seven days a week because the army needs the cannon and ammunition we produce."

"I suppose it's good your father taught you so many of his skills before he died." Mama sighed.

"Papa's training is the reason I have a foreman's job." He reached across the table separating them to touch her arm. They both missed his father's steady insight and wisdom. "My pay isn't at his level, yet we live in a comfortable home and there's no danger of starving."

"Don't be so certain. Food prices have risen since Fort Sumter fell into our hands." Trembling hands set her sampler aside. "I still wish you hadn't given Nolan's whole family their freedom papers."

"That was three years ago, Mama." Jay tamped down his rising frustration. They'd had this conversation many times since he'd reached his majority. Though, in fairness, his family had lost a difficult amount of money because he freed their enslaved workers, his father had left them in good standing in other ways. Finances seemed to weigh heavier on his mother since the war started. "I've seen too much to feel good about slavery. I wish the law didn't prevent me hiring the whole family afterward."

"Nobody makes better coffee than Corinna did."

"Agreed. I was sorry to see Nolan's whole family leave Richmond, but the law demanded it."

"We lost all that money." Mama picked up a teacup from the table beside her, jostling it so that tea splashed on her sleeve.

"Nolan didn't get any of that money Papa paid." Jay gentled his tone. His parents had grown up with enslaved folks in their households. "He's in a better position now. Esther and her daughters take good care of us."

"We pay them."

"Of course we do." He reasoned that Mama's grumbles on the matter were based on fears of what the war might bring. "The Bible says that a 'laborer is worthy of his reward.'"

"Don't quote Scriptures to me, son. Plenty of pastors agree with me."

Jay scratched his head. Nothing was to be gained by upsetting his mother further. After a short silence, he threw another log on the fire. "How is Aunt Trudy? I haven't seen her for two weeks." Not that the woman was his aunt but his mother's dearest friend. She'd insisted as long as Jay could remember that he call her Aunt Trudy. That she was no relation to him made little difference. He loved the older woman. "Have I ever mentioned that you have impeccable taste in friends?"

"I do at that." A smile tugged at her lips. "She may have news."

He didn't doubt it. Seemed there was news everywhere these days. "What is it?"

"The information is hers to tell." Mama picked up her fabric.

His mother enjoyed sharing gossip. It was unlike her to keep silent about anything, especially these days. "Well, I suppose I must wait until after church tomorrow to discover it."

Eyes on her fabric, her smile broadened. "That you will."

~

First her brother. Now her father. Beatrice bent over her petticoat. With a heart as heavy as the gold coins her father had given her that evening, she finished the second lining. She'd retired earlier on this Saturday evening than was her custom to start sewing individual pockets within the linen lining for each coin.

Chaotic thoughts swirled, making it difficult to concentrate on the task.

To be sitting in a Northern city—in fact, the *capital* of the North—and planning to smuggle money to benefit the Confederacy was a betrayal in itself. Certainly, her heart had been as torn as her nation to learn of her brother's choice to serve in the Seventeenth North Carolina regiment. She'd felt more sympathy to the plight of her Southern relatives after his decision.

It was within President Lincoln's power to end the bloodshed by withdrawing his troops. That was her prayer.

If citizens in Southern states wanted to leave the Union to begin their own country, why not allow it? Why must so many young men die on battlefields? Citizens fought against their own countrymen. Was keeping the Union worth the cost?

Stitches around the first coin were complete. She held up the fabric. Shook it. No rattling, though the coin sank against the thread. One row of stitches wouldn't hold it in place. Reinforcing it with a second row fixed the problem. It also added another five minutes to the task for each coin.

An added burden. Everything seemed more difficult now, including travel. The Union had taken control of Virginia's Fort Monroe, where she and her family had bid Will a tearful farewell earlier this week. They'd shown their passes at various points. No doubt it would be the same on the way to Richmond.

A knock sounded on the door. "Bea? Are you up for company?"

Annie.

Gold coins were scattered across the chaise where Beatrice worked. "One moment." Shaking hands gathered them into the linen bag her father had given her. Clinking noises as they rubbed together caused her to cringe. Where to hide them? Her desk. The drawer caught on the bag's fabric. She freed it and then slammed it shut.

"Come in."

Her eyes fell on her petticoat as the door opened, the outline of the coin visible. "Annie. Meg." She folded the undergarment to hide the money. "I was just sewing."

Annie clucked her tongue. "Ask Donna to make garment repairs. You have enough to do to prepare for your journey."

You have no idea. "I don't mind. You know how sewing soothes me. Here, make yourself comfortable." She shifted on the chaise to allow Annie room to sit.

"*Knitting* soothes you, dear sister." She tucked her legs under her. "But I doubt I'd bother Donna with the task either. Mother taught us to be independent."

Meg settled on the armless spindle-backed chair beside the desk.

Beatrice's eyes shifted to the drawer containing the coins, mere inches from her cousin's hand resting on the desk. "Are you ready to travel?"

"I will be by Wednesday." Her brow wrinkled under wisps that had escaped the combs holding back the mass of auburn curls. "I must confess to some confusion about your father's decision to send us off so quickly."

"Bea expressed her desire to see Jefferson Davis's inauguration." Annie's lips pursed. "I guess it *is* a historical event, yet I have no mind to support it with my presence."

"Father says our route will take us longer with all the passes required." It seemed best to ignore her sister's derision. How she wished everything were as clear to her as it was to Annie. "He'll speak to business associates who have traveled South in the past months and then make our arrangements."

"I'm surprised he agreed to allow us to travel to the capital of the Confederacy during the war." Meg's shrewd green eyes studied Beatrice. "Though I know my cousin can be very persuasive."

"True." Annie laughed. "Are you afraid, Meg?"

"No." She tapped her fingers on the desk. "We'll suffer no greater inconvenience than delays."

Bea relaxed under Meg's calm assurance. There was something about her older cousin that instilled confidence.

"Part of me wishes to go with you." Annie leaned back against the lounge beside her sister with a sigh. "Yet I can't bear to miss John's visit, if he can manage it."

"It's the right decision." Beatrice hated to see her sister's loneliness. At the same time, she wished to find a man who loved her as much as John did Annie.

"He's proud to serve the Army of the Potomac in General Morrell's Brigade." Annie fingered the fringe on her shawl. "For now, he's defending Washington City, yet it's too far to come for one day. Who knows where they will send him next?"

"It's the uncertainty, isn't it?" Meg rose and placed her hand on Annie's shoulder.

"I'm…afraid sometimes." A tear fell down her face. "He's brave. Courageous. He'll not shirk his duty."

John was a strong man, outside and inside. Bea reached for Annie's hand. "I pray for his safety daily. And Will's."

"Thank you." Annie's voice wavered. "I hate that they fight on opposite sides."

"They were best of friends before the conflict." The fact festered like a thorn imbedded in a thumb. Beatrice hated it too.

"Our marriage has made them brothers"—Annie's voice fell to a whisper—"yet a great chasm separates them while this war rages. I pray their friendship is strong enough to withstand it."

Meg's glance darted from one sister to the other. "How did they meet?"

"They roomed together at West Point" Annie said. "John had to leave his education behind when his father suffered apoplexy. They stayed in touch afterwards. I'd feel better about the state of their friendship if Will could have attended my wedding." Annie swiped an embroidered handkerchief across her wet cheeks. "Here I am, making us all sad when we need to prepare for your journey. How can I help?"

"Nothing tonight," Bea said. "Tomorrow after church is soon enough. Father sent Aunt Trudy a telegram this morning to inform her that we're coming."

"You will come back to me soon, right?" Annie's smile wavered.

"She asked for a long visit, which I hope will restore her spirits." Beatrice hugged her. "I'll return soon enough. Besides, you'll be busy collecting food for our soldiers, remember?" Her conscience smote her for smuggling to the Confederacy after all she'd done to support the Union.

Nothing could change that now. She pushed the guilt away. Late nights spent sewing loomed ahead.

Jay only half-listened to his mother and her closest friend's upcoming plans to sew for the soldiers as they sat on the sofa arranged perpendicular to his cushioned armchair. He sank back, marveling yet again that Trudy Weston's parlor managed an air of elegance and comfort in equal proportion, a feat few accomplished. The room, decorated in shades of mauve and green, complimented the wallpaper pattern that reminded him of raindrops. He felt at home here. He wasn't certain that was due to his earliest memories of eating warm oatmeal cookies with milk as his shoes dangled a foot from the floral pattern on the rug. Aunt Trudy exuded an air of hospitality to everyone who entered her home, young and old. A score of guests were easily accommodated in this parlor, and there was a smaller family parlor on the second floor.

Today, there had been only the three of them for a delicious lunch, which surprised him. The widow often lamented that company of friends was the only thing that erased the echo of her lonely footsteps in empty rooms even with a paid staff that clearly adored her.

Come to think of it, he hadn't received many invitations that included meals lately. Perhaps his mother's concern about food costs was well-founded.

Jay wondered idly why Trudy had never remarried. Her husband died when Jay was but a babe. His mother described him as a gruff gentleman with a kind heart. It was exactly like Trudy to see through a person's facade to the true nature.

"Mary, I believe we're neglecting your wonderful son."

Shifting on the sofa, Trudy leaned toward Jay. "I'm happy you're not at the foundry today."

"As am I." Jay grinned. "I'd hate to have missed that delicious meal...not to mention the hospitality of your home, which has no equal."

"Why, thank you, my boy." Trudy's blue eyes sparkled beneath short, wiry gray curls. "Though I believe Clara's baked ham carved the way to your heart in this circumstance."

"You may be correct." With his appetite satisfied, Jay didn't stir himself to argue. "Mrs. Williams is an excellent cook. Please give her our thanks for a fine meal."

"With pleasure." Her smile widened. "How are things at Tredegar Iron Works? Are you all keeping up with orders? Cannons and such?"

"Doing our best." Jay scooted to the edge of his chair. Finally, a topic unrelated to sewing for soldiers. Or making bandages for soldiers. Or taking delicacies to wounded soldiers in the city's many hospitals that had opened in the past year. "We're busy. Our shops daily produce three-hundred pounds of canister shot and fifty twelve-pounder shell and shrapnel. We also average sixty-four six-pounder solid shot and sixty-five six-pounder shrapnel every day. That's not to mention the heavy ordnance—ten-inch, eight-inch, and forty-two pounder guns."

Mama gave a slight shake of her head.

On the verge of spouting more praises, Jay closed his mouth. He could talk about workings of the foundry and auxiliary shops the whole afternoon and not repeat himself. Though his mother knew more than most about his work, he never shared his company's secrets with anyone. There was so much to do that he worked seven days a week when military orders or other duties demanded it. His men liked the overtime pay. Even the enslaved men appreciated the extra hours, for that pay went directly to them, not their owners, who rented them to the company for months or a year at a time.

"Forgive me, ladies." His mother was right. A parlor wasn't an appropriate setting for such talk. "My enthusiasm for my job sometimes gets the better of me."

"Not at all. I'm very interested." Trudy glanced at Mama. "What they produce is vital to our brave soldiers."

"Indeed." A gleam brightened Mama's eyes. "So much so that our government ordered the Tredegar Battalion to remain a Home Guard."

"Yes." Jay stared at a rose pattern on the rug. Being stuck here because he was a skilled foreman still stung. He wanted to fight for his country as much as his friends who slept in camps. It was difficult to tamp down his keen disappointment to be staying home in Richmond with those too old or too young to serve as soldiers. At twenty-four and a bachelor, Jay was the prime age to fight.

"They accepted Joseph Anderson when he offered to serve." Mama crossed her arms. "He's the owner of the ironworks...he even calls it J.R. Anderson & Co. You'd think they'd order him to stay in Richmond, not make him brigadier general."

Another thorn in his flesh. Yet he understood this decision. "Mr. Anderson—I mean, Brigadier General Anderson, went to West Point. He has the education required to lead. The South needs all the good men it can get." John Tanner had assumed direction of their operations, along with Dr. Robert Archer.

"True." Mama's stony face relaxed. "Our filled hospitals attest to that need."

"Agreed. But I propose to change the topic of our conversation." Trudy's eyes brightened.

"Of course." Mama clasped her hands. "At last, we'll learn your news."

"You may recall that I've invited my nieces in Washington City numerous times for a prolonged visit."

He nodded. He'd never voiced his concern over young

women traveling to Richmond during the war because their father was unlikely to consent to the plan.

"I've received a telegram from my brother." Her blue eyes sparkled. "Hiram cannot come, but he's sending his daughter, Beatrice, and his niece, Meg."

"Why not wait until summer?" Or until the hostilities ended? Richmond's population had swelled since the war began. The city didn't need two Yankees in its midst. Some did not welcome the Northerners. It seemed foolhardy.

"Beatrice wants to attend the inauguration."

His skin tingled. "She supports the Confederacy?"

"I don't know that she does or doesn't." Trudy shrugged. "She has roots in Richmond. Her brother lives on a North Carolina plantation—he's the one who was captured and finally exchanged earlier this month."

"Right. Lieutenant Will Swanson. Now I recall the family." Will's bravery had impressed Jay. "I haven't seen Will for ten years. His sisters were younger. Beatrice and Annie?"

"Correct." Trudy inclined her head. "Annie married a Union soldier last month. Beatrice is now a beautiful young woman of nineteen."

Jay cringed. Someone like her would likely look down her nose at a man in his prime not in uniform. "Have I met the cousin?"

"Years ago. Mrs. Margaret Brooks—Meg as she likes to be called—is related to them through Bea's mother. Meg's a widow from Chicago. A very pleasant woman of about twenty-five."

Another Yankee. "When do they arrive?"

"Arrangements are being made. Hiram will send another telegram if it's within the week."

"They will be here several months, son." Mama looked at him out of the corner of her eye. "We'll have plenty of occasions to become better acquainted."

He darted a sharp glance from one woman to the next. At

last he understood. The pair were up to their matchmaking again. Their last attempt hadn't gone well. The young woman they'd chosen for him last time had married and moved to Tennessee a few months after the courtship ended.

This time wasn't going to be any different. Annie and her husband supported the Union. The younger sister, despite her interest in Jefferson Davis's inauguration, must be of the same mind.

He stifled a groan. Why did his mother imagine he'd be interested in courting a Yankee?

CHAPTER 3

The chugging of the wheels across the railroad tracks on Friday afternoon threatened to lull Beatrice to sleep. Traveling on a dreary day wasn't how she wanted to spend Saint Valentine's Day, especially with no suitor on her horizon. Sighing, she rested her forehead against the rattling windowpane and stared out at the Virginia valley. The wintry scene was shrouded in misty rain. Beauty hid beneath the fog.

Or smoke. Coal smoke outside mingled with cigar smoke inside to nauseating effect.

She had never traveled to Virginia without her mother, who'd died nearly three years ago. The loss struck her afresh as she stared at the gloomy countryside, though part of her was grateful her mother hadn't lived to see the tragic division in their country.

"Bea, are you crying?" Meg, sitting beside her on the hard seat, pressed a folded handkerchief into her hand. "What is it? Do you miss Annie and your father already?"

"Forgive me. I'm thinking of Mother." She wiped her cheeks, appalled that her emotions had gotten the better of her in public.

"I understand that sorrow. There are moments when grief cuts deeply." Meg waved away smoke permeating the railroad car. "Want to talk about it?"

Bea shook her head. "I need to think about something else."

"Well, unless I miss my guess, your aunt will keep us busy in the coming weeks."

"True." *How I wish Mother were part of those plans.*

"It was good of your father to ride with us on the Potomac River until we reached Alexandria."

"Yes." Annie had awoken feeling poorly and elected to stay behind. "He wanted to ensure that we understood how to speak with the pickets and guards we'd meet along the way. You were right—checking everyone's passes caused delays at every point. We must be three or four hours behind schedule. I hope Aunt Trudy isn't worried."

"It can't be helped. I believe we've made it through the last one." Meg peered around her at the gloomy countryside. "At least, I hope so. Can't see where we are in this fog."

"Sorry we were two days late leaving Washington." Turning to the window, Bea hoped to hide her blushes. The extra sewing, all done at night because Annie claimed every spare moment of her days, had delayed the trip. Bea touched her blue traveling dress and was alarmed to feel the outline of a coin. Not only that, the weight of the petticoat underneath made it sag past the hem. Her sweet mother would be mortified at this lapse of manners. Beatrice must push down both sides of her half-hoop skirt while walking to mask the view of her underclothing to the public.

They couldn't reach Richmond soon enough. The task ahead weighed her down more than the coins.

She peered around. Men read books and newspapers. A mother cradled her sleeping boy against her side. No one seemed to have noticed the coins hidden in her gown. The only one who met her gaze was the conductor as he offered a drink from his water bucket to the suited gentleman in the seat behind her.

"Water, miss?" The conductor held a dipper over a wooden bucket.

"Yes, please. I'm parched." Bea accepted the dipper and drank the last drop. Cold water, though that wasn't surprising in this drafty car. Heat from the coal stove didn't reach them as well as its aroma did. "May I have another, please?"

"Of course, miss." He gave her another dripping scoop.

Beatrice leaned over to keep her skirt dry…a vain attempt because even the small hoop skirt filled the confined area between seats.

"How much further?" Meg eyed the dipper in her cousin's hand.

"To Richmond?" At Meg's nod, he peered outside over their heads. "Hard to say just exactly where we are. I reckon upwards of twenty miles."

Not close enough. Bea glanced at Meg, who gave a reassuring smile before drinking her fill.

"It'll be dark when we get there," the steward said. "Not too late for supper, though, unless the army wants to delay us somewhere along the road." He lowered his bushy gray eyebrows. "I don't know as I've seen you two before. Sisters, are you?"

"Cousins." Meg smiled at him. "Our mothers were sisters."

"Were?"

"They've both passed on to their reward now."

"Sorry to hear that." He glanced at Beatrice. "You folks got kin in Richmond?"

"My aunt lives there," Bea said. "We'll stay with her."

His bearded face relaxed. "That's a relief. I hear hotels are filling up, what with the inauguration coming up and all. You all have a mighty fine visit together." He hefted his bucket and stepped to the seat in front of them.

Beatrice arranged her cloak over a wet spot on her dress with a sigh.

She had a sudden premonition that more awaited her in the Confederate capital than she realized.

Jay paced in front of the Central Railroad Depot at Broad and Sixteenth Streets. No moon tonight. Just the gas streetlamps to light the blackness of the night sky, darker due to cold, misty rain that continued to fall.

Richmond citizens had crowded a different railroad station this evening. The remains of Captain Jennings Wise of the Richmond Blues arrived at the Petersburg Depot on Eighth Street over an hour before. He had died at a battle on Roanoke Island, which was now in Union hands. Jay had been too far away to honor the fallen officer with his presence.

Fort Henry on the Tennessee River had surrendered to General Ulysses S. Grant two days before Roanoke fell.

The South couldn't win every battle. Nonetheless, those losses stung.

He slapped his hands together and then rubbed them. Mr. Swanson's telegram had said to expect the ladies to arrive at three o'clock. His mother had accompanied Trudy in her carriage to the depot at the appointed hour while Jay was still at work. He'd been invited to a small family supper that evening with his mother. Plans changed when he received a frantic message at work from his mother of a delayed arrival. He left the foundry as soon as possible and escorted them home to wait in the warm comfort of Trudy's parlor. It had taken a quarter hour to calm their fears that the train had been attacked by Northern forces.

Jay consulted his pocket watch. A quarter past seven. He hoped the older women's worries weren't justified. There'd been battles and skirmishes this winter up near Winchester, the last he'd heard about from his friend, Oliver Fudge, who was one of the local men camped there. The ladies' train was miles from that location.

He blew on his hands. What a cold Saint Valentine's evening. Not that he was courting anyone who expected him to call. Perhaps that was for the best. These days, his job demanded most of his waking hours.

Another long look down the tracks revealed nothing but mist. What caused the delay? Perhaps there had been a derailment. He paced under the awning of a nearby shop as panic rose. Two women traveling alone. Armies from both sides of the conflict camped in Virginia. Anything could have happened.

Or maybe it was simply a problem with a citizen pass that forced them to disembark and talk to someone in authority.

No. He didn't like that possibility. What else? He rubbed his jaw. Crowded trains. The sheer numbers of travelers were higher with the inauguration coming.

On the other hand—

"Mr. Nickson?"

He swung around. "Ah, Harold." He was grateful the tall black man, Clara's husband and Trudy's butler and driver, distracted his worries. Jay gestured for him to wait under the awning next to him. "Did Mrs. Weston send you? Your coat is drenched. Did you walk?"

"Yes, sir, since you have both our horses. Mrs. Weston can't sit still, not knowing what's happening with Miss Bea and Mrs. Meg. I offered to come for news."

"Nothing yet. The station master only reminds me that travelling isn't as easy as it was a year ago. As if everyone in Richmond isn't aware of the war." He clamped his jaw.

"Sure enough. Mrs. Weston will blame herself to her dying day if anything happens to those sweet young ladies—her words exactly." Harold shook water from his hat. "I expect they'll come any minute. Are the horses and carriage still stabled down the street?"

"Yes. I'll fetch them once the train arrives." It comforted Jay to have someone share the worry. Nasty weather kept pedestrians to a minimum. Being alone with his thoughts the past two hours had been miserable. "I can't understand why Beatrice's father allowed them to travel this distance without an escort."

"Mrs. Weston explained that to me." Harold squeezed droplets from his slouch hat. "Her father is a wealthy banker and can't leave Washington right now. Miss Beatrice's brother lives in North Carolina. Her new brother-in-law is camped with the Army of the Potomac somewhere in Virginia, so no man in the family can travel with them. Both Miss Bea and Mrs. Meg have been here. Do you remember them?"

"I remember Bea as a young girl. She and her family split their visits between Aunt Trudy's home and the other two families outside the city, both with plantations."

Harold replaced his hat with a shiver.

"I'm happy for your company, but you'll catch cold if you don't get warm." Uncertain of the free man's welcome for an extended period inside the depot, Jay tugged on his lower lip. "Wait for me at the stable. Tell them I asked you to hitch up the horses the minute you hear the train's whistle."

"I'll do that." He glanced up the street and back. "Thank you kindly, Mr. Nickson."

Jay clapped him on the shoulder and said a prayer that neither of them would wait long. Then he added another plea for the travelers' safety as he entered the train depot to warm himself for a few minutes by the wood stove.

The train chugged into the station a half hour later. A weight fell from Jay's shoulders when a beautiful blonde moved to the train's exit, waiting her turn to descend. She scanned the thin crowd with a puckered brow.

Smiling, he raised his arm. Her gaze riveted to him, and relief lightened her face. She spoke to the older woman with auburn curls beside her. Meg Brooks was also lovely, yet it didn't slam across Jay like Beatrice's beauty. Why had he not recalled her looks?

Because she'd been a mere girl when last he'd seen her, a child of fourteen.

And Jay had been courting Miss Amelia Walters, and he'd had eyes only for her. Miss Walters was now Mrs. Theodore Dimmick of Nashville, Tennessee. Soon after the wedding, his father had passed from a lung ailment, and Jay had thrown himself into his job.

Not good memories. He strode toward the ladies. As Beatrice took the first step down, her foot caught in her low-hanging petticoat, and she pitched forward.

Jay lunged toward her.

She grabbed for the handrail and missed. Her shoulder struck Jay's chest. He wrapped his arms around her, saving her from tumbling to the ground. The scent of lilacs mingled with coal smoke.

"Oh, my apologies." Wide blue eyes stared up at him.

His heart stuttered and then thundered. He hadn't held a beautiful woman in his arms for a long time. Too long, he realized, because it was difficult to speak. Or maybe that was due to her surprising weight. That a woman with such a trim figure weighed enough that his legs started to buckle surprised him. He set her down gently.

"No apology necessary." He stared down at her classically

beautiful face framed by a profusion of blond curls. "Those steps are quite steep—"

"Bea, are you all right?" Lifting her chin, the other woman, Meg, stared at his arm still around her cousin.

He removed it and stepped back.

"Thank you, sir," the woman said, "for your kind assistance—"

"Meg, this is Mr. James Nickson." Beatrice inclined her head toward him. "We called him Jay growing up. Aunt Trudy's dearest friend is his mother, Mary."

He grinned. "Of course, it's been several years since you've seen me. I'm pleasantly surprised that you remember me, Beatrice."

She smiled. "I'm equally happy you remember me. Is my aunt waiting in the carriage?"

"She awaits you at her home." No need to belabor the long wait beyond everyone's control. "She is a bit worried so we'd best hurry. Please take a seat inside the station. I'll collect your baggage and fetch you when the carriage is ready."

"I didn't mean to worry her." Beatrice glanced from Meg back to him. "Let's stop at the telegraph office first, for she's not the only one concerned. I'll send a telegram to my father and Annie, and then we'll go to Aunt Trudy's. I've no doubt some military man will want to see our passes while you are occupied."

He hesitated, torn between a desire to assist them and to get them home to a supper that must have been warmed over and over.

"We will manage." Meg linked arms with her cousin and began to walk away. "No need for concern. We'll be ready when you are."

Something in the widow's manner reassured him. She seemed capable of handling whatever crisis might occur.

Perhaps Hiram Swanson had made a considered decision when he sent the pair to Virginia together.

Striding toward men unloading trunks and boxes from a car, Jay turned his damp collar up. Away from Beatrice's beauty, his heart rate resumed its normal rhythm. He shook his head at such foolishness, for he had no intention of falling in love with a Yankee in the midst of a war between their two countries.

No matter how sweet and beautiful that Northern woman might be.

CHAPTER 4

"It wasn't necessary for you all to delay your supper waiting for us." Beatrice dabbed a bit of gravy on dry roasted beef. How Clara managed to keep the supper as flavorful as she had was a wonder…and a testament to her culinary talents.

Bea stole a glance at the handsome man sitting opposite her in her aunt's intimate family dining room. He sliced through the beef as if starved. Brown hair, parted on the side. She liked that he was clean-shaven in a day when many men wore mustaches and beards. Six-feet tall, if she had to guess. He had the broad shoulders and muscular arms of a man who worked hard, but it was his compassionate green eyes that captivated her.

"Truthfully, I couldn't rest until I knew you and Meg were safe." Trudy, seated at the head of the table to Beatrice's right, sipped her tea. Wiry gray curls were gathered back and tied with a blue bow matching her gown.

"My apologies our late arrival caused you anxiety." Beatrice touched her aunt's lacy sleeve, which extended over her wrist.

"We never felt in danger." Meg, at Bea's side, inclined her

head at her hostess. "Delays were the worst of our inconveniences. Thank you for including me in your kind invitation."

"Not at all. I consider you, as Bea's beloved cousin, part of the family." Her rose-patterned teacup made no sound as she set it on the matching saucer. "I suppose, in these uncertain days, travel inconveniences are common."

"I fear they are, Mrs. Weston." Meg's glance dropped to her half-empty plate. "I traveled to Chicago last autumn to sell my home and met with delays on my return to Washington City last month."

"Now, you called me Aunt Trudy as a child." A twinkle lit the older woman's blue eyes as she leaned forward. "I insist that you revert to it."

Meg laughed. "Indeed, I will."

A pretty black woman brought an empty tray and began clearing the table.

"Clara, how lovely to see you again." Beatrice smiled at the friendly woman who was her senior by at least a dozen years. "I knew you still worked here as soon as I tasted this delicious meal."

"Thank you, Miss Bea. I remember your sweet mama always complimented my cooking." A smile lit her dark eyes. "It sure is good to have you here, safe and sound."

"I can't agree more." Jay gave a shaky laugh. "And thank you for another delicious meal."

Beatrice smiled at his gracious manners as Clara took his empty plate. A perfect Southern gentleman, just like her father and brother—even if he wore casual clothes to supper. Mrs. Nickson had explained her son's lack of a vest and coat as soon as they arrived. He had come straight from work to meet their train.

The clock in the hall struck ten times.

"Trudy, the hour grows late." Mrs. Nickson exchanged a

concerned glance with her son. "I'd never leave right after supper under normal circumstances..."

"Don't give it another thought. Our friendship is too strong for that." Trudy stood.

"But I was clearing the table to bring in the cherry pie." Clara glanced at Trudy.

Everyone paused in the act of rising.

"Will it keep until Sunday's dinner?"

Clara nodded.

"Then, if there's no objection ..."

Bea shook her head.

"No objections here." Jay shook his head with a grin. "Especially as it sounds as if an invitation to dinner after church is on its way."

The camaraderie between them cheered Bea's dwindling spirits.

"Of course, dear boy." Trudy winked at Bea. "You observe how he has me wrapped about his little finger."

The banter surprised a laugh from her.

Jay grinned at Bea. "I'd be honored to escort all you lovely ladies to church on Sunday."

"Since you ask so gallantly"—Bea inclined her head with a smile—"we accept."

"The first of many plans." Mrs. Nickson's glance slid from her son to Beatrice.

"Yes, we'll try to plan entertainments despite the unpleasantness." Trudy took Jay's arm and led them from the room.

Beatrice clutched the back of the chair. What harsh realities had the war caused her relatives?

At the door, Jay clasped her hand. "We'll all rest easily tonight knowing you are safe."

"Thank you." Her heart warmed at the sincerity of his tone. "And thank you for meeting us at the depot. I can't express how lovely it felt to see a friendly face waiting just for us."

"Yes, thank you." Meg extended her hand to him before turning to his mother. "You've been very kind."

"Think nothing of it." Mary gave her a warm smile. "We will see you all on Sunday."

They left on a chorus of good-byes.

"After this trying day, I want you to rest tomorrow." Trudy led them to the stairs. "No need to stir from your rooms early in the morning. Sleep as long as you like."

Beatrice suddenly felt her exhaustion. Tomorrow morning was soon enough to begin unraveling these heavy coins from her traveling petticoat.

After an hour of snipping stitches the next morning, only ten gold coins lay tucked inside a coarse linen bag when someone tapped on the door. Beatrice's glance darted at the pile of torn threads. "Who is it?"

"It's Meg. Bea, are you awake? It's past ten." The knob rattled. "Is your door locked?"

She sent up a prayer of thanks that she'd locked the door earlier after Mabel, Clara's daughter, brought her a cup of chocolate. "One moment."

Within seconds, the money bag lay hidden in a vanity drawer. Loose threads were wadded with her petticoat and tucked into her trunk.

Heart racing, she scanned the room. The unmade bed was a rumpled mess, as if she'd left it moments ago. A glance in the mirror revealed that her chaotic blond curls matched the turmoil of her mind. How would she accomplish all her father asked when her loyalty was divided?

A question for another hour. "Coming." She unlocked the door.

Meg took one look at Bea's hair and giggled. "Did you just leap out of bed, cousin?"

"Looks like it, doesn't it?" Beatrice clamped her hands over her wild hair. "Takes a few minutes to tame these curls."

"We inherited our mothers' curls, didn't we?" Meg's auburn hair was already brushed and held back with combs.

"Annie didn't." She sighed, envious of her sister's beautiful, straight brown locks. "Come in. Sorry I'm not dressed yet." She touched the fastened buttons on her robe.

"I thought I heard you moving around an hour ago. We share a wall."

Beatrice glanced at the pink wallpaper. So they did. She'd have to monitor her movements late at night and in the early morning. "I didn't mean to awaken you. Mabel brought me a cup of chocolate."

"She brought me one as well." Meg scanned the spacious bedroom with its high bed, dressing table, desk, chest of drawers, and chaise lounge. An open trunk lay near the wardrobe. "My room is similar, though decorated in yellow tones instead of pink."

"Aunt Trudy remembered this is my favorite color. She's a treasure." Her heart swelled with gratitude. "Sit wherever you like." *Or go back to your room so I can get on with my father's work.*

"I couldn't disarrange the covers more if I sat on that rumpled bed," Meg teased, choosing the seat at the dressing table where the coins were hidden.

Beatrice forced a laugh, nerves leaping in fear that her cousin might explore the vanity's contents.

Meg looked at the empty cup. "Did you remember to bring the package with you?"

"Wh-what did you say?" How had Meg discovered that Bea had smuggled in money for the Confederacy? Her heart hammered a staccato rhythm.

"Coffee." Her brow furrowed. "Your aunt asked you to bring

ten pounds of coffee since prices have soared here." She got on her knees in front of the trunk and reached inside.

Beatrice grabbed Meg's hand before she touched the petticoat.

She gasped, giving a pointed stare at Bea's vicelike grip.

"My apologies." How could she explain her unprecedented reaction? She'd never kept secrets from her cousin before this war. She laid Meg's hand on the floor. "I mean, I did remember to bring the coffee. Extra coffee beans, in fact. My trunk is very heavy."

Meg lifted a corner and blinked. "It *is* heavy. With an aroma of coffee. The beans aren't roasted?"

"No."

"Good. Hanging up your clothes to air will likely remove a lingering coffee aroma. You'll be glad to get that bag out of there and delivered."

"Indeed." *More than you know.* Only her thoughts focused on another bag. Beatrice evaded her cousin's speculative glance. Meg was too perceptive by far.

"I'll be happy for a cup to start my day tomorrow." Meg peered into the trunk. "I prefer it over tea or chocolate."

Bea closed the trunk and sat on it, hoping her rude behavior didn't hurt her cousin's feelings. What else could she do?

"It's common to feel out of sorts after a long day of travel. We're both tired." Meg stood. She brushed at a wrinkle in her blue dress. "Let me know if you want me to request a luncheon tray in your room today."

"Forgive me." She rose and stared at the white collar of her purple dress. "I didn't sleep well. I'll be better by lunch."

Meg touched her shoulder and then let herself out.

Regrets at upsetting her cousin warred with her resolve to keep her father's secret.

The sooner Bea rid herself of this burden, the better. Now to figure out a way to get the money to her uncle's plantation and then arrange a quiet meeting with him. Aunt Trudy's decision to marry a business man brought about a family squabble, one that had seemingly ended with his death. Or perhaps it merely simmered below the surface. Continued friction prevented a close relationship. A pity because the siblings—except for normal spats—had been the best of friends as children. Trudy rarely saw her brother and sister.

Perhaps Jay could be persuaded to drive Bea to Uncle Isaac's mansion. Something deep inside her had responded to the admiration in Jay's eyes when he saved her from falling from the train. A little flirtation might pave the way. They'd need an escort. Meg was the best—and worst—choice because part of Bea balked at Jay spending time alone with Meg while Beatrice sought a private audience with her uncle.

Jay had dazzled Bea already. And he was as kind as he was handsome…

She shook her head. Better to think about the task at hand first.

The other choice in ridding herself of the gold was to drive to the President's House and give the money to Jefferson Davis herself—a daunting possibility, for she'd never met the man.

She'd rather allow Uncle Isaac to take care of the matter.

She opened the trunk and picked up the petticoat, which weighed about thirty pounds even after she'd removed ten coins. Tracing the outlines that remained even after removal of the coins convinced her the garment must be burned to hide her activities.

Bea couldn't get the bag delivered quickly enough.

Jay stole a glance at the lovely lady by his side. It had been three years since he'd sat at church beside a woman who snagged his interest to such a degree that he didn't even know the sermon's topic.

Was Beatrice as impressed with the history of St. John's Church as he was? Patrick Henry had delivered his famous statement in support of the colonies some hundred feet from the pew where they sat. *Give me liberty or give me death.*

Who'd have guessed the colonies that pulled together to defeat the enemy less than a century before now considered *each other* enemies? The Founding Fathers never saw this coming.

Truth be told, nor had he.

These sober reflections reminded Jay to protect his heart against falling for a Northerner, no matter how lovely.

A Southerner from his slouch hat to his boots, Jay didn't want to hear statements in support of Lincoln's army. A soldier of the Tredegar Battalion who stood ready to protect Richmond as needed, he hated slavery yet loved his homeland. If fate demanded it, he'd fight for Virginia and his loved ones to his dying breath.

Give me liberty or give me death.

"What did you say?" Beatrice whispered.

"Sorry. My thoughts are loud today." Heat crept across his face.

Her blue eyes widened. Then her lips curved. "Mine can get that way too."

CHAPTER 5

Jay shifted closer to the warmth emanating from the parlor's fireplace. Trudy's maids had arranged one sofa in front of the fire with armchairs on either side. The other lunch guests—two couples his mother's age and a widower with his school-aged son and daughter—had left half an hour before. Most men of fighting age had mustered into the army and were likely sitting around a campfire to stay warm in the damp chill.

If only he were there to shiver with them.

Instead, he sat near a cozy fire opposite of Beatrice in the semicircle and was glad for the opportunity to observe her as she knitted. A Yankee, a fact unaltered by her relation to a respected Richmond family. He'd guard his tongue with her and Mrs. Brooks—Meg, as she'd insisted.

"A delicious dinner." Mama sank back against the sofa. "Would Clara share that recipe for baked ham with my cook? She's a talented cook herself, but Clara knows something about seasonings that Esther doesn't."

"I will ask. She'll appreciate the compliment." Trudy turned to Beatrice on her other side. "Thanks for bringing coffee from Washington. It has grown very expensive of late."

"My pleasure." Her blue eyes shone. "It's not my preference, though I sometimes enjoy a hearty cup on winter mornings."

"There's enough to last for weeks." Trudy studied the stitches. "What are you knitting, my dear?"

"A baby blanket for my sweet niece." She caressed the expanding yellow square. "Hannah is two months old, and it's unfathomable that I haven't met her. Then again, her father held her for the first time this month."

"What a joy that must be. I remember Will from your childhood visits." Compassion stirred in Jay's heart for the Confederate officer. "I was certainly sorry to learn that his fort was forced to surrender."

"A tragedy." Mama pursed her lips.

Beatrice bent over the yellow square as if to end the conversation.

Meg studied her cousin's slumped shoulders as she sipped her tea. "Aunt Trudy, you mentioned the hospitals are filled with wounded soldiers. What can we do to help? We're making a long visit, and I don't intend to sit idle."

"You'd help our dear soldiers?" Mama asked.

Jay raised his eyes heavenward at his mother's shocked tone. He loved her dearly, but sometimes a bit of restraint would be welcome.

"Of course." Meg's gracious nod held no offense. "Isn't that right, Bea?"

"Yes, we were all involved back home."

"For *Northern* soldiers, surely?" Mama's incredulous glance darted between them.

"There is plenty enough to do." Trudy patted Mama's hand, no doubt to encourage her to think before she spoke further. "Mary and I take food and delicacies to the hospitals three days a week."

"We sew at the homes of other women from church once a week." Mama studied callouses on her fingers.

Jay's senses heightened at seeming uncertainty in Beatrice's expressive eyes. "Perhaps all that volunteer work is too much for guests in Richmond."

"Not at all." Beatrice raised her eyebrows. "Compassion fills my heart for all the wounded in this war. I'm happy to help. Does anyone need knitted socks?"

"We're still enduring the cold of winter, my dear." Trudy smiled at her. "That brisk wind tore open my cloak this morning. Chilled me to the bone. I'm certain our patients and even soldiers on the field need warm socks."

"I can vouch that socks are needed." The fire toasted Jay's toes through his leather shoes. Guilt gnawed at him to be enjoying the heat. He'd trade this comfort to be camping with his friends in the Twenty-first Virginia. The last letter from Oliver had reported they were back at Winchester and camped on the Romney Road. Even his friend's dreary details about marching in snow, shivering in the cold, hadn't deterred Jay's desire to join their brigade, the Second Brigade of the famous Stonewall Jackson's Division, no less.

"The way you're scowling at the crackling fire, it almost seems you wish you were out in this weather with them." Beatrice tilted her head as she studied him.

"I do."

"My son's job is important to the Confederacy." The pride in his mother's voice was unmistakable but did nothing to lessen his frustration. "Our government refused to allow him and his fellow workers to go to the battlefield and insisted they remain here as Home Guard for our city." Mama straightened her shoulders. "Why, he's—"

"Mama, no need to bore our guests with such details." Jay interrupted before she provided information they didn't need to know. He was a long way from trusting the cousins, though it pleased him that they wanted to help Southern soldiers while staying in Richmond. Whether this stemmed from a desire to serve the South or mere politeness while in the vicinity, he could not say. A chill went through him that one of them might be here to spy. Probably not since they were here by invitation, yet it was best to guard the South's secrets. "Let us speak of more pleasant topics entirely."

Beatrice studied him and then looked at the growing rows of yellow stitches.

"I must say that I enjoyed the morning's service." Meg's bright tone brought a welcome change of topic. He contented himself with listening to the women chatter about the sermon, the people at church, and St. John's history.

He planned to warn his mother to refrain from discussing his work as soon as possible…on the carriage ride home, in fact.

~

Rain pelted the shutters. Beatrice glanced out the parlor windows into the dreary, gray afternoon and wondered if Jay felt himself branded a coward for choosing to protect his own city, especially since the government prevented him from leaving. She sensed his frustration at remaining in Richmond. She rather applauded Jay's courage in performing his duty.

Another thing she didn't understand was Jay's watchful attitude. He seemed almost suspicious of her and Meg. She'd ponder that later. Arranging a visit to Uncle Isaac's home was her highest priority. The coins weren't all freed from their fabric yet, or she'd ask Jay to drive her to the plantation today, despite the dreary rain. Blankets and coals for their feet would keep them warm in the closed carriage whenever they went.

Perhaps it was best to hint at her desire to visit.

At the first lull in the conversation, Bea leaned forward. "Aunt Trudy, have you seen Uncle Isaac lately?"

"It's my custom to spend a day there at Christmas, but the war has made many things harder." Her back stiffened. "No doubt you recall our relationship is a bit strained."

"Yes." Questions died on her lips at her aunt's demeanor. The tension had something to do with Aunt Trudy's marriage to Uncle Parker, who died before her birth. Or maybe the continued strained relationship had something to do with Uncle Isaac's inheritance of the entire plantation. It still stuck like a burr in Bea's father's soul all these years. "I'd like to see him and Aunt Meredith. And, of course, Aunt Victoria and Uncle Michael as well. But I'm especially eager to see Uncle Isaac."

Trudy's brow furrowed. "I've no plans to visit in the near future. Perhaps when the weather warms."

"My father wishes me to go there." Torn between a desire to do her father's bidding and not hurt his sister in the process, Bea chose her words carefully. "You need not alter your plans."

"You'll need passes from the Provost Marshal to travel outside Richmond." Jay studied her.

"Oh. I didn't know." Her heartbeat quickened.

"An unfortunate circumstance of war." Trudy gave a heavy sigh. "Anyone visiting Richmond these days seems to be under scrutiny."

Meg shifted in her chair. "Two young women on a family visit surely cannot be of concern."

"You'd think so." Trudy eyed her. "But Richmond citizens are not as hospitable as before the hostilities began. I doubt you will suffer ill effects."

Mary touched her friend's arm. "Acts of kindness for our soldiers will go a long way to relieve our neighbors' worries about their loyalty."

"True." Resting his elbow on the chair arm, Jay tapped his fingers against his mouth.

"I know nothing of obtaining passes." Almost nothing, at any rate. Bea's brother-in-law had helped her and Annie get them in Washington City. "Father arranged for our travel here." Time to charm Jay into helping them. She widened her smile and angled toward him. "Will you help us, Jay?"

He blinked as if dazzled.

Good. He wasn't immune to her femininity. Her many suitors had taught her the power of a soft smile accompanied by a gentle touch on the arm.

"Certainly." He straightened. "I'll accompany you to the Provost Marshal's office. General Clayton and his staff bear responsibility for passes."

"I hear Mr. Benjamin's staff also writes passes." Mary's brow furrowed as she looked at Beatrice. "He's the Secretary of War, you know."

"Request a pass that extends to summer's end, at the very least." Aunt Trudy gave Jay an approving nod. "Bea promised a long visit."

"I'll happily escort both of you." Jay's glance lingered on Beatrice. "Though it will be next week at the earliest due to my job's demands. I'll attend the Inauguration on Saturday. It will be an honor to escort all of you to that momentous event"—his brow lowered—"should you wish to attend."

"That will be lovely." The Inauguration of President Jefferson Davis. Bea gave her head a tiny shake. The very reason she'd rushed to Richmond...and she hadn't given the event a thought since she arrived.

CHAPTER 6

The following Saturday, Beatrice sat between Meg and Aunt Trudy in the crowded galleries reserved for women at the Capitol. Driving rain pelted the roof. Frowning at splatters on her gown despite the carriage dropping them off near the building's entrance, she tried to suppress a shiver. Citizens standing outside in the downpour must be miserable, for umbrellas weren't strong enough protection from the elements.

Indeed, she was grateful for the seat and doubted Jay had been as fortunate. Men filled the rotunda. For his sake, she hoped he stood within sight of his president.

One gray-haired man stood, stoop-shouldered, with glistening cheeks as he stared at Jefferson Davis. Misery fought with determination in his expressive face. Perhaps the old man's thoughts propelled him back through their country's history, possibly to the Revolutionary War that had freed them from Great Britain.

And now that same great nation raised arms against its own citizens.

A sobering reflection on this grave occasion.

Her focus shifted to the Confederate President, inaugurated

today to serve a six-year term. The man dressed in black sat on the Speaker's chair. Mrs. Davis and those in the cabinet sat opposite, awaiting the ceremony.

The officials stood. It was time for the oath, which was to take place outside. Bea and Meg followed those who ventured outside to witness it. They raised their umbrellas and huddled close for warmth as Davis walked along a path between mounted men who had cleared the way. The waiting crowd of perhaps two thousand lifted their voices to cheer for their president.

He climbed the bunting-draped stand and stood in the rain as the crowd cheered. The applause lasted for minutes before the people quieted.

Beatrice held her breath as Davis took the oath, then lifted the Bible and kissed it. The opening statement of his speech reminded listeners that it was George Washington's birthday and that they were assembled to usher in the permanent Government of the Confederate States. She raised her eyes to the impressive statue of the mounted first president above Davis in the middle of Capitol Square. It was unlikely that President Washington, even in his wildest nightmares, foresaw such division in their country.

The downpour eased during the speech, which was interrupted sporadically by cheers.

Bea didn't doubt President Davis recognized the magnitude of the moment as he stood, erect and tense. If the Confederacy won, history would paint him as the hero his countrymen already considered him. If they lost, he'd be viewed as a traitor.

She'd witnessed the oaths of two presidents on opposing sides. Both men, she had every reason to believe, served their countries to the best of their ability. To all appearances, both held strong convictions, believing they'd chosen the right side of the conflict.

Only one would emerge victorious.

What about her own loyalties? She'd collected and shipped food to Northern soldiers. She'd sewn a variety of clothing for them. Last week, she had done the same for Confederate soldiers. Every man deserved warm clothes, surely, no matter what side he supported.

Beatrice respected the decisions her brother, Aunt Trudy, and Jay had made to support the South. They lived here. She wasn't as certain of her feelings about her father's change of loyalty.

Davis's speech ended. She bowed her head for the prayer afterwards.

No doubt this was a historic event. The chilly atmosphere hung heavy with its solemnity. Future generations would speak of it with praise or derision. Which one?

A shiver slid down her spine. What was coming next?

Jay, his heart filled with national fervor after the day's ceremony, accompanied his mother to fetch Beatrice, Meg, and Aunt Trudy. They had all been invited to attend the reception at the Executive Mansion that evening. It had been impossible to stay dry during the inauguration, though his mother and Aunt Trudy had remained in the gallery during the speech to guard against catching cold.

"Thanks for returning for us, dear boy." Trudy gestured to a seat in front of the fireplace. "The girls will be down soon. At least, I believe they're aware of the passing time." She smiled and smoothed a nonexistent wrinkle from her gold brocade gown. "One hopes you both recovered from the afternoon's chill?"

"Not yet." Mama grimaced. "After such an uncomfortable day I would not leave the house in this weather for a less important levee."

"Agreed, my dear." Trudy glanced at the clock. "It's February. One can only be happy it isn't snowing."

The parlor door opened, and Bea swept in with a radiant smile. The blue of her satin gown with its white lace overskirt enhanced those beautiful eyes in a way that stole Jay's breath. He vaguely noticed Meg, who entered the room behind her in a less elegant violet wool trimmed with black lace. It surprised him to see her don half-mourning, as she hadn't worn it other times. Perhaps she didn't own a fancier dress.

"You both look lovely." Jay strove to look at each young woman equally as long, but it was a losing battle. It wasn't only the elegance of Bea's dress or the curly blond cascade across her shoulders that made her so lovely in his eyes. It was something undefinable yet uniquely hers that drew him.

"Why, thank you, kind sir." Bea curtsied playfully. "My cousin and I labored for hours to draw out just such a compliment, right, Meg?"

The other woman laughed. "I'll leave the compliments for my beautiful cousin. I merely wanted to look my best for this momentous occasion."

"Speaking of which, Harold has the carriage ready." Trudy lifted a gold cloak from the back of a sofa. "Shall we don our cloaks? I'm anxious to congratulate our new president."

The inauguration and the continued rain dominated the conversation on the carriage ride. Mama and Trudy, the only ones who had met President and Mrs. Davis, gave their impressions of the couple.

His attention was captured by Beatrice's lovely face as she listened to her aunt. Then misgivings took over. He was escorting Northerners to the Executive Mansion. Was he daft?

Confederate secrets were unlikely to be topics of conversations at an inaugural reception. However, concerns about the women's loyalty reminded him not to let his guard down with the lovely ladies, especially Bea. She dazzled him with her smile, her sweet nature.

And her flirtation.

For, as he thought over her request to help her obtain necessary passes, he realized she had flirted to convince him to agree.

Just as Amelia had dazzled him with her flirtatious ways three years ago. Unfortunately for Jay, she had also captivated his friend. That was how she'd come to be Mrs. Dimmick instead of Mrs. Nickson.

Perhaps Theodore Dimmick had done him a favor.

It was the first time he'd considered that possibility. He stole a glance at Bea, hoping she didn't prove to be cut from the same bolt as Amelia.

~

Beatrice tried to quell the nervous twitch of her hands. Standing in a reception line for the better part of an hour jittered her nerves. She was now close enough to the Confederate President and Mrs. Varina Davis to catch a word or two of their conversations with Richmond citizens ahead of her.

Swirling thoughts made Bea's temples ache. She, a Northern citizen struggling with her loyalties, was about to meet the Southern president.

Tonight, she must pretend to support the South. With her whole heart, she prayed for calmer heads to prevail and end this war without further bloodshed. If that meant the country was forever divided, so be it.

Dangerous sentiments, perhaps, in such company, though some might agree.

Finally, the waiting ended, and Aunt Trudy stood before the Davises.

"And may I present my dear niece, Beatrice Swanson." Trudy gestured to her with a proud smile.

Beatrice curtsied.

"Her cousin, Mrs. Margaret Brooks."

"You are in mourning, Mrs. Brooks?" Varina Davis's tone was gentle.

"Yes, ma'am. My husband." Meg swallowed and lifted her chin.

"My condolences, my dear." Mrs. Davis clasped her hand briefly.

Meg inclined her head.

"And this is my son, Jay." Mary beamed at him. "He works at Tredegar and serves in its battalion."

"Ah. There are those of us who might wish to serve on the battlefield yet are needed on the home front." President Davis shook his hand. "You serve your country by supplying the needs of our military. Remember we need our Home Guard, Mr. Nickson."

"Thank you, President Davis." Jay's loose fist tapped against his chest. "May I say how happy I am that you lead our country?"

"Most kind of you. Thank you." The president looked beyond them.

The line of folks extended around the circular entryway to the main door. Feeling herself politely dismissed, Beatrice followed her aunt into a crowded parlor. There had been no opportunity to mention her errand for her father…not that she had expected a moment of privacy with the president at such a public event. It seemed she must rely on her uncle to take care of the matter for her.

Jay murmured something about seeking refreshments and melted into the crowd.

She sighed. He hadn't arranged to take her to the provost marshal's office yet. She'd discovered the pressing demands of his job left him little free time. Her hopes of his driving her to Uncle Isaac's plantation began to fade.

"My dear sister-in-law." Meredith Swanson stepped toward Trudy from a sea of faces and clasped her hand. "How lovely to see you at the home of our new president. Darling,"—she turned to the tall man with salt-and-pepper hair following her—"you were just saying that you wondered if your sister had come to the reception, and here she is."

"So I was." Isaac Swanson's smile didn't warm his brown eyes. "Trudy, we missed you at our Christmas celebrations this year, though they weren't as festive, as is our wont."

"This war seems to have taken over our very lives." Trudy inclined her head and offered him her hand. "Isaac. Meredith. A pleasure. Of course, you remember my dear friend, Mary Nickson."

"How lovely to see you again, Mary." The pretty brunette clasped her hand and then looked beyond her with a gasp. "Is that my dear niece?"

"How good it is to see you, Aunt Meredith." Beatrice returned her aunt's hug, whose trim waist had thickened somewhat since she'd seen them at her mother's funeral. She'd always found more in common with her aunt than her uncle. Perhaps it was because Aunt Meredith was ten years younger than her husband.

"What's this? I didn't know you'd be here so soon." Isaac beamed at her.

"Uncle Isaac. You look more like my father every time I see you." She lifted her cheek to receive her uncle's kiss.

"He looks like me, my dear. I am the eldest son." Isaac patted her shoulder.

"I'm certain you both remember my cousin, Mrs. Margaret Brooks." Beatrice took Meg's arm and drew her into the circle that had somehow displaced her. "Meg and I are in Richmond to make a long visit with Aunt Trudy."

He quirked an eyebrow at his sister.

"Isaac, I hadn't found the time to send around a note to you about the girls' visit." Trudy spoke in a brusque tone that held a hint of apology. "This war…the dead and wounded…had put me in such a state that only family could restore me."

"A carriage ride of an hour or two will bring you to me." Isaac's eyes narrowed. "Please feel free to call whenever you need to be around family."

Pursing her lips, Trudy gave a slow nod.

"As for Bea's visit, I knew she was coming. My information came from Hiram." His chin jutted higher. "I imagine his latest letter was delayed, for I didn't know Bea was already in Richmond."

"You must come for Sunday supper in the spring." Scarlet crept up Trudy's face. "How are your sons? Are they here?"

Beatrice scanned the crowd for her older cousins. Even though the difference in ages wasn't great, she hadn't been as close to Benjamin and Steven as Will had been. They were nowhere in sight, but then neither was Jay. Where was he with their punch? Her throat was parched.

Meredith's smile faltered.

Jay walked up carrying two cups of milk punch. He halted a respectful distance away.

"No." Isaac grasped the lapels of his black coat. "Both our boys serve our beloved South with the Twenty-first Virginia. They're in the Second Brigade of General Stonewall Jackson's Division."

"The South needs more brave men like them." Trudy's eyes gleamed.

"That it does." Isaac thrust out his massive chest. "I told Meredith it was a shame we raised only two sons, or we'd have more to send."

Meredith's face blanched.

"Here is Mary's son, James Nickson." Beatrice spoke quickly

to ease her aunt's consternation, probably caused by fear for her boys.

"Yes, you've met him." Trudy took Jay's arm and drew him closer. "Jay stole away to claim refreshments for us." She laughed. "It looks as if one of us should have gone with you."

"My apologies." Jay grinned as he gave the milk punch to the older women. "I couldn't manage more than two cups in such a crowd. It's good so many came to support President Davis."

"I'll accompany you on the return trip." Beatrice's breath hitched when he smiled his thanks.

Isaac considered him. "Are you on furlough, son?"

"No, sir." His neck flushed deep red. "I serve with the Tredegar Battalion."

"Ah." Isaac's shoulders relaxed. "Our government is in desperate need of the munitions produced by your works. Richmond's citizens know that. Under those conditions I respect your service in the Home Guard."

Jay's jaw tightened.

His uncharacteristic silence mystified Bea, who was growing more attuned with Jay's feelings each time they met. "Uncle Isaac, I hope you and Aunt Meredith will soon join us for Sunday supper."

"Of course, my dear." His glanced darted to his sister. "But let's first invite you all out for luncheon tomorrow after church services."

"Thank you, but this weather is too uncertain for me to travel so far." Trudy gave a stiff smile. "Perhaps in a few weeks."

"I regret to hear it." He turned to Beatrice. "That doesn't mean the rest of you can't visit for the afternoon. We'll serve you supper before sending you back to the city."

Beatrice blinked, knowing that her aunt's refusal included all of them. How could she accept without treading upon Aunt Trudy's hospitality?

Yet this was the opportunity she needed to talk with her uncle alone.

"I cannot come either." Mary touched her friend's sleeve. "Though I thank you for the kind invitation."

"Jay, perhaps you will not mind escorting these two lovely ladies to our home tomorrow?" Isaac's glance darted between the two younger ladies.

"Do come." Meredith smiled. "We have been as dreary as the weather. A family visit is exactly what we need to cheer us."

"You youngsters have my blessing to go enjoy the day." Trudy's lips pursed as she searched Bea's expression.

Jay looked at Beatrice with a wrinkled brow.

"It will be a pleasure." A weight lifted from her shoulders that her aunt blessed the outing. "Meg?" At her cousin's nod, she turned to Jay. "Will you escort us tomorrow?"

CHAPTER 7

Jay settled back into his seat opposite Meg and Bea in the closed carriage the following afternoon, relieved to finally be on their way to Isaac Swanson's plantation. He had been a schoolboy of fifteen when he'd last attended a social occasion at Trudy's home in Richmond where the Swansons were also present—and then he'd spent more time with Benjamin and Steven in the gardens with others their age. Of course, all three boys had their eye on the neighborhood girls at the party and teased each other about who would be first to work up the courage to talk to one of them. He'd won.

"I apologize for our late start." Bea pulled on the fabric of her embroidered linen handkerchief.

The scent of lilacs wafted from the dainty cloth. "No need for regrets." His heart hammered when those mournful eyes the color of cornflowers in May stared up at him. An urge to hold her, rest her head against his shoulder in comfort for whatever sadness assailed her—no, it wouldn't do to fall for a Northern girl. "You can't help forgetting something from your aunt's house." She hadn't changed her pink dress after church to save time. They all wore their Sunday clothes. So what had taken her a quarter hour to accomplish? Good manners overrode his curiosity.

Bea crumpled the linen and then smoothed out the wrinkles against her brown wool cloak.

After a quick glance at her, Meg looked out the window. "It has snowed, rained, or otherwise been so dreary of late that one wonders if the sun has forgotten how to shine."

"Agreed." Jay was glad for Meg's insight in shifting the conversation. Bea was preoccupied with some dark thought. He wondered at its cause. "I'll wager you haven't been in Virginia in the winter months. January and February are often like this."

"No, this is my first winter visit. Bea, are you worried that your uncle will fret over us if we are late?"

"Aunt Meredith is more likely to worry."

Jay frowned. "Muddy roads will no doubt slow our progress." It had been a taxing week with another one looming ahead…just like they'd all been of late. He shifted his exhausted frame against the thin cushion. A blazing fire was what he wanted more than a hot meal right now. No, not such a good idea. A warm fire might lull him to sleep.

"At least it's not raining." Meg studied the gray sky. "No promises about our return ride. It's cold enough for those dark clouds to bring snow."

"Thank you both for accepting Uncle Isaac's invitation." Bea's handkerchief was a crumpled mess. "Yesterday was such a long day that I'm certain a relaxing afternoon was more in order than an hour's drive in the cold."

"It's my pleasure." Jay laid his hand over those restless fingers.

Her hand stilled as her gaze flew to meet his.

"Spending the day with two beautiful ladies"—he grinned to lighten the moment—"makes me the envy of all my bachelor friends."

Bea giggled. "Thank you, kind sir."

He reluctantly removed his fingers from her small gloved hand.

"Do you remember my cousins?" Bea asked.

"We last met when I was fifteen." He grinned. "Shall I tell you a bit about that day?"

Bea tilted her head.

"Benjamin was fourteen and Steven was soon to be twelve." He crossed his arms and set about amusing the ladies with a story from his boyhood, when the awkward ways of youth were far from impressive to the girls.

~

Beatrice dislodged a peach slice from the pie with her fork. The plantation's familiar formal dining room with its cherry wood furnishings wasn't as comfortable as she remembered—or perhaps it was the tense atmosphere. It wasn't possible to eat another bite past the growing knot in her stomach from this morning's decision.

"Tell me more about the ironworks." Isaac pushed his empty plate aside. "You produce enough artillery shells for our soldiers?"

"Thousands of shells." Glancing at Beatrice and Meg, Jay shifted in his cushioned high-backed chair. "I prefer not to brag."

"Hard work deserves a chance to boast." A wide grin accompanied Isaac's hearty tone. "Tell me more."

"We give all our railway engines a name and then monitor them."

"Good. You take pride in your workmanship." Isaac folded his hands. "But what about ammunition?"

Jay flushed. "We produce a good quantity of canister shot, shell, shrapnel, and solid shot. Heavy ordnance, of course."

"Mounted guns."

"Exactly." Another glance at the women.

"Where do you get your iron?"

Jay rubbed his jaw. "The war has given us challenges of late."

"That it has."

Beatrice studied Jay's flushed face. They'd been talking for some time, and anyone could see he'd rather not discuss his demanding job on his day off. Or did his reasons run deeper? Perhaps there were secrets at the ironworks kept from citizens. That made Jay even more fascinating than she already found him. She toyed with a bit of pie crust as the possibility took root.

"Is everything to your liking, Beatrice?" Meredith glanced at her plate. "The maid can bring you a different slice."

"No, please don't." Beatrice held up her hand, appalled to be singled out. "I confess to being far from famished. Please thank your cook for a delicious meal." She didn't know any of the staff's names.

"Then, if everyone is quite finished"—Meredith waited for their nods—"why don't we enjoy our coffee in the comfort of the parlor?"

Here was her best opportunity. Beatrice stood. "Uncle Isaac, might I have a word? My father asked me to speak with you."

"Of course, my dear." The corners of his mouth lifted as if he'd expected her request. "If you all will please excuse us, we will soon join you in the parlor."

Within minutes, Beatrice sat in front of her uncle in his study with a large wooden table between them. Books filled three sets of shelves along the wall to her right. Journals lay stacked on the bookcase behind the desk as if someone often perused their information. Curtains were open on the windows lining the left side of the room, allowing in scant light from the dreary day.

"Beatrice, I know why you're here." Isaac studied her. "Your father told me that you'd have something for me."

"Not exactly."

"What do you mean?" His chair scraped against the rug, and he stood. Pressing his hands on the table, he leaned over a stack of paper on the desk. "Where is it? Never tell me you lost all that gold."

"No, nothing like that." She raised her hand, palm forward. "Neither am I comfortable in keeping my father's money in my possession."

"I understand." The chair creaked against his weight as he sat. "Leave it to me. Hiram did send gold? I told him that was best."

"It's gold."

"Excellent. Give it to me. I'll relieve you of this burden and see that all is done properly."

She drew a deep breath. "I didn't bring it."

"Didn't bring—" He smacked his forehead. "I begin to wonder why Hiram trusted a young woman with such responsibility."

"Because he knew I'd do what needed to be done." The back of her neck burned. She still didn't know how she felt about aiding the Confederacy. That didn't mean she'd not comply with her father's request...because it helped Will.

"Yet you left the money back in Richmond." He rapped his knuckles against the desk.

"I didn't like to bother you with it." She lifted her chin. "Especially since I'm staying a short carriage ride from the Executive Mansion." Everything in her was muddled. Only one thing had been made clear during her prayers for guidance this morning at church. This was her task, not her uncle's.

"Wait." He gave his head a slight shake. "Did I understand you correctly? You plan to give the gold to President Davis yourself?"

"Yes." She straightened her shoulders. "This gift is from my father. I will represent him in this matter."

"You're one determined young lady. Yet there is another consideration." Studying her expression, Uncle Isaac leaned back in his chair. "Your father wrote of some qualms about your loyalty."

Her face flamed, and she stood. "Uncle Isaac, I am loyal to my country." He didn't need to know that her thoughts were a mass of jumbled emotions. Who deserved her loyalty? Her home was in the North. Her brother's home was in the South... not to mention her sweet baby niece, whom Bea had yet to meet. "I love my father. I will do as he asked."

"You place yourself in needless jeopardy." He pressed his fingertips together. "If, say, a Federal officer discovers that you gave gold to the Confederate government while in Richmond, you might end up in a Northern prison the same as Will."

A jolt skittered through her body. "No one will know." Her voice came out in a whisper.

"There are Union spies in Richmond. This we know." His fingertips turned white from the pressure. "They turn up in the most unexpected places."

"No doubt." Her eyes widened. Did he suspect *her*—his own niece—of spying? She barely knew her own heart. "Nevertheless, I feel this is the right way to proceed." His doubts actually strengthened her resolve.

"Very well. I will readjust my day's plan for tomorrow to ride into the city and accompany you there."

"Not necessary." She rose. "Though I thank you kindly for your offer."

He stood, his hands clasped behind his back.

"I am so pleased we were able to talk over this matter." Something didn't feel right about the whole situation, though she didn't understand why. "Now we can enjoy our day without its shadow over our heads."

"Spoken just as your mother might have done." Isaac gave her a reluctant smile. "You not only inherited her beauty and compassion, but also her independent nature. You do her proud."

Tears sprang to her eyes. "Uncle Isaac, you could scarcely have chosen a more welcome comparison. Thank you."

"My pleasure. One more thing before we return to the parlor." His smile faded. "Your father has charged me to look after you and Meg while you are in our fair capital city. Should trouble arise, send for me."

"I will." As she followed him out, she wondered at the tension in his erect posture. They had ended the discussion on a positive tone. Did he have lingering doubts about her loyalty?

Unlikely. Father trusted his brother. She'd do the same.

Perhaps Uncle Isaac could help obtain passes. No, she'd ask Jay once more for his help. No need to bother her uncle.

Especially as she remembered her father's half-uttered concern about the reasons he didn't inherit the land that Uncle Isaac now called home.

Meg sneezed again.

Glancing at Meg's flushed cheeks, Jay folded his arms. Unless he missed his guess, the weather had taken a toll on the widow.

"Bless you." Concerned, Beatrice looked at her cousin's watery eyes on the carriage ride home. "Do you feel badly, Meg?"

"A little." She touched her handkerchief to her nose. "No need to fret."

"This dreary chill is enough to make us all ill." Rain struck the roof. Beatrice peeked around the shades. "Too dark to see anything but low hanging branches."

"If the road doesn't become too muddy, you ladies will be home in half an hour." As much as Jay enjoyed their company, he was ready for the day to end.

Bea rubbed gloved hands over her cloaked arms. "I do hope Harold is not too cold, driving in this weather."

"I have an umbrella. I'll sit with him and hold it over us." Jay gave her a blanket from the seat beside him. Exhaustion overtook him at the prospect. "The rain just started."

"Before you climb up there, I have a question." Determination lit Bea's eyes.

He paused with fist poised to bang on the roof.

"Will you take me to get a pass so I can travel around Richmond? As a Northerner, I know it's good to carry one at all times." She put her hand over her mouth. "How is it we were able to travel to Uncle Isaac's plantation today?"

"In our rush to accept your uncle's invitation, we forgot. I thought about it when we reached the plantation." He shrugged, relieved that concern hadn't come to fruition. "The weather may have been on our side. Perhaps the usual stops were not guarded. Perhaps God smiled on weary travelers. I don't know. I keep my pass on me. Let's pray it's enough."

Beatrice exchanged a look with her cousin. "Perhaps it's not necessary."

"It's necessary," he said. "Don't neglect it."

"I won't." She folded her arms with a shiver.

Shouts from the forest outside started his adrenalin. Yankees? "Get down."

Immediately alert, the ladies hunkered below the window.

His rifle was at home. Nothing to be done about that now.

A loud rap sounded on the carriage door. Bea gasped. Blue eyes flew to his. He touched her shoulder in a comforting clasp.

"I need to see your passes."

"I've got it here." Jay paused with his fingers on the door.

"Stay inside," he whispered. "They may want to talk with you directly."

"Good evening, folks." Jay stepped out into the rain as he perused the armed group. Confederate gray uniforms, he confirmed with a relieved sigh.

"We need to see your passes, sir." One bearded young man stepped forward.

"Certainly." He retrieved it from his inner pocket. "Jay Nickson's the name. I'm with the Tredegar Battalion and only had one turn at picket duty." He hoped to build a rapport with the men.

"You ain't missed much. Standing guard ain't fun in the rain and snow." The soldier held the pass up to the lantern light on the side of the carriage. "This is good, Mr. Nickson." He gestured to the carriage. "We've looked at your driver's papers. Who else is in the carriage?"

"Two ladies. Mrs. Margaret Brooks and Miss Beatrice Swanson. Relatives of Mrs. Gertrude Weston in Richmond."

"We'll need to see their passes."

"They're in town for a visit. They attended the Inauguration." It didn't hurt to hint they supported soldiers like the ones surrounding him. "With all the festivities going on, we forgot to see the Provost Marshal."

The man frowned. "What are you doing on this road so late on a Sunday evening?"

"We've come from a visit with Mr. and Mrs. Isaac Swanson, Miss Swanson's uncle."

"The tobacco plantation owner?"

"The very same."

Meg went into a coughing fit inside the carriage.

"The widow is very ill." Whether Meg had a real coughing spell or was acting, the officer's eyes widened. He could use the man's uneasiness to his advantage. "We must get her in out of this chill before her condition worsens."

The young man exchanged a glance with the soldier closest to him, who shrugged. "He works at Tredegar. No need to get the ladies out in the rain. Especially with one feeling so poorly. Don't want to get sick ourselves."

Someone inside gasped for air and then coughed again.

Meg's act was good enough for the stage. Or she was really sick. Whichever was true, he read the indecision on the soldier's face.

"Get the old widow out of the cold." The officer gave Jay his pass. "And see to it that they have a pass before venturing outside the city."

"I will. Thank you kindly." Not bothering to correct the soldier's assumption that Meg was elderly, Jay climbed inside before the fellow changed his mind. As soon as the door closed, Harold took off at a smart clip.

Meg coughed. The ladies were seated again.

He held a finger over his lips to discourage questions and listened for sounds of pursuit before speaking. "Understand why you need a pass now?"

Wide-eyed, Beatrice nodded. "That was quite a convincing act, Meg."

He agreed. "It saved us the inconvenience of being taken to the authorities. Quick thinking. I will take you to the provost marshal at the first possible moment. I promise." He banged on the ceiling. "Now to give Harold some relief from the rain."

The carriage slowed to a stop.

"We'll have you home as quickly as possible." Umbrella in hand, Jay shoved his beaver hat closer to his ears and stepped out into the cold. "Harold, I have an umbrella. Let's shelter under it."

"Much obliged, sir."

The wet seat soaked his trousers as soon as he sat. With any luck, he'd be in his own comfortable bed within the hour.

"It's a cold rain," Harold observed as they took off. "That umbrella helps."

"Good." The bell in Tredegar's yard would ring at half past six to begin the work day. Too early by far because it followed too many days with little rest. He shivered as rain soaked his double-caped coat.

Getting stuck in the mud on this miserable evening was the last thing he wanted. No, meeting another set of soldiers was the last thing he wanted this close to the city.

Providence had been with them earlier. He whispered a prayer of thanks and added a supplication for no further delays.

Harold slackened the reins. The horses responded by picking up speed. No doubt they were ready to be out of this weather, too.

CHAPTER 8

A sense of urgency awoke Beatrice to a dreary dawn. They'd been fortunate last night. Jay and Meg's quick thinking had saved them.

Getting the passes and giving her father's gold to President Davis were her top tasks. Uncle Isaac should not share in a gift he hadn't sacrificed to give. As the eldest son, Isaac had inherited her grandfather's thriving tobacco plantation. According to her mother, her father had expected to inherit at least one hundred—and perhaps as much as five hundred—acres of the thriving two-thousand-acre property. As a young girl, her family had dreamed of a second home on the land. It didn't happen.

No one had explained why Grandfather modified his will. It had shoved a wedge between the brothers. The conflict between the North and the South had actually united them again enough to plan a financial gift to the Confederacy.

The uneasy feeling all was not right with the inheritance had festered for years, and now grew to certainty in the cold light of morning. Even a brief meeting with her uncle yesterday left her unsettled.

Uncle Isaac was hiding something from his siblings. Had he been the one to convince Grandfather to change his mind as his death approached? Father had never accused him of it to her knowledge. Might something be done at this late stage?

It was worth investigating.

Bea pushed those reflections aside to figure a way to avoid a visit to soldiers at Chimborazo Hospital and go out on her own. Her aunt and Mary took food to wounded at Winder Hospital on Mondays, but sharp-witted Meg accompanied Bea. If she hadn't been sworn to secrecy by her father…

No, not a good idea. Her cousin must never learn of his gift to the Confederacy.

Lord, You helped us get past the guards yesterday. Please clear a way for me to keep my promise to my father.

Beatrice threw back the covers and shivered. Strange. The maid hadn't been in to build up the fire. Kneeling, she poked smoldering embers and laid a skinny branch on top. Before it caught flame, there was a knock on the door, and a maid with a bobbed cap peeked inside.

"Come in, Letty." She smiled at the black girl of perhaps sixteen. "No need to tiptoe. I am awake."

"Oh, Miss Beatrice, that's my job." She knelt beside her and chose a section of a rolled-up newspaper from the wood box. "It's sorry I am to be so late this morning. Mrs. Meg is feeling poorly. Mrs. Trudy is with her now."

Beatrice dropped a stick onto the pile. "How is she?" What kind of cousin was she to be so preoccupied with her own problems that she'd forgotten Meg's flushed cheeks of the previous evening? Aunt Trudy had sent her to bed immediately.

"A fever. Not too high. Likely from being out in the bad weather the past two days." Letty glanced up from coaxing the flames. "You don't feel poorly, do you, Miss Beatrice? Mrs. Trudy will never forgive herself if both of you take sick under her care."

She lifted her chin. She wasn't a child, after all, and neither was Meg. Then she recalled her aunt's compassionate heart. "I feel fine. Nothing worse than a bit of weariness after a hectic few days."

"Mrs. Trudy will be happy to hear it."

"I'll go to Meg now." Beatrice shrugged into her wool robe and hurried into the adjoining bedroom.

"You're certain you don't want me to send around for the doctor?" Trudy sat on the edge of the ornately-carved wooden four-post bed.

"A day or two in bed will put me to rights." Meg sank deeper into the feather pillow, her red nose and cheeks in stark conflict with her white nightgown. "Oh, Bea, there you are. I hope you didn't also catch a chill."

"I am as healthy as the proverbial ox." Beatrice sat gingerly on the yellow-and-cream quilt covering. "I'm sorry you did."

"It can't be helped. I'll miss visiting the soldiers at Chimborazo Hospital today and sewing group tomorrow at the very least. I regret that, for I love nothing more than feeling useful since Thomas …"

Beatrice's breath caught at this rare insight into Meg's feelings.

But Meg didn't continue.

Trudy took up the conversation. "After Parker passed, I questioned if there was any reason for me to live. My days, my life had been entwined with his. What future could there be without him?" Trudy's whispered tones vibrated with emotion. "I finally came to realize that the Almighty wanted me here or He'd have taken me too. My life had a purpose beyond Parker's death." She covered Meg's hand with her own. "Never doubt your worth, even now. You are very dear to us."

"As you are to me." Meg's eyes glistened.

"I will send a note around to Mary to postpone our plans."

Trudy exchanged a glance with Beatrice. "We shall all have a quiet day together."

"Please don't change anything." Meg blew her nose. "I shall feel much worse if you don't go to cheer up the wounded men in my stead."

"If you are certain—" Trudy's brow furrowed.

"I am."

"Then I will send someone after a bottle of Elijah Baker's bitters. It will soon make you feel much improved." Trudy stood. "I'll get ready now. Bea, you can join us at Winder Hospital today. I ate early so Clara has kept your breakfast in the warming oven. Go to the kitchen whenever you are ready to eat. Phineas, Mary's driver, is taking us in her carriage. Harold isn't complaining of a chill, but I've given him the next two days off to rest, hoping to ward off any ill effects."

Meg sneezed.

"I will stay with Meg, Aunt Trudy." A lump rose in her throat that she couldn't be honest with her relatives. Her errand couldn't be over soon enough.

"As you wish, my dear." Trudy kissed Bea's cheek. "I will see you upon my return. In the meantime, ask Letty for whatever you need."

"Thank you." Meg waited until she was gone before looking at Beatrice. "Sleep is all I want. Don't stay home on my account."

"What can I do for you?"

"Please don't fuss. A warm bed, a supply of handkerchiefs, and a good cup of hot tea are all I require." She blew her nose.

"Then I'll fetch your tea. Here's a stack of handkerchiefs on the bedside table." Bea pointed to them nestled beside the gas lamp, its white globe painted with yellow daisies. She bent to kiss Meg's flushed cheek and then hurried away.

Her cousin was asleep when she returned. Tepid tea would be there beside the handkerchiefs when she awoke.

As Bea donned a yellow print dress to mock the continuing

dreary weather, she was struck by the opportunity to spend the day on her own. Just as she had hoped and prayed—and then forgotten in concern for Meg.

Now, how was she to arrange to get to the Executive Mansion without arousing suspicion?

An hour later, breakfast eaten, Beatrice still didn't know how to accomplish her solitary trip. Someone had driven her anywhere she wanted to go while in Richmond. Other than walking—which was too far, especially carrying a heavy bag concealed beneath her cloak—she had no idea how citizens living in the city got around. Was there an omnibus similar to those in New York City? Beatrice didn't know nor did she believe it advisable to carry so much money on such a vehicle.

Frustration mounted as her bedroom mantle clock ticked away the minutes. Meg might sleep for hours. Aunt Trudy planned to return in the middle of the afternoon. There was time to get there and back...if only she figured out how to go.

Even if she wanted to request a ride from Harold, he was off today. Clara told her at breakfast he went back to bed after learning he didn't have to work, so he probably was a little worse off for yesterday's dousing. A pity that two of the four who went suffered ill consequences from the weather. No doubt Jay was at work unless confined to his bed. His dedication impressed her.

In fact, a lot of his character traits impressed her. All except one. For every moment that he seemed drawn to her there was a moment where she felt him withdraw. Troubling, as she couldn't think of anything she'd done to cause such a reaction.

She couldn't afford distracting reflections. Mid-morning already. What could she do?

If she were in Washington City, she'd borrow her father's buggy and handle the reins herself, a skill she'd learned as a schoolgirl from her mother, who had raised her daughters not to depend on others to do what they could easily do themselves.

Wait. Aunt Trudy had a buggy, rarely used in winter because only the back and sides of the one-seated vehicle were enclosed. Facing the cold was worth the reward of removing this millstone from her neck.

However, she'd never hitched a horse to any vehicle. She tapped a finger on her lips. Clara's son worked in the stable with his father. She'd have to ask for help…which meant explaining her errand.

An ice cream to cheer Meg? No, hot liquids soothed a sore throat.

A bank errand? Perfect. She'd exchange part of the silver given to her by her father for local Confederate currency. Her glance faltered on the chest hiding the gold. Where had Father obtained it? He kept silver—what he'd given her—in his own bank's vault.

The less she knew, the less she had to keep secret.

Pulling out a piece of paper, she wrote a note for Meg and Aunt Trudy explaining she had an errand. If she returned with none of them being the wiser, she'd burn the letter later.

~

Beatrice guided the buggy carefully down Broad Street's long hill. Though Clarence, Harold's son, had assured her that Morning Glory was their gentlest mare, she was nervous of wagons, horses, carriages, and pedestrians on the road. Capitol Square, where President Davis had given his stirring speech two days before, was near Clay Street, the location of the Executive Mansion. That was all she knew. It had been dark when they'd arrived at the reception.

Her confidence grew every time Morning Glory heeded the slightest movement in the reins.

A strong odor of tobacco permeated the atmosphere, a mute testimony of the industry's prevalence in the city. Beatrice touched a lacy handkerchief to her nose. No use. It didn't block the pungent smell. Folks around here must be accustomed to it, for no one ever mentioned the aroma in her hearing.

Heads turned her way. Well-accustomed to male attention, Beatrice tried to convince herself their stares had nothing to do with the heavy money bag tied to her shoulder.

She patted her stomach where the bag lay concealed beneath her cloak. No, it didn't show through the folds. That slight lump gave nothing away.

"What's she doing, riding in that open vehicle in the middle of winter?"

Beatrice stiffened at a strange man's comment from the sidewalk.

"Couldn't say. She's a Yankee though. Her and another Yankee are staying at Mrs. Weston's house." Another man spat tobacco juice on the sidewalk. "Probably here to spy on us."

"Can't trust any of 'em."

"Truer words were never spoken."

Insulting. Beatrice's face flamed as she passed them. The pair, some ten paces from her, must have known she overheard.

Every instinct wanted to respond. To tell them that was no way to treat a lady. Something held her back. Better to ignore the hurtful words. It was the first time out alone in Richmond. Had the presence of her Southern escorts protected her from such abuse?

If these men knew her errand today, they'd change their mocking stance.

Still, she was unaccustomed to disrespect at the hands of strangers.

Lifting her chin, she determined to forget the incident. Those men weren't worth another thought.

Capitol Square loomed up ahead on the left. The Executive Mansion was in the opposite direction, but where?

She turned right on one of the numbered streets. Luck favored her, for an impressive three-and-a-half story gray mansion stood a block away.

Not luck, but Providence. *Thank you, Lord. Please continue to guide me.*

Three soldiers, armed with muskets resting on their shoulders, approached her. "What's your business here, Miss ..."

Her heart hammered against her ribs at the weapons. "Swanson. Miss Beatrice Swanson. My business is with President Davis."

The oldest one, perhaps in his mid-thirties, strode over and leaned against the buggy. "Does he expect you?"

"No." Her shoulders straightened at his abrupt manner. "You may inform him that I'm here."

Jay smothered a yawn as he followed the men out of the gun foundry for their lunch break. Tredegar had finished the Navy's huge order for armor plates earlier that month. Many had worked almost exclusively on the two-inch plates to give four inches of armor on the Confederacy's *Merrimack* since September.

In addition, Lieutenant John Mercer Brooke had designed a heavy rifled cannon with a wrought iron ring on the piece at the breech. They'd received orders for the first two Brooke guns in September, orders which had expanded twice in the fall.

The smell of heated iron was nearly as prevalent in the yard as in the many buildings working with the metal. He sneezed as the brisk air struck his face. This cold was poorly timed, for he'd not leave at the end of the normal ten-hour shift any day this week. They had too much to do. He'd stay himself and offer overtime to any man who wanted it, no matter how much he'd prefer an early night.

When Mr. Swanson asked for details of what they were producing, he'd kept his mouth shut for good reason. If citizens knew of the armor plate that made the *Merrimack* an ironclad vessel, the enemy would know it, for it didn't seem possible to keep secrets in this capital city. Spies lurked around every corner.

That's one reason his superiors had added spying on visitors to the ironworks as well as his workers to his tasks. He hadn't found reason to suspect his own men of sharing secrets. Visitors were another matter altogether.

For all he knew, Bea and Meg were Union spies, using their visit to amass sensitive information important to the military and whisper it to authorities in Washington City.

Folks were plenty mad at Yankees, and Jay didn't blame them. Too many had lost husbands and sons. Though the South had won some major battles, they'd lost Fort Henry on the Tennessee River and Fort Donelson on the Cumberland River just this month. The loss of Roanoke Island on the North Carolina coast struck a chord with Richmonders, especially with the death of Captain Jennings Wise of the Richmond Blues.

Jay fell in behind the back of the lunch line. Another sneeze. As slowly as he was moving today, forty-five minutes wasn't a long enough break. He'd wolf his food down to make it back on time.

"President Davis has important matters that demand his attention." The look the officer exchanged with a fellow soldier was nearer to a sneer. "It may be hours—even days—before he can spare a minute."

To talk to the likes of you. He may as well have said it aloud, so plain was the look on his face.

"It's important I see him." Did her manner of speech give her away as a Northerner? "I will take but a moment of his time. Perhaps you can show me somewhere I can wait." Preferably inside the warm mansion.

"I'll need to see your pass."

Not good. There was no Southerner at her side to vouch for her. "I haven't obtained one yet."

Another soldier approached from the other side and took the reins. Then he extended a hand to help her down.

Finally, a Southern gentleman. "Thank you," she said, once her feet were planted on the grass. "I'll get a pass today. I met President and Mrs. Davis at the reception on Saturday evening while with my aunt, Mrs. Gertrude Weston." Glancing at each face, she was filled with chagrin when none reacted to the name. Perhaps they'd recognize the other names. "My Uncle Isaac Swanson and his wife, Meredith, who own a plantation east of the city, were also there. I was also accompanied by Mr. James Nickson and his mother, Mrs. Mary Nickson. Mr. Nickson is with the Tredegar Battalion."

Something in the leader's manner changed. "Wait here."

Two of them sauntered toward the mansion's small front porch leaving two others standing a respectful distance away from her. Several soldiers rode around the building, their horses at a slow trot. Dismounting, they joined a small group of uniformed men gathered there. Because the soldiers had halted her buggy before reaching the mansion, the back of the home was in plain view and caught Beatrice's eye. Fruit trees graced the steep terraced garden in back—the type of garden that invited guests to linger. Classic columns along a large portico in the rear of the home gave the impression of grandeur.

Very pretty indeed. If it hadn't been such a gloomy, cold day, she might have been tempted to explore the beautiful gardens. As it was, her shoulders sagged under the heavy sack of gold. The soldiers near her buggy watched as she strolled to a nearby bench.

The sooner she rid herself of this burden, the better.

Her attention swung back to the soldiers as one of them mounted the steps and went inside.

She had no intention of going home without a pass. Perhaps she'd ask President Davis for his assistance.

If they let her see him.

CHAPTER 9

"You told my guard that what you have to say is important." President Davis gestured for Beatrice to sit on the armchair angled toward his in the parlor after a brief greeting. "I'm certain you can appreciate that my days pass quickly with all the tasks awaiting my attention."

"I do understand." She wanted this interview over too. "I'll be brief. My father, Hiram Swanson, is a banker in Washington City. His son—my brother, Lieutenant William Swanson of the Seventeenth North Carolina—was captured last year when his forts surrendered, Forts Clark and Hatteras. My father was loyal to the Union until he witnessed his son held for months in a Northern prison."

"My regrets to your family." He spoke graciously. "Has Lieutenant Swanson been exchanged?"

"Yes. Early this month." She realized that, from the way she began, he expected her to ask for help with Will's release. "I didn't come to ask for help but to bring it. My father's change of heart prompted him to send a gift to the Confederate government." She removed her cloak and drew the straps holding a bulging bag from her shoulder. "He gives his donation in gold because it retains its value in times of financial uncertainty."

"This is a welcome surprise, Miss Swanson." He accepted the bag and opened it with a smile that eased the tension on his face. He reached inside eagerly. A golden coin in his hand shimmered under the gasolier, a gaslight chandelier. "I recall you from the reception. You were there with your aunt?"

"Yes, Mrs. Gertrude Weston." This was going better than she'd expected. She reminded him of the others attending with her, adding her uncle and aunt's names to show the family connection.

"Nearly the whole family there to welcome me in as the Confederate president." His eyes gleamed as he stared at the gold coins. "Thank you for your gift. May I send an acknowledgement to your father?"

"Please don't trouble yourself." Her cheeks flushed. She hoped he wouldn't find her rejection as rude as it felt. "He lives in the North, after all, and—"

"Understood. Well, is there anything I can do for you?"

"Just one thing." It was the opening she'd waited for. "My cousin and I require passes. We plan to be here into the summer months. Can you…I mean…do you…?"

"Say no more." He strode to a table and scribbled on a paper. "Take this to the Secretary of War's office. He will take care of the matter. Ask one of my soldiers to escort you if you like."

"Thank you, President Davis." She stood, thankful that she'd done what her father asked.

The mantle clock chimed the hour for the second time since Beatrice arrived at the crowded office on Bank Street—unescorted for she had simply inquired the building's location from the soldiers standing guard near her buggy.

Bea fought to keep her rising frustration from showing in her expression. After waiting an hour and a half, she wanted to push her way to the front of the line and wave her note from President Davis in the officer's face.

As another man left General Clayton's office with a discouraged expression, she decided it was best not to stir the pot. Glimpses of the general had revealed his silvery hair atop a stern, commanding face. It seemed he refused as many passes as he granted.

Perhaps Bea should have waited for Jay to accompany her.

No. Her father had done all he could to smooth her path to Richmond, and she didn't need another parent. There were other women waiting in the cramped space. She wasn't helpless.

A woman dabbed wet cheeks with a handkerchief as she stepped away from the provost officer's desk.

Bea glanced at the general, who had already seated himself and moved on to the next person. The woman's tears hadn't moved the general enough to change his mind. Perhaps a confident approach was best. After all, the note from President Davis all but granted permission for her and Meg to travel in and around the perimeter of Richmond through the summer.

Her father's gift had paved the way for them.

Another quarter hour passed before a harried man ushered her forward. "Are you here to obtain a pass?"

"Yes."

He gestured an empty seat in front of General Clayton, who stood.

"Yes?"

"Good afternoon." Bea blinked. She understood he was busy but had expected more than the brusque greeting. "My name is Miss Beatrice Swanson, and I'm here to request a pass to travel in and around Richmond."

"Where are you from, Miss Swanson?" His stare pierced through her.

"Washington City." She lifted her chin as they both sat. "My cousin, Mrs. Margaret Brooks, and I are making a long visit to my aunt. Perhaps you know her. Mrs. Gertrude Weston lives in the Church Hill area of Richmond." It didn't hurt to let the officer know that her aunt lived in a wealthier part of the city.

"I know of her. We've never met." He leaned back in his chair. "Why are you visiting in the middle of the hostilities?"

"We have often made such visits and saw no reason to stop." Bea met his suspicious gaze without flinching. She told him about herself and her relatives and that her uncle's plantation near Seven Pines was a destination they'd visit.

"I've met Mr. Swanson. So he's your uncle. An easy claim to verify." He raised bushy eyebrows.

"It is." Bea bristled at the general's blatant distrust. "In fact, I met with President Davis this morning. He learned that Mrs. Brooks and I haven't yet obtained a pass and wrote you a note to set your mind at ease over the matter."

General Clayton snatched the note from her outstretched hand and scanned it. "You'd have saved us both precious minutes by showing this to me immediately. Perhaps you will remember that in future dealings."

Bea recalled her upbringing in time to bite back a retort. Her mother would have gently put him in his place. "Of course. We are requesting that the pass extend through the summer months."

"President Davis has written of your request." He paused and gave her another piercing stare. "One wonders why."

Good. The leader hadn't explained his reason for granting her request. Bea straightened her back. She had no intention of mentioning her father's gift. To anyone, ever.

He waited a few seconds. Then, after dipping his pen into the ink well, he wrote on two pieces of paper. "These passes allow you and Mrs. Brooks to travel within ten miles of our city. They expire on September first. Should you desire to go back to

Washington City before then, come back here first. We also want to see you if you want to travel outside the limits set by the pass." He blew on the wet ink before giving her the forms.

"Very good." September seemed the distant future, and she could not foresee traveling further than Uncle Isaac's plantation. She and Meg had originally discussed leaving in June, but her aunt urged them to stay longer so they agreed. Bea was happy to remain in Richmond and away from her father, who had placed her in a dangerous position. It was hard to forgive him for embroiling her in his scheme, especially with all the trouble it might cause her. Her resolve to maintain her silence strengthened like steel. "Thank you for your time."

He inclined his head and then looked beyond her.

Dismissed, she left holding the papers aloft to dry.

The task had taken more time than she'd had to give. Her aunt's staff would worry when she missed lunch. Perhaps Harold might even look for her, believing that she lost her way on city streets.

They didn't know she had lost her way when her father asked her to betray her country.

CHAPTER 10

"Did you hear?" Ward Ellis's deep voice carried across the open field of Gamble's Hill.

Jay, lagging behind his fellow soldiers in Tredegar Battalion on the green field where they'd just finished a routine Saturday drill, quickened his pace to learn the latest war news. He'd gone to bed exhausted after supper without reading the Richmond newspapers all week. Today was the first day of March. What had he missed?

One of the six men walking ahead of Jay tossed his musket over his shoulder. "Hear what?" Victor Poole's bored tone was typical. He didn't care about events unless they directly affected him.

"President Davis declared martial law in Norfolk and Portsmouth a few days ago. Now it's Richmond, with General Clayton in charge. It even affects those within ten miles of our city."

Jay gave a low whistle.

The men stopped and turned at the sound.

"Didn't see that coming." Jay joined the group.

"No." Ward rubbed his hand across the musket resting

against the shoulder of his gray jacket similar to everyone else's in the battalion. "But I figure it's because there's too many Yanks in our city."

"Probably spying on us." Though shorter than Jay by a couple of inches, Victor was a large man and not afraid to fight. He'd be a formidable opponent for a Northern spy.

Jay cringed. "Without a doubt, some of the Yankees are spying on us." In the past, some of their company's secrets had become known to Federal forces, notably about the Southern submarine ships. Jay and his fellow workers must prevent sensitive information from falling into the wrong hands.

"Send 'em all back up North." Victor grunted.

"No one wants to eat with the enemy." Ward kicked at a tuft of grass.

"Not all Northerners are our adversaries." Jay's face turned hot despite a stiff breeze. He had dined with Bea and Meg on several occasions. They sewed for Southern soldiers. Visited Confederate wounded in hospitals. Surely those weren't the actions of an enemy.

"To me they are." Victor scowled.

"Agreed." Dirt flew under Ward's boot. "Anyway, I reckon the new rules are aimed at Yankees and our citizens who support the Union, but I don't know as we're not opening a can of worms."

Jay's thoughts flew to Bea, whom he hadn't seen since dropping her and Meg off on Sunday night after visiting her uncle. He'd best warn them to keep their loyalties to the Union to themselves or they'd come under the scrutiny of General Clayton and his marshals.

A can of worms indeed.

"Elizabeth, I'd like you to meet my dear niece, Miss Beatrice Swanson, who will be with me through the summer." Trudy drew Bea closer to a pretty brunette some twenty years her senior. "Bea, this is my friend of many years, Miss Elizabeth Van Lew. She and her mother live on Grace Street."

"How do you do?" Beatrice said.

"Very well, thank you." Elizabeth's smile eased the strain on her thin face. "You're one of the nieces who live in Washington City?"

"I am. My sister Annie chose to stay close to her husband, who was camped near us."

Something flickered in her eyes. "Her husband is a Union soldier?"

"Yes." Bea looked around to see who was listening in the crowded church yard. Jay talked with a group of men a few feet away, and Meg chatted with an older woman.

Her aunt inclined her head at Beatrice.

A warning. Perhaps it was best not to provide regimental details. "He's a Union officer."

"I haven't had the pleasure of meeting Annie's husband, my new nephew." Trudy smiled. "Which only reminds me that I haven't held my great-niece either."

Bea jumped on the subject change. "My brother and his wife were blessed with my niece in December. Hannah is—"

"Nearly three months old." Trudy covered her mouth with a gloved hand. "It's true what they say about the passage of time—it flies past on eagles' wings."

"Indeed it does," Miss Van Lew said. "Your family has been blessed."

Meg wandered over to stand beside Bea.

Trudy took Meg's arm and introduced her.

"How lovely to meet you, Miss Van Lew." Meg inclined her head.

"It's a pleasure to meet you, Mrs. Brooks. Is your husband with you?"

Meg's smile was gentle. "Always, but only in my heart. Unfortunately, I lost Thomas."

"My condolences, my dear." Compassion filled Elizabeth's face.

Bea hooked her arm with Meg's. "We are all the richer for having known him."

Meg drew a deep breath. "Indeed."

"Are you also from Washington City, Mrs. Brooks?"

"I'm staying there for now with Bea's family, who kindly opened their home to me for the duration of the war." She patted Bea's hand and then withdrew her arm. "Chicago was my former home."

"A fair distance away." A woman waved to Elizabeth across the cemetery. "I must speak with someone before I go, but it was lovely meeting both of you. Trudy, perhaps you will all come for supper soon?"

"We'd be delighted. Thank you." Wide-eyed, Trudy's fingers touched her lips. "Give my best to your mother." She watched Elizabeth walk away. "Well, ladies, I believe you impressed her. I haven't been invited to dine with the Van Lews in two years."

Jay joined them as Miss Van Lew walked away. He and his mother had been invited to garden parties at her beautiful home on rare occasions. There'd been talk of the Van Lews being Northern sympathizers last year. He didn't know if he believed the rumors, but he didn't disbelieve them either. Even a few longtime residents of Richmond, as the Van Lews were, had made statements in support of the Union since the hostilities began. "So you met Miss Van Lew?"

"A gracious woman." Bea tilted her head up at him with a smile. "She plans to invite us to supper one evening."

"Happy to hear it." Bea and Meg must have impressed Miss Van Lew.

"As am I." A gust of wind blew Trudy's cloak open. "Brr. I'm ready for this blasted cold weather to pass." Trudy looked at Jay. "You're still invited to dine with us, dear boy, even though your mother is feeling poorly."

"Thank you, and I will happily accept. I don't see Harold with your carriage. May I offer a ride in mine?" Jay gestured to his closed carriage with Phineas waiting on the driver's seat, reins in hand. "Mother has suffered a chill for nearly a week and is happy to spend another day in bed. She hopes to join your sewing group on Tuesday."

"Harold is still feeling poorly so we walked here. And Meg spent five days in bed this week." Trudy accepted Jay's assistance into his carriage.

"It's good to be up and around again." Meg rested her hand on Jay's arm and released it as soon as she was seated. She scooted over by Trudy.

Only Beatrice stood on the grass with him. "How about you?" he asked, extending his hand to her. "I hope you didn't suffer any ill effects from last weekend's bad weather."

"None at all." Smiling, she placed her gloved hand in his. "And I have some news for you."

That radiant smile did something to his heart. He somehow managed to remember to help her climb the carriage step.

Once he was seated beside her, she turned to him. "Did you forget to take us to the provost marshal's office?"

"I apologize to you both." His heart sank to disappoint her. "This week was so busy that—"

"Aunt Trudy explained that you sometimes don't eat supper until eight o'clock." Bea clasped her hands together.

"It's usually closer to seven." Jay glanced at Trudy. How much had she told the cousins about his job? "But it's important to get your passes at the earliest opportunity because—"

"I already have them." Her blue eyes sparkled at her triumph.

His glance darted from Bea to Meg and back again. "You already have them?"

"Meg was sick, and I knew something had to be done after the soldiers stopped us last Sunday."

"What's this?" Trudy flapped her hand across her reddening face. "You didn't tell me you were stopped by soldiers."

"Yes, it happened just outside the city on our return trip." Bea gave her aunt a rundown on what had happened.

When they reached Aunt Trudy's house, Jay helped them all outside and then placed a hand on Bea's shoulder to halt her as the others hurried inside. "So you went by yourself to the provost marshal?"

"I did."

"Did you have any trouble?" He'd learned that passes weren't always given on the first or even the second attempt.

"A long wait." She hesitated. "And a short meeting with a rather gruff man."

"General Clayton?"

"Yes."

"I'm proud of you."

She blushed and took his arm.

Bea's independent spirit pleased him. This sweet woman captured his attention more with every meeting and now had tucked her small gloved hand on his sleeve. His feet barely touched the cobblestone sidewalk leading to the porch.

CHAPTER 11

"You must be mistaken." Mary Nickson's voice carried across the parlor at Amy Waterman's home, where the women of St. John's Church gathered to sew on Tuesday.

Bea noticed Meg's shoulders tensing and halted mid-stitch.

"It's true." Faith Bartlett leaned across the other large table in the room. The mother of eight had earned the gray streaks in her brown hair. "Former U.S. Congressman John Minor Botts has been arrested."

"Taken in the middle of the night, from what I hear." Katy Ann Everett tucked a wisp of blond hair, arranged in a bun at the nape of her neck, behind her ear.

"Was there a warrant?" Trudy's eyes darkened, a threaded needle poised over a shirt sleeve.

"A warrant isn't necessary these days." Faith put down the cotton fabric and stuck her needle into it. "The suspension of habeas corpus and martial law gives the government the power to arrest whomever they please."

"No warrant?" Trudy frowned. "Then what was the charge?"

"I heard he was arrested because he's a Union man." Katy

Ann, a mother of two in her thirties, glanced around the room with narrowed eyes.

Heart racing, Beatrice stared at the fabric in her hands, which would soon be a handkerchief. A man was arrested because he supported the Union? The man had broken no laws. Why was this allowed?

Meg bent over her nearly completed shirt, her expression hidden.

"He's not the only one." Amy Waterman, a brunette and the mother of two sons, turned from her seat beside Bea. "That whiskey distiller, Franklin Stearns is his name, was also arrested. They say he supports the Union."

Bea gave her head a slight shake. Jay had warned them on Sunday not to be vocal in support of the Union. Since he hadn't explained the reason for his warning, Bea hadn't told him that her mind was a confused muddle. And now this. What was happening in Richmond?

"That surprises me, to be sure." Mary leaned back in her chair, her face ashen. "Was anyone else arrested?"

"There were others. Folks I didn't know." Faith stared out the window, where the sun was hidden behind gray clouds yet again. "A butcher. A night watchman. A grocer. An ice dealer."

So many? Bea hid her shaking hand beneath the fabric. Were she and Meg also in danger of arrest?

"They've closed the distilleries. No liquor is to be sold." Amy glanced up. "Legally, anyway."

"That will stop the public drunkenness that's been such a problem of late." Trudy gave Mary a troubled look. "Good riddance."

"The best news I've heard." Mary nodded. "Anything else?"

"We're all to be in our homes by ten o'clock." Katy Ann threaded her needle.

"And stay there until dawn." Amy frowned. "The streets will be patrolled to make certain folks obey the law."

"Oh, and you'll need a passport if you have to travel outside the city." Katy Ann stared out the window.

Gray clouds thickened on the horizon.

"Do they realize the inconvenience they cause?" Mary muttered.

Sounded like the whole city was in prison to Bea. She glanced at Meg, who sewed at a rapid pace. Her flushed cheek was all Bea could discern of her cousin's face.

~

A letter from Oliver Fudge lay on the hall table when Jay arrived home from work on Friday. "Mama? I'm home." He peeked into the dining room. His mother's place was cleared, and the table was set for one. Late for supper again, the same as every weekday since last summer. No wonder he was tired.

Supper could wait. He carried his friend's letter upstairs to his bedroom, where the wood furniture and muted green wallpaper and bed coverings were the most masculine décor in the house besides what was in his father's library. He sighed. How his mother liked to decorate. Needlepoint samplers graced every hallway and room. Predominantly pink tones in the parlor and dining room gave the areas a feminine flair that both he and his father, before he passed, had learned to tolerate to keep her happy.

Flopping into a green cushioned armchair, Jay scanned the letter with growing concern. Then he washed his face and hands from the bowl and pitcher on a chest before running down the stairs.

"I'd know those pounding footsteps anywhere." Mama emerged from the parlor on the left side of the stairs. "Your meal awaits you in the dining room. I'll fetch my sampler and join you."

Jay sat at the head of the table in front of chicken croquettes, peas, and applesauce in a separate bowl. He asked a silent blessing on his meal and began eating before his mother entered with her sewing basket.

"How was your day?" he asked.

"Good." She set the basket on the chair beside her. "Trudy and I took the girls to Chimborazo Hospital again. The girls helped the nurses care for our wounded. Trudy and I fed those who are missing arms and hands." She shook her head. "Such a pity."

Hearing that the Northern women were caring for Southern wounded warmed Jay's heart toward them, especially Bea. Her kind, generous nature appealed to him.

"I didn't expect those girls to enter into charity work for our soldiers as they have done." Mama guided a needle threaded with blue thread into cream-colored fabric. "It's a nice surprise."

The arrests of suspected Union supporters had continued. As long as Bea and Meg kept their Northern sympathies locked up inside, they should be safe. He hoped.

Mama sighed. "Both Trudy and I think her nieces' connections to the Weston and Swanson families will protect them."

"I hope so." He prayed for their safety every night. "Yet Meg has no actual relation to Aunt Trudy."

"We've decided not to belabor that point in future introductions." Mary tugged blue thread through the fabric. "I invited Trudy and the girls to lunch after Sunday services."

"Glad to hear it." His spirits lifted at the prospect. "We've been at their home every week since Bea and Meg arrived."

"It was easier at first, when they were learning our routines." Her attention didn't stray from her needlework. "We'll likely resume our custom of taking turns. The price of food has soared. It's not right for Trudy to bear all the expense."

"I agree." Though Father had left her well-cared for, it wasn't fair for one person to make all the sacrifices in any relationship.

"I've also invited the Bartletts and the Robersons."

"Good." One couple his mother's age and one a few years his senior. His mother had chosen well.

"What news is there from Oliver?"

"They've moved their camp to Berryville Road a week ago."

"They certainly move around a lot." She looked up. "Is there a reason for it?"

"The army doesn't always inform privates of reasons for their orders, but Oliver figures he knows what it is." The familiar feeling of dread returned. "They moved camp often because the enemy was near."

"Oh, dear." The needle slipped from Mama's fingers. "Of course, I realize the Union army has been in Virginia for months. It's just..."

"That the enemy camps near the men I grew up with?" He clenched his jaw.

"Yes," Mama whispered. "It might have been you."

"But it's not me." Fate had given him a different task, one just as important. President Davis had helped him see the truth.

"I hope you don't mind if I'm grateful your job keeps you in Richmond." Mama fished for her needle among the folds of her skirt.

"Not at all."

His answer seemed to satisfy her and she began sewing again.

Jay's thoughts, however, returned to his friends at camp. Was the Union army headed for Richmond?

"The weather has warmed." A week later, Bea lifted the lacy sheer drapes that were so often closed during the day in her aunt's parlor. Her aunt was out and Bea still hadn't found an opportunity to ask her about Grandfather's will. "The sun is shining. Surely that's a hopeful sign spring is coming. Let's walk this afternoon."

Five minutes later on the sidewalk, Bea turned to Meg. "Let's stroll the neighborhood and then take Broad Street toward the city."

"Sounds lovely. This is the nicest day we've had since we've been here. I don't mind where we go."

"I believe that's Miss Van Lew's home. It's on Grace Street." Bea nodded to a mansion on their right. "Look at the lovely terraced garden."

"Those magnolia trees are beautiful. The landscaping was well-planned for the hilly terrain." Meg turned. "Look at the lovely view of the James River they have from the gardens."

"Here's the front of the home." Bea's breath quickened from the exertion of climbing the hill. She stopped to admire the three-story mansion with its stately pillars.

"Wouldn't it be lovely to sit in a rocking chair on one of those wide porches?"

Bea burst into laughter. "I hardly think rocking chairs are the style I expect to see there."

"But it's exactly my style." Meg grinned.

"Miss Swanson. Mrs. Brooks."

They turned to see Elizabeth Van Lew strolling toward them from the corner of Broad Street. They hurried to meet her.

"Miss Van Lew." Bea smiled. "How good to see you again. We're taking advantage of the pleasant weather and stopped to admire your lovely home."

"Why, thank you. Please join me for a cup of tea. My errands took me longer than I anticipated. I'm ready to sit and catch my breath." Elizabeth tilted her head. "Quick conversations at church aren't long enough to get acquainted. We'll enjoy refreshments and warm ourselves by the fire."

Bea wasn't cold or thirsty, but she did want to befriend her aunt's neighbors. She looked at Meg, who nodded. "A cup of tea sounds lovely." They joined her on the walk leading to her home.

"You may both refer to me as Miss Elizabeth, if you like." She lifted her dark skirt a few inches while climbing the porch steps.

"Thank you." It was a gesture of friendship. "Of course, you are welcome to call me Beatrice or Bea."

"And I prefer to be called Meg." She reached the top step as Elizabeth opened the door.

Though she was accustomed to large homes, Bea was surprised that the entry hall was wider than hers back in Washington City. They were led to an elegantly furnished parlor, where Elizabeth asked a maid to bring refreshments.

"How do you like our city?" Elizabeth asked once they were seated near a cozy fire.

"I've always loved Richmond. My father was born and raised on a plantation near here. I love that my Southern roots tie me to this city." Bea struggled to find a gracious reply. "But right now, with all the turmoil of martial law..."

"It has somewhat changed the welcoming atmosphere." Meg's bracing smile lightened the sting of her words.

"I quite understand. These are troubling times." Elizabeth studied them. "Have you experienced any negative comments directed at you as Northerners?"

Bea recollected the men on the street who'd spoken of her in derogatory tones. She hadn't told anyone about the incident, and it seemed best to hold her silence with a recent acquaintance. They had talked twice with Miss Elizabeth on the church grounds, and even Aunt Trudy had seemed surprised by her attention.

"Is it so obvious then that we are from the North?" Meg maintained a pleasant demeanor.

"To those who live here." Elizabeth smiled. "Does the number of arrests of suspected Union supporters alarm you?"

Bea looked at Meg. This wasn't typical afternoon tea conversation, and refreshments hadn't arrived yet. "I don't like to see anyone arrested and held without a trial." Her thoughts flew to all Will had endured as a prisoner of war.

"I agree." Meg studied their hostess. "Most folks here assume we are for the Union simply because of where we live."

"Not everyone." Elizabeth rested her folded hands in her lap. "Assumptions can be dangerous in our current environment."

Bea shifted against the comfortable cushion. Their hostess steered them toward murky waters. Was she trying to trap them?

Meg's green eyes narrowed. "You aren't trying to get us arrested as Union sympathizers, are you, Miss Van Lew?"

"Far from it, Mrs. Brooks." Elizabeth met her gaze squarely. "You've sewn for Confederate soldiers, visited Confederate wounded in our hospitals. Are you compassionate women who seek to ease their pain, no matter what side they fight on? Or is it an act to steer local authorities away from learning your true feelings?"

"You are well informed." Meg squared her shoulders.

Elizabeth inclined her head. "I merely seek the truth."

Bea wished she were as certain of her loyalties as her cousin and her sister. But she wasn't. She saw both sides. Mostly, she wanted the division to end. Yet Elizabeth's probing statements stemmed a new fear. "Do you believe we are in danger of being arrested under this new martial law?"

CHAPTER 12

After lunch on Friday, Mr. Furbisher, the foundry superintendent, sought out Jay and motioned for him to join him outside the gun foundry.

What now? It had been a grueling morning, and Jay didn't need additional headaches. He joined his superior in the yard outside the L-shaped gun foundry. "You wanted to speak with me, sir?"

"It's not good." Mr. Furbisher cracked his knuckles. "Just what are you and your men doing in there?"

"Besides filling orders for train wheels, we've lately been casting cannon, sir." Jay wondered what he'd done to warrant the stern tone.

"Not very well, son, I can tell you that much."

Jay took a step back. "What do you mean?"

"We've had reports of cannons exploding." Mr. Furbisher's graying beard fairly tingled. "*Tredegar* cannons delivered last month."

Steel pounded against steel in the background as the terrible news pierced his soul like the frigid air penetrated his coat. Had their cannon cost soldiers their lives?

"Part of your job is to watch your men and other workers. It's vital to protecting our company and our soldiers who use our equipment." Mr. Furbisher's eyes narrowed. "Seen any sign of deliberate sabotage?"

"None," he managed to stammer. Had he missed something? His heart sank for the disastrous loss. His foundry's skilled workers had accomplished a fair amount of work to melt gun iron, prepare flasks, and then cast the cannon that ranged in size depending on the order. Then each was sent to the gun mill, a general iron foundry, and a brass foundry. Mistakes could have occurred during any of those processes. If he had been more diligent in monitoring his workers' actions, might he have prevented this tragedy?

"We've received cannon pieces back so they can be recast," Mr. Furbisher said. "Our foundries have been running daily since the conflict started. We're tired, but that's no reason to deliver inferior cannons."

Heat coursed up Jay's neck. Mr. Furbisher was right. There was no excuse for inferior workmanship.

"I want you here every day to oversee your men while they recast those cannons." Wrinkles deepened in the man's brow. "You're not the only ones working this schedule. I'm going to all the foremen. I'm not certain where the problem started. All I know is that we must fix it."

"Yes, sir." A knot developed in Jay's stomach. Poor workmanship was unacceptable at any time. During war, it was inexcusable.

"Our next cannons will be tested," Mr. Furbisher said. "If any fail, our company will be charged to replace them."

A grave situation, indeed. "Our country's battalions must be able to trust our munitions."

"Agreed. I'm glad you understand the gravity of the situation. Inform your men. Keep your eyes open for sabotage as much as for poor workmanship. There may be those among us who desire to harm the South. We can't allow it." Mr. Furbisher strode away and then turned back. "Remember that our battalion has a parade and drill at half-past four tomorrow on Gamble's Hill. Full dress uniform. Arms must be ready for inspection."

"I'll be there."

"Good." The superintendent strode inside the gun mill.

Jay rubbed the back of his neck. They had worked so hard to meet the orders. Where had the mistake occurred? Was one of his men deliberately passing on faulty goods difficult to catch?

Entering the gun foundry, his gaze swept the men bent on their tasks. His mind tumbled over each of the men and rested on two who resented extended hours, despite Jay leaving it up to each one to work for overtime pay.

He rubbed the back of his neck as he considered two men stoking the furnace. He owed it to his company and his country to give everyone a hard look.

Another troubling matter was that Dr. Archer—make that Major Archer, for he led their company's battalion—believed that Richmond was in danger of attack. He'd asked that their three-hundred men battalion add two eight-inch howitzers and two twenty-four-pounder rifled siege guns. He also wanted an additional company of one hundred men. To the best of Jay's knowledge, Major Archer's requests had been declined.

Recent rumors were that General Joseph Johnston had fled from Union General McClellan's army so quickly that he left behind food and supplies, including heavy guns and ammunition. At least some of the heavy guns had been destroyed to keep them from falling into enemy hands.

Jay slapped his forehead with the palm of his hand. Here they were working extended days to supply guns, and their army had left some of the precious artillery behind.

Recasting the exploded cannon was an embarrassment to his company. Jay couldn't change what had already happened, but he planned to make certain everything sent out of his gun foundry was quality work. New orders had to be filled. Tredegar workers were running behind as it was.

He sighed to lose his only day of rest. Not only that, it was his only opportunity to see Beatrice.

Perhaps it was for the best. He couldn't deny his growing feelings for the sweet, compassionate woman.

A Northerner. He must never forget that they stood on opposing sides of the conflict. Trouble was, the more time he spent with her, the less that seemed to matter.

But it mattered.

"It's my belief that the Unionists living in Richmond are the main target, though Northern visitors will certainly be watched." Elizabeth studied Bea. "Your aunt is a respected woman in this city. While you remain a guest in her home, I believe you are safe…unless you begin spying."

Bea's heart pounded at the remembrance of her solitary meeting with President Davis. Then she calmed herself. No one knew. "I'm not a spy." Just a smuggler. Her chest tightened with guilt.

"If I claimed to support the Union"—Meg lifted her chin —"that wouldn't be a popular statement in this city."

"The number of Union supporters in the Confederate capital may surprise you." Elizabeth stiffened as footsteps approached the closed parlor door. "You were admiring my home. I'm quite proud of the alterations my father made to it."

"Oh?" Meg's eyes narrowed as the maid carried in a tray.

"Yes, our home was a brick-and-stucco Federal design when he bought it." Elizabeth smiled at a pretty maid of perhaps twenty. "Thank you, Jane."

"Your father's alterations have made it a beautiful home," Bea said. Was the maid an enslaved woman? Bea followed her hostess's quick change of topic but she wondered at its reason as Elizabeth poured their tea.

Elizabeth gave her a cup and saucer as Jane slipped from the room. "Beatrice, I've heard rumors that Jay Nickson is courting you."

She blushed. "No, that is not true." His flattering attention hadn't yet led him to suggest an outing. She was ready with her answer when he did, for she welcqmed an opportunity to become better acquainted. "His job demands most of his waking hours."

"Ah." Elizabeth's eyes twinkled. "I've seen the way he looks at you. It is only a matter of time before he asks to court you."

Bea exchanged a startled glance with Meg, surprised at the personal turn the conversation had taken. She was not in the habit of discussing her feelings, not even with her sister Annie, though she hoped Miss Elizabeth was right about Jay's feelings. Sometimes it almost seemed as if he didn't trust her. Perhaps because she was a Northerner?

"Mr. Nickson and his mother have been kindness itself to us." Meg smiled at Bea. "We appreciate their friendship more than we can say."

"Yes, they are all that is pleasant." Elizabeth sipped her tea. "His job must be a very important one to keep him from home until late in the evening. Does he talk about it?"

"No." Was Miss Elizabeth probing for secrets? "Only that he's a foreman." That was likely common knowledge.

"What is it you want to know?" Meg's expression turned serious.

"I find myself curious as to what they are doing there seven days a week." She shrugged. "One wonders about such things in uncertain times."

"No need to wonder if he's a reliable boss. He is committed

to his company." Bea was certain that anyone who knew Jay understood his loyalty.

"Aren't you curious what he does all day?" Elizabeth gave her a coaxing smile. "I'll wager that he'd be proud to show you around his building."

Meg raised her eyebrows. "I am also curious to see the famous ironworks."

"Of course, you are." Elizabeth nodded. "Surely there's no harm in mentioning your interest."

Bea squirmed in her cushioned chair. That Meg considered the outing a good idea swayed her. "In my experience, men like to boast of their accomplishments. Not Jay." After hearing so many military men boast of their regiments or weaponry, she'd been happy with his silence about his job. Now she wondered. Either he didn't have an important job or he wasn't a braggart... or he'd been sworn to secrecy.

A possibility that made him even more intriguing.

"I've noticed the same inclination to boast in military men." Elizabeth clasped her hands together. "Jay is a soldier in the Tredegar Battalion, isn't he?"

"Yes." For someone who didn't know Jay very well, she was remarkably well-informed. To what purpose? Bea stood. "Meg, Aunt Trudy will be home before us and begin to worry."

"You're right, of course." Meg stood with a smile. "Thank you for the refreshments and lovely conversation, Miss Elizabeth. I hope we will see you again soon."

Elizabeth walked them to the door. "I am certain that you will."

"Men, please come on over." No more delays. It was the end of their shift. Jay rocked back on his booted heels. He didn't want to tell his workers the bad news. Many of them were enslaved men rented to Tredegar for the income they could bring to their masters. Tredegar had bought some of them. Others were free men. Were it up to him, Jay would hire them outright, as he had done in his own home. He couldn't change the foundry's system, but his actions were within his control. He treated each man with respect.

Men sauntered to the arched gate where he waited.

"I have bad news. Some cannons that were made last month have exploded. Ours." Jay, too restless to remain still, paced in front of them. "I don't need to tell you that this is a smear on the Tredegar name."

The only sound was the popping of machinery in the background.

"Are they saying we done it?" A tall, thin man folded his arms.

"No, Seth, not specifically." Jay forced himself to stop pacing and turned to face his workers. Seth stared at his boots. Avoiding Jay's eyes? It was possible someone here was the guilty party. They were an easy group to blame since they'd only started making the guns in February. "Mr. Furbisher said that we all need to make this right. Our armies are our most important customers, and they depend upon our guns."

"What's to be done?" Zeke's brow furrowed from his stance near the back. He'd been with the foundry longer than Jay.

"Cannons will be recast." Expressions varied from sorrow to guilt to near defiance. With an overload of orders, it was safe to assume no one wanted to redo what had already been done. Jay noted the guilty expressions as men to keep an eye on. "Pieces of exploded guns are being returned. We'll melt them down and start over."

A few groans were quickly smothered.

"I wish it hadn't happened this way." Jay shoved his hands into his coat pockets. "But that's the situation we're in. I'll be here every day until this crisis is behind us. No doubt there will be opportunity for extra hours."

A few hands raised.

"Good. Thank you." Jay still didn't know what blame lay at his own feet, whether mistakes or intentional acts on the part of his workers. "Let's take extra care with these next guns."

Heads nodded.

"Go home and get some rest." If there was any shame cast on his foundry, he bore it. "We'll start on this tomorrow."

CHAPTER 13

Saturday, the day after their unexpected meeting with Elizabeth, Bea waited until Meg left on an errand before going to her aunt's study. "Aunt Trudy? Are you too busy for a talk?"

"Never too busy for you." Trudy set down her pen on the mahogany table. "Just writing a letter to Hiram."

"Oh? Have you heard from him recently?" Bea's last letter from her father had been tucked in a drawer, unanswered, for a week. He had thanked her for taking care of his 'errand' and asked her to continue her good work. She imagined he meant her to aid the Confederate soldiers, something she didn't mind doing. If he meant for her to continue giving gifts to the Confederacy, she didn't want to know.

"Yesterday. He's far more interested in events in Richmond now that you're here, my dear." Trudy laid her spectacles aside. "He also said he hasn't heard from you directly for two weeks."

"I wrote to Annie and asked her to read my letter to him." Bea wandered to the window and pushed aside the heavy brocade curtains. She'd never liked her uncle's study with its mahogany wood furniture and burgundy curtains. It seemed a dark room.

Trudy joined her at the window. "He's learned about President Davis's passage of martial law."

Bea rested her head on the cool windowpane. "He isn't ordering me to come home, is he?" Maybe her reluctance to write Father stemmed from her strong desire to stay here.

"No, though he asks my assurance that you and Meg are safe." Trudy placed a hand on her shoulder. "Why don't we sit?"

"What did you say?" Bea sat on a leather chair opposite her aunt. A gaslight lamp sat on a table to the side of them.

"That, in my estimation, you are safe. You aren't involved in any activities that arouse suspicion. Quite the opposite, in fact."

"True." Bea stared at her folded hands.

"Do you want to stay?"

"Very much. It's good to be in Richmond again." Bea studied her aunt's anxious face. "This place has always felt like a second home."

"You don't know how much that means to me." Trudy clasped her hands together. "My home has been empty far too long…and the fighting only makes the loneliness harder to bear. I hate visiting our soldiers in the cemeteries. And now I fear all the death will make it difficult for our country to heal from what we've done to each other."

Bea's throat tightened with unshed tears. Her aunt had never spoken of the country's division.

"I need you here for as long as you want to stay." Trudy extracted a dainty handkerchief from the sleeve of her gown. "You can leave tomorrow if you like. Or remain until the war's end. It's up to you. I want you to feel safe."

"I feel safe here." Her aunt's anguish was hard to bear. "Meg and I have decided to stay through August unless the situation becomes dangerous. In that case, we'll take you with us to Washington City."

"All right." Trudy gave a quick nod. "We have a plan. Now, what did you want to talk about?"

"I don't want to stir up old tensions." Her aunt was already upset. Maybe she should wait on the discussion.

"Between me and Isaac?" Trudy lifted her chin.

"Yes. And between my father and Uncle Isaac. There's been a rift between them for years."

"What do you want to know?"

"I'm curious why Grandfather changed his will."

Trudy looked away. "Yes, we're all curious about that."

"So you didn't know ahead of time?"

"No." Trudy shook her head. "Not until the reading of the will."

"Did Grandfather write the new will while he was ill?"

"It wasn't written by my father's hand." Trudy's jaw clenched. "Isaac claimed Father dictated it to him."

Jay walked to the Weston home on Sunday for a simple family supper. His mother was already there. For whatever reason, no other guests had been invited. Jay was glad, for he didn't need a crowd.

Nothing conclusive had arisen in his diligent spying on his workers. Both Seth and Zeke had volunteered for extra hours. Jay spent a good portion of his day near the pair, for one or the other looked around to locate him more often than was than their wont.

Their actions made him suspicious. That didn't mean either was guilty. It didn't mean they weren't. Jay watched everyone.

With a grueling week ahead, he was anxious to push the worries of work aside for a pleasant evening in the company of the most beautiful woman he'd ever met. Thoughts of Beatrice had enabled him to make it through the shame he felt for his company's faulty cannons. So far there was no reason to place blame on him or his men specifically. Regardless, something had gone very wrong.

No one was more determined than he to make it right.

Welcoming smiles greeted him from the women gathered in the cozy parlor. Bea's smiling eyes caught his glance and held it.

"You're earlier than expected, son," Mama said.

"I was ready to leave the foundry behind"—Jay kissed her cheek—"for the company of beautiful ladies." He looked at Bea, whose smiling blush gave him hope that she returned his regard.

"My dear boy, it's good of you to come cheer up an old woman." Trudy extended her hand, which he briefly clasped. "We missed you at church."

"Indeed." Bea patted the sofa beside her.

A promising gesture. His heart lightened at the unspoken invitation. The folds of her pink dress rustled against his leg as he sat next to her. "I regret missing the service. And your company."

"Yours is an important job." Bea tilted her head. "What do you do all day?"

It didn't hurt to speak of general information that was widely known. "Our gun foundry has skilled workmen who melt gun iron in furnaces."

"Gun iron?" Bea twirled one of her curls against her cheek.

"Yes, it's specially manufactured." Her twirling fingers mesmerized him. She was certainly a beautiful woman. "We typically make parts for the railroad—train ties, wheels, and the like. Lately we've been casting cannon." No secret there. Everyone knew they produced them.

"Are they very large?"

"They can be. The size depends on the order."

"I was right. Yours is an important job." She smiled at him.

"Just doing my job." He shifted on the cushion, troubled by

all that entailed right now. "Our soldiers have the most important job." Exploding cannons made it difficult for their army to trust their munitions.

"But you have the necessary skill and training needed at Tredegar," Mama said. "Unlike the average soldier."

"No such thing as an average soldier, Mama." How he wished to join them in the camps and on the battlefields. "They have courage to fight for their convictions. Those men have my greatest admiration."

~

"I agree." His insight impressed Bea. "But you are also a soldier."

"Home guard." His smile didn't reach his eyes. "My buddies in the Twenty-first Virginia are camping out near the enemy tonight. It's not the same."

The enemy. Jay spoke of Northern soldiers as the enemy. It disturbed her to hear soldiers like her brother-in-law described as the enemy. Her thoughts flew to Will. Was he back with his Southern regiment, preparing for another battle? There had been no correspondence from him since his return home, so he might not have received her letters sent from Richmond.

"Pardon me, Miss Trudy." Mabel peeked around the door. "Mama says to tell you supper is ready."

"Thank you. We will be along shortly."

The girl nodded and left the door open.

They all stood as Trudy took her friend's arm. "Mary, let's lead these young ones to their meal."

"Let's do." They entered the hall at a sedate pace.

Bea's heartbeat quickened. By that simple act, Aunt Trudy had released Jay from his responsibility to escort his hostess into the dining room. She looked up at him as Meg slipped from the room.

"May I?" Jay offered her his arm.

"You may." Returning his smile, Bea rested her gloved fingers in the crook of his elbow, feeling solid muscles beneath her hand. His job must be an active one. He was a strong man. "We haven't seen you much lately."

"Perhaps we can remedy that." He halted, putting distance between them and the others.

That sounded hopeful. "Yes?" She tilted her face up at him, delighting in the warmth of his arm.

"If you are willing to wait until later in the day, we can go for a ride on Saturday."

"Horseback?" Her voice squeaked. She had never learned to ride horses.

He laughed. "No. If it's a pretty evening, we'll ride in our landau to see beautiful views of the James River. We can also walk near the Capitol where the inauguration took place."

"Among the linden trees." She had been courted by several men. Never had her heartbeat quickened from a mere invitation for a drive. Perhaps it was her heart's response to the man who wanted to court her.

"Yes." His feet bounced as if buoyed by her reaction. "My battalion drills at Gamble's Hill every Saturday. After that, I'm done for the day."

"My father insists that I be chaperoned." It was as if butterflies danced in her stomach. He wanted to court her. Miss Elizabeth had been right.

"I'd love your cousin to join us." He flushed the color of ripe beets.

Aunt Trudy cleared her throat from the entry to the dining room. "Are you two coming?" Her tone was stern, yet there was a twinkle in her eyes. "Our food is getting cold."

"I'm sorry—"

"My apologies—"

They spoke at the same time and then burst into laughter.

"Come along." Trudy beckoned them. "Continue your conversation at supper."

~

"So, what were the two of you whispering about in the hall?" Mama's glance darted between the couple.

"We planned an outing for next Saturday," Jay allowed his glance to linger on Bea's blushing face. "Meg, will you join us? If I get done with my drills early enough, I will take you both to supper and then for a drive."

"I'd like that above all things." She gave Beatrice a mischievous grin. "That is, if this plan meets with Aunt Trudy's approval."

"Indeed, it does, my dear." Trudy eyed her niece. "Do remember to be home well before curfew. Those fellows patrolling the streets mean business."

"We will." A smile touched Bea's lips as she looked over at him.

"Of course." He'd forgotten the ten o'clock curfew. No matter. They'd have several hours together. "I'll remember."

Beatrice clasped her hands to her chest. "Meg, Jay will take us on a lovely drive to see the James River by moonlight."

Her excitement made the ride sound all the more enchanting.

"Then let us hope for a clear, warm evening." Meg's gaze darted between them. "Thank you for including me."

They'd had enough rain to last for weeks, in his opinion. Meg's acceptance lent his heart wings. Escorting Bea for the evening was something to anticipate amid all the bad news running rampant. He considered his acquaintances who were still in the city, seeking a possible escort for Meg. Troy Hanson, a bachelor at Tredegar, would enjoy an evening's entertainment.

Jay glanced at the widow's serene face as she looked at her

cousin. She had worn partial mourning to the reception at the Executive Mansion. Remembering her few comments about missing her husband, he rejected the idea of inviting a friend along to chaperone him and Bea and be a companion for Meg. Somehow, he knew she wouldn't like it.

"What do you hear of war news, Jay?" Mama sipped her coffee.

"There have been no new letters from Oliver." Jay looked at Beatrice and Meg. "Oliver Fudge is a school pal who serves in the Twenty-first. He's written in the past of marching in snow and rain, struggling to warm himself on cold nights by the fire. A rugged life, to be sure." He didn't want to ruin everyone's happy mood by mentioning rumors that the city was in danger of attack. Not imminent but like a wisp of smoke on the horizon. They all had enough bad news. He'd not add to it.

"I went to the market yesterday. They charged me fifty cents a pound for butter." Mama shook her head.

Evidently, his mother thought he'd given enough war news.

"Who'd have thought?" Trudy frowned at her cup of tea.

"Twenty-five cents a pound for bacon too. Jay needs a hearty breakfast before work." She looked at him across the table. "The price of beef is no better. Thirty cents a pound—for poor quality meat, let me tell you."

"The fellows at the shop were telling me that coffee is now one dollar and fifty cents a pound." Jay never shopped at the market and was glad to have something to offer to the conversation. He caught Bea's gaze lingering on him and returned her smile, glad their courtship was about to begin. What made it even better was that she seemed to feel the same.

"Outrageous. Why, some women are roasting rye or even corn to make coffee." Mama's delicate porcelain cup clinked against the saucer. "And using dried willow leaves to make their tea."

Jay nearly laughed aloud at Bea's involuntary shudder. "I

believe I'd sooner drink plain water," he said. Though if he were thirsty enough for the taste of tea, he conceded that he'd try the willow leaves after all.

"Did you hear that salt is in short supply?" Trudy gave a little smile before eating a dainty bite of chicken pie.

"That's unfortunate." Mama frowned.

"You're not going to like this, my friend," Trudy said. "The city is purchasing it from Saltville. It's to be rationed now."

"Rationed?" Mama's frown deepened.

"One pound a month per person."

Mama gasped. "So little?"

"It's only five cents a pound." Trudy put down her fork. "I'm glad my nieces are visiting."

Beatrice sputtered, as if trying not to laugh. "For the extra salt?"

"It's an extra two pounds of salt each month." She giggled.

Everyone joined in the laughter at her joke.

"The blessings these ladies bring are unceasing." Jay chuckled.

Mama darted a look from Jay to Beatrice. "That they are."

CHAPTER 14

Bea's last conversation with her aunt about Grandfather's will had upset the older woman so much, Bea decided to talk with her uncle instead. To do that, she had to see him. Jay was too busy to escort her to the plantation, and she hesitated to ask Meg to accompany her. If the truth was too ugly, she preferred to keep it between her, Aunt Trudy, her father, and her siblings.

There might be another way to see her uncle.

Bea watched for an opportunity to talk with Aunt Trudy alone. When Meg went out for a solitary stroll, Bea found her aunt sewing in front of the parlor fire. "Can I talk to you?"

"Of course." Trudy held up a small dress. "I'm sewing a dress for Hannah to send with your blanket."

"It's beautiful." Bea fingered the soft material. "Frances will love this gift."

"I hope so." Trudy set aside the yellow fabric. "Now. Tell me what's on your mind."

"Do you have plans for Easter?" Bea pulled a chair closer to the fire and then sat.

"I usually entertain guests for luncheon. They normally leave in the middle of the afternoon." She sighed. "Everything has changed so. I suppose we can host a small party, if you like."

"Back home, we always paint eggs with children who attend our Easter parties."

Trudy's eyes brightened. "We can do that. I'll ask the Bartletts—they have eight children. And the Robersons have two children. Is that enough?"

"Ten children will make a fun party." Bea laughed. "Just the right number for them to enjoy one another's company and not so many that I'll feel overwhelmed. I'll ask Meg to help."

"And I'm comfortable watching the festivities. I'm quite looking forward to it." Trudy's smile widened. "Mary and Jay will be invited, of course."

Another opportunity to see her beau. "I'd love that." Bea clasped her hands. Now for the bigger request. "May we also invite Uncle Isaac and Aunt Meredith?"

"Well...I don't know..." Picking up the fabric again, Trudy fidgeted with it.

"Please?" Bea laid her hand on her aunt's lacy sleeve. "I don't get to see them often."

Trudy eyed her. "All right. I'll send invitations today."

"Thank you." Bea hugged her, knowing it was a sacrifice.

No matter what, she would ask Uncle Isaac about the will that day.

~

"That's the sound of marching." Two days later, Beatrice halted on the brick sidewalk leading to Broad Street. "I've heard the same unmistakable sound outside my home in Washington City." This time it must be Confederate soldiers.

"They're marching into Richmond." Meg stared toward the street.

Bea's heartbeat quickened. Since both sides had cause to demand her loyalty, she still didn't know where to give it.

"Bea?" Meg gave her cloak a gentle tug. "Don't you want to continue our stroll?"

"Is it safe?" Bea lowered her voice.

"You brought your pass, didn't you?"

"Yes." Bea cinched her reticule closed.

"Then we've nothing to fear." Meg studied her. "Don't you need some fresh air? I know I do after sewing several hours in Mrs. Grover's parlor."

"It was stuffy in there."

"The odor of pipe smoke lingered." Meg's steps faltered and then quickly resumed. "There they are." She nodded ahead. "Southern soldiers."

An impressive sight indeed. Soldiers walked four abreast with muskets resting on their shoulders. Wool blankets the color of charcoal were tied at the ends and slung over their necks. Knapsacks on their backs carried personal possessions. Haversacks toted their food.

Not so different from the Union soldiers that had marched past her home last summer.

"Let's continue our stroll." Meg tugged on her gloved hand. "We're to entertain ourselves while Aunt Trudy rests. My choice of entertainment is to walk."

"Fair enough." What harm was there on the city sidewalks while a Confederate army passed beside them?

Outside St. John's Church, soldiers filled most of the boulevard. Some tipped their hats gallantly as Bea and Meg walked by.

"Should we wave our handkerchiefs at them?" Bea whispered.

"No." Meg smiled toward the men. "That's for the man you want to smell your lilac perfume and dream of you before a battle."

Jay wasn't going to battle—a blessing in her eyes if not in his. A handkerchief seemed a nice thing to offer a hero...but were these men *her* heroes? While they marched past with smiling nods and cheery waves, it almost seemed as if they were.

Bea turned toward the city, and Meg strolled beside her to the rhythm of marching feet. They skirted women and girls offering dippers of water to the soldiers. Others gave small cakes of cornbread or muffins, just as she, Annie, and other staff had done last summer.

"Looks familiar." Bea skirted around women beside large black kettles. "It's a good feeling."

"To give? It certainly is." Gazing ahead, Meg's body froze.

Bea searched the people milling ahead but recognized no one. What stole the color from her cousin's face?

Meg rushed forward without a word. Bea followed as closely as the crush of people allowed. They pressed toward the soldiers as her cousin sped further away. Then she was gone.

Panicked, Bea peered in every direction. Finally, she spotted auburn curls toward the bottom of the steep road. Meg stood near a woman with a bonnet pulled low over her forehead. The stranger spoke without looking at her and then disappeared down a side street.

Meg glanced in the stranger's direction as if undecided whether to follow.

Bea hurried to her cousin's side. "Who was that woman?"

"I thought I saw a friend. It was a mistake." Without looking at Bea, Meg turned back toward the soldiers, who raised their hats at cheers from the crowd. "Residents are making the soldiers feel welcome, aren't they?"

"Indeed, they are." Something wasn't as it seemed. Bea looked down the road the stranger had taken. Folks following the Confederate regiment moved on and climbed another steep grade of Broad Street.

If there was someone Meg knew in the crowd, she was hidden well.

"Bea? Meg and I are in the parlor."

Bea turned at the bottom of the stairs and sat by her aunt in front of a cozy fire. "Sorry, I started a letter to Annie and then fell asleep after our walk. How was your afternoon?"

"Good. I caught up on my own correspondence. I have news —we received an invitation from the Van Lews." Trudy picked up a card from the table beside her. "Mrs. Eliza Van Lew is the mother of Elizabeth, whom you've met. Eliza is a widow of some years and her daughter lives with her. They've invited us all to a soiree at their home on Saturday."

"Saturday?" Bea's smile wobbled. Surely her aunt didn't expect her to change her plans. "How unfortunate that Meg and I are already engaged elsewhere."

"I remembered, of course." Trudy scanned the invitation. "Elizabeth mentions several other families who are invited. Some you know from church. Mary and Jay, of course. The Bartletts, the Robersons, the Watermans, the Carringtons, and the Everetts are also coming."

"This is the first evening party we've been invited to since President Davis's Inauguration." She and Amy Waterman had talked on several occasions at the sewing group. She also found much in common with Katy Ann Everett. Why did it have to be the one evening that Jay singled out for their courtship to begin?

"Sad but true." Trudy sighed. "Food shortages and soaring prices have hostesses limiting entertainments to small groups… or eliminating them altogether. This invitation doesn't include supper. I will say the Van Lews don't often invite me to their parties, so there may not be another opportunity. Mary and I can attend to represent our families if you prefer to keep your plans as they are."

"I love parties. It's only that Jay has planned this special evening for us." *For me*. That made her choice easy. "If I must choose, I would prefer to go with Jay." *Then I won't have to share his attention with anyone except Meg.*

"Jay may decide to change our date." Meg tilted her head. "Since you know he's included, why not consult him?"

"You want to go, don't you?" Bea's hopes plummeted as her evening with Jay slipped from her grasp like Virginia clay.

"My spirits have been as gray as the winter weather. No doubt I would have enjoyed the party." The corners of Meg's mouth lifted in a semblance of a smile. "Supper and a drive with you and Jay will be fun. I quite look forward to it."

Remorse that she'd not consulted her cousin first battled with resentment at foregoing her time with Jay. Surely, he'd ask again, right?

"Meg's suggestion is a wise one." Trudy nodded. "I can send a note around to ask Jay to stop by tonight."

"Please do." Bea snuggled into her chair, happy for an opportunity to see him again before Saturday. And either way, she'd likely have him as an escort for the evening. Her spirits lifted at the prospect.

CHAPTER 15

Jay had lived near the Van Lews all his life yet could count the number of parties he'd attended in their home on two hands. This family was above his standing in the city's social circle. No doubt about it—his mother's friendship with Trudy Weston was the reason he'd been included. Upon learning of the soiree, he and Bea had rearranged their supper plans to Sunday. He looked across the parlor where several women mingled, Bea among them. A happy smile lit her face at the animated conversation. It had been a wise decision.

His interest wandered from his conversation with Andrew Waterman and Dave Everett as he pondered the differing groups gathered. Wealthier men who made a living in the tobacco business. Others who owned shops in the city. Jay had met a baker in the garden outside before the evening chill had ushered most guests into the parlor.

Bea glanced at him as if she had known where he stood. He returned her smile. That peach-colored dress enhanced the delicate beauty of her face.

"Is that right, Jay?"

He started at Dave's question. "Sorry, I didn't hear your question."

"Yes, your attention is centered across the parlor." Andrew chuckled. "You escorted Beatrice Swanson here tonight, right?"

Jay nodded. "Along with her aunt, cousin, and my mother."

"Who is her cousin?"

"Mrs. Margaret Brooks. Tragically, she lost her husband." He searched the room. "She's standing near the window with Miss Elizabeth Van Lew and a couple of men. I met the baker earlier but I don't know the other gentleman's name." Neither man wore expensive jackets and vests.

"The baker is Cade Yancey." Dave nodded toward a tall man in his thirties. "He owns a bakery on Marshall Street. The short, balding man is Paul Lucas. He's a carpenter and owns a furniture store also on Marshall Street."

"Small business owners standing a few feet from the Carringtons and the Roysters." Andrew sipped his punch as he scanned the guests. "Not something you see every day."

"True." The Van Lews had invited wealthier couples along with those of humbler trades. Jay wondered if they had done this at previous parties then smiled a little. He himself worked at the Ironworks, and Andrew lived in Union Hill, a neighboring community not as elite as this area of Church Hill.

"Shall we join the ladies?" Jay met Bea's gaze across the smoke-filled room.

"Reckon we should." Dave looked at Katy Ann, his wife, who sat in a circle of chairs with Bea.

Jay passed Trudy and his mother, who sat among another small group of ladies with Mrs. Eliza Van Lew near the fireplace. The large party of neighbors somehow provided comfort and a sense of normalcy in the midst of the war's turmoil.

The evening was winding down early due to the curfew, now only half an hour away. Beatrice's heart lifted at Meg's happy expression. They'd spent little of the evening together as both drifted to join different conversations. Even though she'd donned her purple wool in half-mourning again tonight, Meg had seemed to release a bit of the grief she wore like a cloak. It was a breath of fresh air to Bea, who couldn't wait to write Annie. They both had long prayed for Meg to emerge from her mourning.

"Folks are beginning to leave." Jay touched her elbow. "I'll send word for Phineas to bring the carriage for us."

"Best not to risk being late." Bea sighed to see the soiree end, for she'd met new people. Jay had been attentive even when not at her side. She had enjoyed a lovely conversation with both her hostesses. Mrs. Eliza Van Lew had graciously asked about Bea's family. And not once had Miss Elizabeth asked about Jay's job. "We'll gather our cloaks."

Jay strode from the parlor. A middle-aged couple followed him. Bea scanned the dwindling crowd, where women outnumbered the men because of the war. No one spoke of this reality in her hearing, yet the missing neighbors were almost a presence in the room.

"There you are." Meg touched her sleeve.

Bea nodded to the open parlor door where two women exited. "Jay is asking Phineas to bring the carriage."

"Then we must give our thanks for the lovely evening." The light in Meg's green eyes dimmed.

"You enjoyed it?"

"Oh, yes." A delicate flush tinged her cheeks. "I met several people that I hope to see again."

"Anyone in particular?" There had been a couple of bachelors in attendance, including a widower in his thirties.

"None of that." She shook her finger. "Thank you for altering our plans to include this soiree. A change of scenery, new folks to talk to, delicious delicacies…it's what we all needed to end this Virginia winter weather."

"Ladies, shall we find our hostesses?" Trudy reached for Bea's gloved hand as Jay joined them.

"Our carriage awaits." He offered an arm to Beatrice and his mother on his other side.

Trudy reached for Meg's hand and they all walked together to where the Van Lews stood near the door. "Eliza. Elizabeth, thank you for your kind hospitality."

"Our pleasure." Eliza Van Lew gave them a gracious smile. "I hope you will come again."

"It was a lovely party." Bea released Jay's arm to extend both hands first to Mrs. Van Lew and then to Miss Elizabeth.

"Thank you, Beatrice." Elizabeth smiled. "We don't have as many entertainments now, but we both enjoy it."

This dratted war had altered life too much. "Of course." Bea stepped back as the others gave their thanks.

Jay fidgeted at her side, and she realized fifteen precious minutes had passed since he'd left for the carriage.

"We will look for you at church." Bea turned slightly as she spoke to remind her aunt of the time.

That was all it took.

Jay helped the others inside the carriage first and then leaned over. "Our good-byes will be brief at your aunt's home, so let me say how much I look forward to tomorrow evening."

"As do I." Bea smiled up at him.

He clasped her hand and helped her inside.

She loved how he managed to take care of everyone's needs and still remain attentive to her. She gave his fingers a slight squeeze before releasing his hand.

His smile broadened as he climbed in behind her.

Tomorrow couldn't come soon enough.

CHAPTER 16

On Sunday, Jay escorted the ladies into the landau with a tip of hat at his driver. "Thanks, Phineas, for getting the horses from the stable across the street." Darkness had fallen while they ate. "We just finished our supper."

"I peeked inside the window, Mr. Jay." The graying man grinned. "I fetched them when you was about finished with your pie."

"Good man." Jay clapped him on the back and then seated himself beside Bea.

"Thank you for a lovely supper." Bea tucked her hand on the inside of his arm.

"Yes, thank you for inviting me along this evening. Supper was delicious. Not certain we'll see the James, though." Meg gestured at a gas street lamp.

"Yes." He regretted the clouds. It was more romantic to ride under the moonlight. "But we can ride to the public square."

"And walk along its paths?" Bea asked.

"Whatever you wish."

Bea seemed eager to explore the grounds. Jay hoped that

meant she wanted to spend more time in his company. "Phineas, please drive us to the square."

"On our way." He grinned back at them. The team set a sedate pace, almost as if the horses were full from dinner too.

"We'll begin at the Washington Monument." Jay settled back in his seat.

"Sounds lovely." Bea glanced at Meg. "Of course, we stood in the rain at the Inauguration and saw it then."

"It's more serene this evening." Meg's attention seemed snared by the buildings and sidewalks they passed. "I look forward to examining it from a closer view."

"As I do."

Jay entertained them with stories from his days at the Mechanic's Institute, back when he never imagined their country could divide. He enjoyed the company of the woman at his side, who listened with flattering attention at his silly stories and whose hand was tucked comfortably on the crook of his arm.

As if it belonged there.

Her hand remained there as they later stood at the feet of the bronze statue of President George Washington and the sculpted figures surrounding its base.

"I like that the sculptor designed it so that our first president is seated on a horse," Meg mused as she stared at the mounted figure. "It reminds me he was first a general."

Two couples strolled up, arm in arm.

"The cornerstone was laid on Washington's birthday in 1850 and then unveiled on the same date in 1858." Jay admired the sculptor's skill. "You may notice the sculpture of President Thomas Jefferson is there for his contribution to our independence."

"Patrick Henry is my favorite." Bea tilted her head. "His words stir my heart even to this day, 'Give me liberty …'" Her gaze dropped to her gloved hand on Jay's arm.

"'Or give me death,'" he finished. The speech inspired him yet again, all the more because the words had been spoken in his own church.

~

Bea removed her hand from Jay's arm. Patrick Henry's stirring words had inspired a revolution. That quote seemed equally fitting for those suffering in slavery today. Many fought and died for that liberty.

Suddenly, Bea's fog of confusion melted away. Her father and brother weren't supporters of slavery yet had other reasons to lend their loyalty to the South. As did her aunt...and Jay.

She respected that they felt their homeland, the state they loved, was under attack and they must defend it.

Even so, Bea had her own mind and her own heart. She wanted the Union to win this war.

What did that mean for her and Jay? She was beginning to fall in love with him. She had longed to fall as deeply in love as Annie loved John.

Now that she found a beau worthy of her heart, must she give him up?

"Bea?" Meg touched her arm.

She was glad no one was able to read her thoughts. "I'm sorry. Did you say something?"

Meg laughed a little. "We were talking about the monument. Are you feeling all right?"

"Yes, I'm fine." She caught Jay's concerned expression. "Are you two ready to stroll the grounds?"

As an answer, Jay offered an arm to each of them. Bea placed her hand on his coat sleeve.

"The Bell Tower is not too distant." Jay quirked an eyebrow at her.

"Let's walk to it." Even if the future of their relationship was uncertain, she decided to enjoy the evening.

They passed couples, a family, and men smoking cigars. Light from streetlamps touched Jay's handsome face as he bent toward her. Lingering glances accompanied by a gentle touch of his hand warmed her so that she never suffered from the night breeze. He managed to include Meg in their conversation.

He was kind and compassionate. Loving. Faithful. Strong. Fun. The type of man her heart had searched for.

A wrought-iron fence marked the boundaries of the square. The trio strolled from one end to the other before Jay faced them both.

"Ladies, I fear that it's time to get you safely home."

"So soon?" Bea surprised herself. Several men had courted her, and she'd never cared to linger with any of them after an outing. Until now.

"Unfortunately, there's that pesky deadline. We'll have more evenings like this one, I promise. They will be all the more enjoyable as spring takes root."

"It has gotten chilly. I hadn't noticed." Bea shivered and then laughed with the others.

"I believe that means you've enjoyed yourself, Cousin." Meg's glance darted over the people in the area.

"Ah, and here's Phineas." Jay waved. "Arriving just as we need him."

"You are blessed by those who work in your home." Bea waited as the landau approached.

"Blessed is the right word for it." He clasped her hand for a moment before helping her into the vehicle.

Her heart beat a staccato rhythm. The touch of his hand affected her as no one else's. Why did he have to support the Confederacy?

~

While glad of the welcoming light from lanterns hanging on either side of the arched front door, Jay was sorry that their first evening together was at an end. He wanted to kiss Bea, but it was far too soon. They needed to become better acquainted. She had snuggled against his side on the ride home but had been quiet. Meg filled the lull in the conversation with comments about the beautiful city square.

Jay decided to wait until he was alone with Bea to suggest another evening out. Something in him balked against planning it with a chaperone present.

He helped Meg from the carriage first.

"Brr." Meg shivered. "Chilly. Thanks for a lovely evening, Jay. I'll see you inside, Bea." She hurried up the walk as the housekeeper opened the front door.

Jay held out his hand to Bea. "This evening has flown. I hope you enjoyed it."

"I did." She put her small hand in his and took her time getting out of the landau. "It was wonderful."

"Good." The way she looked up at him with the streetlamp touching her face made him want to kiss her all the more. Only the housekeeper's watchful presence on the porch held him back. "Perhaps we can go to a play next time. I'll invite my mother and Aunt Trudy as well."

"That sounds lovely." She squeezed his hand and then removed it. "I would love to ride to Tredegar one afternoon. I'd enjoy seeing where you work. Meg has also expressed an interest."

Jay took a step back. Bea was a Northern lady on Southern soil. Was her motive for their courtship to learn the company's secrets? "No one visits without a pass." After four suspicious fires last May, he and others in his company had added guard duty of the grounds for weeks. He was unlikely to forget that threat.

"You can request passes on our behalf, can't you?"

"Beatrice, come inside." Aunt Trudy stood on the porch with a shawl over her shoulders. "Let your young man get home."

Bea gasped. "I forgot the curfew. I'll see you tomorrow then." With one last smile, she hurried up the path.

Jay tilted his pocket watch toward the lantern light as the door closed. Ten minutes before ten o'clock. It was no more than a five-minute carriage ride to his home.

He leaped over the landau door. "Let's hurry home, Phineas."

"We'll be there before the cat can lick his ear, Mr. Jay."

They took off at a smart clip.

"Halt." A man in shadows called the command in a gruff voice.

The landau stopped.

"Are you aware there's a curfew?" As the stranger stepped under the streetlamp's light with two other men, a silver badge in the shape of a shield with the letters 'C.S. Detective' glinted on the man's chest.

General Clayton's marshals. Best tread carefully. "Yes, sir." And it wasn't ten o'clock. "I live two streets away—"

"I'll need to see your passes. First, your driver."

Phineas extracted a page from his pocket and gave it to the marshal.

He scanned it under the light and then returned it. "Your turn."

"Of course." Jay gave him the paper. Three armed men. He wouldn't give them any reason to use their weapons or arrest him and his driver.

The bearded man held it toward the lamplight. "James Nickson. It says here that you work at Tredegar."

"Yes, sir."

"A Tredegar man escorting Yankees." The guard's eyes narrowed on the last word.

Jay stiffened.

"Them Northerners better watch their step." He returned Jay's pass. "Wouldn't want them out past curfew."

Anger shot through Jay at the veiled threat.

"No, sir. That wouldn't be a good idea." The marshal's voice softened as he refolded the document.

The hair stiffened on Jay's neck. The ladies had done nothing wrong. Why were they under the guards' scrutiny? Military police had arrested many folks on the suspicion of supporting the Union. His heart thundered at the possibility.

"Move along," the detective said. "Don't let us catch you out after curfew again."

"No, sir." Jay resisted the urge to point out that they were only out after curfew because they'd been stopped.

Phineas didn't slow down until they were inside their carriage house. "Them fellas sure do mean business."

Jay sighed. "I believe they do." He'd best remember to have Bea and Meg back home well in advance of ten o'clock in the future. No, it was better to wait until he had a day off to escort Beatrice during daylight hours. Once this problem with the faulty cannons was behind him, his presence at work wouldn't be necessary seven days a week. He'd honed in on Zeke and Seth as the only ones exhibiting strange behavior. Still no evidence of wrongdoing though.

Those concerns were pushed away as fear for Bea and Meg took over.

The ugly threats from the guard plagued him as he climbed into bed. He'd need to issue another warning for the ladies to watch what they said and did—especially not to show support of the Union, for he didn't doubt where their loyalties lay.

He flopped to his side with a heavy sigh. Another problem plagued him. Bea had asked to see the ironworks. To what purpose? The army sometimes requested special equipment or ordered specific new designs to aid in combat. Designs hidden from citizens. Those military secrets must stay within the company's walls.

He tossed in his bed. Beatrice seemed to care for him the way he was growing to care for her. This wasn't simply a flirtation for her, as he had suspected in the beginning. He searched for a reasonable explanation for her interest in his company. Sharing that information with her father? With Northern leaders?

Not on his watch.

No matter how much he cared for her.

CHAPTER 17

By mid-week, Jay still had no evidence that any of the cannons leaving his gun foundry were less than perfect. He inspected each one, rubbing his hand over the entire surface, searching for the slightest blemish.

He glanced at his workers watching his inspection with varying expressions. Some men were anxious, as if desiring his praise. Others stood with folded arms and relaxed stance.

Seth concentrated on building up the furnace fire and darted a glance at Jay every now and then.

Zeke pushed his slouch hat down over his eyebrows. It shaded his face so Jay couldn't discern his expression.

He could find nothing wrong, so Jay released the cannons for the next phase in the process.

Zeke looked over as the cannons were hauled out.

Jay answered a few questions as he walked the length of the building. All seemed well…but it didn't. There was something he couldn't put his finger on.

When it was time for lunch, Jay strode over to Zeke. "One moment."

"Boss, I gotta eat. It's beef stew today."

"I know." The sound of booted footsteps grew faint behind him. "This will only take a moment."

"What is it?" Zeke took a step back.

"You've been here for years." Jay widened his stance. "Do you think there's a problem with our work?"

"No, suh." He shook his head. "Whatever caused those cannons to explode, it happened after we was done with them."

Jay rubbed his jaw. Was Zeke too emphatic, hiding some secret? Or was he defending his coworkers? "What do you think happened?"

"Don't know." Zeke stared at the floor. "What do you think?"

"Not sure." Jay eyed him. "Seen anything?"

"Nope." He shuffled his feet.

This wasn't getting anywhere. Best let the man enjoy his break. "Well, come to me if you suspect anything. That's all I ask."

Zeke looked up, his face a still mask. The turmoil in his eyes jolted Jay.

"Enjoy your stew." Jay stood silently until the door closed behind Zeke.

Some men weren't at Tredegar of their own accord, reason enough for them to want the Union to win the war.

That didn't mean they were responsible for the sabotage…if it *was* sabotage. Perhaps an inexperienced worker made mistakes with tragic consequences.

Jay's gaze swept the foundry, empty except for him. He'd stay late tonight and look for anything out of place.

His biggest challenge since the war began was spying on his men. How he hated it.

~

Bea peeked over her tea cup at Jay's expressive face. Exhaustion reigned in the slump of his proud shoulders as they sat before the parlor fire. Was that the cause of his uncharacteristic silence?

She, Meg, and Aunt Trudy had dined at his home at his mother's invitation. Now all were seated in the parlor with the three other women carrying the conversation.

A week had passed since Jay had escorted her and Meg to supper and a drive. The whole evening had surpassed her hopes. Her only disappointment was Annie's absence.

Her sister had always been a chaperone for her, and after their excursions, they'd give one another their honest impressions of the gentlemen. How she missed her sister's insights, though it was doubtful Annie would be happy she courted a Southern gentleman during the war. She had penned a long letter about him to her sister with a separate one for her father and hadn't received replies.

Now, Jay brooded over his cup of tea. Perhaps he had misgivings about courting a Northerner.

Annie, what's your opinion? Write to me quickly.

Elizabeth Van Lew had stopped to talk with her and Meg that morning while the other women were occupied inside the white frame church. She seemed genuinely pleased for Bea's courtship, expressing a keen interest in any news. The conversation was interrupted with the arrival of Mrs. Eliza Van Lew, who possessed a more timid nature than her daughter.

Jay had been preoccupied about his job, piquing Bea's curiosity, though she was confident she would see the place with her own eyes before too many days passed.

He had also mentioned taking them to see a play. Far more exciting.

"Dear boy, did you get home before the curfew last Sunday?" Trudy took off her shawl and folded it.

"We would have been home with minutes to spare." Jay frowned. "Yet Phineas and I were still stopped."

Bea flushed. It was her fault because of her reluctance for the evening to end.

Mary shrank into the chair's cushion. "You didn't tell me."

"I didn't like to worry you, Mama." His gaze bounced from her to Bea. "But it's best you all know."

"Supporters of the Union are still being arrested." Trudy shook her head. "I can't say I want anyone passing on our secrets."

"Most still wait in prison." Mama's teacup rattled against her wedding ring. "Sometimes I don't recognize my own city."

"Bea. Meg." His fists clenched. "The guards knew I'd escorted you."

"We are being watched, then?" Bea put a hand to her throat.

Meg ran her fingers through her curls, her face downcast.

"I fear so." His brow wrinkled as he looked at Bea. "The guard warned that neither of you should be out past curfew."

"Then there is no help for it, ladies." Trudy straightened her shoulders. "I'll write your father, Bea, and make arrangements to send you home."

"Please, don't send us back to Washington." Bea's throat tightened at the very suggestion. "I don't feel as if I'm in danger, do you, Meg?"

"If I believed we were in danger of arrest, I'd leave in the morning." Meg straightened her shoulders. "From what I've observed, the marshals are arresting Unionist citizens of Richmond. They may not like us as Northern citizens, but we're here as invited guests."

"Exactly." Bea watched some of the worry ease from her aunt's expressive face. "Some folks don't like us, it's true. I've made friends at the sewing group and at church. As much as I miss Annie, I've no desire to leave. I'm where I need to be." Jay's courtship was part of her desire to stay. So was her aunt's need for the companionship of family.

"Fair enough. Since you both feel strongly about staying." Trudy's gaze darted between them. "Even so, it's best we all stay near home in late evening. Jay, you say that it wasn't quite ten o'clock when you were stopped?"

"That's right—and I agree." Lines furrowed a rut in his forehead as he turned to Bea. "The guard all but promised you'll be arrested if caught out near curfew. Have you been vocal in your support of the Union?"

"No." If only Jay understood how these threats strengthened her loyalty to the North.

Meg shook her head.

"I thought that my reputation, that all I've done for my community would protect them." Trudy's face paled.

"No doubt it does," Jay said. "Both that and their charity towards our soldiers will bring a quick release in the unlikely event of an arrest." He pressed his fingertips together. "But let's guard our words."

"I've said nothing to warrant such scrutiny." Bea's mouth tightened.

"Nor have I." Meg clasped her hands, knuckles white. "Tensions are high. It's natural for authorities to wonder about us. As long as we continue as we started, we'll be safe."

"Bea and I discussed us all attending a play." The corners of Jay's mouth turned down. "Unfortunately, that will wait since we'll curtail evening activities. But I don't believe you ladies have visited Pizzini's."

"No." Bea glanced at Meg, who shook her head. "Is that a restaurant?"

"Ice cream." He grinned. "An Italian confectionary. They serve the best ice cream I've ever eaten."

"I will look forward to it." Her heart lightened that, though they'd miss the play, Jay had other ideas for their entertainment.

Confederate soldiers continued to march through Richmond, making them a common sight in the following days. Bea and Meg had decided to heed Jay's warning and remain close to home in the evenings, yet their days were as busy as ever with hospital visits and sewing for the soldiers.

Annie's response to her courtship was carefully worded. She agreed that Jay seemed a wonderful man yet cautioned Bea about their differing loyalties. Bea tried to tamp down her resentment. How comforting it must be for her sister to marry a man who shared her allegiance.

On the other hand, the tone of her father's letter was optimistic. Jay's job of arming the military impressed him, as did his service in Tredegar Battalion. He wanted only the best for his daughter and awaited to learn more of him.

She had no doubt he'd also written instructions to her aunt. Yet her father's enthusiasm battled Annie's caution, leaving Bea's emotions in a state of confusion.

Except when she was with Jay.

He often came over for an hour in the evening. They talked in the parlor while Meg wrote letters at a nearby table. They went for a brief drive one pleasant evening as the weather warmed. He took them to Pizzini's when he managed to get off early. Bea savored the ice cream almost as much as Jay's company.

Another letter from Annie advised her to tread cautiously. Take the courtship slowly. Perhaps her sister, who knew her so well, understood that Bea's admiration for him grew with each encounter.

Her father's next correspondence cautioned her to always have a chaperone. His Southern roots ensured he had no qualms about division between them. After learning of arrests of those with Union sympathies, he'd considered asking her to cut her visit short. Jay's courtship swayed him. She could stay.

Bea had no intention of informing her family of the guard's veiled threat to Jay. As the days passed and nothing happened, her fears lessened.

A reply from Will was typical.

I'm happy for you, Sis. Since you rarely write about your beaus to me, I imagine this man is special. We can't fight without artillery and ammunition so I reckon that makes your beau a hero. All I can say is he'd better be good to my sister.

That caused her to laugh. His comments were just what she needed. That her brother agreed with her that he was a hero strengthened her resolve.

She was sitting in her aunt's pew on the first Sunday in April —Jay was working again—when a soldier interrupted church services. He asked to address the crowd. Permission granted, the clean-shaven man of perhaps thirty strode to the front.

"Ladies and gentlemen." He gave a respectful nod. "I come to you on behalf of our army. Three trainloads of hungry soldiers have arrived in Richmond. They are Major General James Longstreet's men and haven't eaten for a day. If you have food to spare, I'm asking that you help feed our brave men."

Bea's heart went out to them. That might have been her brother, who was back with his regiment in North Carolina.

Amidst the murmurs all around them, Trudy leaned toward Bea and Meg. "What do you say, ladies? Shall we help?"

"Of course." Bea glanced at Meg. "Can we leave during services?"

"It seems important." Trudy turned to Mary on her other side. "We'll prepare baskets of food."

"I'll do the same."

Other women and girls left the building with them.

They went straight to the kitchen when they arrived home. Clara and her family weren't back from church yet. A delicious aroma of baked ham hung in the room.

"I'll make biscuits. They're filling." Meg left the kitchen for the stocked pantry in the basement.

"She cooked for her husband. Rebecca taught me to make lemon cookies." Bea raised her hands, palms up. "That's all I can do."

"No doubt that's some soldier's favorite cookie." Trudy waved her hand. "I haven't cooked since Parker and I were newly married—that's more years ago than I care to admit—but I remember how to make an excellent stew. The men will have their cups with them to use as bowls."

"Biscuits, stew, and cookies." Bea nodded as Meg came in with a sack of flour. "A good meal."

"We'll share our lunch and slice up the ham for our boys. This will be fun." Trudy laughed. "Cooking in my own kitchen again."

Bea giggled. "I'm going to watch you two so I'll learn two more dishes. Think my future husband will appreciate my culinary skills?" Her thoughts flew to Jay.

"I think we can be certain of it." A puff of flour flew into Meg's face as she opened the sack. She sneezed and then giggled. "Though, as you can see, I may not be the best teacher."

Jay was surprised to find that Zeke wasn't at the foundry the next day. He strode over to Seth, who melted iron at the furnace. "Seth, is Zeke ill? He isn't here this morning."

"Ain't heard that he's ailing." Seth barely raised his eyes from his task. "I ain't see him since yesterday."

Neither had anyone else in the gun foundry. Jay checked at his quarters and then at the hospital on the grounds. No Zeke.

Where was he? Jay crossed the grounds to his superintendent's office, hardly noticing the pleasant rays of sun warming his face. "Mr. Furbisher?" He knocked on the door. "Might I have a word with you?"

"Come in, Jay." Furbisher shuffled a stack of papers. "I was just coming to tell you the good news. Recent tests of our cannons have been without incident. Things are looking up, my boy."

The news heartened Jay, but he couldn't relax yet. "I came with news of my own."

"Oh?" Mr. Furbisher gestured for him to sit.

"One of my men didn't report to work this morning. He's not sick." The only vacant chair was a wooden one to the side of the desk. Jay sat in it. "I've just come from the hospital."

"Who is it?" His brows furrowed.

"Zeke."

"A good worker."

"One of my best."

Mr. Furbisher rapped his knuckles on his desk. "Think he might be a runaway?"

"Maybe."

"How long has he been gone?"

"He worked yesterday." Jay couldn't remember seeing him after their noon meal break.

"Think he had something to do with the faulty cannons?"

"I don't know." Jay scratched his head. "I've watched him and everyone else. I've searched for tools that might be used to mar the weaponry and found nothing hidden or out of place."

"No evidence of wrongdoing?"

"None." Mr. Furbisher's stare pierced through Jay. "Zeke's been acting suspiciously. Maybe because he was planning an escape to the North."

"I'll talk to Dr. Archer." Mr. Furbisher sighed. "We don't have time to search for him. If he's left the city, we're unlikely to find him. Zeke may have made it to Union soldiers at Fort Monroe."

After he left the superintendent, Jay whispered a prayer that Zeke was safely at Fort Monroe, where so many runaway slaves had taken refuge during the war. He added a prayer that no one in leadership at Tredegar ever found him.

Later that week, Jay and Bea strolled along populated and steep hills of Richmond's main streets. Dusk was an hour away. As long as he took her home before dark, Bea didn't require a chaperone.

Zeke hadn't returned to work. Inquiries from Mr. Furbisher directly to Jay's men hadn't shed any light on his whereabouts. Seth, the man who worked closest with Zeke, probably knew something but wasn't telling. Jay prayed Zeke had reached safety.

"Such a beautiful spring evening." Bea's fingers tightened on his arm.

"I ordered the weather just for you," he teased, loving the happy glow in her blue eyes.

She giggled. "Thank you, kind sir. I'll take another one just like it tomorrow."

"I'll see what I can do." He laughed. "I'll be back to working six days in a week or two."

"A welcome change. And I do understand." She stepped over a missing brick in the sidewalk. "My father also works long days. This war has affected many people."

"That it has." Jay scanned the street for the military guards. No sign of shield-shaped silver badges identifying General Clayton's detectives on horseback. Good. Pedestrians were mostly the average citizen hurrying to who knew where.

"Has there been any bad news?" Bea's brow furrowed.

"A battle in Tennessee on Sunday." His heart ached at the fight's tragic losses. "Lots of men died on both sides. We lost General Albert Sidney Johnston."

"I'm sorry." She kept her gaze on the sidewalk. "Was it a Union victory then?"

"Looks like it." His jaw clenched. Was she sorry that lots of men died or that the South lost a beloved general? "We've got a steep hill to climb before the street levels somewhat. Do you want to turn around or keep walking?"

"Walk." She surveyed the steep grade. "Daunting the first time, isn't it? Meg and I have strolled along this boulevard on several occasions. Besides, Annie and I walk daily back home."

"How is your sister?" Taking her hand, he guided her around a cart as they crossed a side street and headed up the steep grade. He released her warm hand reluctantly.

"She misses John, who marched South last month. He doesn't tell her many details about where he's camped and what he's doing." She sighed. "That actually scares her more than if she knew for certain the opposing army was near him."

"I'll wager he merely means to protect her."

"I agree with her. I'd prefer to know as much as my husband was free to tell me." She blushed a becoming shade of pink. "That is, were I married and my husband a soldier."

The old familiar shame crept over him.

"You're Home Guard. That doesn't mean you aren't brave." She stopped halfway up the hill and turned to him.

His spying at Tredegar took a certain amount of courage. "You are too kind."

"Not kind at all." Blue eyes held his gaze. "It's not only the soldiers facing the enemy who are heroes in this conflict. Wars have many different kinds of heroes. To the men relying on the cannons you provide, you're one of them."

He turned away in humiliation. Exploding cannons battered

his heart. She couldn't know about those. Another secret between them. "The sun has set. We'd best turn back."

She bit her lip. "Perhaps someday you'll trust me enough to tell me what's bothering you."

"I trust you, Bea." Just not with war secrets.

~

Dare she believe herself trusted if there were secrets he wasn't telling her? Bea rested her hand on his arm as they descended the hill. "Have you planned a tour of Tredegar for me and Meg yet?" She hadn't spoken of it since that evening on the square. It seemed a good time for a change of topic.

"No." Jay's voice was a little gruff as he gave her a side glance. "As you can imagine, much of what I do needs to remain confidential."

That stoked her interest. Especially with Elizabeth Van Lew's hints about the company's secrets. "What *can* you tell me? I won't be bored, I promise."

"Trust me, you'd be yawning before we reached the top of the next hill." His laugh sounded a bit forced. "Besides, I'd rather hear about your day."

"The ladies' group sewed in Mrs. Ellis's parlor today." This hill seemed steeper than the last. "I took my yarn and knitted socks for the soldiers while the rest cut and sewed trousers."

"Did you mind?"

"Not at all. I like to keep busy. So does Meg."

"Was she there today?"

"No." She frowned. Meg had claimed errands as her reason for missing two hospital visits last week and two sewing group sessions this week. "She had shopping to do."

"You didn't want to go with her?"

"I offered. She said it was better that we didn't both miss

sewing for the soldiers." The sky had deepened to a dark blue. "It's getting late."

"There are plenty of folks on the streets, but let's not worry your aunt." He lengthened his stride.

"Clara saved us a piece of pie. I hope you can stay. Just leave by nine o'clock to be safe." Her breath came in gasps. She wasn't accustomed to the fast pace.

"I will. Is it cherry?"

She smiled at the question. She'd learned that it was his favorite. "Clara seems to bake them fairly often when you're expected."

"And all these years I thought it was Aunt Trudy's favorite." He laughed. "I'll definitely come in for dessert."

"I hoped you say that. Let's rest a moment." They'd reached the top of the hill at the corner where they turned for her aunt's home.

"My apologies." He touched her shoulder. "I'm so accustomed to a fast pace at work that I didn't notice it."

A church bell rang on the hour. "It only means that we've worked up an appetite for dessert."

He chuckled. "Lead me to it."

CHAPTER 18

"I'm going out this morning." Meg sipped coffee with her breakfast of a corn muffin a week later.

"Aunt Trudy is sleeping late to rest up for Easter tomorrow. Uncle Isaac and Aunt Meredith will be here for lunch." Bea hoped for an opportunity to learn more about Grandfather's will. It upset Aunt Trudy to speak of it, suggesting the matter was far from closed. "The Bartletts and the Robersons are bringing their whole families, so it will be a lively occasion."

"That it will."

Eyeing her, Bea ate a forkful of scrambled eggs. After she'd swallowed, she said, "I'll go with you today."

"No need." Meg rose from her seat at the dining table. "I won't be long."

"Is everything all right?"

"What do you mean?" She rubbed a finger over the tablecloth's lacy design.

"You've become very secretive of late." Bea's brow wrinkled. "You went out three days this week with no explanation. I'm worried."

"Don't be." The corners of her mouth turned up. "It's only that I am concerned for a friend."

"Can you tell me more about this friend?"

Meg shook her head.

Bea studied her troubled expression. "Let me help."

"There's nothing you can do." Stormy green eyes pleaded for understanding. "I will tell you all whenever I can. Until then, can you trust me?"

"Yes." Something was wrong. Perhaps with her late husband's family? Thomas's brother had been a bit of a problem at times. He lived in Colorado the last Bea heard. "On one condition."

"What is it?" Meg lifted her chin.

"That you will accept my help whenever you need it."

"It's a promise." Meg hugged her and then bolted from the room.

Bea listened to the rustle of her dress on the stairs.

Then she rested her forehead in her hand with a long sigh. More secrets. It seemed this war manufactured them daily.

How she hated it.

Tomorrow would be Jay's first day off in over a month. He could think of little else than celebrating Easter with Bea and the small party gathered at the Westons as he rode to drilling practice. His friend, Troy Hanson, hailed Jay as he tied his horse to a hitching post.

"You ready for a day off?" The shorter man with blond hair peeking under his hat clapped him on the back.

"I'll say." He rubbed his lower back. He'd be able to sleep an extra hour even with church. "How about you?"

"My mother and younger brothers claim they forgot what I look like." He grinned.

As the pair walked toward Gamble's Hill, Victor and Ward fell into step beside them.

"You fellas hear the news?" Victor jerked his head at Ward. "We've been talkin'."

"About Yorktown being under siege?" Jay wanted to trust that the Confederate army would keep the Union army far from Richmond. Important battles taking place in Virginia made it difficult.

"Hope that situation doesn't turn hotter for us but, nah, not that," Victor said.

"I haven't had time to read the newspaper." Troy shifted his musket to his left shoulder. "What's the news?"

"Congress authorized the conscription of all white male citizens between the ages of eighteen and thirty-five." Ward thumped his chest. "That's me."

"That's all of us." The news rocked Jay's stomach. "For how long?"

"Three years." Victor's heavy tread stomped out an ant hill.

"There are exceptions. Certain occupations critical for the war are exempt." Ward's shoulders slumped. "Like us. Same old thing."

Jay glanced at Troy. His friend agreed with him about an obligation to remain on the job.

"Well, I'm tired of it. They need soldiers." Victor shoved his hat over his thick eyebrows. "Here's one man that don't need much convincing to find a regiment and join it."

"I struggle with it too." Jay searched for a way to calm the disgruntled man. "Thing is, our comrades on the field need our cannons, our ammunition. Without them, they can't win battles."

Victor grunted.

"Truth is, there are different kinds of heroes. To the men relying on the cannons you provide, you're a hero." Bless Bea's heart. She'd given him the words he needed to help his comrades resist the urge to muster into the army. "It takes all of us to win this conflict."

"Someone tell you that, Jay?" Troy raised his eyebrows. "That doesn't sound like the way you'd say it."

"Maybe not." Jay grinned. "But it sounds like the truth to me."

"Not to me." Victor raised the business end of his musket to the sky. "Don't be surprised if you don't see me around much longer."

Jay eyed him. "I hope you reconsider. We need your skills."

"I'll think on it." He quickened his pace. "That's all I'll promise."

"Reckon that's the best we can hope for." Ward watched Victor trot ahead to where the others waited. "We're all doing the best we can." He ran to catch up with his buddy.

Troy gave a low whistle. "Ain't that the truth."

Yeah, and the recent spying on his men gave Jay a sour taste in his mouth.

Troy tapped his arm. "Who said that to you? About the heroes."

"Beatrice." He couldn't keep a smile from his face as he spoke her name. She was growing more dear to him with each passing day.

"So you're still courting that Northerner?"

His smile died. "Thanks for not calling her a Yankee."

"There are those who will." Troy gripped his musket. "She doesn't ask about your job, does she?"

"She's interested in what I do all day." His jaw tightened.

"There are things most folks know about us, and other things they don't." Troy's brow creased. "Remember the submarines."

"I'm not likely to forget." The back of Jay's neck grew hot. Who at Tredegar could forget that successful initial battery test of the submarine designed by William Cheeney last fall? It blew up a barge on the James River in view of several civilian spectators. Tours at the time with trusted individuals included views of a second submarine ship under construction at Tredegar—a mistake, for the Confederate submarine was entangled in nets around Union ships soon after. Someone had warned the Union navy to set out nets.

"We better guard our secrets now."

"Don't worry about me," Jay said.

"She ever ask to tour our place?"

Jay was spared having to answer when they reached the large group. Troy's warning confirmed his decision. There'd be no tours to give clues to developmental stages of torpedoes and other weaponry. He no longer suspected her of spying, yet who knew what remarks she might make, innocently or not, to an unknown spy?

He glanced at his armed coworkers. Some undoubtedly yearned to answer duty's call on the battlefield. They were all doing the best they could. Bea's encouraging words had a ring of truth.

The problem with the exploding cannons remained a mystery. All his spying on his men bore no fruit. Nothing pointed to anyone in the gun foundry as the culprit.

Cannons delivered to the army were safe now. Mr. Furbisher had ordered Jay to stop pursuing the matter, as his next tasks were to make train wheels and axles.

He wondered if he'd ever know the truth. That was why he'd refused Bea's praise. If he or one of his men made the mistake, Jay bore the blame. Certainly not the actions of a hero.

Zeke had not returned.

~

Bea anticipated Easter more than she had in a long time, partly because Jay was going to church tomorrow. Not only that, he had suggested a drive to Hollywood Cemetery and to see the falls on the James River later in the day. Bea didn't know who all was going with them yet.

It was only her, Meg, and Aunt Trudy who sat down at supper the Saturday evening before the holiday. Meg had been out several hours during the afternoon and was quiet at the meal.

Bea awoke later that night to the sound of weeping.

Meg was a private person, yet Bea was not about to ignore her sobs.

After pushing back the covers, she donned her robe. A moment later, she tapped on the door as softly as possible to keep from awakening anyone. "Meg, it's Beatrice." She spoke in a whisper. "Please, can I come in?"

Silence.

"I heard you crying. Please. You said you'd let me help."

"One moment." Footsteps approached. A lock released, and then the door opened.

Bea slipped inside and gasped at the broken woman before her. Tears trailed down her cheeks. Her auburn curls, released from their habitual combs, were in wild array. A pink robe was loosely belted over a white nightgown.

Meg closed the door and reached for a handkerchief.

"What is it?" She hadn't seen her cousin in such distress since her husband's funeral. "Do you miss Thomas?"

"Always. How I wish he were here." She poured water from the pitcher into the bowl on a chest of drawers and splashed her face. "That's not causing my distress tonight."

"What's troubling you?" Bea took her hand and led her to the chaise lounge. "Let's sit. Tell me."

Meg blew her nose and then studied her. "First, I have a question for you."

"Of course." Bea perched on the edge of the chaise.

"If the police or the government questioned you about someone's activities in a time of war—let's say it's Jay or me—and threatened to put you in jail if you didn't tell them what they want to know, would you tell them?"

Bea blinked. "Wh—what?"

"Would you tell them?" Her fierce tone demanded honesty.

She met Meg's unfaltering gaze. "If you're asking if I can keep a secret, the answer is yes. I kept my brother's secret for months, knowing it was for his protection. A dear friend of our family, Mrs. Rose Greenhow, was suspected of spying for the Confederacy. I was surprised but not stunned when it was later confirmed. While it was under investigation, we didn't speak of it with acquaintances." Her father's change of loyalty, his gift to the Confederacy, and her part in it must remain confidential, especially from someone as fiercely loyal to the Union as Meg. "Secrets abound in times of war. Yes, Meg, you can trust me."

"You would choose to stay in jail to protect me or Jay?" She leaned forward.

"I'd stay in jail." Bea lifted her chin. "Sometimes love comes at a cost. I will pay its price."

"I believe you. I had to be certain. If called upon, I will do the same for you. When you decide a course in your mind before it happens, you are less likely to flounder in the midst of trials." She trudged to the window and stared outside. "Not everyone does this."

"What happened?" The direction of the conversation alarmed her.

"Have you heard about the spies imprisoned in this city's jails?"

"I read about it in the newspaper." After Rose Greenhow's experiences, spies captivated Bea's attention. And Bea hid her own activities in smuggling money into the Confederacy. "Two men were condemned to hang. They gave information to the authorities that implicated other spies."

"That's correct. Their testimony was used against someone I've met."

Bea covered her mouth with her hands.

"After Thomas died, I worked at different jobs to distract me from my grief. One job provided new experiences. I met new people. It yanked me out of my despair."

"In Chicago?"

"Yes." Meg kept her face toward the window. "Have you heard of the Pinkerton Agency?"

"It seems so." Bea's brow wrinkled. "Oh, yes. It's a detective agency. Father mentioned them. Why?"

Meg turned. "Because I was one of Pinkerton's scouts."

"You...worked for Pinkerton's?" Bea's body went limp.

"I didn't meet all the other scouts. We work in secret. I met two of the condemned spies. One of them is a friend."

"You *worked* with them?" Bea rubbed her forehead with a shaking hand. If those other detectives were in prison, Meg must be in danger.

"Not exactly, though I did help sew dispatches into the waistcoat of one of them."

"To hide information." She could scarcely believe her ears. A member of her own family was a *spy*. Then her breath caught in her throat. Might her father be included since he helped Rose Greenhow last year?

"It's best you don't know specific details." Meg bent to lay another log on the fire. "A trial ended today. Since the others were sentenced to hanging—though they did not hang—it seems likely Timothy Webster will receive the same sentence."

"Is that why you were crying?"

"A lot of good has come to the Union because of his activities, his courage. I hate what's happening with them...all the arrests." She stared into the orange flames. "Remember the friend I saw in the crowd when we walked that afternoon?"

Bea had forgotten the incident. "Did you talk with her?"

"Not that day. She ran from me, so I knew she was in trouble. I walked the streets a few times until I finally spotted her again. She entered a shop. I went in after her." The fire crackled, escalating the tense atmosphere. "We had a brief conversation, and she told me that she was being watched and to stay away."

"Did you?"

"Of course. It's fortunate I heeded her warning because she was arrested with Timothy earlier this month." Meg slumped onto her rumpled bed. "I cried for the treachery dealt my friends by those whom they should be able to trust. I fear this will end badly for Timothy and perhaps for Hattie. Almost as bad is my inability to lift a finger to help them, for to do so would implicate me." She lifted tormented eyes to Bea. "I must remain silent. I've prayed for their safety, for guidance. But I'm now convinced there is nothing I can do to alter their fate."

"Then the bravest thing you can do is maintain your silence." Bea, her body shaking in reaction to all she'd learned, crossed the room to sit beside her.

"I've felt like such a coward." Meg hugged her. "How did you know what I most needed to hear?"

She stared into the flames. "Are you spying on the government here?"

"No." But there was neither shock nor indignation in her response. "I worked with Pinkerton's while in Washington City last autumn. My job was to interview female runaways, deserters, and refugees. Mr. Pinkerton told me in December that he didn't need me any longer. So, I'm not officially spying on the Confederacy."

"I don't want the danger your friends face to strike you." Bea's throat constricted. "Maybe we should go back to Washington."

"No, I want to stay here." Meg sat on a corner of the chaise. "I can do some good in Richmond. Don't worry. I'm always careful."

Bea was certain that her cousin was listening for information useful to the Union.

More secrets. This was one she'd have to keep until the war ended, whenever that might be. *Please, God, let it end soon.*

CHAPTER 19

Bea was happy when the Easter meal ended because she gathered the children to paint Easter eggs. She giggled at her own mistakes, which invited the boys and girls to laugh when their own red, orange, and yellow brush strokes went awry.

Meg showed surprising talent with her artwork as she sat around the parlor table in the midst of laughter and fun. Dyes made from beets, oranges, and lemon peels were used to paint designs of crosses, churches, and bunnies.

Bea invited the adults to join in. Jay laughingly refused from his seat with the men.

Aunt Meredith surprised her. She painted eggs with the children while her husband admired them, clasped hands resting on his stomach. Isaac didn't have much to say to his sister but had learned all his niece had been doing during her weeks in Virginia at lunch.

Yet there had been no time alone with him.

While the children painted their last egg, Bea leaned over Meg's shoulder. "Can you take over? I want to speak with my uncle."

"Certainly. This is fun." Meg rose from her chair and began walking around the table with praise for each child's work.

Bea seized the opportunity. "Uncle Isaac, it's a lovely day. Would you like to see the gardens?"

"I'd welcome it." He offered her his arm.

Bea, meeting Aunt Trudy's apprehensive gaze with what she hoped was a reassuring look, left the parlor with him. "The back door is just down this hallway." Then she blushed, realizing he must know the design of his sister's home.

"I recall the way." Isaac opened the door. "Now, I believe I have my niece to thank for today's invitation. Meredith is enjoying herself."

"I did mention to Aunt Trudy I wanted an Easter Celebration." Heat spread up her face that he wouldn't be here today without her prompting. It was a humiliating circumstance she hoped to get to the root of. "One wonders why a sister doesn't see more of her brother with a mere ten miles separating them."

"That's all water under the bridge, my dear." His chuckle seemed a bit forced. He gestured toward the white metal bench, ornately crafted with a grapevine design. "My siblings seem to resent my father's change of heart on the matter of distributing his property."

Bea sat and arranged her skirt to give herself a moment to gather her courage. "My father expected to inherit acreage." It was bold of her to question him, but no one seemed to be doing it. "What changed Grandfather's mind?"

"I know little about it." He looked away from her, toward a spreading magnolia tree in the yard. "My father informed me his will had changed a month or two before his death."

Wait. That wasn't true because Aunt Trudy said Grandfather dictated the will to Uncle Isaac. Best keep that knowledge to herself and see if he'd reveal something else. "Wasn't he ill at that time?"

"Not so ill he didn't know his own mind." Isaac gave her a

piercing stare. "What are these questions? I thought you brought me out here to tell me news of your father. Has he sent more gold?"

"No." Bea paled at the possibility. As a Union supporter, she wanted nothing more to do with her father's smuggled gifts to the Confederacy. "Nor have his letters hinted at it."

"Isaac?"

Bea's body jerked at Aunt Meredith's voice. She hadn't heard her footsteps on the dry grass. Her uncle had lied to her, proving something was amiss.

"Yes, my dear?" Looking at his wife, Isaac rose.

"The guests are beginning to leave."

Bea stood, reluctant to let the topic rest for another day.

"Then we must hurry inside to say our goodbyes to everyone." Isaac turned to Bea. "I regret that our time is at an end. Remember, send a note around if there's anything you need from me."

How about the truth? She mustn't say that. "Thank you."

Bea followed them inside, wondering how the changed will came about.

Did Aunt Trudy have a copy?

~

Jay settled back in his open carriage with Beatrice at his side, looking lovely in yellow—her dress, Easter bonnet, and matching parasol. Within half an hour of the guests leaving, Jay, Bea, and Meg were on their way to the falls. Her aunt and his mother chose to stay home, out of the bright spring sunlight. Opposite of them, Meg's cream-colored parasol shaded her blue dress. Since she usually wore half-mourning on special occasions, it gladdened his heart that she didn't today. It wasn't a pastel shade such as Bea's, yet perhaps it was a step toward healing. Phineas drove them again today. The man who was old enough to be his father didn't have a family and was often a mentor for Jay.

"Tell us again where you're taking us." Bea's beautiful face turned upward toward the sun. "Meg was in the garden with the children when you told me."

"Ah, that's right." His right leg jittered faster than the horses. "I had promised you both a nice view, and today we will see the Falls of the James River. Phineas likes the falls, don't you?"

"That I do," Phineas said.

"A waterfall?" Meg peered toward the calm river.

"Not exactly." He never tired of looking at the peaceful waters down the hill from his home. "More like rapids. There's a stretch of about seven miles where the altitude drops to create them. I've always fancied it gives the water a wild appearance."

"I saw it as a child." Bea's dress brushed against his thigh as she shifted the shade of her parasol to include him. "I'll see it today with new eyes."

"On our way back," he said, "we'll stop for a stroll at Hollywood Cemetery."

Meg's brow furrowed.

"Reserve judgment until you've been there." He chuckled. "There are plenty of walkways and roads for our carriage. Oh, and I'll show you where two of our presidents are buried."

"Who?" Bea shifted toward him. Her knees grazed his for a moment until she settled into a comfortable position.

"Presidents James Monroe and John Tyler."

Bea's rapt face made it difficult to gather his thoughts.

"The cemetery is a popular spot for strolls," he added. "One often sees couples walking there in the early evening."

"It's late afternoon, so I suppose I will feel welcome." Meg's smile seemed a bit sad.

"You're always welcome." Jay silently cursed his choice of

words. He hadn't meant to exclude the widow. Was she lonely? "I have a friend at the Ironworks. Troy Hanson's a pleasant fellow. Good company. Shall I invite him on our next outing to help you chaperone us?"

"Thank you for the thought. At some time in the future, perhaps I will be pleased for the companionship of a good man. But not yet." Her parasol tilted, hiding her face.

Jay looked at Bea, who shook her head.

"It's a beautiful spring day." Bea lifted her face to the sun. "What can go wrong?"

The war. Jay's smile died. Oliver's recent letters divulged that local boys in the Twenty-first Virginia, led by Lieutenant Colonel John Patton, had met their first enemy fire last month at Kernstown. Some were wounded. They fought bravely until ammunition ran out. Jay imagined the fear that put into his old buddies, how they must have prayed for deliverance. The enemy pursued them for more clashes and skirmishes.

"What's that black smoke up ahead?"

Jay followed Beatrice's gaze with a sinking heart. Enthusiasm for the day had blinded him. Down the hill were the many red brick buildings of Tredegar sprawled between the river and the Kanawha Canal. New tracks in the yard allowed railroad companies to send cars right up to the doors for loading. New buildings like the boring mill and foundry leaped out to his practiced eye, but he hoped they didn't notice. The company had been busy since the war started with enlarging a building here, constructing a new one yards away. Looking at it through Bea's eyes, the foundries, boring mill, gun mill, spike factory, machine shops, locomotive shop, and so many more churned out plumes of charcoal gray smoke impossible to miss.

He suppressed a groan. The ladies had requested a tour of Tredegar. The last thing he'd intended to do was provide it.

"That must be the Ironworks." Meg shifted in her seat, giving herself a better view of the acreage.

"That's where you spend your days?" Bea stared at the impressive array of red brick buildings that started in the valley near the river and expanded up the hillside.

"It is."

"An impressive sight." His dismissive tone sliced through her eagerness. "Aren't you proud to be part of it?"

He glanced down the hill and then back at Bea. "I am."

"Will you tell us what we're looking at?" Meg tilted her parasol so that the fall of auburn curls around the side of her face was all that was visible.

He stared at his feet.

"Yes, please show us." Bea placed her hand on his folded arms. "We know nothing of the Ironworks. Why not tour the grounds while we're here? Go inside the buildings?"

Jay shook his head. "No visitors without passes. I can't acquire those for you."

Her hand fell back on her lap. A twinge of resentment rose. Secrets tended to make folks curious. No wonder Elizabeth Van Lew wanted to learn about it.

"Which building do you work in, Jay?" Meg's body was turned toward the expansive array before them.

He pointed. "See that L-shaped building?"

Bea craned her neck.

"It's near the river in a section where several foundries, mills, and shops are so close that some share a wall."

"I see it." Meg pressed against the door. "As Bea said, it's an impressive sight."

"What is the smaller building off to the side?" The ambling pace allowed Bea to study the property. "The one without plumes of black smoke."

"That's the main slave quarters." Jay pulled his hat down over his brows, shadowing his eyes.

"Some of Tredegar's workers are slaves?" Bea asked. The knowledge left a sour taste.

"I'm afraid so." His jaw clenched. "Some they rent from owners for a period of time—say a month or a year. Others have been purchased."

"How unfortunate." To Bea, it was a smudge against the company as black as the smoke billowing against the clear blue sky. She glanced at their driver's stiff back, wondering how the free man felt about it.

"I don't like it," Jay said. "I believe in paying a man—or woman—for the work they do." His neck flushed.

"Your mother told me that you gave free papers to the servants working in your home upon reaching your majority." Bea studied him. He had freed those in his home yet worked with enslaved men. "I gathered your mother was not pleased with your decision."

"She worried about the money we lost." He shook his head. "Yet not one of those folks received a nickel of what my father paid years ago. It's not right."

"I agree." Trees lined the lane now that the ironworks was behind them. "My mother was an abolitionist and instilled those beliefs in us at an early age."

"It's different for me. I grew up around slavery. Folks around here grew up seeing it. They accepted it, so I did too, as a child."

"What changed your thinking?" Bea was happy that they agreed on this crucial matter.

"Seeing folks mistreated. Crying out in pain." His hands clenched. "It horrified me, especially as I was too young to help them. Then I found a copy of *Uncle Tom's Cabin* along the road, as if someone had flung it from a carriage window. I knew many around here hated the book. I read it in secret."

"A powerful story. Annie and I read Mother's copy."

"Powerful indeed. It riled me up so much that I asked my father to release our slaves. He refused."

"So at the first opportunity, you did it yourself."

"Yes." He finally looked at Bea. "Working with good men at Tredegar changed me, too, as did my friendship with Phineas here."

"If you recall, we became friends after you made changes in your household, Mr. Jay." Phineas's stiff posture relaxed.

Jay's eyes widened. "I reckon we did, Phineas. I never realized."

"I know. Changing a man's heart is the hardest kind of change there is." The team slowed as if in response to its driver's words. "You're a good man and a courageous one."

"Did you suffer for your decision? You did the right thing and paid for it?"

"Friends called me daft." He shrugged. "And other names. A few turned their backs on my family. We're no longer friends." He leaned forward, elbows resting on his knees. "One man at church drew me aside after services and confessed that my example convinced him to draw up free papers for his own staff."

"Amazing." Bea began to comprehend the daring required to go against the tide. The bad feeling that had overtaken her moments ago blossomed to admiration. He had begun changing what he could years ago. "I admire your courage."

His body relaxed as he smiled at her. "That means more to me than you know."

The break in the trees was up ahead. "Do you ladies want to walk along the bank for a better view of the falls?" Jay's hopes rose that Bea considered him a courageous man. Perhaps there was a chance for their courtship to flourish, for love to blossom like the wild daisies on the hillside behind them. His admiration for her grew daily.

"I hoped you'd offer." Bea's blue eyes shone. "It's beautiful here."

"Let's walk." Meg rested her hand on the door.

"Phineas, let's stop here for a while." His arm brushed against Bea's lacy sleeve as he leaned forward.

"Good idea." The carriage halted on grass beneath the shade of a towering maple tree.

"Excellent spot. Thank you, Phineas." It was cooler under the shade of the massive tree, likely a mature tree during the country's revolution. Jay stepped from the carriage and helped Meg down. Then he looked up at Bea. She stared into his eyes with an admiring look that stole his breath. Hope surged up his chest. His hands nearly encircled her tiny waist when he lifted her to the ground. Why, she weighed little more than a schoolgirl.

She rested her gloved hands onto his shoulders without looking away.

For a long moment they gazed at one another. Then his gaze dropped to her mouth.

Her hands fell to her sides, and he released her immediately.

When she turned, her slipper caught in her dress's lacy overskirt. Gasping, she tumbled toward him.

He wrapped his arms around her as she fell against his chest. "Are you all right?" Then she looked up, those pursed lips mere inches from his. He ached to kiss her.

"Pardon my clumsiness."

Her nearness, her rosy cheeks, were too tempting. He bent his head.

"Bea, are you all right?" Footsteps in the grass behind them broke the couple apart. "Did you fall?"

She stepped back, hands covering her red cheeks. "You know what an awkward creature I am."

"No, I can't say that I've noticed that." Meg compressed her lips though her eyes sparkled. "You've dropped your parasol."

"Allow me." Jay retrieved it. Seeking to ease her embarrassment, he gave it to Bea with an exaggerated bow. "Your parasol, my lady."

She giggled. "I always seem to be falling around you. Thank you for catching me. Again."

Jay grinned at her reference to the time she'd stumbled on the train step. "Carriages, trains. I pray I'm always there to catch you on the rare occasions when you fall."

She tucked her hand inside his outstretched arm. "That's my prayer too."

Sounds of the rapidly moving water soothed Bea as she strolled next to Jay to the water's edge.

"The river is calm down by your aunt's home." Meg stared at the tumultuous river. "It's hard to believe the James is so wild a short drive away."

"Boats can only go into Richmond a short distance. If they venture too close, the falls push them back." Jay made a pushing motion with both hands in demonstration of waves against the boats. "It's deserted here…probably due to Easter celebrations. I'm glad because it's peaceful."

"And beautiful." It thrilled Bea to discover nature's beauty anew with him at her side.

"This is my favorite spot to view the falls. My father often brought me out here as a boy." Jay gave her a side glance. "I ride out here when I'm pondering a situation. Though I bring my mother to Hollywood Cemetery to decorate my father's grave, this is where I come when I most miss him."

Touched that he'd brought her to such a special location, Bea reached out her hand in silent comfort.

He pressed it against his cheek for a moment and then, with a glance at Meg, released her.

Bea said, "I feel my mother's presence most in our large parlor, where we have hosted many tea parties and soirees over the years." Rhythmic splashes took her back to when her mother served as a gracious hostess to many neighbors and friends. "I still miss her, especially in these turbulent days. I miss her wisdom, her insight. Nothing will ever make me forget her."

"Nothing." He clasped her hand, touching her heart in shared sympathy.

The horses neighed behind them as footsteps approached. Phineas stopped at the bank several yards away.

Jay picked a rock and tossed it over the rapids. It skipped twice before flopping into the water. "I'm out of practice, Phineas."

"Too much hard work." Their driver tossed a stone over the river.

"Four times." Jay whistled. "I can match it. Give me a minute."

The men took turns skipping stones. It looked like fun. Bea tilted her head at Meg, who raised her eyebrows with a twinkle in her eyes. "Teach me how to do that." Bea surprised herself.

"You're teasing." Jay stepped back.

"Why should you men have all the fun?" Bea rested her parasol against a tree.

"It's easier to learn on the calm part of the river." He studied her. "Are you serious?"

Bea tossed a stone. It splashed with a single plop. She frowned. "Show me." There had to be some kind of trick to it.

"And me." Meg joined them.

Jay's glance darted from one to the other. Then he grinned. "Select a round, flat rock like this one. Turn your body a bit and then throw it like this." His arm whipped nearly perpendicular to the water. The rock danced across the rapids four times before disappearing into them.

"Good one, Mr. Jay." Phineas nodded.

"I can do that." Bea selected a similar stone and tossed it. One plop. "Hmm."

Meg's attempt yielded the same results.

"You ladies probably never played baseball."

"No." Bea giggled.

Laughing, Meg shook her head.

"Well, you're throwing the stones in an upward motion like this." He demonstrated with a stone that plopped straight into the water. "Throw it like this." He whipped another rock from his side. It skipped three times.

"Let me try." Bea tried again. It splashed once.

"Better." Jay lifted her arm. "Have your elbow up a bit when you throw."

She enjoyed his instructions and decided to take a while to learn the skill. Then Meg began tossing stones, and Bea changed her mind. She wanted to be first to skip the stone.

The ladies laughed at their efforts. Bea was the first to skip a stone twice. Then Meg threw one that skipped three times and laughed like a schoolgirl.

"You win." It was good to hear her cousin's joy after last night's tears. "I hope we remember how to throw them for next time."

"You won't forget." Jay's grin broadened. "If you do, I'll be here to remind you."

Meg nodded indulgently, and Bea blushed, happy that her cousin approved of her beau.

Jay checked his pocket watch and sighed. He wasn't ready for their day to end. "It's time to find Meg and return to the landau."

"I guess we have been walking for a while." Bea gave the arm she held a brief hug. "It's been a lovely day."

Children's laughter accompanied them on their stroll along the walkways of the Hollywood Cemetery. A family sat near a set of gravestones with a picnic basket nearby. Jay turned to her. "I'd like to end our afternoon together with a stop at Pizzini's Confectionary, if they're open."

Bea looked up at him. "Ice cream is always a welcome treat on a hot afternoon."

The color of her eyes nearly matched the brilliance of the sky above them. "Where's Meg?"

"Reading the headstones up ahead." Bea didn't spare her cousin a glance. "She feels we are well chaperoned with the other couples and families in the area."

The way Bea looked at him invited his kiss. He bent towards her slowly, allowing her an opportunity to halt him. This time, there were no interruptions as their lips met for the first time. The aroma of her lilac perfume assailed his senses, and the sweetness of her kiss stole his breath.

"We'd best find Meg." A delicate flush complimented her radiant smile in a dazzling way. "I know she is as ready for refreshments as we are."

Her smile proved she didn't regret their kiss. He was glad Amelia had betrayed him with his friend. Beatrice was much better for him and to him.

Jay dreamed of a future with her in Richmond. She seemed to like Virginia. Her father and sister lived a mere hundred miles away, less than a day's train journey in times of peace. It was perfect.

His feet barely touched the grassy hillside as she beckoned her cousin.

CHAPTER 20

Bea lifted the curtains to watch Meg hurry down the sidewalk toward the city. Good. She'd waited a week for an opportunity to talk to her aunt alone. Bea's frustrating conversation with Uncle Isaac on Easter left her hungry to know more.

Her aunt was ascending the stairs when Bea came down.

"Aunt Trudy? Do you have time to talk?"

"Of course. Let's chat in the family parlor." Trudy continued up the stairs. "It's cozier."

Indeed, it was. As Bea sat opposite of her aunt in the small room decorated in shades of green and yellow, she wondered why they didn't spend more of their time here.

"Now, my dear." Trudy rested her folded hands in her lap. "What's brought the frown to your face?"

"I spoke with Uncle Isaac on Easter." Best take the topic head on. "I asked why you, as siblings, don't see one another more often."

"Very direct of you." Trudy blinked. "What did he say?"

"He mentioned that you were unhappy with Grandfather

changing his will. He also told me Grandfather changed the will and then informed him afterward."

"Isaac wrote it." Trudy paled. "He lied to you."

Bea straightened her shoulders. "I wondered if you have a copy of the will."

"I never saw the new one. It was read aloud to me." She looked toward the window as if seeing something far away. "I confess the shock prevented clear thinking that day. Hiram, who had the presence of mind to read it, told me it was written by Isaac. It struck us as odd. That was the beginning of the rift between the brothers."

"Do you know what the old will said?"

"All the children were familiar with it. The daughters were to receive two-hundred fifty acres each, and Hiram twice that amount. Isaac's inheritance was one thousand acres as he made his living directly from it. One can imagine our surprise after Father died." She held up her open palms. "What were we to do? Isaac said he followed Father's wishes."

"But you suspected differently?"

"I did." Trudy studied her. "I'm sorry to speak ill of my own brother, but I might have built my home on that land after Parker died to be near family. It was a great loss."

"I wondered about that." Never had her aunt spoken so openly of her disappointment. "Do you have a copy of the old will?"

"Perhaps it's among Parker's documents." Trudy's brow furrowed. "Why are you so interested? We can't change what's been done."

"I want to make sure all was done as Grandfather wished." For Bea wasn't convinced at all.

"Timothy Webster will hang today." Meg barely closed the door to Beatrice's room before blurting out the news.

Bea, fumbling with the final button on her frock, gasped. "Are you certain?" It had been over a week since their magical day with Jay down by the river, and dreams of him consumed her thoughts. She was ashamed to have forgotten the spy's plight.

"Yes." Meg sank onto the chair beside the desk. "He was sentenced to hang this morning at the New Fair Grounds—also known as Camp Lee. To my knowledge, Nathan Hale was the last American to be hanged for spying."

"I am more sorry than I can say." Bea sank onto the bed, facing Meg. The condemned man was a spy…just as Meg used to be. Might still be if given the opportunity. If she was caught… Bea's pulse raced.

"There's nothing I can do to save him." Meg wrung her hands. "It's been decided. Death by hanging on the twenty-ninth of April."

"Tragic."

"Such a courageous man," Meg said. "Fearless in some ways. But smart about it too."

"Is there anything I can do?"

"Yes." Her hands clenched. "I will attend this morning's hanging. Will you come?"

It was Tuesday, so Aunt Trudy expected them to join the sewing group while she and Mary took food to the wounded at Camp Winder. There was no question that Bea preferred to knit socks over witnessing a man's death. "Is your attendance a way to lend your support?"

"There's a chance he'll recognize a familiar, sympathetic face in a crowd turned against him. I must try, though I understand if you don't want to attend."

Bea tried to swallow a hard lump in her throat. She'd never watched an execution…for good reason. Yet Meg needed her. "I'll go." The words felt wrenched from her heart.

"Miss Elizabeth will be there, though she didn't ask me to go with her. She may slip away from the crowd as soon as…it's over."

"Miss Elizabeth? How surprising. You two talked by the schoolhouse after church on Sunday. Is that what you discussed?"

"We spoke briefly." Meg walked to the window and looked up toward a gray sky. "Your aunt usually leaves at nine. We'll borrow the buggy and leave then. The time…I'm uncertain… let's get out there as soon as possible."

The thought of breakfast turned her stomach. "I'll be ready."

"Wear drab clothing with a hat that covers your hair and shades your face. A veil if you have it." Meg's frock was black. "Folks mustn't notice us."

A shiver ran through Bea. She was going to a hanging of a spy with someone who used to work at the same detective agency. Yes, she'd cover her hair and wear a partial veil.

After Meg left, she prayed for their safety and protection… and for the condemned man's soul.

The crowd pressed toward the gallows with scoffs and jeers from Richmond citizens overwhelmingly against the spy. Beatrice shuddered at the terrible scene. She edged closer to Meg, glad they stood in the back.

A tall man of perhaps forty was led toward the scaffold. His brown mustache twitched when he halted before the gallows. Meg stiffened.

"You don't have to watch," Bea whispered, her gaze fastened on the poor man.

Meg lifted her veil.

Timothy Webster mounted the steps with guards. A noose was placed around his neck. He scanned the crowd as he said good-bye to several people standing near. Bea thought he glanced their direction.

A clergyman bowed his head and prayed.

Meg lowered her veil during the prayer. When a black cap was placed over Mr. Webster's head, she tugged on Bea's hand and nodded toward the woods where their buggy awaited.

They backed away as all eyes were riveted to the gallows. Following Meg's lead, Bea lifted her skirts to run over the rough grounds, half fearing they'd be arrested for showing support of the spy. She glanced back. No one pursued them. It seemed all eyes were on the condemned man.

~

This can't be happening. Jay scanned the newspaper article again in his bedroom that night. Union gunboats had threatened New Orleans, an important city to the South. They had broken through heavy chains stretched across the Mississippi River. Confederate forces hadn't been able to defend the city against the gunboats and left it. The Louisiana city fell on the twenty-fifth of April, four days before.

A disaster for the South. He rubbed his temples in a circular motion. At least Yorktown, though under siege, was still holding. Norfolk, another important port in Virginia, wasn't under attack—as far as Jay knew.

According to Oliver's latest letter, the Twenty-first Virginia was camped across the Shenandoah River. The desire to fight with them had eased with the extra hours he'd worked over the past two months. He now saw his job as the most important contribution yet exhaustion had taken its toll. Trying to finagle a few hours to court Bea every week had taken priority over less important things like sleep.

The fall of New Orleans jolted the war back to the forefront of his mind. Virginia wasn't the only state suffering. The Tennessee battle at Shiloh Church earlier that month had been the worst so far. The losses in dead and wounded soldiers were difficult to recover from.

Too many losses, too close together. It scared him to think of the fighting in Virginia towns like Yorktown, which he'd visited.

He had a bad feeling that worse losses were on the horizon. Richmond, as the Confederate capital, was a Union target. Rumors escalated that the Union army was headed here. He prayed that never happened, for the city's Home Guard was inadequate to protect it. His battalion had about three hundred men. Fighting on the battlefield and fighting in a city were very different. While he wanted to protect Virginia's citizens, he didn't want fighting on streets outside his home.

The very possibility made his blood run cold. He tossed the newspaper into the fireplace, where it rested among the lingering ashes of last winter's fire.

Beatrice had certainly chosen a dangerous time to visit her aunt. Martial law arrests of Union supporters scared him for her sake. Ever since the night the guards threatened Bea and Meg, Jay had been diligent to have her inside her aunt's home before half past nine. No need to take chances when guards watched them. In fact, guards monitored the streets in daylight hours, so they likely knew of the volunteer work the ladies did on behalf of Confederate soldiers. It would make sense if their charity work shifted the guards' suspicion from them.

He bowed to pray for their safety and that the women would be careful in all they said and did while in the Confederacy's capital city.

Restlessness drove him to his feet. He stood at the open

window. Past curfew, a group of men paused at the street corner. Light from the gas street lamp glinted off a shield-shaped silver badge. Guards.

Jay quickly extinguished the lantern and then peered outside again. The men were gone. Spooky how quickly they'd left. In fact, the empty streets were eerie in themselves.

Scaring law-abiding folks didn't set well with Jay, though he agreed spying must be squelched.

One of those spies had hanged today. He never felt good about hangings, and this poor man had slipped from the first noose and struck the ground hard. Authorities made certain that the second rope was strong and secure.

Movement outside. Men climbed the hilly street toward St. John's Church, near the Van Lews' home. There'd been talk that the Van Lews cared more for the Yankee prisoners than for the Confederate's wounded. It seemed unlikely, as most of the folks at their recent soiree had been vocal in their loyalty to the South. It was nice of Miss Van Lew to invite Bea and Meg, strangers to Richmond. Come to think of it, Elizabeth Van Lew had been quite gracious in her attention to them at church. Not surprising, really. The Van Lews were known for their kind generosity.

All seemed quiet outside. He turned from the window and slumped in his chair. Beatrice never bragged about Union victories, even in the privacy of her aunt's home.

She was a Northerner.

He was a Southerner. Devoted to Virginia.

No doubt her allegiance was given to the Union.

Except, her brother served the Confederate army as a lieutenant. He'd been a prisoner of war for months. Had that changed her mind?

The more time they spent together, the more he wanted a future with her. Was there hope if they held opposing allegiances? He needed to know which side commanded her loyalty. He vowed to look for an opportunity to question her when Meg wasn't around. Somehow, he already knew the widow was loyal to the Union.

CHAPTER 21

Bea and Meg toted empty baskets along Broad Street toward the grocer's on the first Friday in May. Families, servants, and workmen dressed in plain clothing mingled among women in hoop skirts and men wearing patterned vests under expensive coats. "I can't believe we've been in Richmond two and half months," Bea said.

"The weeks have flown," Meg said.

Bea adjusted her hat to shade her eyes from the bright morning sun. Passing wagons and carriages failed to block the sun high in the sky.

"I'm glad Jay's courting you."

Her cheeks warmed at the knowing look in Meg's eyes. "He's a good man."

"Agreed. Attentive to you. A fine Christian man who is loyal, hard-working, and courageous. You're blessed indeed."

"Yes." Bea considered how he went against popular opinion to give his staff their freedom. "Oh, Meg, I have such fun with him." She thought of the concert he'd taken them to. "I'm glad he shares my love of music."

"You're falling in love with him." Meg grabbed her arm. "Watch out for the lamp post."

Dazed, Bea stepped around it. Did she love Jay? "I've never been in love."

"With all the men Annie tells me have courted you, I'm surprised to learn that." They descended one of the hills of Broad Street.

"None of my courtships lasted longer than a month." Bea's brow furrowed. "I ended them as soon as my interest waned. None were right for me."

"And Jay is?"

"I think so." Everything was more fun with Jay. They enjoyed many of the same activities, shared many of the same values. His faith was important to him, a must, to her way of thinking. "I am more certain with every meeting."

Meg's answering smile seemed forced.

"Don't you like him?"

"I love him as a possible husband for my sweet cousin." She halted as they reached a street corner. "My concern is his Southern loyalty."

A man in work clothes emerged from a building. "Southern loyalty?" He placed his hands on his hips. "Lady, everyone around here is loyal to the South." He took a menacing step toward her. "Right?"

Bea drew in her breath at the implied threat. No one dared to threaten Hiram Swanson's daughter. Nor was she in the habit of addressing men who hadn't been introduced to her.

"Yankee."

His derisive use of the word seared across her like a slap in the face.

Meg tugged her arm.

Perhaps it was better to leave without a word.

"Yankee women." He spat tobacco juice. "You're not welcome here."

Meg tugged harder, and they hurried up the hill without speaking.

"Don't be out after curfew." Derisive laughter taunted them.

When they reached the crest, Meg glanced over her shoulder. "Good. He didn't follow us."

"Was he a guard?"

"I don't know. No badge."

"Let's walk home a different way." Bea shuddered at the man's belligerence.

"Agreed." Even Meg's hands shook. "He was very brazen."

A young mother with several children stared at them as they passed.

"Shh." Meg shook her head. "Don't talk about anything that might set us apart."

If citizens of Richmond hated Northerners so much, did her courtship with Jay have a chance of prospering?

~

"Sorry I had to work today." Jay searched Bea's brooding face. "It changed our plans."

"I enjoyed the church singing." She stared at the sidewalk as they strolled arm in arm.

They'd attended an evening song service within walking distance, so her aunt had decided they didn't require an escort—as long as they came right home after church. It was early enough that Meg went for a stroll on her own when they left.

"I hoped you would." He was glad she loved music as much as he did. "Is something troubling you?"

She darted a look at him and then resumed her study of the path.

What had he done? He'd worked late every night last week. Was that it? "Can you tell me what's wrong?"

"Well, I want to ..." She craned her neck in every direction.

"But I've learned it's best to keep my thoughts to myself in certain settings."

His back stiffened. What had happened? Other folks milled about the shaded streets nearby as the sun approached the horizon. Not a place for private discussions. "Perhaps we can talk in your aunt's garden."

"Yes, let's sit a while." She quickened her step. "We're almost home. I'll tell her we're back."

Home. She thought of Richmond and her aunt's house as home. A promising sign. They arrived, and Jay wandered the garden near the mature magnolia trees as he waited. Bea soon emerged through the back door followed by Clara, who carried a tray with a pitcher and glasses of lemonade.

"Now, is there anything else you'll be needing, Miss Beatrice?" She set the tray on a round table that matched the ornate white metal garden furniture.

"Nothing, thank you. Has my cousin returned from her walk?"

"Just before you did. I'm surprised you didn't encounter her on the street."

"I didn't see her." She looked at Jay, who shook his head. "Thanks, Clara."

They sat on the garden seat for two with Bea's attention riveted on her lemonade.

"What's wrong?" Jay leaned forward. "You can tell me anything." Even if she planned to end the courtship, it was better to know than to guess at the trouble.

"Do you believe we should be courting?" She raised troubled blue eyes.

His heart sank. So she did intend to sever their relationship. "Do you want to end it?"

"No." She tilted her head. "But folks around here…they don't like Northerners."

"Some don't." Oh, boy. This didn't sound good. "Did someone…say something unkind to you?"

She tilted her head. "You won't like it."

His gut clenched. "Tell me anyway." He ground his teeth as she told him about a belligerent man on the sidewalk who threatened them. "I wish I had been there." The man would have been on the ground, courtesy of Jay's fist. "That had to be upsetting."

"It was." She bent her head, hiding her expression. "It made me wonder if you've suffered consequences for courting me."

"Nothing that matters." A few fellows had taunted him after last week's drill practice. "Do you feel unsafe in Richmond?"

She sighed. "Not usually. The man lashed out at us because we were talking about Northern and Southern loyalties."

He groaned. "Folks are unusually sensitive right now. Their husbands, brothers, fathers, and sons are dying in battle. That's not easy to forgive."

"No." She looked away.

"Please be mindful of what you say in public." His heartbeat quickened. "Not only are there people who will make nasty comments, they may also complain to the guards about you."

She gasped. "I'll be careful."

"Maybe you should go back to Washington City."

"No." Her brow furrowed. "Aunt Trudy needs her family around her."

"She's been more content since you came." He rubbed his hand through his hair. "But your safety comes first."

"I've been praying about that." Her eyes pleaded for understanding. "Meg and I had a long talk after the incident. Then we prayed about the situation, asking God to show us when it's time to leave Richmond." Her eyes pleaded for understanding. "Jay, I feel I'm meant to be here now. Meg feels the same."

"I don't like men speaking to you like that." Jay strove to squelch his anger.

"I don't either. But things are tough at home too. There are plenty of Confederate spies and sympathizers in Washington. Remember my family friend, Rose Greenhow?"

He nodded. The woman still resided in prison as far as he knew.

"I'll continue to pray for guidance." Her posture straightened. "Please pray along with me."

"I pray for you daily."

"I know." She touched his hand. "As I do for you. I'll pray for wisdom until this war ends."

This was the perfect avenue to broach his questions about her allegiance. "Bea, I need to know where your loyalties lie in this conflict between our countries."

"Our countries." Her voice wavered. "Aren't we part of the same country?"

Sadness engulfed him. "Not anymore."

~

Bea stood and stepped away from the garden seat, hoping their relationship was strong enough to discuss this vital topic. "It's not an easy matter to decide."

"Are you for the South, then?" He stood as well, eyebrows nearly reaching the sweep of brown hair that fell toward his forehead.

"No." Her face heated. "I'm not against them either."

"I don't understand."

"Annie knows her own mind. She has never wavered in her support of the Union…not even when we learned our brother fought for the Confederacy." She closed her eyes. "Back then, I didn't know what to think. How can I go against my own beloved brother?"

"How indeed?" His green eyes narrowed.

"Then Annie married John, Will's best friend from West

Point. This war has turned the best of friends into enemies." Bea made a cutting motion with her hand. "I hate it."

"I hate it too." A fist pressed to his chest.

"Then my aunt. Yes, let's talk about her. She freed her slaves years ago yet is loyal to the South. Aunt Trudy's opinion means a great deal to me." She had become almost a second mother to Bea.

"She was born and raised in Virginia. Most folks believe in states' rights and profess loyalty to their own state, even when they disagree on some matters. You'll find few who believe every law is beneficial."

"Like you?" She looked up at him.

"Like me." He rubbed his jaw. "As you know, I don't agree with slavery."

"Yet you'd fight for it."

"No, I would not." He stepped back. "I will fight to protect my country, Virginia, and its citizens."

"I'm so confused." She ran her fingers under her curly locks.

"And you." He cupped her face. "I'd fight for you."

"I believe you." How long she'd waited to find a strong, compassionate man like Jay. She had no doubt he'd protect her at the cost of his life, if fate demanded it. She pressed her cheek against his hand.

He enfolded her in his arms.

She snuggled closer, reveling in the strength of his arms. It felt as if she belonged there. He leaned to kiss her, and her heart responded to the depth of his caring for her. When he cradled her against his chest, she stayed there, treasuring the soothing comfort of his embrace until, mindful of watchful eyes, she moved away to sit on the bench. Away from the warmth of his arms, all that divided them descended with an iron force as hard as the metal seat.

He sat beside her.

"My loyalty is to the Union." After the passion of his kiss, she kept her eyes lowered. "You say that you will fight for your country."

"I am willing to die for it."

"I don't want that. I wish the battles to end today." She wrung her hands. "At this very moment. No more dead soldiers. No more wounded."

"No more hateful words that slice like a sword."

"Exactly." She sighed. "Yet I fear we've come too far down this path for the two countries to simply agree to part ways."

"I fear we have." Jay rubbed his hands against his legs. "Too much blood has already been shed."

"Have you considered..." Bea spoke hesitantly, but she had to ask. "...moving your allegiance to the North?'"

His jaw set. "You know I can't."

The chasm between them deepened. "You work with slaves. Others around you surely would fight to keep slavery going."

"Without a doubt." He stood and rested his hand against a mature magnolia tree branch a few feet from the benches. "The reasons that soldiers pick up a musket vary. Some do it for pride's sake. Others for their state or their country. Some—on both sides, no doubt—are coerced to muster in, or shamed into it. Some want to and are prevented from fighting."

"I don't doubt your courage, Jay." She took a step toward him. "We disagree on this one point—"

"There you are." Meg rounded the corner. "The sun passed over the horizon half an hour ago. You two probably didn't notice, as dusk falls so softly on spring evenings."

"My apologies, Meg." Jay turned to her. "I didn't realize the late hour. Is my mother ready to go home?"

"I'm afraid so." Her glance darted between the silent couple. "I can wander about the yard for five minutes if you like."

Bea looked at Jay as the shadows closed in around them.

He focused on her cousin. "Yes, please give us a moment, Meg."

She gave a nod and began a slow stroll toward the magnolia trees near the edge of the yard.

"This chasm between us is not too deep to span." Jay held her hand to his chest. "Other couples have overcome far greater differences."

"Do you think so?" For the first time since he'd kissed her, hope stirred.

"I do. I—" He turned his head at the sound of footsteps on the dry grass.

"Meg is by the magnolia trees." Aunt Trudy's voice. "Are Jay and Bea with her?"

Bea squeezed his hand and then released it. "We're here, Aunt Trudy."

"Good evening again, Mama," Jay said. "Aunt Trudy."

Bea admired his impeccable manners when she knew he'd wanted to say more to her privately. Would he have professed his love?

Hard to know. But she felt its strength even without the words.

CHAPTER 22

That night, Jay paced in his room long after the house was quiet. It was near midnight. His conversation with Bea haunted him. Though he had to be up in five hours, he could not rest.

Concerns about their differences had kept him from pursuing a courtship with her in the winter. Her kindness, her beauty, her compassion had all captivated him, yet her suggestion that he switch his loyalties slashed his core.

He'd never take up arms against the South. It wasn't in him to betray his home state, his country. He'd sooner cut off his right hand. How could she ask it of him?

Bea didn't share his loyalty. Well, she did...but it was directed to the North.

Could their relationship thrive under such conditions? Or even survive the tumult surrounding them?

Someone had called Bea and Meg a derogatory name. Not that the word was bad—it was the way it had been spoken. Then he'd threatened them. The first threat leveled against them came from the guards themselves. Was the man who'd spoken to them a guard? Perhaps not. Maybe a brother of a guard. His fist clenched at the thought of a Southern gentleman frightening the ladies.

No, that scoundrel could not be called a gentleman.

Jay's pace escalated as he considered the danger they faced. The Union army threatened Virginia cities near Richmond—Jay still prayed that Yorktown would hold strong. Fear mounted among Richmond residents that the Northern army had its sights on the Confederacy's capital city. He was confident in Lee and Stonewall Jackson's leadership to keep them away.

Jay knelt and prayed for the Confederacy and for the protection and safety of his loved ones. His fervent prayers for Bea brought peace to his soul.

Both Bea and Meg had decided, after praying for guidance, to remain in Richmond. After his own prayers, Jay agreed. There was no doubt that their visit was a tonic for Aunt Trudy, whose sensitive heart was breaking at the deaths suffered by both sides.

Jay slumped onto his bed. He and Bea agreed on one important matter. They both hated slavery. He remembered the day he'd discovered its ugliness. He had been ten when Elsie, one of the kitchen maids, ran away. Jay had wondered why she wanted to leave their comfortable home. Then he overheard his father describing Elsie's "escape" to the marshal. It seemed an odd description. Prisoners escaped from jail. Children ran away from home. Elsie left during the night without telling anyone her intentions. When his father asked the marshal to pursue her, Jay learned the young woman hadn't been free to leave.

That morning, his attitude underwent a change. Then, after reading *Uncle Tom's Cabin,* he'd grown to hate slavery. Was this common bond enough to bridge the gap between them?

He didn't know, because his Virginia roots were older than the United States. He was not about to betray his home.

The clock on the mantle struck one. Jay raked his hand through his hair. Amelia had been as sweet as honey when she was with him yet had not hesitated to betray him. Had she told him her interest waned and broken the courtship, he'd have respected her decision. The way she broke their courtship was with an announcement of the betrothal at a party. The humiliation and pain of the moment had stayed with him.

Did Bea love him? She'd never said so in as many words.

Or did she want to steal secrets through his connection to his company? Was that her interest in him?

Until he knew that answer, it seemed best to avoid courting her.

~

An article in yesterday's Richmond Daily *Whig* about the wounded at Camp Winder had convinced Bea and Meg to take soup to feed a portion of the twenty-five hundred men who suffered for lack of food. Aunt Trudy and Mary intended to join those sewing bed clothing for the soldiers while the cousins planned to take a laundry pot full of vegetable soup to the camp.

So, Thursday morning found the younger women peeling potatoes at the kitchen table while Clara cooked the soup outside.

"Have you talked with Jay this week?" Meg tossed quartered sections of raw potatoes into a large kitchen kettle.

"Quarter those again to feed more men." Bea peered into the kettle. "Not since Sunday evening."

"The atmosphere in the garden seemed tense." Meg took a handful of sliced potatoes from the pot. "Is everything all right between you?"

"I don't know."

"What's wrong? You've been quiet all week."

"I'm confused. My feelings for him grow with every conversation but"—she rested the knife on the wood surface—"he's a Southerner."

"He's been a Virginian throughout your courtship," Meg observed. "You didn't seem concerned before."

"I didn't know my own mind when our courtship began."

Meg's gaze flew to her face and then lowered to her task.

"I see both sides of the conflict. When it started, it seemed reasonable to simply allow the Southern states to establish their own country. It was what they wanted. No one *had* to die in battle."

"I wish we could have resolved our disagreements without fighting." Meg's head bent over her work. "I prayed for it, as did countless others. It wasn't to be."

"So many people I love support the South." She met her cousin's sympathetic gaze. "And it bothers me Jay is so secretive about what his company is producing."

"They produce locomotives, wheels, freight cars, cannons, ammunition." Meg shrugged. "Everyone knows that. It's the other things they produce…specific types of warfare…that have folks asking questions."

None of it sounded interesting when explained that way.

"I heard snippets about submarines being built at Tredegar last fall, so yes, they have secrets." Meg tossed a pile of quartered sections into the half-filled kettle.

So Jay's refusal to share his company's secrets was actually heroic, because Union spies would pass the information to the authorities so something can be built to counter it. Elizabeth Van Lew had seemed very interested in Jay's job. Bea gasped. Could Elizabeth be spying for the *Union?*

"Bea? What's—"

The outside door opened, and Mabel stepped inside. "Mama says we need more potatoes if you got any ready."

"We do." Bea stood to lift the heavy kettle. "Is this enough?"

"We have tomatoes, green beans, and carrots that we canned

last summer." The girl studied the contents. "I'd say just about. If you can finish what's piled on the table, we'll add those to the cooking pot. I'll bring this pot right back."

"Fair enough." Bea selected one of the four potatoes remaining as Mabel slipped outside. "We're almost done here."

Meg watched Mabel leave and then turned to Bea. "Is something wrong? You seem upset."

"No, I'm fine." Bea wanted time to consider Elizabeth's loyalties. If the Southerner was a Unionist, Bea didn't feel quite so alone.

"Good." Meg looked up as Mabel returned. "How will we transport all this soup to Camp Winder?"

Mabel set the empty pot on the table. "We got that all figured out. Harold and Clarence—that's my brother—are coming with you. They'll load the empty laundry kettle onto the wagon and then fill it with hot soup once it's inside. Can't fill it all the way 'cause it'll slosh out on the ride over."

"Looks like you all have thought of everything." Bea smiled at her, impressed.

"With Mrs. Trudy's generous heart, you all probably know we've done this before."

"Yes, I imagine so. Thanks for all you do." Bea sank back in her chair as the last potato went into the pot. "Meg, I'm going up to read Annie's letter before we go."

"Of course. I'll knock on your door when everything's ready."

Bea hurried upstairs and was soon settled on her chaise to enjoy news from home. Annie's note was dated Saturday, May third.

My Dearest Sister,

How I miss you! It's been weeks since I waved goodbye to you in the wee hours of a winter morning. Now, I wish I'd traveled with you, but more on that later. This is the longest we've been apart. Father misses his youngest daughter and is including his own letter with mine.

It seems the battles have escalated with the warmer weather. Three letters from John arrived the same day. He warned me not to send you too much news about his division in the Army of the Potomac, but they've seen more action than I wish him to have. He was in our vicinity until March, and how I long for his swift return! Now, dearest sister, he is in Virginia, far closer to you than he is to me.

The page trembled in Bea's hand. The Army of the Potomac was as close to Richmond as that? To attack it?

It seems that we should have waited to send you to Aunt Trudy. With the opposing armies crisscrossing Virginia, it may be safer for you to remain there until the situation calms instead of mounting the first train north, as I want you to do.

As for your courtship with Jay, I cannot help but worry that your loyalty to the North and his to the South will cause clashes between you. Father does not seem concerned about that aspect of your relationship, so perhaps I worry too much. (I am the older sister, after all!) Meg and Aunt Trudy are with you. Speak to them of any concerns that arise in your courtship and write to me, of course. I confess I barely recall meeting Jay so I can give no opinion as to his character, but he had better be all that is good and kind to my sister or he will answer to me. (And Father, John, and Will.) I trust your good judgement.

It grows late, so I will close. You're always in my prayers. Be careful, sweet Beatrice. You are very dear to me!

Your loving sister,

Annie

Bea tapped the page against her lips. Her sister was

concerned about this important disagreement between her and Jay. Father wasn't, likely because his own loyalty had shifted. Of course, the savvy banker's correspondence would give no indication of it. His opinions held great sway over her and she felt the familiar confusion taking over as she opened his letter.

Dearest Daughter,

My attention to what is happening in Virginia has been unwavering since you left for Richmond. The news of the Army of the Potomac's presence in Virginia is widely reported and, of course, we know that the Confederate army is also there. There have been skirmishes and battles that may lead to Richmond. My concern is for you, Meg, and my sister.

Here is my dilemma. The armies are broken into corps, brigades, divisions, and regiments. The large units often divide and go in opposite directions, making it difficult for me to know whether it's safe to ask you to return home immediately. If I were to do that, I might be sending you into the path of a skirmish that just broke out north of you. I'm in a quandary over the situation. I have prayed for guidance. In my heart I believe you are safer staying where you are. Your aunt Trudy is there. Your uncle Isaac is also watching out for your safety, so I'm not concerned on that account. He stands ready to help you in any way necessary. It is only that I am a protective father who wants to ensure his family is safe. That includes your North Carolina family and my baby granddaughter.

Of course, your new beau is watching out for you as well. I like the sound of that young man, and I believe your mother would be pleased with him as well.

Bea closed her eyes against the tears that threatened. If only Mother were here to lend her approval. It took a moment to collect herself.

If you feel safe where you are, then stay. If not, pack your trunk and leave with Meg for your home in Washington City. Take a train west to Tennessee and then head north through Kentucky to Cincinnati and then come east through Pennsylvania and home. Such a meandering trip must include overnight stays in various cities as you change trains. I've learned it can take up to a week, so I don't prefer such a journey for you. As much as I miss my sweet daughter, I want you to stay as long as things are going well. I'm proud of the charitable work you are doing there. Keep up the good work and be careful, dearest Beatrice.

Your loving father,

Hiram Swanson

Bea scanned his letter again, searching for what he meant and was not saying. Her uncle stood "ready to help her in any way necessary." It seemed as if her father believed her volunteer work at the hospitals and the sewing group stemmed from a desire to aid the Confederacy.

Did it? She'd knitted socks to keep a shivering man's feet warm, not melted iron to fashion bullets. Spending time with wounded and dying was something she'd do for soldiers on either side. Her compassionate nature didn't allow her to turn a blind eye to their pain if it was within her power to ease it.

Or was she still confused about her loyalties?

Why must Father always make her doubt herself? She dropped the letter and crept to the window. Her father's change of attitude always put her in a state of confusion.

Looking out over the garden where she and Jay had their first disagreement didn't calm the turmoil in her heart. They had been interrupted before reaching a resolution, if there was such a thing in this circumstance.

A knock on the door was followed by Meg's voice. "Bea? We're ready to go to Camp Winder."

"I'll be down in a moment."

She pinned on her hat with one last look at the garden where Jay had kissed her.

He valued her feelings and opinions. Her father seemed to view them as an extension of his own.

~

Bea arrived home with Meg later that afternoon and stopped to drink lemonade waiting for them in the parlor. "Looks like Aunt Trudy is still out. I'm exhausted, but I must say that serving all those hungry men lifted my spirits."

"Yes, helping others is its own reward, isn't it?" Meg eyed her. "I believe I'll go for a stroll."

"Aren't you tired?" Bea raised her eyebrows. "We stood on our feet for hours."

"No, I'm fine."

Bea sighed. "Then I'll get my shawl. Those gray clouds look threatening. It might rain before we return."

"I'm not worried." Meg looked out the window. "Besides, I won't be gone long. Take a nap. There's no need to accompany me."

"Where are you going?" Curiosity overcame exhaustion.

"To see a friend." Meg stared out into the garden.

"Your friend in jail?" If so, her cousin needed support.

Meg shook her head. "It's still too risky to visit the jail. Someone else."

"Then who is it? Are you visiting Elizabeth Van Lew?" The more she had considered Elizabeth's loyalties, the more likely it seemed that she supported the Union. As for spying, Bea had no proof. "I've noticed you two are becoming friends."

She turned away. "It's best you don't know."

"Why?"

"You can't tell what you don't know." Her jaw set.

Bea studied her. "You don't have to keep secrets from me. I already know enough. You can trust me. Let me help." Suspicions that her cousin was involved in spying again caused her knees to grow weak. Even so, Meg didn't have to face the danger alone.

She turned back to the window as clouds blocked the sun.

The room darkened. Bea wrapped her fingers around her cold, empty glass and waited for her decision.

"All right. Walking with you will attract less attention than a woman walking alone. You can come on one condition." She turned toward her with a serious expression.

"Anything."

"When I give the sign, I want you to let me go on ahead. Step into a shop."

"If it's open. Some have been closing."

"Then stare into shop windows as you wander along. My errand is a short one. Maybe two minutes. Then I'll return to you. Can you do that?"

"Yes." Bea agreed without hesitation even as she wondered at an errand that only took two minutes to accomplish.

"Meet me back here in a quarter hour."

"I'll be here." Not knowing what to expect, Bea was back in the parlor with her shawl and reticule within ten minutes.

Meg carried in a basket with her reticule swinging from her arm. "I told Clara to expect us back in about an hour."

"Where are we going?" Bea followed her down the cobblestone path to the street.

"I thought we'd stroll along Main Street."

"All right." She began to understand why Meg had been a successful scout. Her lighthearted smile suggested she hadn't a care in the world. Respect for her cousin mounted with each step.

A brisk pace took them past the ornate homes of the Church Hill neighborhood. Soon they approached the hotels, banks, and shops leading into the heart of the city.

"Look inside that grocer's window." Meg indicated the store with a nod. "He has coffee. Didn't your aunt mention her need of more coffee beans?"

She hadn't. Annie had sent enough coffee to last another month. Bea met Meg's smiling glance. After the briefest of nods, Bea understood. "Yes, it's in short supply. I'll step inside and see how many pounds are available for purchase."

"I'll come back for you."

"Of course." Bea entered the shop. Meg's meaning was clear. Make a leisurely purchase, and she'd return soon.

Bea ordered five pounds of unroasted coffee beans from the stranger at the counter. She turned to browse the shelves while he weighed it. Five pounds would feel like double the weight by the time she carried it home.

There was no one else in the store. Where was Meg?

"Will that be all, miss?" The bald man with a gray mustache dropped a sack on the counter.

"Hmm…" She wanted to extend her time until Meg returned and searched the shelves of dried spices and seasonings for inspiration.

"Oh, good. You found the coffee."

Meg was at her side before she realized anyone was there. "Yes. Aunt Trudy will be pleased, won't she?" Bea was surprised how easily she entered into the game.

"Indeed."

The exorbitant price was paid with local bills she'd exchanged for silver back in February.

"I love the smell of roasting coffee beans more than I love the beverage." Meg placed the sack in her basket as they left the shop.

"Agreed." Bea realized the comment was for the grocer's

benefit. As soon as they were out of earshot, Bea lowered her voice. “Did you take care of your errand?”

“Whatever do you mean?” Meg’s pleasant look belied the warning in her eyes. “Are you ready to go home?”

More than ready, Bea realized as she nodded. Whatever Meg was doing, it required strong nerves and quick thinking.

They turned toward their Richmond home. Bea whispered a prayer that Meg soon trusted her enough to tell her about her friend.

In the meantime, she’d keep a watchful eye out for her cousin.

CHAPTER 23

"Are you certain? Norfolk has been abandoned?" Jay reeled from the news that his fellow citizens left the Confederate city and its naval base. "That allows the Union to waltz in and take it over."

Troy bit into a sandwich. "Appears to be a mistake to me, but I'm not a military leader."

Jay's appetite for his ham sandwich evaporated. "We have a few minutes before lunch ends. I want to walk along the river." Too bad his favorite place to view the falls was too far away. He did his best thinking there.

"I'll come with you."

They left the crowded yard where workers ate. Long strides left the billowing black smoke behind them.

"I knew that General Johnston had left Yorktown. It ended the siege but not in the way we hoped. By now, Union soldiers must occupy it. What else has happened?" Jay halted at the river's edge.

"Not been reading the newspapers, have you?" Troy frowned.

"Not for a few days." The news was all bad anyway.

"I don't have a girl," Troy said, "so I reckon I have more time than you."

It was Monday and a week since Jay saw Bea. He had penned a note to her, apologizing for his inability to escort her to church. He had planned to take her and Meg to a restaurant for supper last evening and sent his regrets. He had arrived home from work at half-past five yesterday and been asleep by eight o-clock. This grueling schedule made him feel the aches of an old man.

"It's said that President Davis was called away from a reception Friday evening. It seems that enemy gunboats are headed up the James River." Troy gazed at the calm river with a troubled expression.

"What?" Jay stood in front of the peaceful James. "There have been so many rumors in the past. It can't be true."

"I don't know." Troy's mouth set in a firm line. "On Saturday, the First Lady took her children and left on a train bound for Raleigh."

Jay's heart thudded. President Davis must trust the news to send his family away. What about the safety of the rest of the city's citizens?

"Did you realize the Confederate Congress left the capital a couple of weeks ago?"

Jay blinked. He had known, but it hadn't concerned him. "You don't think...?"

"I don't know." Troy raised open palms toward the heavens. "Seems a mite too convenient to be a coincidence."

"The big boats can only go so far, you know." Jay stared up the river. "The falls will stop them."

"Yeah, but they'll be in the capital before reaching the falls."

"Why are we still at work?" Jay jerked around to face the foundries. "Our battalion is needed to guard the city."

He shook his head. "It's been deemed more important that we arm our soldiers."

"There are forts all around the city." Jay's blood pumped through his veins, spurting energy where exhaustion had reigned. "Surely we'll be sent to defend them."

"No. Not yet anyway." Troy's mouth tightened. "We have heavy guns at Drewry's Bluff."

"That bluff is seven miles from Richmond." Jay swiped his hand across his mouth. Seven miles. They feared Union gunboats would come that close? No wonder the Davis family had left. How was he to protect Bea and his own family while sweating in heat from coal fire furnaces all day?

"Rumor is we blew up the CSS *Virginia."*

"What?" His heart sank. Losing that ship would be a great blow to the Confederacy. He hoped they all didn't live to regret it.

"It was too big to pursue the gunboats on the river. They didn't want to risk our ship falling into enemy hands." He heaved a heavy sigh. "It's believed our guns at Drewry's Bluff will stop the gunboats."

"It better stop them." What a disaster. He stared down the James to where it seemed that enemy boats were headed toward them. Their guns at Drewry's Bluff should blast them from the water…or make it so hot they decided to turn back toward the Peninsula.

Jay closed his eyes in silent prayer for Bea, his mother, and all those he loved in the city. *God, please keep the enemy from breaking through our defenses and reaching us.*

~

It had been nine long days since Bea's unfortunate conversation with Jay about their conflicting loyalties, and she sat before her open bedroom window with one lantern lit on the other side of the room. Passing guards could see no more than her silhouette as she stared into the darkness.

She and Jay might have resolved something as a couple…or at least ended their discussion on a positive understanding…had they not been interrupted.

A tap on the door interrupted her sadness. "Come in."

Meg peeked around the door. "Do you want company?"

"Of course." Not really. She wanted to wallow in her sadness. Matters between her and Jay remained unsettled. His note postponing their supper plans at his favorite restaurant had further depressed her spirits.

"I'll join you." Meg carried the desk chair over to the window. "Pleasant breeze."

"Yes."

"You miss Jay."

"I do." Bea stared at a flickering flame in a gas street lamp on the street behind the house. "He's working long days again yet he managed to see me at least twice a week the last time that happened. And he canceled our supper plans last evening."

"Postponed them. We'll do it when his work schedule allows."

"Meg, I fear he is avoiding me."

"Why?"

"We had a disagreement." Bea shook her head. "No, that's not exactly it. We discussed the war."

They sat in silence a few moments.

"My confusion doesn't help," Bea said.

"Confusion?" Meg raised her brows, glancing at two men walking the streets. "It's past curfew. Those must be guards." Her voice dropped to a whisper. "Let's sit away from the open window where our voices carry."

Bea stared at the men, who were looking in their direction, with a mixture of annoyance and fear. No, the guards shouldn't hear this conversation.

"Continue to whisper." Meg settled next to her on the lounge on the other side of the room. "What has confused you?"

"This conflict. The division between the North and the South." Bea waved her hands in a sweeping gesture. "I support the Union, but there are so many reasons for differing views."

"Nearly as many opinions as there are people." She sighed.

"Good people that I respect fight for the South. Support the South. Aunt Trudy, for instance, hates slavery nearly as much as my mother did."

"Yet going against her homeland is not in her nature."

"Exactly."

"I suspect Jay shares those feelings."

"I believe he'd rather cut off his own arm than turn his back on Virginia."

Meg arranged her robe over her nightgown.

"And my—others have expressed similar sentiments." Bea was horrified that she had almost mentioned her father's change of heart. Meg's empathy made it easy to talk with her. Bea vowed to keep stricter control on her words.

"This is a confusing time to be alive, no doubt about it. I pray our country survives it." Meg's reverent tones were spoken as a prayer. "Has Jay professed his love for you?"

"Not in so many words." She couldn't keep a smile from her lips. "Yet I know he loves me."

"What about your feelings? Do you love him?"

"I do." Bea rarely expressed her innermost feelings even to Annie, but tonight she was lonely, and Meg understood loneliness. "But it's as if there's a broad river between us."

"Bridges are built all the time. I didn't agree with Thomas about every matter. We weathered the storm." Meg patted her shoulder. "I'm not saying it's easy. You'll need to discuss the matter honestly. Respect one another's opinions and beliefs. If you choose it, you and Jay can weather the storm together."

A weight tumbled off her shoulders for the first time since Jay said goodbye.

"There's something else we need to discuss." Meg closed the

window and returned. "I read every Richmond newspaper and I fear hard times are coming to this city. Along with both armies."

Bea smothered a gasp behind her hand. Standing, she turned to hide the fear that must line her face.

"Brace yourself." Meg sat on the edge of the chaise as she told Bea about Varina Davis leaving Richmond with her children and the threat of the gunboats. "It's likely they'll be stopped before reaching us."

"I never want to see this city destroyed."

"Agreed." Meg stood and began to wander about the room in a restless manner.

Bea's hand on her throat felt icy cold. "Or the people I love to be harmed in any way."

"I pray that never happens." Meg walked to the now closed window in the shadowy room. "You have recent letters from Annie and your father. Do they advise you to stay in Richmond or return home?"

"I'm certain my father wishes he had never agreed to this visit." Maybe not since she brought his substantial gift to the Confederacy with her. She found his letter in the desk and held it toward the lantern light. "Here it is. He says for us to head West and then north to Cincinnati if we leave Richmond. Annie also believes it safer for us to remain here."

"May I read it?" Meg held out her hand.

"Sorry." Bea folded the letter and tucked it away. "Some of it is private."

"Then burn it." Meg dropped her hand. "Don't keep anything that the authorities may use against you or your family."

Bea's cheeks burned. Did Meg suspect that her father's loyalty was now to the Confederacy?

"I've also had letters from Annie and your father." Meg returned to the window. "Uncle Hiram is very concerned for your safety."

"We're safer here, aren't we?"

"I believe so."

She agreed. "Meg, you've been out without me a few times since that day you had to see your friend. Can you tell me what you did?"

Her face tightened. "It's best you don't know."

"Can't you trust me?" Bea's voice rose in her desperation to understand.

"Please, remember to whisper." Meg sighed. "I do trust you, Bea. It's dangerous. Your father will not thank me for placing you in the middle of it."

Bea stared at her. So she had been correct.

Meg looked away. "Please forget what I said."

Silence between them grew awkward. "Does what you're doing require you to be in Richmond?"

Meg looked back at her, eyes wide. "I don't want to leave Richmond."

Bea suddenly didn't want confirmation that her cousin was spying on the Confederacy. How did she get the information to Union authorities? Meg was right. Bea wasn't ready to know the details. "I don't want to leave Aunt Trudy and Mary." She flushed. "Or Jay."

"Of course not. We're doing a lot of good here."

"Are you conflicted about our charitable work here?"

"You mean taking food to wounded Confederate soldiers, changing their bandages, writing their letters to loved ones?" Meg tilted her head. "Sewing clothing for them?"

"All of it."

"If I did, I couldn't force myself to be kind to the soldiers. But I am a Christian first. I believe in treating others with kindness, even if they hurt you. Everyone needs food, clothing." She spread her arms wide. "Those suffering in the hospitals deserve our kindness, no matter their allegiance. No, I want to ease their pain and pray for them. Listen to their stories of loved ones back home."

"I feel the same." It comforted her that her cousin, though loyal to the North, had no qualms about treating those who disagreed with kindness.

Respect for others went a long way to pave the path toward reconciliation.

CHAPTER 24

Gunboats were approaching Richmond, and here Jay was, stuck at Tredegar. Sometimes it seemed as if the foundry bound him with chains.

It had been three days since he'd learned that Union gunboats were headed up the James toward them. Five gunboats. He'd waited in vain for his battalion to be sent to forts encircling the capital. He wanted to protect the city.

On the other hand, that they hadn't been called upon was a hopeful sign of the army's confidence in halting the advance.

Drewry's Bluff was located ninety feet above the river at a sharp bend. Earthworks, barracks, and mounted guns guarded the fort there. Rumors were that Southern infantry guarded it, along with the crew of the recently destroyed CSS *Virginia*.

The ground shook beneath the building. He and his men looked at each other. An earthquake?

Jay ran through the arched brick exit into the yard. Men from surrounding buildings emerged at a run.

"What happened?"

"What was that?"

"Are them Yanks attacking us?"

Jay's heart thundered. Gunboats?

Troy wobbled over on vibrating ground. "I'll bet those Union ships made it to Drewry's Bluff."

"Sounds like it," Jay said. The ground shook again, and a faint booming sounded in the distance. "Think they'll get through?"

"I didn't expect them to get that far."

"Too close for comfort." Jay followed others to the river's shore.

"I'll say." Troy's face was ashen.

"No doubt we're peppering bullets into the boats." Jay imagined he was there, smelling the gunpowder and lead, blinded by smoking guns.

"Wish I could see it," Troy said.

"Me too," Jay straightened his shoulders, "with my musket pointed at the enemy."

The ground continued to rumble. More men joined them by the river, some silent, some wondering aloud how many minutes it would take for the Southerners to convince the Yanks to turn back toward the peninsula.

Jay enjoyed their confidence and then thought of Bea and his mother. He presumed they weren't so confident. There was no ignoring the ground's vibrations. He closed his eyes and said a quick prayer for their safety as well as for the battle happening south of the city.

The plank floor of the hospital ward shook. Bea braced herself against the rough wood of the wall in between patient beds. Terror gripped her heart. They must endure an earthquake on top of all their troubles?

"That ain't no earthquake, miss." Colt, the Tennessee man to whom she'd been feeding egg gruel, sank back against his pillow. "When shells strike the ground, it feels just like that."

Cannons? Bea nearly collapsed against the wall that shook again.

"Don't take on so. Battle sounds are faint." Colt fell back against his pillow as all forty beds in the building rattled, most of them occupied by patients. "They ain't close enough to do you no harm."

"Not yet." A wounded man in the next bed scowled.

"Now, Tom," Colt said. "No need to frighten Miss Beatrice any more than she already is." Colt shot her a look of apology.

"She's fine. For now. Them Yanks are trying to get to Richmond. Too bad I can't get out of this cot yet and give them the whooping they deserve. Give me a few days."

Tom's bandaged shoulder wound required closer to a few weeks to heal. Yet it was the lack of fear in the soldiers' eyes that slowed her pulse. She pushed herself away from the whitewashed wall with a glance out one of the ten open windows that ran along this side of the building. Ten matching windows ran down the opposite side, interspersed with three doors each, aiding in ventilation. Some folks milled around looking south. She hoped it wasn't as bad as it sounded. "Thank you for calming my fears, gentlemen. I've never experienced this."

"I'd like to say you get used to it." Colt looked at the empty bowl shaking on his bed as the floor boards jiggled again. "But I doubt you will."

An honest observation. "I believe you." She appreciated learning the truth from soldiers who had lived through it. "Cannons or not, there are a few more hungry men who need their breakfast. Tom"—she looked at the disgruntled man with the shoulder wound—"you're next. The surgeon has suggested beef tea for you."

"Figures. I ate that yesterday. And the day before that." He sighed. "And the day before that."

"I understand you're tired of it. Beef tea has lots of nourishment." The beds clanked for about five seconds. She planted her feet to wait it out. Tense men from Tennessee regiments were trying to ignore it, possibly for her sake. She'd match their efforts. "And that will make you strong again."

"If you say so."

"I'll get it for you." It pleased her to see the corner of his mouth twitch upwards. She scooped up the dirty bowl and utensils and left the whitewashed single-story building identical to rows of other hospital wards. Crossing the wide avenue that separated the wards, she peeked inside the next one to find her cousin.

"Meg, do you need anything from the kitchen?" The door shook on its hinges with another blast. Where was the fighting? It seemed too close for safety's sake.

"A bowl of egg gruel. Thanks." Meg hurried to the doorway. "Difficult to ignore the building's vibrations. Are you all right?"

"Not much choice, is there?" Her cousin's tense demeanor must be mirrored on her own. "These men are hungry, and we've got a job to do."

"I needed to hear you say that." Meg's face relaxed. "Remind me sometime to tell you how courageous you are."

Smiling, Bea hurried toward the kitchen.

"Probably at Drewry's Bluff."

A male voice carried from another aisle between buildings. Bea peered to the left but didn't see anyone. Slowing at the stranger's comment, she tucked a curly wisp behind her ear.

"Reckon Union gunboats made it to our fort there. Our boys are convincing 'em to turn back," another man replied.

"All the way to New York Harbor."

"That ain't far enough, if you ask me."

"Once we get those ships off the James, we got the Yankee infantry to worry about." A new voice this time.

"We ain't got to worry about nothin'. Our boys will send the traitors back where they belong."

Bea's face flamed at the disgust in the stranger's voice as

much as from his threat. Was Annie's husband one of those Union soldiers the Southerners scoffed at? Annie's latest letter revealed he was near the Peninsula, but where?

If John were ordered to attack Richmond while Beatrice was there, wouldn't he find a way to warn her? Maybe not. Even as a second lieutenant, he wouldn't know detailed orders until his commanding officer deemed it necessary to tell him.

Either way, John needed her prayers. She whispered a quick prayer for his safety as she picked up her skirt with her empty hand and set her sight on the open kitchen door. Her stomach rumbled from the appetizing aroma of beef stew that would be lunch for some patients in about four hours.

As she told Meg, there were hungry men to feed.

~

Jay arrived home at six o'clock that evening. There was finally some good news—the Union boats had turned back in a fury of shot and shell from his fellow Southerners.

After that, all he'd been able to think about was Bea. She must be terrified. It wasn't safe for her to return to Washington City. He didn't want her to go anyway.

His mother was frantic, something he should have anticipated given her nervous state in recent months.

She and Trudy had planned to join the sewing group today, but the commotion started first. The friends had waited together for the girls to come home from Chimborazo Hospital. By the time they did, the ground had stopped shaking.

It took a quarter of an hour to calm his mother enough that she nibbled at her supper.

Jay didn't take time to eat. His mother's fears were convincing proof Bea needed him.

As for the difference in their allegiances, he had no answer and hoped to avoid the topic. He was more certain his love was the enduring kind with each passing day.

It was half past seven before the smell of coal smoke was washed from his hair. Long strides took him to Trudy's home in record time.

Harold opened the door before the knocker clanked twice against the metal. "Mr. Jay, welcome. Such awful rumbling as we had this morning was sure to bring you this evening."

"Good evening, Harold. It was quite a disruption." Jay stood with him in the spacious entry hall. "It's safe now. Our boys drove them back."

Harold studied the dark green rug. "I don't want to see nothing bad happen to Mrs. Trudy and her guests."

"Agreed." Jay scanned the hall and the ornate stairway. His greatest concern at the moment was for Bea. "I know it's late to call, but I'm worried about the ladies. Are they here?"

"Mrs. Trudy asked for a supper tray in her room. I'm of the opinion she does that when she wants time alone to pray. We don't expect her downstairs until breakfast." He glanced toward the stairs with its gleaming wooden handrails. "Miss Beatrice is in the garden with Miss Meg. Let me just go around and see if they're receiving guests."

Jay ran a finger under his collar as the tall man disappeared down the hall. As a frequent guest in this home, he'd expected to be escorted to the garden directly. Yet he'd avoided Bea for almost two weeks when he could have spared an hour here and there to see her.

His concern for her fear had driven their disagreements away. Did she even want to see him?

Harold's quick steps approached. "The ladies will be pleased for your company in the garden."

A hopeful sign. Lifting his chin, he strode down the hall to meet her.

Bea, with an indrawn breath, looked up at Meg as Harold left the garden and reentered the home.

"Do you want to see him?" Meg sat beside her on the white metal bench.

"Yes, I've longed to see him." She'd looked for him to call every evening that week to no avail. "But why didn't he return to finish our conversation before this fearful day?"

"A question for Jay. This may not be the best hour for that discussion." Meg patted her hand. "Defense of this city and protection of his loved ones is likely uppermost on his mind. Unless I miss my guess, that includes you, cousin."

Footsteps on dry grass.

"I'll stay a few minutes and then give you time to talk. Just talk quickly. The sun is setting now." Meg turned in the seat to face him. "Jay, how lovely to see you."

Bea stood, uncertain whether to extend her hand after his long absence. Her heart skipped at his apprehensive expression. He wore a brown jacket with a patterned vest the color of sand and looked more handsome than ever.

"Good evening, ladies." He took off his hat and held it against his chest. "I'm happy to find you looking so well. My mother is rather the worse for the scare our city endured today."

"I'm sorry to hear it." Bea made a sweeping gesture at an iron chair close to hers and sat. He hadn't reached for her hand, as had been his custom after their courtship began. Perhaps Meg's presence caused his awkwardness. "Meg and I were at Chimborazo Hospital when it began."

"Chimborazo?" His forehead wrinkled. "So early in the morning?"

"Yes, we were there yesterday. The number of sick and wounded is rising. They asked us to return today and help feed the men breakfast." Bea considered the daily happenings she hadn't shared with him yet. Some were minor and hardly worth mentioning, but she loved telling him everything about her life. She thought of her father's gift to the Confederacy. And Meg's spying. No, not everything was suitable to tell Jay.

"Ah, you were with soldiers. Then you were in a safe place to weather the battle." Some tension eased from his face. "Were you afraid?"

"It's frightful to be close enough to a battle that the ground trembles beneath your feet." Meg glanced at her cousin. "Bea's reaction helped me."

Bea was touched. Looking back, she was glad she'd been able to push her fear away to focus on the needs of her patients.

"How so?" Jay's eyes widened.

"She remained focused on our task. We couldn't alter the battle. She reminded me that wounded and hurting men were hungry. We took care of them."

"I'm proud of you, Bea." A gleam lit his green eyes. "Both of you, of course. You overcame difficult circumstances. Thank you for all you do for our wounded."

Warmth spread through her at his praise. How wonderful to be with him again. "What about you? You were at work? How far away was the battle from you?"

"Only seven miles. A river battle that was too near us for complacency." Shadows turned his green eyes nearly gray. "I pray the enemy never comes closer."

Bea didn't dare look at Meg after Jay's reference to the Union army as the enemy.

"Perhaps the two of you would like to stroll the garden while I enjoy the colors left behind by the setting sun." Meg gave Bea an encouraging nod.

"Yes, I'd like that." She arose. Bless Meg for giving them an opportunity to speak alone.

Jay extended his hand.

She placed her ungloved hand in his, reveling in his touch. "Crowds of folks were gathered at the street corners today when Meg and I strolled along Main Street. No doubt they sought the comfort of their neighbors in shared fear."

"Shared fear is fear halved," he said.

"It is." She smiled at the wisdom behind his words.

He bent his head toward her. "Tell me, truly. Are you all right?"

"About the battle?"

He nodded.

"It scared me, but my patients assured me I was in no immediate danger. I trusted their instincts." Dusk fell as Bea strolled with him along the familiar imbedded stone walk around the half-acre garden. "Remember that I live in Washington City. There were rumors that our city faced attack after the battle at Bull Run."

"'Our' city." His fingers twitched against her hand. "Thanks for choosing that word. It's a good reminder."

"Of what?" She flicked a glance at his profile.

"Of all that separates us."

She pulled her hand away and halted. "What separates us, Jay? Explain it to me."

"Your loyalty is to the North."

"You've been avoiding me." Her lips tightened. Was this ugly war, after causing her father to topple from his pedestal in her eyes by embroiling her into smuggling for him, also to rob her of the man she loved?

"It's been hard...busy work days..." His face turned crimson.

"I recall when those long days didn't prevent you from stopping by for pie after supper or to stroll with me in the evening." She put her hands on her hips. If he wanted to end the courtship, he must say it.

"No." He rested his hand against a mighty oak. "It's this war that's trying to divide us."

"War has a way of doing that." Her tone was more bitter than she'd intended.

"True."

"Do you have feelings for me?" She tilted her head, studying the conflicting emotions crossing his face. She loved him, but she wasn't about to tell him first.

His hat tumbled to the ground as his hands cupped her face. "I love you, Bea. More each day. More than you know. I thought I'd never have the chance to tell you."

She gave a shaky laugh. "I love you, Jay Nickson."

It was true then. She'd not guessed wrong. For so long, she'd longed for love, a love like her parents had enjoyed. A love like Annie and John shared. Now, she'd found it.

With a Southerner.

"Now what?"

His gaze dropped to her lips. He lowered his head and kissed her breathless. She put her arms around his neck and leaned against him, rejoicing in the feeling of coming home she found within his arms.

When he pulled himself away—with considerable effort, or so it seemed—she allowed herself to rest in his arms. "I've missed you so."

"Oh, Bea. I do love you." He gave her a lingering kiss and then studied her face in the deepening darkness under the tree. "I don't want the war to divide us."

"Never."

He held her a moment longer. Then he stepped away. "Tensions mount to a fever pitch. I've heard gentle Southern women who wouldn't swat a fly ask their beaus to kill a Yankee for them."

Waves of shock tremored through her at the hate directed toward her brother-in-law and his fellow soldiers.

"I don't want you to be threatened, or worse, harmed, by

anyone in the name of patriotism." Tormented green eyes closed briefly.

"Were you in Washington City, you'd be in danger if you spoke of your Southern loyalties to the wrong person."

"Precisely my point." He ran his hands through his hair. "Was our love doomed from the start?"

"Not doomed. We'll face difficulties, certainly." Bea needed to think. To pray. "Let's each pray for guidance."

"Excellent idea."

"It's getting dark." His face was in the shadows. "I know the others will welcome a chance to visit with you. Will you come inside for some cobbler?"

"Sound delicious, but I had best get back home." He stooped and retrieved his hat from the grass. "It's doubtful I'll be at church again Sunday. May I take you for a drive later that afternoon?"

"Perhaps we should wait a bit." They needed time to think, to pray, for this relationship presented challenges.

Bea's heart sank as a shield seemed to descend over his expression. She watched him stride away from the house, wondering if the war had achieved its divisive purpose yet again.

CHAPTER 25

"Good afternoon, Miss Elizabeth." Bea shifted her heavy basket to her other arm as she returned the other woman's smile.

"Did you come from the shops?" Elizabeth peeked at her full basket covered with a blue-cloth.

"The grocer's. My aunt worries that certain foods are becoming scarce in the city." She touched the basket filled with cans, eggs, spices, and seasonings. This was her purchase for them, and she felt pleased with her gift. "Tea has grown expensive, and I found some."

"One learns to do without luxuries when necessary." Elizabeth sighed. "Why are you out on your own?"

"Meg is filling sandbags at the Petersons'." A fully-loaded wagon passed on the road heading west with children walking behind it. The rumors of invasion had folks packing up and leaving Richmond. The battle two days earlier lent credence to the fear. "Dust from the sandbags caused me to sneeze so I volunteered to pick up a few items for my aunt."

"Emotions are running high with this talk of the enemy invading. President Davis was wise to declare another National

Day of Humiliation and Prayer yesterday. We all need prayer." Elizabeth's eyes darted from one crowded corner to another. "I'm headed home. Why don't we walk together? I'd welcome your company."

"I'd like that." The tense atmosphere had Bea looking over her shoulder. Many had eyed her as she'd hurried past. The welcome she had experienced here as a child was long gone. "Thank you."

Elizabeth set off at a rapid pace. "Have the rumors scared you into advancing the date of your return home?"

"No." She tugged on the brim of her hat to shade her eyes. "I promised Aunt Trudy I'd stay through the summer. We talked about it after Thursday's battle. I'd rather be here to assist her if something dangerous occurs anyway. Meg agrees."

"Your aunt is a fortunate woman to be so loved. And perhaps there is another reason you remain in Richmond."

Catching the sly glance that accompanied the observation, Bea remained silent. Jay's presence was an excellent reason to stay, should he give their love a chance to blossom. She was still praying for him, for she knew her own heart's desire.

"May I ask you about Jay?" Elizabeth asked. "I didn't see him at church last week. Is he well?"

"He is busy at work."

"Ah, yes." She darted a look at Bea. "Buildings have been constructed at Tredegar since the hostilities began. One wonders what they are doing now."

"Casting cannon and making ammunition." Bea's suspicions that Elizabeth was a spy strengthened each time the older woman mentioned it, making Bea glad that he didn't give tours…or details.

Not even to Bea. She was surprised that refusal no longer bothered her, rather it proved him to be a man of principles.

A group of plainly dressed women on the corner glared at them as they passed. Bea didn't recognize anyone. She nodded to them. No one smiled, inclined their head, or nodded to return her silent greeting. The sunny May day suddenly gave her a chill.

"This war won't last forever." Elizabeth darted a look at the women. "Though there are days when it seems it will never end."

Curious. Those women hadn't seemed to like Elizabeth. Bea had never met them. Perhaps they didn't like Miss Elizabeth associating with her as a Northerner.

"Look at her." One contemptuous voice followed them. "Walking our streets while supporting the Yankees."

"She's one of them," said another. She might as well as have spat the words like tobacco juice, so venomous were they.

Bea inched closer to Elizabeth.

"Pay them no attention." Elizabeth lifted her chin.

"I'm not accustomed to such comments being directed at me." The back of Bea's neck heated. She wondered what the women's reaction would be if she responded to their hateful words.

Elizabeth's head jerked. "Of course not. Don't give them the satisfaction of knowing they hurt you," she whispered.

That advice stiffened Bea's backbone. "You are correct, Miss Elizabeth. Things will change in due course." She raised her voice so that it carried to the women behind them.

Laughter and scoffing comments followed them for several paces.

"Don't allow their criticism to wound you"—Elizabeth darted a glance her way—"yet there's no cause to invite their scorn."

Bea flushed. Would she always be ridiculed?

Or was their scorn directed at Elizabeth?

The sun sank toward the western horizon as Jay mounted his horse for his ride home on Saturday. He'd gone back to work after drilling to talk with someone and got caught up in the activity. They worked at maximum capacity in shifts. A sense of urgency crackled in the atmosphere as the enemy's army approached the city. What a nightmare.

Bea had refused to return home, a decision that, after much prayer, he felt surprisingly peaceful about.

How he missed her. If only it weren't too late to call on her.

The streets were overflowing with people and vehicles, causing him time and again to slow his horse's trot to a walk. Three wagons packed with every household item imaginable ambled past him toward the west. The fear he read on the faces of families walking beside the loaded wagons told the story. It might be late in the day to leave the city, but dread lent its own wings to their flight.

It had been reported that Union General George McClellan's army was at White House Landing, a mere twenty-three miles from Richmond, just a day's march away. Perhaps his mother would want to visit his sister's home in Tennessee.

Folks in his city had reason to fear. Yet he must report to work in the morning, not guard his loved ones from one of the forts that surrounded Richmond. Why did his battalion drill weekly if there was no intention to use them in defense? Could the soldiers nearby protect the city?

More weary travelers walked beside loaded wagons. Innocent citizens and soldiers alike paid the price of war.

He finally reached home and rode his horse to the stable in back.

"Long day?" Phineas accepted the reins.

"Yep." Just another in a long succession. Jay dismounted, nearly too exhausted to speak.

"Going back right after breakfast?"

"Six o'clock." He sighed.

"I'll have old Daisy here saddled and waiting." Phineas rubbed the mare's mane.

"Appreciate it." Daisy had been a filly when Jay courted Amelia, and he'd granted her the privilege of naming it, thinking she'd ride her after their wedding. Another mistake that weighed on him. In fact, he rarely referred to his horse by name. Likely another mistake, for he had treated Daisy as a remnant of a soured past relationship.

Mama ushered him to the dining table as soon as he'd washed his hands and face. Chicken stew for the fourth night this week.

Mama had eaten supper earlier and fidgeted in her chair adjacent to his at the head of the table. He didn't comment on the meal, but Mama knew him well. "Food prices are worrisome."

"We can afford it, Mama." His salary was more than adequate to keep his mother in comfort and to take care of a wife. Bea was accustomed to a luxurious lifestyle beyond his means, yet she'd not lack the fine dresses that she favored. He prayed for guidance as his love for her continued to grow. The war had done enough damage already. It mustn't also create a rift between them.

"Not everyone is so fortunate." Mama ran her fingers along the table's smooth edge. "It's not only the cost. Many businesses are closing. Farmers aren't bringing as much produce."

Her unspoken worry might as well have been written in his bowl. "Our army is between us and the enemy." He tried to keep his tone even as he ate another bite of soup. No need to feed her fear.

Her hands fluttered. "There's talk of burning the tobacco we have stocked in our warehouses to keep it from the enemy. The cotton, too."

"That's not a good idea." Jay pondered the possibility. He'd grown up with the aroma of tobacco everywhere he went in the city. The odor so permeated the atmosphere that he only noticed strong whiffs. The wealth of many—surrounding plantations included—depended on tobacco. "I hope the authorities make a different decision."

"This is the first time I haven't felt safe in my own home."

His spoon struck the bowl. Stayed there. The whispered words tore at his heart. He wanted to protect his mother, Bea. Aunt Trudy and Meg. Their safety weighed on his shoulders.

"We were at Chimborazo Hospital today," Mama added. "A veritable stream of wagons, families and possessions inside, headed through our city from the east."

Sights he'd witnessed on his ride home. If he read her right, she wished to leave Richmond. He propped his elbows on the table and folded his hands. "Do you want to go to Blanche's home?" His older sister lived in Chattanooga with her husband and two children.

"Is it safer there?"

"Maybe." The tablecloth muted the rapping of his knuckles. His mother had always been calm and capable. The war had frayed her nerves from the first battle. "Tennessee has suffered its own struggles." They'd lost Forts Donelson and Henry in February. That battle at Shiloh was last month.

Mama fidgeted with her cup. "Chattanooga isn't a bad idea."

"True." Joe was a courageous man yet, being a preacher, chose to honor his convictions not to fight and stay home. "Joe will watch over you. I'll send you if you like."

"You won't go with me?" Her eyes widened.

"How could I? They need all of us to complete the orders coming in." He spoke in a gentle tone. "Blanche wrote about Confederate troops constructing forts and batteries near the Tennessee River to protect the town."

"That's one of the reasons I'm considering it." She rested her forehead against her hand.

"I don't want you to travel alone on the train. I'll ask who from our staff would be willing to accompany you."

"I'll pray about it." She stood and then sat again. "I want to talk to Trudy. You work tomorrow, correct?"

"Yes." His aching body longed for a different answer. "No church for me."

"I'll invite Trudy, Meg, and Bea here for supper, and we can talk about it together."

"Very well." His mother always discussed major decisions with her childhood friend. He had hoped to take Bea for a drive after work, chaperoned by Meg, of course. She hadn't agreed to the outing. Perhaps it was just as well, for now they had other important matters to discuss.

CHAPTER 26

"Do you want to go to Tennessee?" Trudy sank back in a cushioned armchair in the Nicksons' cozy second-floor family parlor.

Bea studied Mary's stiff expression, its tension mirrored on Jay's handsome face. They had enjoyed a pleasant conversation over a delicious supper of fried fish without speaking of the threat to the city once, a minor miracle since the approaching army likely occupied everyone's mind. Those threats prompted Jay's mother to consider a trip to her daughter's home.

"I don't know." Mary waved her hands toward the ceiling. "Of course, I long to see Blanche. I last visited her family before Fort Sumter was fired upon."

Thirteen months ago. Bea met Jay's concerned gaze. Battles in the past year had left dead and wounded soldiers on both sides. Forgiveness, after everything finally ended, would be a long time coming for folks who'd lost husbands, sons, fathers, and friends.

"It will be good for you to see them." Meg's soothing tone held kindness.

"Little Joe turned seven in January. Donald will be five in

July. Because my Christmas visit had to be cancelled, perhaps it's best I stay with them a month or two now." Mary gripped the arms of her chair. "Do you feel safe here, Trudy?"

"I am not certain that *safe* correctly describes my feelings. I have prayed for this war, for the soldiers dying on both sides, until I have no words left." Her gaze shifted toward the window, where a rainy evening had ushered in premature dusk. "I suppose the correct description is *protected.* Whatever happens, my Savior will be with me. I will not suffer it alone."

Her aunt's conviction calmed Bea's spirit. "I admire your strong faith."

"It didn't come easily. I battled for it." Trudy clasped her hands in a prayerful pose. "Parker's death was particularly difficult for me. I grieved not having a son to carry on his name, a daughter who inherited his gentle spirit. It was loneliness such as I've never experienced." Her sorrowful glance fell on Meg. "I believe you understand that difficulty, don't you, dear?"

"Indeed."

"I asked God many times why He didn't take me at the same time." There was a sheen of tears in Trudy's eyes. "He let me know I still had work to do."

"My children were raised when I lost Fred, and I wondered the same thing." Mary sniffed, her puffy eyes on her son. "How I wish I could consult him now."

"He was wise in many ways," Jay said. "I'd love to talk with him about all the turmoil in our country. As to your present decision, I believe you'll be safe with Blanche." Jay touched his mother's forearm. "It's my opinion, you'll also be safe in Richmond. Generals Lee and Jackson will keep the enemy away."

"For now." Bea didn't realize she'd spoken her thoughts aloud until everyone looked at her.

"Do you know something we don't?" Mary asked.

Bea recoiled at distrust in the woman's eyes. It had never been there before tonight. "No, ma'am, I do not."

Mary turned to Trudy. "And what of your Yankee guests? Are they protected as well?"

"I've prayed for their protection. I trust in it." Trudy stiffened. "I'm certain you meant no offense, Mary, but please do not refer to my nieces that way."

"My apologies. I meant no offense." Mary's tone softened. "I worry that Bea and Meg are in danger. A mere suspicion that people are Unionist is enough to lock them in jail these days. These ladies are from Washington City and Chicago. Shouldn't they go home until this present danger subsides?"

It was as if a cold, wet breeze entered through the open window, allowing the unfriendly women on the street corner to lash out again. Had she been in danger?

Shoulders back, Jay held Bea's gaze until her heart eased. "Were they still in Washington City, I'd advise them to stay, but I believe they are as safe as we are."

"Which is to say, not safe at all." Mary clutched her stomach.

"Actually, we had a long conversation after our boys stopped the Federal gunboats on the James River." Trudy's soothing tone encompassed them. "We each had individually prayed for guidance, and we each came to the same conclusion. They are safe in my home."

"If something happens, I'd rather be here." Bea flushed at the admiration that lit Jay's green eyes. "I don't want Aunt Trudy to face it alone."

"We both agreed." Meg smiled at her adopted aunt. "In the meantime, we'll do all we can to help the wounded and sick at the military hospitals."

"Miss Mary." Bea angled toward Jay's mother. "I appreciate your concern. My sister Annie feels it wiser for us to remain here. After praying for guidance, my father feels we are safer here. It comforts him to know Aunt Trudy has family with her."

"That Hiram." Trudy smiled. "We were always close as children. He and Charlotte stood by me when the rest of the family scorned my marriage to the owner of a tobacco warehouse."

"My mother told me Uncle Parker was goodness itself to you." Bea hated the rift that still existed. "She and Father loved him. Why did the others disapprove?"

"They preferred I marry the son of a plantation owner." A long sigh escaped. "They even had a fellow picked out for me. Once I met Parker, there was never another man for me."

Bea met Jay's eyes. She understood the conviction, for there was no other man for her either. She prayed Jay would soon accept their differing loyalties as she had. "Your family didn't object to his character?"

"No, my dear. Only his profession. It was an honorable one. That's what mattered to me."

"So you were able to work out your differences with Uncle Parker?" Bea tilted her head toward Jay. She was becoming more certain that she and Jay could meet their challenges squarely. If only he was as certain.

"Oh, yes." Trudy's glance darted between the couple. "Once we made the decision to marry, nothing swayed our resolve. We loved one another."

"Parker was the perfect husband for you," Mary said. "I knew it from our first meeting."

"Your support solidified our friendship for all time." Trudy gave her an affectionate smile.

"You've been supportive to me, also." The tension on Mary's face shifted to kindness as she looked at Bea. "I have no such worries about your courtship."

Mary referred to her and Jay. It seemed her earlier reference to herself and Meg as Yankees didn't brand them as outsiders after all. Her father approved of the courtship as did Jay's mother, which was important to Bea.

Jay looked at Bea and…was that hope in his eyes?

"Trudy, why don't we move to the downstairs parlor? It's

larger. We can talk about my trip while these young ones play a game."

Evidently the friends wanted to talk. Bea's spirits lifted at the suggestion. "Yes, let's play a game. How about spillikins?"

Jay laughed. "I didn't expect you to suggest playing jack-straws, which is what we called the game."

Meg giggled. "I haven't played that since I was a child."

"Me either. I played it last when I was here." Bea laughed. "I'll warn you that I used to be pretty good."

"Challenge accepted." Jay laughingly extended his arm to her.

She reached her hand toward him with a smile. He covered her hand with his warm, callused hand and tucked it in the crook of his elbow. They needed to have a conversation whenever they found themselves alone again. The joy in his hopeful expression was the best gift she'd received in a long time. Suddenly she was filled with hope for the future.

Even with the Union army approaching Richmond.

CHAPTER 27

Bea was happy to help Jay find someone traveling by train in the direction of Chattanooga as he had asked Sunday evening. None of his staff had felt comfortable traveling to Tennessee, possibly because he'd requested they stay with her until her return trip. It seemed that he had lowered his expectations and was now searching for someone to simply travel one way with his mother. He'd figure out how to get her home later.

Jay had held Bea's hand while they all prayed together before parting. Their game had been filled with laughter and fun. Bea loved Jay's hearty laugh, and she heard it often. She suspected that the lighthearted atmosphere was the tonic they all needed. Her spirits had soared. Last night's sleep had been the deepest, most refreshing she'd enjoyed for weeks.

She and Meg went to the sewing group at the Watermans' home on Monday. "Do you know if any of our church families are traveling by train to Tennessee?" Bea settled beside her hostess and selected a strip of cloth.

"Is someone leaving?" Amy asked.

"Mary Nickson plans to stay with her daughter for a few weeks."

"I remember Blanche." Katy Ann Everett took a seat opposite Amy. "I hated to see them move away when Joe found a job at a new church."

"You knew her?" Bea didn't recall meeting Jay's sister, his senior by six years. Blanche married at seventeen. It seemed likely the two had been introduced when Beatrice was a child.

"We were in school together." Amy glanced at Katy Ann. "The three of us are the same age."

"What's she like?" Bea dreamed they'd be sisters one day.

"She's much shorter than her brother." Amy stared out the window into the gray, rainy morning.

That wasn't saying much, considering he stood at about six feet tall.

"She's got brown hair that she braided and pinned around her head like a crown. Her eyes are green like Jay's." Katy Ann placed a rolled-up bandage into a basket in the center of the table.

"Friendly," Amy added.

"Oh, she never meets a stranger." Katy Ann smiled. "So Mrs. Nickson is going to stay with her?"

"That's her hope. Jay asked Meg and me to help him find someone traveling that way. Surely with all those leaving by train, at least one family is going in the general direction of Chattanooga."

Amy looked at Katy Ann. "Do you know where Celia Ellis's sister lives?"

"Somewhere in Tennessee."

"Celia told me yesterday she's going to her sister's home this week. She didn't mention how long she'd be staying." Amy selected another long white strip.

That sounded promising. "I'll tell my aunt."

Mama was at Trudy's home when Jay arrived there at half-past six.

"Jay, how wonderful. Come join us." Trudy rose from the dining table to greet him and then sat again.

"Thank you." His spirits rose at Bea's smiling gesture at the empty chair beside her. "Good evening, ladies."

There was a chorus of greetings. Jay's glance lingered on Bea's glowing face as he took the seat beside her. Her peach dress complimented her blond curls. This woman was as kind and compassionate as she was beautiful.

"Harold, please ask Clara to bring a plate in for Jay."

He inclined his head and left.

"Mama, I sent Blanche a telegram this evening about your potential visit." If there was a reason for their mother to stay here, he'd soon learn that news from his sister. Otherwise, he'd continue to make plans.

"Thank you, son."

"I have good news." Bea smiled at him.

"What is it?"

"She learned from Amy Waterman that Celia Ellis plans to go to Tennessee." Seated on Trudy's left beside Meg, Mama grimaced. "She waited until supper to mention the news."

Bea's lips formed into a pout.

"Thanks, Bea. You saved the day, and so quickly too." He fought against hugging her in gratitude, even as he wished his mother had allowed her to share the news. Mama's temperament had changed during the war, and she didn't mind letting her son know whenever she was unhappy. "Where in Tennessee? When will she leave?" He'd gladly pay Mrs. Ellis's train fare.

"It's too late to call on her this evening." Mama's mouth

pinched as Clara set a generous wedge of chicken pie in front of Jay.

"That is so under normal circumstances." Trudy exuded calm resolve. "What if she plans to leave tomorrow morning?"

"Tomorrow morning?" Mary half rose. "I can't be ready so quickly."

"Exactly so." Trudy patted her arm. "We must find out for certain. If memory serves, Celia's sister lives in the southern part of Tennessee."

"Chattanooga is only a few miles from the Georgia border." Mary's face brightened.

The perfect solution. Jay's heart lightened in gratitude to the woman of his dreams.

Bea drummed her fingers against the linen tablecloth, her meal forgotten. That Mary resented her waiting until evening to surprise them with the happy news was evident from her indignant attitude. Bea struggled against a twinge of resentment herself, directed at Jay's mother. Why had she stolen Bea's privilege to tell Jay of the potential travel companion?

Such a small thing. She should let it go.

"I don't know Celia well. Her husband is away serving our army." Trudy pressed her fingers together in a steeple. "They're raising her niece, who is about seven."

"It may relieve her mind to take you with her, Miss Mary." Bea thought the little girl's presence would shift Mary's focus off herself during the trip. "I agree that a quick unplanned evening visit is better than a missed opportunity." Waiting until Jay was with them to share the news caused this problem, which she regretted.

"Thank you, my dear. I'm sorry if I seemed ungracious. My agitation over the matter is no excuse for what must appear as ingratitude. Your kindness is appreciated." Mary's expression softened. "Jay, Phineas drove me here in the landau. We can leave as soon as you're ready."

A forkful of chicken pie paused on its way to his mouth. He turned toward Bea. "Perhaps everyone would like to go. The Ellis family lives on the outskirts of the Church Hill neighborhood, so it's not far."

"I didn't want to inconvenience everyone," Mary said. "I'd appreciate the company. Will you all join us?"

Bea nodded. If this didn't work, they'd plan something else, and she wanted to be part of helping Jay solve the problem. His green eyes were filled with loving concern for his mother, a trait that pleased her. She understood family loyalty.

"Thank you, but I will stay behind." Meg folded her linen napkin without looking up. "I'll take a stroll instead."

Another errand. What was her cousin up to now? "Shall I accompany you?" Bea asked.

"No." Meg gave her a reassuring smile. "Go with them."

"All right." Her cousin didn't often venture out alone after supper. It worried her.

"Don't go far, my dear." Trudy stood. "It's past seven. Remember the marshals on patrol."

"I won't forget." Meg stood as everyone rose from the table. "I will see you when you return."

"Are you ready, Bea?" Jay stepped closer with a smile that lit his eyes.

"I'll fetch my parasol. The sun has decided to emerge from the clouds in time for it to set." She smiled up at him, forgetting everything but his presence as Meg slipped from the room.

CHAPTER 28

Frustration marked the next three days. By Thursday, Jay was ready to pull out his hair. Mrs. Ellis had happily accepted his offer to pay the train fare for her and her niece on Monday. Her sister lived in Cleveland, a Tennessee city less than a morning's train ride from Chattanooga, so she agreed to accompany his mother the entire journey because Jay promised to pay for it. The full amount went into her reticule that very evening as a sign of good faith.

A note from her on Tuesday complained rising food costs required extra funds for all the meals that would be required if she accompanied Jay's mother. Jay'd penned a note of agreement. He steeled himself for her next demand.

On Wednesday, Mrs. Ellis visited his mother in the afternoon and gave them the unhappy news that she had changed her mind about going to Tennessee. She apologized for the inconvenience and left without returning his money.

When Jay returned home after a long, hot day at the gun foundry on Thursday, his mother was all smiles again. "You'll never believe it."

"What happened?" He hung his hat on its hook, fearing her

happiness had something to do with the demanding, ever-changeable Mrs. Ellis.

"Celia brought her niece Sarah this afternoon. Apparently, the child has her heart set on visiting her aunt in Cleveland. Poor girl doesn't realize why we're going." She stood with him at the bottom of the stairs. "Anyway, the trip is back on. Celia asked me to be ready to leave Saturday morning."

"No." Jay's faith in the woman had taken a severe beating. For all he knew, she'd abandon his mother in Knoxville on a whim. "Inform Celia we'll make other arrangements."

She blinked. "But I'm already packing."

"Mama, she's not trustworthy. The kindest thing I can say about her is that she changes with the direction of the wind. I can't trust your wellbeing to such a companion." He worried for the little girl if her aunt was always as flighty as she'd demonstrated this week.

"If not her, then who?" A shaky hand brushed back a wisp of brown hair marked with strands of gray.

"I don't know." None of his staff wanted to travel with his mother. Perhaps her present agitated state didn't make her easy to escort some five hundred miles. He sympathized with them, for these days she had an unpleasantly blunt manner when she was upset, which was more often than usual. He longed for the sweet, strong woman who had raised him. That strength must still be locked inside her. Hidden, indeed. He raked his hands through his hair.

Mama said, "Let's go talk with Trudy after you wash up and eat your meal. I ate earlier. Shall I tell Esther you'll be ready to eat in a quarter hour?"

"Yes, thank you." He ran up the creaky steps.

"Jay?"

He paused half way to the second floor.

"I can be ready to leave tomorrow, but who will go with me?"

Jay pondered the problem as he washed the day's grime away. Who indeed?

"I'll go with you, Mrs. Mary." Meg's serene gaze scanned the street behind Trudy's house from the back porch. Bea, Trudy, and Jay were also seated in rocking chairs as the sun approached the western horizon.

That anyone wanted to travel with Mary in her present disagreeable mood shocked Bea so much that she covered her mouth to block her gasp. Guilt shot through her that she didn't want to go.

"But why?" Mary's rocking chair halted on the porch's wood floor. "It's so much trouble."

"I've considered it since Mrs. Ellis first changed her mind," Meg said. "I prayed about the trip last night and woke up this morning at peace with my decision. I'm quite comfortable on trains. Once you are safely at your daughter's home, I'll return."

"Thank you for this perfect solution." Tears shone in Mary's eyes. "Can you be ready to leave Saturday morning?"

Jay's eyes widened. "Mama, we can't ask—"

"I'll be ready." Meg stood and leaned against the sturdy white railing facing them.

Bea's head reeled at the lightning speed with which Mary had accepted Meg's suggestion. Meg was calm and capable, the ideal companion.

"That's no solution, my dear friend," Trudy said, "as it will require Meg to return by herself."

"It's not a problem. I've been on my own for two years."

"Still, I can't like it." Trudy looked up as the door creaked. "Ah, Clara, bless you. We all need a cold drink."

Clara carried a tray of glasses of lemonade and a pitcher onto the porch.

"Perhaps there is someone who will go with you." Trudy frowned. "You won't be gone long."

Meg laughed. "We've just spent several days trying to find someone who's going to Chattanooga. And no, I'll not travel with Mrs. Ellis."

That surprised a giggle out of Bea, who had lost respect for the woman during the week's negotiations.

Clara handed a glass of lemonade to Trudy. "Take Mabel with you."

Bea blinked at the inspired idea—if the sixteen-year-old agreed. "That would be safer for you, Meg."

"Will she agree?" Meg tilted her face, her gaze fixed on Clara.

She laughed. "I know my daughter. She wants to ride a train. See new places. That girl ain't going to stay in Richmond when she grows up. I give my permission if she wants to go. Let me fetch her."

After the door shut behind her, Jay leaned forward in his rocker, focused on Meg. "I'll go to the provost marshal to obtain passes for all of you to leave the city. First thing in the morning." He raised his palms with a look of disbelief. "Thank you for your kindness."

"Let's not get ahead of ourselves," Trudy cautioned. "Mabel hasn't agreed."

The excited girl burst out the back door with her grinning mother behind her. "Please take me. I want to go."

Bea's heart filled with gratitude as the arrangements were made. Meg couldn't feel that she wasn't part of the family with all the love poured out on her.

"Meg, I'll never forget this kindness to my mother. I'm grateful." The tightness eased from Jay's face. "I understand why Bea adores you."

"I adore her too." Meg's green eyes shone. "And I'm happy to do this small thing for all of you."

"Thank you, my dear." Mary stood and hugged her. "Just

knowing I'll see my sweet daughter and grandchildren has eased my heart's worry."

The relief on Jay's face did Bea's heart good. His mother was a trial at times, yet goodness and kindness were integral to her nature. Bea resolved to pray for the travelers daily until Meg and Mabel were safely back in Richmond.

Bea curled up on Meg's bed the following morning. "Are you certain there is nothing I can do to help you pack?"

"No, for the third time." Meg laughed. "I merely want your company."

"I feel guilty about not going with you."

"Do you want to?"

"Not really."

"Then don't give it another thought. I'll return in four or five days." Meg folded a petticoat.

Bea hesitated. "Will you find Jay's mother to be a difficult traveling companion?"

"No." Meg laid aside her clothing and sat on the corner of the bed. "Mrs. Mary is fearful of the future. Some folks don't handle tough emotions easily."

"True." Bea had noticed the same thing. "She makes unfortunate statements when she's upset. Like calling us Yankees."

"We *are* from the North. That's not a bad thing. She didn't mean it in a derogatory way."

"I never thought of the term Yankee as derogatory until someone called me by the name."

"Words have power to hurt us only if we grant them that power. Some folks make comments intending to ridicule us, it's true, but most speak unaware that their words slice like a sword. I choose to ignore them."

"Not so easy when you're surrounded by Southerners."

"Your grumbling reminds me of someone."

Bea straightened. "Never say…not Miss Mary."

"Not really." Meg squeezed her shoulder and then returned to her wardrobe. "My hunch is that she's not usually this agitated. These are trying times. Don't you like her?"

"I do." Bea bit her bottom lip. "She hurt my feelings."

"I'm certain she doesn't know it." Meg placed a folded handkerchief in her floral carpetbag. "Will you talk to her about it?"

Bea considered. "No. When Aunt Trudy confronted her, she apologized. Her concern is for our safety."

"Exactly."

She walked to the open window. Red roses were beginning to open on a garden bush under the morning dew. Her favorite flower brought vibrant color to the yard. Surely it was a hopeful sign of better days to come. "Have you seen your friend lately?"

"The one in jail?"

"No. The other one. The one you saw when we took a stroll." It had been a quick conversation. Who was this woman and what had they talked about?

"Yes."

"Meg, won't you trust me?" She turned and looked at her. "What if something goes wrong? I won't know how to help you."

"That's a possibility." Meg rubbed taut fingers across her forehead. "In Chicago, someone always knew what I was doing in case there was a problem."

"Please trust me. I won't tell Jay or Annie if you don't want me to."

"All right." Meg crossed to her desk and searched through a stack of correspondence. "But tell no one. Not Jay or even Aunt Trudy. Maybe when we return to Washington City, I'll tell Annie." Meg turned holding a folded sheet of paper.

"Agreed. What's that?"

"Information," she whispered, "that will help Union authorities."

Bea gasped. "How did you get it?"

"You can't tell *anyone.* Lives can be lost. Reputations ruined. Good people might be arrested...even hung." Meg's green eyes became fierce.

"I promise." Bea's heart hammered against her ribs.

"Miss Elizabeth discovered this particular information."

Bea gave her head a tiny shake. So it was true after all. The woman's multiple requests for information about Jay's job, her pointed questions about what the foundry was producing, and the way she'd behaved on the street the other day after those women had hurled slurs at Bea. As if she herself was absorbing the blows. Perhaps the ridicule had been intended for Elizabeth all along.

Things weren't always as they seemed.

"Not everyone in the South believes in this war. Didn't you tell me your loyalties were torn?" Meg sank onto her chair. "None of this is as simple as it seems, is it?"

Bea shook her head. Elizabeth Van Lew supported the Union.

"There are other Unionists in the city," Meg said. "I don't know who they are, but I'm trying to find out."

"To join their efforts?"

Meg was silent.

Bea's stomach quivered at the possible danger her cousin faced if caught. "Is Miss Elizabeth the friend you saw the other day?"

Meg shook her head. "That woman and her husband are letter carriers. They deliver letters—for a fee—to folks in the Union. Mine will be delivered directly to Washington City. They also bring letters back to Richmond."

"Hand-delivered? Not through the mail under a flag of truce?" Seemed risky to Bea.

"Hand-delivered so they're not censored." Meg eyed her. "That's why it costs so much to use their service."

"Did Miss Elizabeth tell you about her?"

"Do you remember Hattie? The one who's in jail?"

Dazed by the dangerous details, Bea managed to nod.

"She told me. Miss Elizabeth doesn't know how I smuggle the information out. She simply knows I can. That's enough. It's better this way."

"Just as she hasn't told you the other Unionists?"

She nodded. "But it's doubtful she knows more than a handful of names anyway. One person tells another, and then that person passes on the sensitive information to someone else who tells the Union leaders."

"Secrets that give Union leaders an advantage." If it quickened the war's end, Bea couldn't fault it, yet she worried for Meg's safety. "Your involvement goes deeper than I imagined." Bea rubbed her throbbing temples.

"What do you fear?"

"That you're spying again."

"And so I am."

CHAPTER 29

Bea looked up from her knitting when Harold opened the parlor door on Monday evening. Jay stepped inside, kindling joy in her heart. She hadn't seen him since the chaos of the train depot. Sadly, there had been no opportunity for a private conversation in the crowded station. His mother demanded all his attention, firing a slew of questions already asked and answered, until she boarded. Bea sighed for the difficult trip ahead for Meg as she hugged her good-bye. Meg's eyes had sparkled with a sense of adventure. She had no money worries, for Jay had given her a substantial amount to cover everyone's trip expenses.

"Good evening, Jay. I pray you have news for us." Trudy dropped her needlepoint into her lap to extend her hand to him.

"Good evening, Aunt Trudy." He took her hand, then turned to Bea. "You look lovely this evening." He clasped Bea's hand to his chest and held it there a moment, his eyes twinkling in her direction. "Sorry I had to work late yesterday to make up the time I missed waiting in line at the provost marshal's office."

"I missed you." An understatement, for her spirits had been

low without him. The steady beat of his heart under her hand gave her a tingling feeling.

He let go of her hand and turned back to Trudy. "I've heard nothing from Mama. I wondered if Meg sent a telegram."

His touch, his lingering glance, brought welcome warmth to Bea's face. It was a comfort to see him, to share this common bond with him. They had far more in common than they had differences.

"I'm afraid not. Please join us."

Smiling, Bea patted the sofa beside her. "We're glad for your company. Meg figured they'd arrive this afternoon if they weren't delayed."

"They had passes to leave Richmond." Jay sighed as he settled next to her. "I couldn't obtain passes for all the cities they will travel through."

"Meg considered the delays for that reason." Bea set aside her knitting. "Our prayers before they left filled me with peace. I'm certain they are fine. Your mother was excited to see Blanche and her family. She'll be happy with your sister."

"My mother does not cope well in unexpected situations."

Trudy's head bobbed. "That's true of her these days. She was a strong woman before fear of this war overtook her. I've no doubt her former strength of character will return." Trudy's lips pursed. "In the meantime, she is easily calmed when feeling herself in capable hands like Meg's."

The knocker on the front door clanged twice. They looked at each other when they heard a familiar voice.

"It's Phineas," Jay said. "I asked that he bring over the telegram as soon as it arrived."

Someone tapped on the parlor door as Jay strode to it.

"Mr. Jay, your telegram is here." Phineas handed him a folded page.

"Thank you for bringing it." Jay clapped him on the back and then scanned the lines.

Bea tensed as she watched his face.

"It's from Blanche." He looked heavenward, and his face relaxed into a grin. "They arrived late, having encountered a long delay at one stop. They are safe. Mama feels comforted just to be there." He crossed the room and offered the page to Trudy. "They will begin their return trip in the morning."

Trudy scanned it. "Expect them sometime on Thursday."

Bea hadn't realized she was worried until learning everyone had arrived safely. With the first part of the journey behind them, the ladies knew what to expect coming back.

Bea took Meg's absence as an opportunity to talk with her aunt once more about the original will. They were both volunteering at different places on Tuesday, so she went down to breakfast early that morning. After greeting her aunt, she helped herself to scrambled eggs and a biscuit from the sideboard before seating herself.

"Aunt Trudy, I wondered if we could talk about the will again."

"If you like." Trudy pushed her half-filled plate to the side. "Though I don't know much more."

"Did you find the old will?"

"I read it again." Trudy fingered a cameo broach pinned on her lacy collar. "It's as I told you. We were all to have received acreage, with Isaac receiving half."

"I don't understand why Grandfather changed it after so many years." The biscuit crumbled under Bea's convulsive fingers. "It hurt my father."

"And I felt it's sting as well." Trudy sighed. "I've always wondered..."

Bea waited for her to continue. "What?"

"If..." Words seemed to catch in her throat.

"If Uncle Isaac had a hand in it?"

"Oh, it's an ugly thought, I know," Trudy's face paled, "but the thought has occurred to me. Isaac had the most to gain."

"True." A weight seemed to descend on Bea's chest. "You remember that he told me Grandfather changed the will and *then* informed him about it."

"Impossible." Her hand jerked against her teacup, sloshing droplets onto the linen tablecloth. "Since it was written by Isaac."

"He lied to me."

Trudy raised her chin. "It seems so. You were strong enough to ask to the questions."

They stared at each other, then Bea ventured to speak. "I think it's worth asking again."

Trudy nodded. "After the Union army is pushed back from Richmond, we'll drive out to see him."

Bea went alone to Chimborazo Hospital on a rainy Tuesday, her thoughts in turmoil. As she cared for her Tennessee boys, she could hardly believe she'd finally convinced her aunt they should investigate what happened. She decided to wait for the outcome to tell her father. The brothers had just started to get along again. She hated to stir up dissension, but the truth mattered…for all of them.

She returned to the hospital on Wednesday amid newspaper reports that the Union army was inching ever closer from the east. General Johnston's army was set up in a defensive line around Richmond, with Union General McClellan's army advancing. The Union's supply base was located at White House Landing, by all accounts a beautiful area on the Pamunkey River less than a mile from the Richmond and York River Railroad.

Uncle Isaac's plantation was that direction, near a village

called Seven Pines. Aunt Victoria lived a few miles to his north on a plantation outside Mechanicsville. Bea wasn't certain where these villages were located in relation to the Union army and prayed for her family's safety and protection.

Aunt Trudy read every Richmond newspaper these days. Her frowning demeanor was easily explained by Mary's absence and the fact that Meg and Mabel were on their return trip. If Trudy worried about her brother and her sister, she didn't speak of it. Bea hoped she hadn't increased her burdens with talk of the will.

Bea didn't volunteer anywhere on Thursday. Aiding the soldiers had become such a habit that guilt riddled her for staying home. Since Jay left work to wait with Bea at the train depot, Aunt Trudy waited for the travelers at home.

"Meg's telegram last night said to expect them on the five o'clock train." As the hard bench grew uncomfortable, Bea gave Jay an apologetic look. "I'm sorry you left early only to have to wait longer."

"I was ready to see the back of that hot place for the day." Grinning, he opened his pocket watch. "Only an hour late so far."

"Only an hour?" She raised her eyebrow.

"I waited far longer for you and Meg."

"You're more patient than I am." Groups gathered on street corners near the depot. One man pointed to his newspaper while another gestured in the direction of Capitol Square. "A lot has happened since that rainy Valentine's Day," she said.

"I'll say." He followed her gaze toward the agitated groups. "Still happening. You picked a difficult season for an extended visit."

Bea strolled to a deacon's seat outside a closed shop. "Does that mean you want me to go home?"

"No." He sat and angled to face her. "I want you to stay."

Forever? Something in the intensity of his green eyes

suggested that was what he meant. As much as she wanted him to say it, this wasn't an opportune moment. Crowded street corners. A bustling depot with men dropping boxes and crates. Not ideal. "I believe I want to hear more about that when things settle."

"You will."

Something in his tone brought a glow to her heart. Even with differing views on the war, they could love each other through the storm.

"Move the boxes into this room." A burly man wearing a hat that nearly hid bushy eyebrows pointed inside the station.

Curious. She didn't remember this much activity after her train pulled out in February.

"Wonder what they're storing in there." Jay's brow furrowed.

From her bench seat, Bea craned her neck. "I can't see."

"You haven't heard?" A stranger nearby turned toward Jay.

"Heard what?" He stood to face the man.

"The secretary of war ordered that official documents be moved to the railroad depot."

Jay's jaw slackened.

"You know, man. George Randolph? The secretary of war?"

"I know the name." Jay darted a glance at Bea. "To what purpose?"

"Ain't heard the reason." The man shrugged. "My guess is it's because the Yanks are getting closer."

They would store the documents there to get them out of Richmond quickly in the event of an attack. The implication was clear. Bea felt the blood drain from her face. Was it possible the Union army approached from one direction while Meg and Mabel traveled to Richmond from another?

"General Clayton closed the gambling houses to keep soldiers at their posts." The man cut a wedge of tobacco and positioned it inside his jaw, focusing on Bea. "Our boys will keep them from Richmond. Just you wait, little missy." He clucked his tongue at her. "You're white as a surrender flag, but don't you worry. General Johnston's army is in between us and those Yanks. He'll turn 'em back."

A distant train whistle blew. Bea had never been so happy to hear one.

"Thanks for the information." Jay nodded to the man. Then he turned and extended his hand to Bea. "Let's see if Meg and Mabel are on this train."

Bea gripped his hand with shaky fingers. This couldn't be happening. The secretary of war wasn't nearly as confident as this fellow.

Richmond really could fall to the North.

Perhaps Jay's mother had been the wisest one, after all.

CHAPTER 30

"Meg, let's go to the sewing group today." Hot but weak tea at the following morning's late breakfast prompted Bea's resolve to ask Annie to send chocolate along with coffee and tea in her next package.

"Excellent idea. I'm rather tired." Meg ate her portion of scrambled eggs and sausage with greater appetite than normal. "That's less strenuous than the hospital."

"Six days of travel will tire anyone." Trudy cleared her throat. "Why not rest? I'll go with Bea."

"No, I'll join you this morning. An afternoon stroll and an early night will restore me."

"I'll walk with you." There hadn't been an opportunity to talk to Meg privately the night before. Jay had stayed until dark to hear about the trip and receive news of his sister's family. He tucked a bulky letter from his sister into his pocket at half past nine as Bea walked him to the door. When she returned to the parlor, Meg excused herself to bed. Bea was eager to learn if her cousin had spotted anything worthy of reporting to Union authorities.

"That will be lovely." Meg gave her a tired smile. "I've missed your company."

Aunt Trudy pushed a half-empty plate to the side. "Bea, I've hesitated to mention a concern, but I feel the need of your prayers."

Instantly alert, Bea noticed dark shadows under her aunt's blue eyes. "What is it?"

"I've learned that Union troops are in the village of Seven Pines. Larger than a regiment or brigade."

Bea gasped. "But that's where Uncle Isaac and Aunt Meredith's plantation is."

"It's a mile east of the village. I'm told army camps are spread out when there are lots of soldiers." Aunt Trudy folded her hands, her wrists resting against the white tablecloth. "I fear Federal soldiers occupy Isaac's land. They've likely been there since the day Mary left—nearly a week ago. I pray for the safety of our family. All those living on the property. Neighbors who were childhood friends."

"Have you heard from your brother?" Ice crystals began to grow in the core of Bea's being. Union soldiers possibly camped on Uncle Isaac's land? He must be livid. It didn't matter at that moment that her loyalty was to the North. It only mattered that people she loved were not safe.

"Not yet." Trudy bowed her head. "You're aware we don't speak often. He reached out to comfort me after Parker died. Offered financial help, business advice, whatever I needed. I was too proud to accept his olive branch. If I had, he might have taken refuge with me when he first sensed trouble."

Bea covered her aunt's hand. It was cold, a surprising contrast to the warmth entering through the open windows. Fear for her relatives stole her power of speech.

"This is your opportunity to extend that olive branch." Meg touched Trudy's arm.

"I've never been one to sit idle when a loved one was in jeopardy." She lifted open palms toward Heaven. "But I don't believe it's safe to go to him."

"Certainly not." Bea's face flushed with a mixture of admiration and terror that her aunt even considered such a risk. "It's too dangerous."

"May we all pray for them around this family table?" Meg folded her hands.

"Yes, dear. Let's do that now." Tears shown in Trudy's eyes. "Pray specifically for their protection should fighting break out. The last thing we want is harm to come to anyone, and we don't want a battle on our land."

Bea, though frightened for Uncle Isaac and Aunt Meredith, was encouraged that Aunt Trudy referred to the plantation as "our land." She'd distanced herself from her childhood home in the past.

"Let's pray." Meg took their hands.

They spoke with bowed heads, enveloping all those living on the plantation in a circle of prayer.

"Are we walking on Main Street again?" Bea matched Meg's leisurely pace that afternoon.

"Too predictable. Let's start out on Broad Street." Meg touched the red cloth covering her small basket. A page rustled. "No need to take the same route every time."

"Cousin, you are anything but predictable." Bea's laugh didn't last long, aware that Meg took an awful risk each time she delivered a message.

She spoke softly. "I worry for your aunt and uncle."

Bea nodded. "Difficult to think of anything else."

"You were quiet at sewing group this morning."

"I didn't know what to say. Since Aunt Trudy didn't talk

about the soldiers on Uncle Isaac's land, it seemed best not to mention it."

"It's likely she's slept less than I did the past week." Meg gave a short laugh. "For someone who slept leaning against a jiggly window in a hot car, that's saying something."

"She's resting now." Bea stepped onto Broad Street. Pedestrians, horseback riders, and wagons were all a safe distance away. "Did you see anything on your trip to report?"

Meg's eyes widened. "It's a beautiful state." She spoke in a whisper. "Bea, you promised. Don't put us both at risk."

Heat crawled up her face. "S-sorry." She blundered. Only in the privacy of their home would she mention it again.

"Blanche is a pleasant woman, beautiful inside and out. Her laugh invites you to join her." Meg's smile was a bit strained. "You'll like her."

"If I meet her."

"You will." Her smile widened. "Did you see Jay while I was gone?"

"Monday evening he came over to wait for news of your safe arrival. We had an hour and a half on our own at the train station yesterday."

"Sorry about that. A private didn't believe our story and took us to his sergeant." Meg sighed. "He finally trusted us and let us go...after we had missed our train. The next one came in early, but it was still an hour wait."

"You're fortunate it didn't leave today instead."

"Granted. In spite of the delays the military put us through, I enjoyed the trip with Mabel. She's a sweet girl." She glanced around. "Let's avoid the crowd at the next corner and walk over to Main Street."

They crossed the road in that direction. Bea said, "I learned yesterday that the secretary of war ordered official documents to be moved to the railroad depot."

Meg turned to her. "To enable them to be sent off quickly in the event of an attack?"

"I assume so."

"I didn't know." She was silent as they walked down the hilly street. "The government knows something they're not telling citizens."

"Meg, a portion of the Union army is at Seven Pines. A brigade, two brigades…maybe a whole corps. We passed that village on the way to Uncle Isaac's mansion."

"I remember."

"Is there nothing we can do for them?" Bea had prayed at every opportunity since learning the news. Uncle Isaac would already be here if he intended to reach out for his sister's help.

"Your uncle?" Meg shook her head. "We can't evade the soldiers who camp between him and us. We'll go as soon as it's safe."

"I don't have a good feeling about it." Bea lowered her voice as they passed two women talking at a picket fence outside a small red brick home.

Meg didn't answer. Her attention was riveted on a couple outside a hotel on the corner.

The man, dressed in a gray coat and vest, was of medium height and had the appearance of a Southern gentleman. The lady wore a green gingham dress of lesser quality than her escort's. A large hat hid her face.

"Let's cross the street at the corner." Meg spoke in a whisper. "Walk on alone and search for an open shop. If you find one, go inside. Don't look for me. I'll join you shortly."

"I will."

Suddenly, Meg wasn't beside her. Light footsteps against the brick sidewalk faded. Bea didn't turn around. The street outside the first row of shops was deserted. Upon reaching the stores, she meandered along, peering into closed shop windows as if longing to purchase every item. All the time, her ears were strained for the lightest footfalls on the pavement.

Five minutes passed. Then ten minutes. Bea reached the end of this row of shops. Slowing her pace, she proceeded up the street, where few pedestrians walked. Where was Meg? An ever-prevalent tobacco aroma grew stronger. Warehouses such as the one Uncle Parker used to own were nearby.

Another five minutes passed. At the next crossroad, Bea peered to the right. The Exchange Hotel, one of the finest in the city, was down that street.

Where was Meg? Bea couldn't leave Main Street and chance missing her. She battled the urge to turn around.

"Bea."

She turned at the sound of her cousin's call. Meg hurried toward her.

"You must have entered a shop back there. We got separated."

She played along. "My apologies."

"No problem at all." Meg's breath came in gasps as if she'd been running. "We're very close to Capitol Square. Shall we finish our stroll there?"

It was a long walk from Aunt Trudy's. "I'd like that." Their legs would be sore tonight.

As Meg chattered about the sights, Bea wondered what had kept her. Did she learn something important or pass on vital information?

She hoped Meg would trust her with what she'd learned.

More secrets to lock inside her heart.

CHAPTER 31

Jay swiped sweat from his brow as he returned to work after his lunch break. It was the last day of May and a Saturday. There had been a lot of days in a row that he'd been there without a break. He really didn't want to be there today, especially as tomorrow was the first time he'd attend church services in weeks. He couldn't wait to surprise Beatrice. They could take a picnic lunch to Hollywood Cemetery if she liked. The cemetery wasn't far from the falls. He felt the need to go to the place where he most felt his father's presence, and he believed Bea liked it too.

As he reached the brick arched doorway to the old gun foundry, the ground shook under his feet.

His fist blocked a groan that came from his soul. *Not another battle.*

Where was it this time?

Loud machinery masked whatever battle audible sounds there might be in the distance.

The ground shook again, longer this time. Men poured out of buildings.

Snatches from multiple conversations assaulted Jay's ears. Heads turned toward the east.

"I heard from my cousin that the soldiers out that direction have been readying for battle. His brigade was going to head them off near Seven Pines. I reckon they're at it now."

Jay heard the words as if from a tunnel.

Seven Pines.

Bea's Uncle Isaac lived just beyond that village. To the east.

He clutched his hair. This couldn't be happening.

~

Bandages she'd just retrieved shook violently in Bea's basket. Sounds of cannons crashed into distant grounds, jolting her body enough that the clean strips of cloth on top of her pile rolled onto the grass. She scooped them up and ran to the ward housing her Tennessee soldiers.

Not another battle. Please, God, not another one.

An unnatural quiet charged the atmosphere inside the ward. Stunned looks shuttered the faces of the men who understood battle.

"You're safe, Miss Beatrice." Colt, the wounded soldier she'd befriended over the spring, sat up in his bed.

Dazed, she set her basket on the edge of his cot.

He stared out the window. "It's coming from the east this time."

East? The area around Seven Pines, where the family plantation was located. *God, please...not my family. Protect them from harm. Give them wisdom as to where to hide. Watch over them. Keep them safe.*

The beds rattled against the wood floor, causing a frightful din. A dozen voices began talking at once. "It seems so close." Or was that due to the fear for her family? Her words came in a whisper.

"I reckon it is." The soldier, whose head wound finally seemed to be healing, turned toward the booming sounds. "What do you say, Tom? Maybe five miles away?"

"Reckon so. Maybe six." The man in the next bed gripped the side of his cot. "I need my rifle."

"Tom, you know any soldier worth his salt ain't gonna attack a hospital." Colt shifted uneasily.

"If them Yanks break through our defenses, I want my weapon loaded and ready. I ain't going down without a fight." Tom's glance bounced around the room, where a dozen conversations took place. "Where is it?"

Her patient's frantic shouts finally penetrated Bea's shock. "Tom, listen to me. Colt's right. No one will attack this hospital." But might Union soldiers march past it into Richmond? Fear for Uncle Isaac and Aunt Meredith wasn't the only worry consuming her. Aunt Trudy's home was a mile to the west. Would they be next in the shelling?

"Mebbe not, but our side might need reinforcements." He tossed back the sheet and then clutched his bandaged shoulder.

"We're safe." There were no surgeons or stewards in the ward to aid her if Tom lost control, as he seemed to be doing. "There's no need to defend ourselves."

"Five miles is nothing. I can be there in an hour."

"I'm certain of it." In prime condition, Bea didn't doubt the man's claim. But three weeks in bed recovering from a bullet wound had weakened the Tennessean. "There's no need. Those defending the city will hold the line."

"What if they don't?" Tom pushed himself to a sitting position with his good arm.

"They will." She spoke with confidence she was far from feeling. What mattered now was that the soldier believed it.

"Think so?" His eyes finally settled on hers.

"I've been praying for God's protection since I learned the

Union army was near." Her gaze held his dazed eyes. "Folks are kneeling in prayer at this very moment, pleading for our safety."

"Tom, we'll defend ourselves and sweet ladies like Miss Bea if we're called upon to do it. You know we will." Colt scooted to the edge of his cot. "In the meantime, let's heal and ready ourselves to join our comrades on the field."

Staring out the window, Tom rubbed his shoulder.

Bea blessed Colt silently for knowing exactly what to say.

A bandage jumped from the basket during a sustained barrage. It rolled down the aisle between the long line of cots, unrolling as it went. She struggled to control her emotions as she chased the fabric they couldn't afford to waste.

At least the battle didn't rage at the edge of her porch as it surely did for her uncle. Rerolling the bandage, she crept to the door. Peered to the east. Gray smoke rose in the distance. Not with the innocence of a family's chimney but with the threat of gunpowder.

God, please protect Uncle Isaac and Aunt Meredith and all who live on their land.

CHAPTER 32

Shot and shell continued to bombard fields and homes on the eastern horizon as the patients able to feed themselves ate. Before Bea went to the kitchen for more food, she stepped inside another ward dedicated to Tennessee soldiers, where Meg worked.

"Bea." Meg waved her over to a bed where she changed a bandage on a young man's hand. A boy, really, who watched Bea's approach with frightened eyes. "Are you all right?" Meg asked.

Not at all, but what good would it do to say it aloud with the frightened boy listening? "Of course."

A tin cup clinked against a side table for several seconds.

"That battle comes from the same direction as your uncle's plantation."

"Yes."

"It's good that your aunt remained at home today."

Aunt Trudy. How had she forgotten her sweet aunt's reaction to the sound of the battle? "We must go to her as soon as we're free."

"I know." Meg sighed. "This ward is full, as are many others, but I haven't seen any doctors in here today."

"Not in mine either." Bea scanned the faces of the men. Some chatted. Others stared out the window. They all knew something she didn't—the horror of battle. And they had a fair idea of what was going on at Seven Pines. "I have three more men to feed."

"I have men who desperately need their medicine," Meg said. "When I finish here, I'll find a doctor. I can administer it once I know exactly what they need." She tucked the edge of the bandage in place and spoke to the young man. "Is that better?"

"Yes, thank you kindly, Mrs. Brooks."

She rose with a final smile for him before addressing Bea. "I'll be at least another hour."

"So will I." Bea glanced toward the window. "Do you think Aunt Trudy will be all right until then?"

"She's a strong woman with a strong faith." Meg gave her a hug. "It runs in the family."

"Oh, Meg, thank you." Bea straightened her shoulders. "I needed that."

Distant booms accompanied Bea and Meg's walk home when they finally left that afternoon.

They found Aunt Trudy in the family parlor, pale and shaken.

"Why didn't you send for us?" Bea scooted a chair closer to her aunt's. "We'd have left sooner."

Meg scooted a chair to her other side.

"Why, those soldiers needed you more than I do." Trudy's hands trembled. "I was fine. I've been sitting here all afternoon, praying for my family and reading Scriptures."

Bea looked at the open Bible on the table, unable to imagine a more productive afternoon for her aunt.

"I've been thinking about my childhood." Trudy touched a cameo broach pinned to her green dress. "How I adored my big brothers. Isaac was strong. Confident. He loved the land. Overseeing the crops. He was always kind to me."

Bea relished this glimpse of her uncle and waited for her aunt to continue.

"As the eldest, he began taking on responsibilities around the plantation at an early age. Father made certain he learned the entire planting cycle. Isaac changed toward me once I met Parker. I told myself I didn't care what Isaac thought. And then my father changed his will." Trudy dabbed her wet eyes with an embroidered handkerchief. "I didn't realize we'd never be close as a family again."

"You miss him." Bea ached for the rift between the siblings. It had trickled down to her cousins, because she'd never felt a rapport with them.

Trudy nodded. "I've felt more alone since the war began. That's why you're here."

Bea squeezed her fingers in comfort.

"But I've decided it's time and past for me to reconcile with my brother." Her sad blue eyes lifted toward Bea. "If he's willing."

"It's time." Unshed tears scratched at Bea's throat. She must be strong for Aunt Trudy.

"It is. That's why I'll go to him at the first opportunity." Resolve overshadowed the sadness in Trudy's eyes. "As soon as the fighting ends. I must try to mend what's broken between us. I can't lose him without at least trying."

"We'll go when the battle ends." Bea patted her hand before releasing it. "As soon as it's safe."

"It's good to have you girls with me." The ground shook, and Trudy gripped the arms of her chair. "Are you hungry?"

"I'm thirsty after that walk in the hot sun." Bea fanned her face.

"Run along to the kitchen, will you, Bea?" Strain showed in Trudy's face but not in her voice. "Clara made a batch of raspberry shrub last week. Nice and tart. Please ask her to bring us a glass."

Open windows allowed distant booms to accompany the shaking floor. "I'll be quick."

Lifting her plain skirt worn without a hoop, as she wore it every time she volunteered at the hospital, she ran downstairs to the kitchen. "Clara, do you have any raspberry shrub left? Aunt Trudy is asking for it."

Clara lifted her hands from a washbowl and dried them. "If I didn't have any, I'd borrow it. I'm worried about her. How is she?"

"Shaken. Yet strong." Bea loved the loyal concern reflected in the cook's face.

"Sounds about right. She didn't want nothing to eat or drink all day." Clara selected a jar of red liquid from a cabinet. "I sure am glad you girls came home. She needs family with her to wait out this storm."

Tears pricked Bea's eyes. She willed them not to fall.

"It sure is a good thing you didn't go back North at the first sign of trouble." Clara raised and lowered the pump handle, and water splashed into a pitcher in the sink. "She needs you."

"Thank you, Clara. I think I know now at least one reason I felt prompted to stay."

"I think I might know another." Clara gave a sly smile and then mixed the shrub with the water. "If you want to get back upstairs, I'll bring this up directly."

"Thank you." Impulsively, she hugged her. "And thank you for taking such good care of my aunt. She considers you all her family too."

Clara hugged her back. "Why, what a nice thing to say."

She turned away, but not before Bea saw a tear glisten in her eye. "I'll tell her you'll be up shortly."

The door knocker clanged as she reached the stairs. She paused as Harold answered it. A soldier dressed in gray stared at her with concerned green eyes.

"Jay." She threw her arms around his neck and pressed her face against his warm chest. "I knew you'd come."

"As soon as I could." His arms closed around her. "You haven't heard bad news from your uncle, have you?"

"No." She held on tighter. "But the battle is there."

"Appears that way." He cradled her head against his shoulder.

"Union soldiers must be scattered all over my uncle's plantation." His heartbeat thudded in her ear, a comforting sound after all the cannon blasts.

"I fear so."

Harold cleared his throat. "Shall I tell Mrs. Trudy you'll be right up?"

Bea reluctantly stepped from his arms. Her aunt needed the comfort of friends too. "No, thank you, Harold. I'll escort Jay to the parlor."

A smile touched the black man's lips as he glanced at their linked hands. "I appreciate it, Miss Bea. Miss Trudy will too."

Her gaze swept Jay's gray pants and coat. "Don't you make the handsome soldier."

He brushed dust from his sleeve. "I came directly from drill practice. Is there any news?"

"None." She held his hand while they mounted the steps. "Listening to the battle doesn't help matters."

"Certainly not." He sighed.

Still holding his hand, she entered the parlor. "Aunt Trudy, Jay came straight from drill practice to see how we're doing."

"The son of my dearest friend. How I miss her today." She rose and held out her hands. "Dear boy, thank you for treating us like family and coming straightaway."

He clasped both her hands in his. "I couldn't be anywhere else."

CHAPTER 33

Jay had intended to stay only long enough to offer his support and then go home to wash, change, and return if invited to do so.

Trudy insisted he stay for supper. She flinched whenever the floor shook—which it did with frightening regularity—so he remained. A few neighbors came and stayed only a few minutes. Women from the sewing group, including Amy Waterman and Katy Ann Everett, also stopped by. Unfortunately, too many folks had their own relatives to worry over.

Jay stayed until the shot and shell stopped at dusk. No one knew if the battle had ended or simply halted due to darkness. Aunt Trudy said she needed a sermon, prayers, and the comfort of dearly-loved hymns as much as ever. Furthermore, she wanted exercise. They'd wait for him in the morning and stroll to church together.

What if the Confederate line fell? Richmond would be overrun.

Thc hairs of the back of his neck stood up. He resolved to remain close to Bea and her family until the danger passed.

Distant cannons blasted their opponents for a second day. It had started around dawn, awakening Bea from a restless sleep. Donning her robe, she sat beside the window and stared toward the eastern horizon while she prayed for her uncle and his family and that the Union army left the area. She also prayed for her brother-in-law, should he be fighting the battle on or near his new uncle's plantation. She was still praying when Mabel tapped on her door to deliver her morning tea.

Occasional blasts rattled the pews at church. Bea, seated between Jay and her aunt, found herself counting the distant cannon shots. Aunt Trudy's mouth tightened every time the hymnals shook against the seat.

The atmosphere was somber. The minister led extended prayer for their soldiers, their leaders, their neighbors living near the fighting, their city, and their country.

After the service, the churchyard was quiet. Solemn, fearful expressions on formerly cheerful faces depressed Bea's spirits.

A white-haired woman gave Aunt Trudy a brief hug. "I said a prayer for Isaac and Meredith yesterday."

"Thank you, Emma." They began walking home.

"Good morning, ladies, Mr. Nickson." Mrs. Van Lew, Elizabeth's mother, stopped them on the street outside her home. "Trudy, have you heard from Isaac and Meredith?"

"Not yet."

The woman squeezed her hand in sympathy. "I will pray for their safety."

"Thank you, Eliza."

They continued toward home. Bea hardly knew what to say to comfort her aunt.

"Listen." Meg halted on the sidewalk.

"What is it?" Jay, moving in front of them, peered in every direction.

Meg stared at Aunt Trudy. "I haven't heard cannons for half an hour or more."

"You're right." Bea's heart thudded. "We were inside the church the last time I felt the ground shake."

Jay turned back to face them.

"Might it be over?" Trudy asked.

"Too early to know." Jay's solemn green eyes held a warning. "It may begin again."

Trudy sagged against Bea. Meg hurried to her other side and put her arm around her.

"Let's get home." Bea met Jay's concerned gaze. "We'll discover what is known about the battle and then see about going to Uncle Isaac's."

"That may not be possible." Jay's tone was both apologetic and adamant. "Let's discover what happened. If we won and the Union army has been pushed back ..."

If we won. Jay referred to the Confederacy. This time she was in complete agreement. She hoped the Union army had lost the battle. Her love for her relatives battled her loyalties.

Love of family won this one.

Hoping to calm Trudy's fears, Jay rode out after lunch to discover the news. Troy Hanson always seemed to know everything soon after it happened. Seven Pines was so close—walking distance from his home, albeit a long walk—that rumors must already be spreading.

Crowds filled the sidewalks everywhere. Pedestrians crossed in front of him, gesturing wildly. He was obliged to stop and wait for one group, as no one seemed mindful of Daisy's hooves.

His gaze followed pointing fingers to a grime-covered group

of soldiers in blue. Weapons had been taken from the Yankees who were walking amid armed Confederates. Jeers from the crowd caused some prisoners to study the ground and others to look around in defiance.

Jay hoped the Northern soldiers would behave themselves, for the air was thick with anger and fear.

And hatred.

"The fighting at Seven Pines is over, isn't it?"

"Most likely."

His ears sharpened at a conversation nearby. He dismounted and looped Daisy's reins over a hitching post. He strolled to the fringes of a crowded corner. These were all strangers to him, but he could at least overhear the news.

"Heard we drove the Yankees back."

Jay widened his stance. Good news, if it was true.

"Yankees will likely still claim victory."

Scoffs and jeering laughter and raised fists followed a stout man's observation.

"But I hear we lost a general."

Jay's heart sank. "One of our generals died?"

A man wearing a burgundy vest with black coat and pants turned to him. "My good fellow, you haven't learned of General Joe Johnston's misfortune?"

It chilled Jay to learn it was the Confederate commander. "Is he dead?"

He shook his head. "Wounded badly enough that he relinquished command. Who knows how long it will take him to recover?"

A difficult blow. "Know anything else?"

"We took prisoners." He pointed to the side street they'd disappeared down. "Lots of wounded coming by the York River train into our hospitals. Not much news yet."

"Did we win?"

The man shrugged. "Maybe. It weren't pretty by any account. Dead and dying still lying in the fields."

Jay's stomach jolted, making him regret his lunch.

"Stood here half an hour to learn that much." The stranger turned his attention back to conversations around them.

Jay had heard enough. His plan had been to seek out Troy. No more. He mounted Daisy and turned her head toward home. He needed to talk to Phineas.

Bea paced across the family parlor and back again. "Where *is* Jay?"

"He knows you're anxious to get to the plantation." Meg looked up from her letter. "He hasn't been gone even an hour."

"It seems twice that." Bea continued to pace. "It's good that Aunt Trudy decided to rest."

"She won't truly rest until she talks with her brother." Meg put down her pen. "And you won't sleep until you know if your aunt and uncle are safe."

"No." She forced herself to halt at the window. Smoke hovered on the eastern horizon. "So many gray clouds around the battle, smoke from cannons and rifles."

Meg joined her at the open window. "Soldiers dead or dying on farmers' fields. Husbands. Sons. Brothers. War ushers in great tragedy."

"I hate it." Bea rested her forehead against the warm pane. "Why must we choose sides against folks who were so recently our countrymen?"

Meg stiffened.

"My father grew up on that tobacco plantation. We all love the land. He loves his brother and must be frantic with worry."

"For his daughter."

"Oh, no, Meg." Bea turned to face her, covering her mouth. "He and Annie don't know we're safe."

"Not for certain." Meg leaned against the wall. "Shall we send a telegram?"

"We can send another once we talk to Uncle Isaac." Bea straightened her shoulders. "I'm going to the plantation."

CHAPTER 34

"Is it safe to take the women to the Swanson's plantation?" Jay ran his hands through his hair. His beaver hat fell onto the stable floor.

"Don't know that it is." Phineas raised his palms. "Don't know that it ain't."

Jay rolled his eyes. "Helpful."

"From what you tell me, we can figure the battle's ended." Phineas ticked off his points with his fingers. "Prisoners are being escorted to Richmond this afternoon. Wounded probably started coming in soon after the whole thing started so that ain't going to help."

"A stranger said we'd pushed the Union army back."

"Then there should only be Southern soldiers along the way. That might be enough to risk driving out there. From what you said earlier, those ladies are powerful concerned about their relatives."

"Bea and Aunt Trudy both mentioned going to the plantation today." They were strong, determined women. "Looks like there's no help for it. Best get going. We must return by curfew."

"I'll go with you."

Jay met his driver's steady gaze. "Thanks. I learned there are still dead and dying on the fields."

"We'll take the closed carriage."

"Good idea. Give me five minutes."

"Let's change into the plain dresses we wear to the hospitals." Meg pointed at Bea's pink satin frock. "We don't know what we'll find between here and the plantation."

"I'll be more comfortable without this half-hoop skirt." She mounted the porch steps. Their time at the telegraph office had taken thirty minutes longer than normal due to a line that extended out the door. "Now the telegram has been sent, it's time to awaken Aunt Trudy so she can prepare for our drive."

Meg looked up the street. "I wish Jay were back with battle news."

"He'll want to go with us." Bea halted at the front door to scan the deserted neighborhood. Everyone must be closer to town, eager for news. "It's nearly three o'clock. We can't afford to wait long. With how worried Aunt Trudy is, I'd rather not wait until tomorrow."

"Miss Bea. Mrs. Meg." Harold stood beside the open door. "It's good you've returned. Mrs. Trudy is asking for you."

Jay rode beside Phineas on the driver's seat. He leaped down almost as soon as the wheels halted at the Weston home. "Let me talk with them. Unless I'm wrong, they'll want to leave soon."

"I'll wait with the horses."

Harold opened the door as Jay took the stairs two at a time.

"Mr. Jay, it's good you've returned. The ladies are ready to go to Mr. Isaac's plantation. They asked me to drive them if you weren't back. I'm happy to do it, of course."

"Phineas has our carriage ready." Jay pointed to Phineas, who stood by the black andiron fence. "Want to ride with us?"

"I believe I'd better come along." Harold lifted his hand to Phineas in greeting. "Did you bring rifles?"

"Two. I decided not to wear my uniform." Jay had changed into work pants, boots, and an old green cotton shirt. If he had to dig the carriage out of the mud, he was dressed for it. "Roads are muddy by all accounts. Rain swelled the Chickahominy River."

"Jay, I'm glad you're here." Bea stepped onto the porch wearing a cotton dress without hoops. The dark blue of the dress deepened the color of her beautiful eyes. "Aunt Trudy is desperate to know that Uncle Isaac and Aunt Meredith are unharmed."

"I'll accompany you." He clasped her gloved hand. "Harold and Phineas will drive."

"I hoped you'd say that." Some of the tension in her face eased. "Harold, Clara packed us a basket with food, water, and jars of lemonade. Will you fetch it?"

"Certainly."

"We don't know what losses Uncle Isaac suffered. We can go back another day if necessary. The meal is for us and them."

"A nice thought." Jay pulled her close for a hug. "Are you all right?"

"Not yet." Bea's head rested against his chest. "Not until I know—"

"There you are, Bea." Meg stepped outside as they stepped apart. "Aunt Trudy is ready to go."

"Then, if you ladies have your passes, let's get started. The mud will slow us down…and who knows what else will delay us."

~

Bea sat opposite her aunt in the sweltering carriage. A welcome cross breeze blew in from open windows. No one had spoken since they left Richmond.

Aunt Trudy desired to use this trip as an olive branch to heal her family. A miracle, if it happened.

At her side, Jay sat with folded arms that didn't hide the rifle resting against the seat, its business end pointed to the floor.

"I smell gunpowder." Meg peered outside. "We're getting closer to where the fighting happened."

Bea leaned out the window. "A gray smoke cloud is almost over our heads."

The sunny day suddenly seemed like dusk.

"So this is what a battle feels like." Meg rested her hands on the side of the window.

"Not exactly." Jay's gaze darted in every direction. "No one's shooting at us."

"Thank the Good Lord for that." Aunt Trudy eyed him. "We'll need to close the curtains."

"Oh, but I'm enjoying the breeze." Bea was looking outside when an unfortunate odor wafted through the windows. "Do you...do you smell that?"

Meg's eyes widened.

"What is that awful smell?" Bea had a terrible premonition she knew the answer.

"Not an odor I ever wanted you to become familiar with, my dear." Aunt Trudy took a deep breath. "The battle happened nearby."

Death? Was that the smell of death? Bea's skin tingled. This was the worst part. Did soldiers ever grow accustomed to this reality of war? What courage it must take to face it, no matter what side a soldier fought on.

The wagon jolted to a stop.

Jay was outside in a flash. "We're stuck in the mud."

"'Fraid so." Phineas jumped down. "We've got two shovels here."

~

What a nightmare. Jay took turns with the other men digging out the wheels. They got stuck twice more. Aunt Trudy asked the curtains to be lowered against the smell permeating the atmosphere.

The sights too. Bullet holes riddled homes, barns, and outbuildings along the country ride. Forested areas now held destroyed trees, some at least a century old. A large branch, rent by a cannon, hung to the ground like a tepee from a trunk twice the size of Jay's torso. It had the appearance of a tree struck by lightning. Tobacco fields lay flattened, destroyed by hundreds of running feet. The farm crops fared no better. Not good, when food was already growing scarce in Richmond.

Jay rode on the top behind Harold and Phineas after they got stuck a second time. Phineas drove on the grass whenever possible.

From his perch, Jay saw a few dead soldiers lying in the fields. He resolved to do something to help if possible. Brave soldiers deserved better than to lie where they'd died.

"Might be trouble up ahead." Phineas guided the carriage back onto the road.

"Soldiers." Harold shifted in his seat. "In gray."

Jay's heart thudded. He had anticipated meeting Confederate soldiers on picket duty in advance of their army. He touched his pocket. A rustle of paper reassured him his pass was where he kept it.

He leaned over the side and knocked on the window frame. Bea's tense face appeared. "Soldiers up ahead. Tell everyone to have their passes ready. They may want to talk to you."

"I'll deal with them if necessary." Trudy's voice was strong again.

He grinned to hear the determined spirit back.

Bea returned his smile before dropping the shade.

"Halt." Five armed soldiers in gray blocked the road.

"Whoa." Phineas stopped the team.

"What's your business on this road?" A bearded man about Jay's age stepped forward.

"We're taking the ladies inside to the home of their brother and uncle, Isaac Swanson." Jay climbed down and handed the leader his pass. "I'm with the Tredegar Battalion in Richmond."

He studied the pass, unimpressed. "I need to see your drivers' passes."

Jay retrieved them from Harold and Phineas, who sat stoically, and handed them over.

"All right." The soldier scanned the pages and gave them back. "Who is in the carriage?"

"Mrs. Gertrude Weston—"

The door crashed open. Jay hasted to extend his hand to Trudy and then Meg and then Bea. He retained his hold of Bea's shaking hand as Trudy walked to the man in charge.

"Young man, my name is Gertrude Weston. I want to thank you and your fine soldiers for protecting our capital."

"Thank you, ma'am—"

"Where would we be without such brave men protecting us?"

His face turned the color of a beet. "We appreciate it."

"No, we are the grateful ones, make no mistake." Her smiling gaze lingered on each soldier. "But we're here because our family was in the midst of turmoil."

"I'm sorry to hear that, Mrs. Weston."

"I know, dear boy. I saw that you were a compassionate soul and fine gentleman as soon as we met." She opened her fan and waved it across her face. "My brother is Isaac Swanson. He and his sweet wife, Mrs. Meredith Swanson...perhaps you've heard of them?"

A man in the back spoke up. "Sarge, they own a tobacco plantation on the other side of Seven Pines."

When the sergeant's mouth compressed, Jay knew they'd be allowed to travel no farther today.

"We simply must make certain that my brother—this young woman's uncle—and his family are safe. It can't be much further." She peered up the road. "Once assured of their safety, we will return home."

Jay scanned the area. Bullets had riddled a nearby home. Large branches dangled from tall trees. Bushes, flowers, and corn stalks had been trampled. Jay was thankful that no bodies lay in the fields within sight.

"Let me see your passes."

Jay gathered them and gave them to the sergeant.

He struck the pages against his palm as he stared at Trudy. "All right. I'll allow you to pass, but you'll have to be back by dusk."

"Thank you, sergeant." Trudy gave him a gracious nod. "May God bless you all and keep you safe."

Every man's face lit at the blessing.

They were on their way toward another smoke-filled sky within five minutes. Jay consulted his pocket watch with a groan. In two and half to three hours, they must be back to this point.

He wiped sweat from his brow. Aunt Trudy had charmed the young men. And her prayer of blessing had been sincere.

Today's trip was for her benefit. She had saved the day, for Jay didn't doubt the soldiers had intended to send them back to Richmond.

~

The smell of gunpowder overpowered more offensive odors as they turned onto the plantation's drive thirty minutes later. Bea raised the shades on both sides and gasped.

"Soldiers passed on this land." Meg spoke softly, looking out the window beside her.

"Indeed." Red splotches appeared on Trudy's face as she stared out the window.

Acres of tender tobacco shoots had been trampled on both sides of the drive. Where Bea remembered seeing a flourishing crop on childhood visits, there was devastation. She closed her eyes against the destruction, gave her head a little shake, and then looked again.

The nightmare was real. Was this grievous loss one her wealthy uncle could recover from?

Fields closer to the house seemed untouched, the green shoots thriving. Bea breathed a silent prayer of thanks that the entire crop hadn't been destroyed.

The carriage halted in a circle drive at the foot of the impressive three-story mansion. Bea's eyes swept the stone steps, the wide veranda with chairs and porch swings, the nearly floor-to-ceiling windows in the front parlor. Her heart leapt with gratitude that no bullet holes marred the stone home.

Jay opened the door and extended his hand to the ladies.

Bea was last to step from the carriage. Not knowing what to expect, she battled the nervousness that quaked inside her. Jay tucked her trembling hand inside his arm and led her to stand beside her aunt.

"Ladies, shall we?"

Before anyone reached the bottom step, Isaac stepped outside. He folded his arms at the top of the wide steps. "Well, Trudy, have you come to gloat?"

She flinched. "I came to see that you and Meredith are unharmed."

This wasn't the welcome anyone wanted. Bea blinked at her uncle's bitterness. Soldiers had destroyed his property. Why lash out at his sister, who'd come to him in love and concern?

"No one came to any harm. We heard the Yankees coming and got everyone out of the fields and into shelter." He swept his hands toward the carnage. "No doubt you saw the destruction along the drive."

"I'm sorry for it."

"Are you?" He descended the steps, one slow step at a time. "Aren't you happy to see me get my 'just reward'?"

Would he be too embittered by his losses to invite them inside his home? She looked up at movement on the porch where servants now stood. Aunt Meredith, at the top of the stairs, held a hand to her throat.

"What are you talking about?" Trudy sounded truly perplexed. "This is my childhood home, Isaac. I never want to see it destroyed."

He studied her, appearing unconvinced.

"Isaac, this business of my marrying a man you didn't like has gone on too long." Trudy lifted her chin. "Let's put it all behind us."

"Am I to believe you're not jealous that I inherited all of Papa's land? Not you, Hiram, or Victoria received an acre of it."

"So is that what's really between us? Not my marriage to Parker, as I thought all along." She fingered the broach pinned to her elegant dress. A gift from her husband.

Bea's eyes narrowed. She had decided to wait until a less emotional day to confront her uncle. Perhaps today was best after all.

"I liked Parker but he wasn't a planter." Isaac reached the bottom of the steps. "After you married him, Papa changed his will."

Trudy gasped. "You mean to say—"

"He decided not to divide the land." His face was a still mask, his eyes stormy. "Hiram chose to be a banker in the North. Victoria's husband owns a large plantation outside Mechanicsville. Parker's business was thriving. I was the only one who stayed to work the land."

"You"—her voice wavered—"you talked him into it."

He didn't answer.

Bea clenched her fists. "My father would have built a home on the land he inherited. A summer home, perhaps. I don't know. But our family would have retained physical roots in Virginia." Her father had grieved the loss of this land. "My childhood, my life, would have been completely different."

Jay placed his hand on her shoulder. Strong. Comforting.

"After Parker died, I would have built a home on my acreage." Trudy stepped forward.

"I worked hard to make this land thrive. And I did it." Isaac struck his open palm with his fist. "Yanks took it away."

Bea flinched for her Northern allegiance. "A tragedy." She had ridden by the tragic aftermath. This wasn't what she wanted. "I hate what happened."

"I'll do what I can to help you rebuild." Two steps took Trudy within arm's length of her brother. "Parker left me in a good position. Please, let's see what can be done."

Tears stung the back of Bea's eyes at the sacrificial gift. A true olive branch.

"You'd…do that for me?" He stared at Trudy, his tone disbelieving. "You'd help me replace the crop?"

"I'd do it for my brother." She spoke softly, as if for his ears alone. "But can't you tell me why Father altered the will weeks before his death?"

A brick the size of a twist of tobacco settled in Bea's stomach. "My father also wants to know."

"Please." Trudy gazed at her brother steadily. "Let's clear the air between us."

"Tell her, Isaac." Meredith stood at the top of the steps. "This secret has eaten at you long enough."

He looked up at his wife a long moment and then turned back to his sister. "I persuaded him to leave me the plantation and the mansion. Everything but his gold. A drop in the bucket compared to the wealth on this land. I convinced him none of you cared about the property."

"I wondered about that." Trudy's face paled. "Past actions mustn't continue to separate us."

"It's somewhat worse than that." He glanced up at his wife. "I convinced him Parker was a greedy man, and he married you to get hold of our land."

"Untrue. A complete fabrication." Bright spots of red splotched Trudy's cheeks.

"I knew it to be false." He didn't meet her eyes.

"A low blow, indeed." Trudy's face was a still mask. "What of Hiram?"

He darted a glance at Bea. "I told Father that Hiram looked down on him because he owned slaves."

Bea gasped. "That's not true. Father loved his father. Grieved for him."

"And Victoria?"

Isaac shrugged. "That was easy. She doesn't need it. Michael's acreage exceeds mine. Father agreed."

"I'd never have imagined it of you." Trudy put a hand to her throat.

Bea moved to stand beside her, hoping her support eased the pain of her brother's betrayal. He'd stolen something precious from all of them.

"If it matters, I've regretted it." Keeping his head lowered, Isaac glanced up. "I wish I had offered to buy it from you instead."

"That would have been best." Trudy studied the grass at her feet and then looked at Bea. "There's pain for you and your family in this. I'm sorry."

Bea didn't trust herself to speak. She wasn't sure if she'd lash out at her uncle or burst into tears. Jay put his arm around her shoulder, a comforting touch that somehow restored her.

"Is there to be no apology?" Trudy lifted tormented eyes to her brother.

"After all these years, I'm almost too ashamed to utter it." He looked at her with dull, lifeless eyes. "I…I'm sorry for what I've done. I can see that it's hurt you."

"Thank you for the apology. And I'm glad to know the truth. I believe Hiram and Victoria deserve to know it also."

His face flushed. "I'll seek out Victoria and Michael. Send Hiram a letter. I don't know what can be done at this late date."

"Perhaps we can all discuss it after the hostilities end." Trudy straightened her shoulders. "There's the matter of the damaged crops to deal with at the moment."

"Half the crops on that acreage are ruined. Another two hundred were lying fallow. It will be a small harvest."

"It will live to thrive again." She clasped his hand.

"You forgive me?"

Bea could barely reconcile this humble man with what she knew of her proud uncle. How long had guilt been eating away at him?

"I only want my family back." Trudy, with tears in her eyes, hugged her brother.

He wrapped his arms around her. "A thousand acres, Trudy, trampled under Yankee feet."

"I'm more sorry than I can say, Isaac." She stepped back but held his calloused hand. "You can start over."

Bea guessed her aunt referred to his past transgressions as much as the land.

"That's what I told him." Meredith's satin dress rustled as she descended the stairs. She hugged her sister-in-law. "I'm so glad you're here. Bea. Thank you for being here."

"We've prayed for you since learning of the danger." Bea held her close.

When Meredith stepped back, Meg extended her hand, which was ignored in favor of a hug. "I am so very sorry for the losses."

"Dearest Meg. It might have been worse." Meredith extended her hand to Jay. "And here's your dependable, strong young man again, Bea. Mr. Nickson, thank you for bringing our family to us."

"My pleasure, ma'am."

Isaac, shame-faced but looking less burdened, hugged Bea and then belatedly greeted Jay and Meg.

Meredith looked at her husband. "Let's go inside for supper. The Yankees didn't get all our food."

"Thank you, sister." Trudy linked arms with her. "We're happy to accept."

CHAPTER 35

Bea rose at dawn the following morning to write a long letter to Annie. When she was finished, she started one to her father. It had been more difficult to write. Learning of his brother's treachery was bound to hurt him.

Yesterday's visit had been cut short by the need to pass the soldiers' checkpoint before dusk. They'd made it there as the sun resembled an upturned bowl in the western sky, too close for comfort. Jay's tense frame at her side hadn't relaxed until they were well past the soldiers.

Aunt Trudy's forbearance with her brother—yet another example of her strength—had started the healing. Uncle Isaac and Aunt Meredith planned to join them for Sunday services. A great beginning, indeed.

Might the future bring a restoration of the original will? Bea didn't know.

Had her father built a second home here, she'd have likely gotten to know Jay much sooner.

The perfect beau. Supportive. Strong. Compassionate to her whole family.

Yesterday had been difficult. Jay had stood beside her, a solid presence. His loving support solidified her desire to marry him.

A tap of the door interrupted her reverie. "Come in."

Meg peeked her head around the door. "Want company?"

"Yes, please. I'm feeling rather melancholy this morning."

"Understandable. Are you all right?"

"I am, though our childhood years would have been completely altered."

"No doubt." Meg sat on the rumpled bed. "There are things we can't change. Some things we must simply accept."

"True." Like her and Jay's differing loyalties. "The hospitals must be filled to capacity with new wounded. Want to go to Chimborazo Hospital?"

"I was about to suggest that very thing."

"Father needs to know Uncle Isaac and Aunt Meredith are all right. Let's send a telegram on our way."

"Good idea." Meg sighed. "We must prepare ourselves. Today won't be easy."

~

Jay stopped by the Weston residence on Monday evening only to learn Bea was still at the hospital. It was nearly half past seven, far later than her normal hour to be home.

He rode to the hospital and found Harold waiting with a carriage for the ladies. Concerned, he wandered around the various wards looking for them. An ambulance driver asked his assistance carrying in wounded, and he agreed. While they carried stretchers, the driver verified all the dead and wounded had been retrieved from the section of road Jay had vowed to himself to help clear. Though he hadn't yet fetched his wagon as he'd planned, due to demands of his job, he figured carrying wounded into hospital tents was just as good.

It was fully dark by the time he finished. Not knowing which of the dozens of wards Bea worked in, Jay made his way back to the waiting carriage. It was gone. Passing more wagons with wounded, he rode back to the Weston residence. After discovering the ladies were safely back, he went home at eleven o'clock. He didn't spot a single guard on the road.

On Tuesday, Jay went to the Weston residence after supper only to learn Bea had retired for the evening.

He left, grateful for the compassionate hearts of women who wanted to soothe the pain within their power to ease, regardless of a soldier's chosen side. He fell more in love with Bea every day and wanted to spend the rest of his days with her. His mother was aware of their opposing loyalties and still approved of her.

Would his father have felt the same?

Uncertainty kept Jay tossing and turning all night. Dawn found him groggy and cantankerous. Heat from the foundry's furnaces fueled his foul mood. Exhausted from the effort to maintain firm control of his tongue, he decided not to go home. Instead, he rode to his favorite view of the falls, where he felt closest to his father.

The rapids blocked out the noise of the city. No one else was there. Little wonder. The whole city was involved in caring for the wounded and dealing with the aftermath of the battle.

He dismounted. "No need to tether you to a tree, Daisy." Lush patches of green grass grew in abundance. "Eat your fill. I know you enjoy this spot nearly as much as I do."

Hands on hips, Jay stood in the shade near the trail. He breathed in fresh, clean air to rid his lungs of the putrid odors from the battlefield.

As a kid, he had rolled up his pants' legs to wade in the water with his father. Laughing, they had splashed each other. They'd skipped rocks over the rapids.

Then, over a picnic lunch, they'd talk. His father had been

the best of men—forgiving, kind, wise, loving, strong—save for one thing. The only topic they had a serious disagreement about was slavery.

His father had grown up around it, just as Jay and Blanche had done. He was accustomed to it. It was Jay's opinion that his father didn't want to think about something he could not change. He had accepted it.

He'd been a leader whom others had willingly followed. Respected in his community. A man of strong faith who rarely missed church services.

Jay had adored him, resolved to be like him. So much so that he'd attended the Mechanic's Institute to better learn his trade and follow his father's footsteps at Tredegar.

"Mama relied on your strength, Papa," he said, wishing his father were there to hear him. "She's floundering. Had you been alive, I know you'd have steadied her nerves, given her the strength to face whatever lies ahead." Jay tossed a smooth stone over the water. It skipped three times.

"You wouldn't like this war. It's divided our nation. Somewhere along the line, folks decided to stop listening to each other. Words—hateful words—stirred up dissension. It led to the Confederacy's attack on Fort Sumter." His heart ached. "I guess the leaders decided they were done talking. We're divided…North and South. I know you'd never take up arms against Virginia. You loved this city, your state. You were proud to live here. There's no doubting your loyalty."

Jay looked up at gray clouds against a blue sky in the horizon. "Papa, I sure wish I knew if you could hear me. Telling you about it helps. I don't know if you care about battles and such in heaven, but I'm certain you still love Mama, Blanche, and me."

It was a relief to speak again with his father, regardless of whether he heard.

"I've met someone, Papa. Her name is Beatrice Swanson. She's beautiful, inside and out. A Christian. Compassionate.

Loving. Kind. Generous. Loyal. There's just one thing." Another rock skipped across the rapids three times. "She's from the North. Her allegiance is to the North, not a popular sentiment in Richmond. Not with you, either."

Overcome with sorrow, Jay turned from the soothing sounds of the rapidly churning river. He couldn't reject his heritage, his state, his neighbors.

Impulsively, he pushed up his sleeves. Sitting on the grass, he removed his boots and socks, then rolled up the legs of his trousers.

He waded into the cold water until it covered his ankles, then waded further until it reached his knees. It was almost as if he heard his pa's voice telling him not to venture further into the rapids, as he had when Jay was a child. He splashed and kicked as if his father were by his side.

"Papa, I'm going to propose to Bea." He splashed the empty spot beside him. "I want your blessing. I ask for your blessing."

Energy spent, he stood still, cold water soaking into his pants.

"You'd love her, Papa. Everything about her except that one thing."

Jay felt no answer. "Lord, what should I do? Do I have *Your* blessing? Beatrice and I can make it past this barrier between us, can't we?"

Suddenly Jay no longer felt alone. He turned around but saw no one. "You're letting me know that, though my dad can't talk with me, You're here, right, God?"

The swift-moving current carried something red. A rose, Bea's favorite flower. He plucked it from the river. "Thank you, Lord. Bea and I share a faith and love for You. Love for our families. Compassion for others. Most importantly, we love one another. Those things bind us closer than the barrier that divides us."

A bird tweeted among the trees. Another answered in song.

Jay waded back to shore. Standing on a thick carpet of grass, he turned back to the rushing river. In the midst of turmoil in his city, the turmoil in his heart eased.

The sun seemed to rest on the western horizon. "Thank you, Father. I needed this talk."

Mounting his horse a few minutes later, he stared at the Falls. Great memories of his pa flooded over him.

He smiled as he rode away, thankful that missing his pa had led him to seek the Lord in this sacred place.

CHAPTER 36

"I haven't seen Jay since Sunday." Exhausted from long days at the hospital, Bea had risen late on Friday morning and eaten breakfast in the family dining room. Aunt Trudy and Meg, who had eaten earlier, sat at the table to keep her company.

"He tried to find you both at Chimborazo Hospital on Monday night." Aunt Trudy sipped her coffee.

"I wish I'd seen him." Bea sighed. "There are so many buildings that I'm not surprised he couldn't find us." The new patients in her ward hadn't seen a surgeon yet. She had washed faces, hands, and arms. Served dippers of water. Dipped soup into the soldiers' tin cups and fed those who needed assistance. Bathed minor wounds and bandaged them. The past four days had passed in a blur.

Trudy rested her head against the spindle-backed chair. "The Union threat continues. Our boys pushed them back but not far enough."

"Widow Rose Greenhow was released from prison in Washington City." Meg scanned a newspaper article. "It seems she arrived in Richmond two days ago. She's staying at the Ballard

Hotel. Bea, isn't she the family friend you and Annie told me about? The one who was arrested for spying on the Federal Government?"

"Yes, her friendship with my mother spread into a relationship with our family." Bea had felt betrayed to learn the widow was a spy yet indignant at her treatment in prison. It had been another secret her father asked her to keep. His advice to stay away from the widow had no doubt saved her and Annie from arrest—though they'd done nothing wrong—because Rose's other visitors had also been arrested. "She and her daughter were held at their home for a while. Then they were moved to Old Capital Prison."

"I've read of her hardships." Trudy shook her head sadly. "All for doing what she could to serve the Confederacy."

"Mrs. Greenhow was a frequent guest at our soirees," Bea said. "I hope she's recovering from her ordeal."

"I'd like to meet her." Trudy fingered the rim of her cup.

"I know she'd appreciate a warm welcome." Bea welcomed the opportunity to see her old friend. "How long will she be in Richmond?"

Meg consulted the newspaper. "The article doesn't say. Let's go today."

"Is that convenient for you, Aunt Trudy?"

She nodded. "Send a note to her at the Ballard Hotel."

~

"I was happy to learn you're in Richmond, Bea." Rose Greenhow smoothed a wrinkle from her purple gown in an elegant parlor of the Ballard Hotel. "Thank you for bringing your dear aunt and cousin."

"I was anxious to see you again after your ordeal." Bea was glad the widow's merry laughter was still as infectious. Her face might be paler than last she saw her, but her hair, parted in the middle and pinned at her nape, was exactly as she remembered. Bea wished her mother, who was about the same age as Rose, could also be here.

"You're a heroine to many in the Confederacy, Mrs. Greenhow." Aunt Trudy, dressed in a green sateen gown, smiled at her from her seat in the hotel's parlor. "One hopes you did not suffer unduly for your loyalty."

"Please, we are of an age. Call me Rose."

"My friends call me Trudy."

Rose gave a smiling nod. "As to my sufferings, they are behind me. Brighter days are ahead, ladies."

"It's good to see you in such good spirits." Seeing her happiness was a comfort. After all the bad news of late, Bea would be able to write good news to her father and sister.

"How can I be otherwise after such a warm welcome to this beautiful city?" Rose leaned closer. "President Davis has already graced me with a visit. General Clayton also."

"Most impressive." Trudy relaxed against the cushioned back. "They are both very busy men."

"I heard General Johnston was wounded in the recent battle." Rose frowned. "We can't afford to lose our generals."

"President Davis appointed General Robert Lee to replace him." Meg, who had been watchful throughout the visit, leaned forward.

"An excellent choice." Rose turned to Bea. "How is your dear brother? Is he still held as prisoner?"

"I'm happy to report he was released in February. We saw him briefly at Fort Monroe before he crossed the bay under a flag of truce."

"I can imagine a bit of what he suffered." Rose patted Bea's arm. "And what news of Annie? And your father?"

"Annie is married—"

"What? I didn't know." Rose's brows shot up. "She married Sergeant Major John Finn, I presume."

"Yes, in January. He's a second lieutenant now." Bea's heart warmed to think of her sister's happiness. "And my father works long hours at the bank, but he is well."

"Your father helped me." Rose laughed. "Hiram was smart to keep nothing written. Everything he gave was all word of mouth."

Bea's jaw slackened. Did Rose just say that Hiram Swanson supplied her with information to help the Confederacy? Her glance flew to the open parlor door. Anyone passing might have heard.

"He was wise not to visit me after my arrest," Rose added. "That would have shifted suspicion onto him."

Bea was suddenly as dizzy as if someone had spun her in circles like in a childhood game. "Even in Richmond, it's unwise to speak of such things in public." She glanced at Meg, whose head was bowed, hiding her expression. "And I'm certain, if my father supplied you with information, it was unknowingly."

"Of course, my dear. I never betrayed him." She patted her hair.

Rose betrayed him now. "Once he heard you'd been arrested, he was quite worried that he'd passed along details, though he was sure they were well-known rumors." Bea's insides turned to ice that a friend so callously spoke of her father's involvement in front of her aunt and—*her cousin*.

A Union spy.

On Thursday evening, Jay had written to Hiram Swanson, requesting his permission to propose to his daughter. It took him two hours to compose the note. In the end, he introduced himself and his family and included references to his job and his home to satisfy the banker that Bea would be adequately cared for.

Were it not for the war and the proximity of Union troops to Richmond, he'd travel to Bea's home to speak to him in person. Jay had only vague recollections of a busy, powerful, broad-shouldered man from Hiram's visits when Jay was a child.

He rode Daisy home early Friday evening. His letter might not reach Washington for a week. Allowing a day or two to pen a response, he'd be lucky to receive a reply in two weeks.

He was ready to propose this weekend. The time was right. He felt it to his core.

He stopped to wait for a train to cross. Several pedestrians on a nearby corner waited with barely veiled impatience. The Union army had moved back a bit yet still threatened the city. In case an important threat loomed, Jay listened to a few phrases of a muttered conversation from the street corner. Spy. Widow Greenhow. Freed at last.

Jay couldn't be bothered with any news less important than another battle. Thoughts of proposing to Bea consumed him. Yet he must wait until he heard from Mr. Swanson so they could begin their future on the correct footing.

He was impatient with waiting for a reply, now that his mind was made up. Perhaps a telegram?

No, a telegram was too brief. Impersonal. It would take too long to reiterate his letter from the night before to a telegrapher. Not to mention the expense.

However, a telegram could reference the letter en route. Should Hiram need all the information before granting his consent, the telegram wouldn't help matters.

Except that he'd know Jay's intentions, giving him a few days to mull it over while waiting for the letter.

On the other hand, Jay might receive a favorable reply tomorrow.

What entertainment could he plan for the proposal?

Most businesses and restaurants were still closed, or he'd treat Bea and her cousin to supper.

His mother always planned gatherings in their home. In her absence, he didn't have a hostess. It was a hurdle. He'd best speak with Esther, his cook.

No, it was better that he not host the event. As host, he'd be obligated to stay with the group. He didn't want to propose in front of everyone.

Where was the best place? Some public place that wasn't closed.

The perfect place occurred to him as the telegraph office sign came into view. Should he send that telegram? Were he a father, he'd want advance notice. Jay looped Daisy's reins over the hitching post.

A telegrapher would have a funny story to tell his family tonight.

CHAPTER 37

The rest of their visit with Mrs. Greenhow took on a nightmarish quality for Bea. The others spoke of the sights of Washington City. All Bea could think about was how to keep Rose from spreading news of her father's involvement in her spying operation. Preventing Meg from passing on the information was her second concern.

Goodbyes were being said. This was her opportunity. "Aunt Trudy, will you and Meg wait for me in the landau? I will be only a moment behind you."

Ever watchful, Meg inclined her head.

"Of course, dear." Trudy's glance darted from Bea to Rose. "Again, it was lovely to meet you. You must come to supper one evening."

Rose accepted the invitation, and the other ladies were soon gone.

"Now, my dear, what did you want to speak about?" Rose looked beyond her as Meg closed the parlor door behind them.

"It's good you feel my father helped you." It wasn't good at all, in Bea's opinion, because it placed him in jeopardy.

"Oh my, yes, Beatrice." She clasped her hands together. "Your father won't remain an unsung hero for long. We will win the conflict, my dear. I know you want this, too. Your father forbade me to ask you to help us. It was great pity, for I'm certain you'd have been a good spy."

"I'm...not so certain." Rose had considered asking for her help to spy on the North? What if Bea had acted on her confusion after learning her brother fought for the South? That confusion continued many months. Her father had saved her from making a serious mistake.

"I've no doubt of it," Rose said. "When you return to Washington, listen for anything not generally known and write to me. I'll see that the information is passed to the authorities."

Heat spread up Bea's face. She must tread carefully. "I am certain you can accomplish that."

Rose patted her hair.

"My greatest concern now is that you protect my father. Please don't tell anyone he aided you."

"But he's a hero here in Richmond."

"But he lives in the North, and, as you know, there are spies everywhere, even here in this great city. We can't risk him going to prison." Hope stirred as Rose's determination to share the glory with her father seemed to waver. "If that information reaches the ears of the Federal government, my father will be arrested, just as you were."

"Of course, I wouldn't want him in prison."

"Exactly." Bea clenched her fists. "Please don't speak of my father's aid." He had confessed he provided no information not generally known to satisfy Rose without actually providing anything of substance. "It will damage his reputation in the North at the very least. At worst, he will be incarcerated or executed." Her thoughts flew to poor Timothy Webster.

"You're right, my dear." Rose patted her arm. "He must wait for his glory until the war ends."

"It's for the best." Bea took her first deep breath since Rose blurted out her father's name. "Thank you, Mrs. Greenhow."

Someone tapped on the door.

"I have more guests coming," Mrs. Greenhow said. "Do you want to stay and meet them?"

"I'd love that, but Aunt Trudy and Meg are waiting for me."

Rose walked with her to the door. "It was lovely to see you again. Give my best to Annie and your father in your next letter."

She agreed and escaped with a nod for the middle-aged couple waiting, strangers to her.

Now to talk with Meg. She'd approach her privately as soon as they returned home.

Unfortunately, only Trudy sat fanning herself in the landau.

"Where's Meg?"

"She had an errand. She assured me she'll return before supper." Trudy bit her lip. "Did Mrs. Greenhow agree to maintain her silence?"

"Yes." No use in pretending she didn't understand her meaning. They'd all heard the shocking revelation.

"Good."

Bea sank against the warm cushioned seat. Her relief had been short-lived.

Where was Meg?

~

Jay stopped by that evening to invite all the ladies to join him at a prayer meeting and singing at a local church. Bea, with an anxious look at Meg, was the only one who accepted.

"Want to stroll a bit?" Jay offered his arm as they left the church later that evening.

"I'd like that." Her smile seemed a bit strained as she slid her fingers into the crook of his elbow.

"Is everything all right?"

"It's been a difficult week." She tugged at her hat as they strolled in the direction of the setting sun, now the shape of a yellowish red half-moon on the horizon.

"You worked at the hospital every day, didn't you?"

"Not today. Meg and I were there twelve hours on Monday. I dressed minor wounds. There are so many wounded that the surgeons couldn't get around to them all. Thankfully, a surgeon came to my ward Monday night, so I felt better about leaving."

"I aided the ambulance drivers several hours myself."

"I'm glad. It was terrible." She shuddered. "No one who hasn't endured those horrible sights and smells can understand. The agony of brave warriors…it stays with you."

"God bless your tender heart. Always." How he loved her. Overcome with emotion at her sacrificial aid to Southern soldiers, he covered her hand with his own. She showed him more every day that she was the perfect wife for him.

"And yours." She hugged his arm.

"Shall we speak of other matters?" They stepped onto a shady side street.

"Yes, please distract my thoughts."

"What did you do today?"

Her shoulders tensed. "I visited an old friend of my mother's."

"Perhaps I know the family."

"Have you heard of Rose Greenhow?"

"The widow who was arrested for being a Confederate spy in Washington?" He stopped. "You know her?"

She nodded.

"Mrs. Greenhow is a heroine."

They began walking again. "I took Aunt Trudy and Meg with me to meet her."

Bea's lips were tight at the corners. "Did the visit not go well?"

"It did." She studied the brick sidewalk. "Mrs. Greenhow received us as graciously, as I knew she would. Aunt Trudy was impressed with her. She plans to invite her to supper one evening. You can meet her then."

"Excellent." Except Bea didn't seem happy about the news. "Is there something else troubling you?"

A quick glance at him convinced Jay of something not right.

"Please tell me."

"It's not my secret to share." Releasing his arm, she opened her fan and waved it across her red face.

"You can tell me anything."

"Once the war ends."

Sounded serious. His knotted tie constricted him, and he tugged at it. Perhaps she'd talk with him away from city streets. "We're close to your aunt's home. Shall we sit in the garden?"

"I can't." She fanned herself faster. "I need to speak with Meg this evening. Are you working on Sunday?"

"No. I'll escort you to church and then take you all for a picnic lunch if you like."

Her expression lightened. "That will be lovely. Thank you."

They halted in front of her aunt's house. "What about tomorrow evening?"

"We'll work at the hospital tomorrow. There's so much to do that I'm exhausted when I return. Can I see you Sunday?"

Disappointment turned to compassion at the tired droop of her shoulders. That gave Hiram an extra day to respond to his telegram. "Sunday, it is."

CHAPTER 38

Someone knocked on the front door while Bea, Meg, and Aunt Trudy ate breakfast the next morning.

"I wonder who that could be so early." Trudy patted the knotted ribbon hairnet covering the bun on the top of her head. "No matter. We are all dressed and ready to meet the day. Bea, aren't you hungry this morning?"

"Not really." Bea pushed scrambled eggs around on her plate. They had alternated between eggs and porridge all week. Armies nearby blocked some roads, making it difficult for farmers to deliver and sell their products. She should be grateful for the meal. Instead, her stomach rebelled against it, for Meg had shunned all private conversations with her.

Protecting Bea's father was paramount to all else.

They all looked up at a tap on the dining room door. "Come in."

"Miss Trudy, forgive me for disturbing your breakfast." Harold stepped inside holding a silver plate that held a folded piece of paper. "It's a telegram, ma'am." He offered the plate to Trudy. "From Washington City. I didn't know as it might be too important to wait until you finished your meal."

"Washington?" Trudy gave Bea a wide-eyed look. "I just had a letter from Hiram two days ago."

Bea could barely breathe. Had Rose's accusations against her father already reached the Union government? Or, worse, had she spouted her praise for his help while still in Washington?

Her father hadn't sent any telegrams since her initial arrival. Bea stared at the page.

"Harold, will you fetch my spectacles from Parker's study?"

"Right here." He pulled them from his pocket and held them out to her.

"What would I do without you?"

"There's no telling, ma'am."

Trudy's lips twitched in an almost smile. Then, the expression faded as she scanned the page, fingers covering her mouth.

"What is it? Is everyone well?" Bea clutched the side of the table.

"What? Oh, yes. Everyone is fine." Trudy folded the message. "If you'll excuse me, ladies?"

"But, may I read it?" Bea knew she was being rude, but her nerves were stretched tight.

"I need to stew on Hiram's message." Trudy halted at the door. "Relax, my dear. All is well."

Bea perched on the edge of her chair. After her aunt had walked out, she turned to Meg. "What do you think that was about?"

"I don't know." Meg pushed back her chair and stood. "Perhaps he has a question for her."

Coming on the heels of Rose's revelations, Bea couldn't relax. "When will you be ready to go to Chimborazo?"

"I will join you later, if I may." Meg paused with her hand on the doorknob. "Don't wait for me."

"But—"

Meg was gone.

Bea wrung her hands. Her cousin was avoiding her. This didn't bode well for her father.

~

Jay rode home later that evening, dejected that Bea was busy. He had so few waking hours that weren't accounted for, what with work and drills, that it was a disappointment not to see her at every possible opportunity.

Someone called his name.

He slowed at pounding hooves behind him. Trees surrounded this section of the street just outside of the city. He turned to see his friend trotting up behind him. "Troy. I didn't get a chance to talk to you at drill practice."

"I wanted to ask if you're still courting Beatrice Swanson?"

"Sure am. Why?"

"Because I started courting Christina Wyatt."

"I thought she was betrothed to Jack Reed?"

"That ended before he mustered into the army last year." Troy flushed. "Are you seeing Beatrice tonight?"

He shook his head. "She's taking care of patients at Chimborazo all day."

"Some temporary hospitals are closing. The crisis is past the worst stage." He dismounted. "Let's walk our horses a minute."

Jay dismounted to walk beside him. "What's on your mind?"

"I thought we might escort our girls together to dinner one evening."

"An excellent idea." Jay grinned. "Once the restaurants open again."

"A few are open now."

"Good. Bea's cousin has been our chaperone. Meg's generous with her time, but I hate to ask it of her every time."

"Same here. Christina's sister is a peach of a girl, but going somewhere with you and Bea will be fun too."

"Can we plan something for next Sunday? Let's scout around for a restaurant open for diners."

"Will do."

"I'll talk to Bea about it tomorrow." Jay mounted. "If I get the opportunity. I hope to have something else to talk with her about."

"Oh?" He quirked a blond brow. "Something important?"

"Yep."

"I'm happy for you." Troy grinned. "I can't wait to meet her and introduce her to Christina."

Jay rode home with a lighter heart. When he arrived, a telegram waited for him on the hall table.

He read it, and joy filled his heart. On a whim, he strode back to the stables to ride out to Troy's home.

"Oh, Bea. Please say yes."

~

After serving supper to those unable to feed themselves, Bea rubbed her lower back and entered the ward where Meg had assisted since noon. She found her cousin giving medicine to a soldier with a bandage wrapped around his head.

"The doctor said that will ease your pain, Benny."

"Thanks, Mrs. Meg. I think I can sleep now."

Meg touched his shoulder with a smile. "Hearing from your girl back home helped, didn't it? She's waiting for you. You'll be home before you know it."

"Are you ready to go?" Bea leaned to whisper.

"I am." She stepped away and spoke to Bea in the space between the many cots and patients. "This was the last task the steward asked me to do. I'll tell him I'm leaving."

Shading her eyes, Bea waited in the hot sun and looked toward the east, wondering how Uncle Isaac and Aunt Meredith were coping with the loss of their crops. Far worse could have happened. Strange how tragic events had become a catalyst for healing among her father's siblings. She was glad they were attending church together tomorrow.

"Long day." Meg joined her. "It's as hot out here as it is inside the ward."

"Yes." They walked along the roads between the wards.

"Is Harold bringing the landau for us?"

Bea shrugged. "I guess Aunt Trudy will send him if we're too late."

They navigated around an empty wagon in the hospital road. Soon they were on Broad Street.

"I don't see Harold." Meg sighed. "I guess walking will build up an appetite for supper."

"Meg, I need to talk to you." Bea turned to her on a forested section of the street.

"About Rose?"

"Please don't believe what she said about Father."

Meg studied her with raised eyebrows. "It was a fabrication?"

"Father told me she asked for his help. He supported the Union but didn't like to refuse, so he shared things that were already generally known."

"That's a relief." Meg pressed her fingertips together. "It broke my heart when Mrs. Greenhow so casually mentioned Uncle Hiram's aid."

"Mine too," Bea whispered.

"Perhaps Mrs. Greenhow believes Uncle Hiram supports the Confederacy," Meg mused as they resumed walking, "and merely means to share the glory. She is as famous as an opera singer at the moment."

"True. Promise me you won't breathe a word of what was said in that drawing room to anyone."

"I've been praying about the situation since it happened." Meg picked up a pebble in the road, rubbing it between her fingers. "Don't worry. Even if Uncle Hiram did share secrets with her, unless I have direct knowledge of what was said and done, I will not betray him."

A weak promise that did little to halt the churning in Bea's stomach. Meg had basically agreed not to pass on this information, but if she learned something more substantial, the door was still open.

Silence descended, uncomfortable in a way it had never been between the cousins.

Meg must never learn that her father had given money to the Confederacy, money that *Bea* had smuggled into Richmond. She'd warn her father to choose his words carefully around Meg in the future. That ought to honor the promise she'd made to both of them, in spirit anyway.

"It's not the promise I hoped for," Bea said, "but I'm grateful for it."

"Please believe I'd never do *anything* to hurt you or Annie. I love you too much."

Bea hugged her, grateful that family love insured Meg's silence.

CHAPTER 39

Phineas drove the landau while Jay entertained the ladies on the way to Troy's house on Sunday after church. Isaac and Meredith had come to church but declined his invitation to the picnic, saying there was much to do at home. Troy was bringing his parents, two school-aged brothers, Christina, her parents, her aunt, and her sixteen-year-old sister to the picnic. Since the party had grown, every family provided something for the meal.

Introductions were made outside Troy's childhood home. Everyone seemed ready to put the ravages of war behind them for an afternoon. It was an excited, chattering crowd that pulled up to a shaded area beside the Falls of the James River.

Esther had outdone herself, frying a batch of delicious chicken the crowd devoured. Christina's aunt objected to sitting on the colorful quilts spread all around and ate in the family's open carriage. Otherwise, everyone entered the spirit of fun that recalled happier days.

Jay relaxed after the leftovers were packed away. The hardest part of hosting was behind him. He missed his mother, not only as his hostess but also because she'd miss the happy announcement.

If there was a happy announcement.

Bea was as pretty as a rose in a pink dress that matched her delicate blush each time she met his eyes. Their eyes met often while in conversation with others. At that moment, she and Christina were in animated conversation down by the river.

Jay quirked an eyebrow at Troy. "Let's join our ladies."

"No need to ask me twice."

Bea looked up when Jay strode to her side. "There you are."

"Here I am." Longing to put his arms around her, he settled for holding her gloved hand. It tightened around his in a way that welcomed his touch. He could hardly wait to steal her away to propose.

"Christina, I learned a new skill this year." Bea gave Jay a teasing glance.

Mystified, he stared back at her.

"Oh?" The pretty blonde, who wore her hair in looped braids beside each ear, tore her gaze away from Troy with an effort. "What's this new skill?"

"Skipping rocks." She giggled.

Jay burst into laughter and gave her a one-armed hug. "She did, indeed. Listen up, Troy. You may need some pointers."

"Yeah?" Troy grinned. "Let's see your skill."

Bea placed her fan on a large, flat rock. Then she selected a flat stone and tossed it out over the rapids.

"It skipped twice." Troy whistled. "I'm impressed."

"Can you show me?" Christina placed her fan on a rock beside Bea's.

Troy's grin widened. The men folded their coats and left them draped over the landau. Dark vests and ties over white shirts squeaked by as acceptable at a picnic—at least Jay hoped so. Soon all four of them were skipping stones. Drawn by their laughter, the whole party joined them. A contest developed to see whose stone took the most skips. Everyone, even Christina's shy aunt, tried a hand at the game.

Dan, Troy's youngest brother, beat them all. He made it to six and, though he tried again and again, never made it that high again.

Laughing, Jay shook his hand in congratulations. The others crowded around the boy.

Jay looked over at Bea, who stood apart as if waiting for him. She met his serious gaze with a tilt of her head.

The time had come.

"Thanks for planning such a wonderful picnic." Bea walked along the shoreline with her hand tucked inside Jay's arm. "I can't remember when I've had such fun. Let's do it again."

"We will." His fervent tone sounded like a promise. "Troy and Christina haven't been courting long, but they seem content together."

"That's a good description."

"Troy wants us to go on outings with them. They will chaperone us and we will chaperone them. What do you think?"

"I'd enjoy that." She squeezed his arm. "Christina is a pleasant person."

"Good. I'll talk to Troy."

"Meg can come if she chooses, right?"

"Of course. She's a lovely woman who graces every gathering."

Bea smiled. "I hope you feel that way about me."

"A hundred times over." He halted under the shade of a mighty oak. "I want to talk with you."

Bea looked back at those still gathered on the riverbank

some fifty yards away. Meg glanced their direction and then contemplated the rushing river again.

"Do you mind sitting on this hollow log?" he asked.

Her gaze held his as she sat beside him in the shade of a tall oak. Her heart raced.

"I wrote your father last week and then followed it up with a telegram."

"A telegram?" Her father had sent one to Aunt Trudy the day before. Why would Jay send a message to her father? Unless... Her heart thudded with hope.

"Yes." Green eyes searched hers. "You see, I can't visit him personally right now because of the war."

She waited, hardly daring to breathe. *Could it be ...?*

"He sent a reply last night." He extracted a folded paper from his pocket. "Bea, he granted his permission."

"He did?" A smile trembled on her lips. *Ask me.*

Jay bent down on one knee. "Beatrice Swanson, will you do me the very great honor of becoming my wife?"

She wanted to throw herself into his arms. But... "Are you certain you want to marry a Northerner, Jay? A woman whose loyalty has grown to become as firmly planted there as this oak tree?" Her fingers brushed the rough bark.

"I came to terms with our differences on this very spot." His jaw set as he sat beside her again. "Can you reconcile yourself to marrying a Virginian loyal to his state?"

"I can." She smoothed his wrinkled brow. "My father is a Virginian. His family's roots are here. My brother owns a plantation in North Carolina. Fights for the Confederacy. These are complicated times."

"They are." He caressed her shoulders. "Can we see past those boundaries? Respect each other's opinions?" His green eyes captured her gaze and held it.

"We can." The love in those eyes brought joy to her soul.

He enfolded her in his arms and kissed her. "I love you, Beatrice Swanson."

"I love you, James Nickson." She smiled at the familiar green eyes so close to hers. "I will marry you."

He gave her a lingering kiss full of love and promise. His words, his embrace, convinced her they'd built a bridge over the chasm that had separated them.

Gazing into her eyes, he helped her to her feet.

"I won't allow this war to steal the perfect man from me because he loves the South." She snuggled against his chest, delighting in the rhythm of his fast-beating heart. He kissed the top of her head as he held her close. "There'll be no division between us. We'll respect one another's different views. Always. The war isn't winning this one."

"No division." His kiss was a seal on their promise to each other.

The grass rustled, and they broke apart.

Bea looked beyond Jay at her smiling aunt and cousin.

"Do I hear wedding bells in the future?" Trudy clasped her hands together.

"Yes, dearest Aunt Trudy." Bea hugged her close. "Wedding bells will peal to bind our families. Did you play matchmaker for us?"

"Guilty." Her blue eyes twinkled. "I told Mary you were the perfect woman for her son. By happy coincidence, he is the perfect man for you. We plotted to get you down here. I regret she's not here to share this wonderful moment."

"Me too." Bea reached for Jay's hand, knowing he missed his mother.

"How Annie will lament not coming with us when she learns your news." Meg hugged her. "I'm thrilled for you, Bea."

"I've never missed Annie more. Jay, you're going to love my sister."

"I'm certain of it." He kissed her hand with a smile just for her.

CHAPTER 40

Happiness bubbled up so that Bea could scarcely contain it. The house was silent, its occupants finally asleep after an eventful day, all but the recently engaged lady whose joy was marred only by an inability to share it personally with her sister, her best friend.

Dearest Annie,

It's been nearly four months since I last saw you, and I've never missed you more. By now you and Father will have received Aunt Trudy's telegram with the wonderful news—Jay proposed today, and I accepted! After seeing your happiness with John, I longed for a good man to grow old with all the more. Who knew that I'd fall in love on a family visit to Richmond in the midst of war? The answer is Aunt Trudy and Mary Nickson, Jay's mother! Our dear aunt confided in me this evening after my betrothed left—how I love to refer to him this way!—that she didn't wait until the conflict ended to introduce us for fear I'd marry someone else. That possibility robs me of my breath, for I can't now imagine a greater personal tragedy.

Jay's proposal was all your romantic heart could desire, dear sister. He hosted a picnic with us and two other families along the Falls of the James River, so we were quite a lively party. It's his favorite spot in Richmond due to happy childhood memories with his parents and sister. I dare to believe this day has added one more happy memory. It was a lovely day that I'll cherish forever.

In fact, Jay and I shared only one unhappiness today—the inability of our parents and siblings to share our joy. On an evening such as this, you and I would be talking and planning late into the night. As it is, it's long past curfew, and I am the only one awake.

A rap on the door raised her hopes that someone else wanted to talk. "Who is it?" Annie was too far away, yet her cousin and aunt were lovable substitutes.

"Meg."

Bea's smile broadened as she opened the door. "Come in. Are you thirsty? I can go to the kitchen. Clara left raspberry shrub in the cellar to cool."

"I don't wish to awaken anyone." She tightened the belt of her robe. "I saw the light beneath your door. I'm glad you're awake."

"How can one sleep on such a beautiful night?" Bea spread her arms wide. "Tonight I'm in love with the world."

"I remember that feeling." Meg hugged her. "Jay is the perfect match for you."

"Do you think so?" Bea sat on the chaise and patted the cushion beside her.

"Yes." Meg joined her. "I believe your mother would have approved."

"You couldn't have said anything I more needed to hear." Tears stung her eyes. "Actually, I'm of the same mind. I've been thinking how differently Mother and Father were raised. Since he lived on a plantation with slaves, they had a different mindset on practices in the South. They had much to overcome."

"Agreed. Yet I've seen few couples happier than Uncle Hiram

and Aunt Charlotte. They respected one another." Meg smiled. "Just as you and Jay will."

"Thank you for that." Bea retrieved a handkerchief from a drawer to dab at her eyes. "I started a letter to Annie. Describing this magical day has only increased my longing for my sister, my family."

"She understands. She did just marry the man of her dreams in January. What are your plans?"

"We won't marry for several months." Dreams filled her heart. "I'll go to Washington City and coax Annie to come back here to help plan. We always dreamed of weddings at my mother's church, where she and Father exchanged vows. That won't happen. Annie was married at John's church in Boston. It appears my wedding will take place in St. John's Church here in Richmond."

"Dreams have a way of changing." Meg squeezed her arm. "It's the perfect location for your wedding."

"Virginia is the perfect setting for our future family." She blushed to dream that their children would live where she'd longed to live as a child. "John will let Annie know when he feels it safe for her to visit Richmond. Then we'll just need Jay's mother to return from Chattanooga and Father to let us know when he'll come to set a date. I'm praying Blanche's family and Will's family will attend. You're already here."

"As to that"—Meg stood and walked to the window—"it's time to let you know my plans."

Bea stood quickly. "Aren't you happy in Richmond?"

"I want to stay in Richmond. I'll be here to celebrate your wedding." Meg glanced at her, then outside as a slight breeze stirred the curtains. "I found a job. I will be working at a bakery on Marshall Street. It's a bit of a walk from this neighborhood, so I'll look for a boarding house."

"What? A job? But why?" Bea blinked rapidly. "I'm certain you're as welcome at Aunt Trudy's as I am."

"I know. She's good and gracious to me. Always." Meg closed the window and stepped back. "But I no longer feel comfortable here."

"I...don't understand." Had her cousin slapped her, Bea couldn't be more shocked.

"I'm a Union spy enjoying the gracious comfort of a Southern woman's home." Her shoulders slumped. "How will Aunt Trudy feel if she discovers I've betrayed her?"

"But..."

"Sending letters with mail carriers isn't cheap. I've used most of the money I brought with me, including Jay's generous gift for escorting his mother to Tennessee."

"That's no problem. I have plenty—"

"No." Meg's chin lifted. "I can't ask you to fund my spy activities."

"You didn't ask. I offered."

"It's too dangerous. Paying for the letters embroils you in the midst of spying on the Confederacy." Meg placed her hands on Bea's shoulders. "Think of it. You're pledged to marry a soldier in the Tredegar Battalion. A man who knows secrets from the ironworks he can't share. If I'm arrested, authorities will look to you and may discover you accompanied me on several occasions when I delivered letters. They don't need much provocation to arrest Unionists in this city. If they suspect you of helping me in any way, it casts suspicion on Jay."

She hadn't thought of that. "I can't do anything that may hurt him."

"Of course not." Meg turned back to the dark window. "The money from the sale of my Chicago home is deposited at Uncle Hiram's bank. I'll ask him to send me a portion. Inquiries into boarding houses show the cost of food isn't the only thing that's escalated. That money will tide me over for a time."

"I don't feel good about this."

"You'll still see me far more often than you'd like," Meg

teased. "You'll see me strolling up the walk and say, 'Aunt Trudy, Meg is here again.'"

"Never." Laughing, she hugged her close.

"Keep me informed of wedding plans. I'll help any way I can." Meg reached for the window.

Bea paused Meg's hand, poised to raise the window. "I need something from you. No, two things."

Her brow wrinkled. "What are they?"

"That you will ask for my help. For money…anything at all. Don't tell me what you need the money for. Just ask."

"Thank you." Her eyes were wary. "What else?"

"That you never spy on or pass along information about my father."

Her eyes narrowed. "We're one hundred miles apart. There's no question of that."

"No, you must promise me." Bea stared at her without flinching. This was important. A spy in the family threatened her father's reputation, his livelihood, and his freedom.

She covered her face with her hands. "How can I know what the future will bring?"

That's why I need your promise. "Please, Meg. He's a good man. Promise me you won't report anything you learn about him."

Meg lowered her hands and raised tormented eyes. "It's never been my intention to betray family. Please believe me. I'll never do anything to hurt you or Annie or Aunt Trudy. That's a promise."

"Meg wants to move into a boarding house?" Jay shook his head in wonder as he sank on the metal sofa in the Weston garden. "Our crowded city has grown expensive. Few boarding homes have empty rooms. I fear she'll search for some time."

"She's welcome to stay here as long as she wants," Bea said. "But I doubt it will be long. Remember that families packed up their wagons before the battle at Seven Pines. They surely left vacancies." Bea's cream-colored fan hid her expression.

"True." He admired how the setting sun cast an auburn glow on her curls. "How did Aunt Trudy take the news?"

"Surprised. Perhaps hurt. Then she reiterated her invitation for her to remain here and pressed upon her that there's always room in her home for family. Meg cried at that."

"You're blessed with a family of sweet, strong, and loyal women."

"I am." Her eyes glowed.

Jay swatted at a bee hovering over red silk roses decorating her hat. "Pardon me. Just trying to protect my fiancée from danger."

"My hero." She laughed.

Her hero. It was what he most wanted to be. This loving, compassionate woman had agreed to become his wife only the day before. Amazing how fast dreams he never dared to indulge in had him walking on air today.

"Did you receive a telegram from Blanche or your mother today?" she asked.

"Actually, Phineas brought it to me at work. Mama reminded me that she was one of the matchmakers."

Bea's smile widened.

"Everyone is thrilled that you're joining the family." He clasped her hand to his chest. "Especially me."

"Oh, Jay, I never dreamed such happiness would be mine." She tilted her face up to his, inviting his kiss.

He gave her the lingering kiss the crowd at the picnic had denied him yesterday, then clasped her near to his fast-beating heart. He couldn't believe this warm, loving woman was to be his wife. The war hadn't won this one. "I love you, Beatrice Swanson."

She snuggled closer. "Beatrice Swanson Nickson sounds even better."

Jay didn't argue. He simply held her closer as she nestled against his chest and thanked God silently for answering his prayers.

Did you enjoy this book? We hope so!

Would you take a quick minute to leave a review where you purchased the book?

It doesn't have to be long. Just a sentence or two telling what you liked about the story!

Receive a FREE ebook and get updates when new Wild Heart books release: https://wildheartbooks.org/newsletter

Don't miss the next book in Spies of the Civil War series!

Byway to Danger

Chapter One

JUST OUTSIDE RICHMOND, VIRGINIA
THURSDAY, JUNE 26, 1862

"Confederate pickets up ahead." Meg Brooks, keeping her voice low, rubbed her fingers against the reticule hanging from her wrist. The hard metal of the loaded pistol calmed her, though it was scant protection against half a dozen men. Trouble from the men was unlikely, and she had shown her pass on many occasions since accompanying her cousin Beatrice Swanson to Richmond in February. Good thing Bea wasn't here today, for Uncle Hiram would not be pleased if Meg dragged his daughter into danger. She sank back against the buggy seat behind her two companions as if she hadn't a care. How she wished it were true. A battle had erupted nearby the day before, and another one seemed likely, if dust clouds from small groups of soldiers riding in different directions beyond those guarding the crossroad were any indication.

"I see them." Elizabeth Van Lew, a wealthy Richmond citizen with no love for the Confederacy, held back on the reins to slow the team pulling their buggy. She stared at the soldiers, absently patting her brown hair, which was arranged in a bun at the nape of her neck. As the oldest of the three women traveling on the Mechanicsville Turnpike, she had taken charge the last time they'd spoken to the guards on this road and seemed prepared to do so again. "Keep calm, ladies. Be ready to show your passes."

A slight gasp drew Meg's eyes to their companion, Eliza Carrington, a few years younger than Elizabeth, who was likely in her early forties. Mrs. Carrington's back stiffened. Meg wondered why Elizabeth's long-time friend had joined their errand when she was obviously fearful.

Pickets strode across the dirt road, blocking their path. "Halt." A soldier took charge and held up a hand while his other hand rested on the musket with the business end pointed downward.

"Whoa." Elizabeth stopped the open, two-seat vehicle. "Good day, gentlemen."

Meg eyed the blue chevron on the soldier's sleeve identifying him as an infantry sergeant. Her glance swept over the others—no insignia, so the rest were privates. Hot afternoon sun beat down on weeds and bushes beside the road that reached to a forested area just beyond. Lingering dust clouds flying from soldiers racing away on horseback moments earlier was the only sign they'd been in the vicinity. She didn't fool herself. With all the activity yesterday, more soldiers were certainly nearby.

"What's your business on this road?"

"We're visiting a friend in Hanover County." Elizabeth spoke with confidence.

Meg, admiring her friend's direct manner, maintained a calm demeanor. Elizabeth and Eliza were Southerners who lived in Richmond. Meg was from Chicago. Best to allow Elizabeth to answer the sergeant's inquiries and keep quiet unless directly spoken to.

"There was fighting at Oak Grove yesterday." The sergeant's glance flicked toward the east.

Meg figured the officer was younger than she at twenty-six, yet he spoke with authority. No novice here.

"Might be more fighting today." His gaze returned to sweep across the women. "Yankees are close."

It was a timely warning, for danger was near. Meg had faced a dangerous man before—not in battle but in her husband's family. Thomas's brother had been a menace to his whole family. As fearful as she was of getting caught in the crosshairs of battle, it was nothing to the danger she'd felt from her former brother-in-law. If she could handle Lance, she could handle Confederate pickets.

"We're not going to Oak Grove." Elizabeth handed him a slip of paper from her bag.

Meg extracted her pass from the reticule hanging from her wrist and gave it to the officer. Mrs. Carrington gave her pass to a waiting private.

"Everything is in order here." The officer returned them. "Not certain it's a good idea to go on."

"We're not afraid." Elizabeth gave him a nod. "You're a credit to your country. Our country needs more good men like you."

Meg, knowing Elizabeth's Unionist support, acknowledged that she actually hinted at a desire to see more men like him serving the *Union* army. Thankfully, he didn't know it.

He flushed and raised his hat at them. "Be careful, ladies."

The temporary blockade of pickets on the road cleared after his warning. Elizabeth, giving the officer a gracious nod, set the horses moving at a walk until they topped a small hill, where they picked up speed. On their right, the forest was farther away with a farmer's field of vibrant green cornstalks lining the road.

Meg, seated beneath the scanty cover provided by the vehicle's hood, immediately missed the shade the forest had provided. She swiped her face with a handkerchief. Blistering June heat wasn't entirely to blame for her discomfort, for blood surged through her veins at interactions with armed enemies.

"Well done, ladies." Elizabeth spoke only loudly enough to be heard over the horse's trotting hooves. "There may be more encounters before we reach John Botts's home."

Suddenly, a rider rode toward them at full speed. Elizabeth quickly navigated onto the tall grass to get out of the soldier's way.

"Something's happening." Meg tried to discern movement ahead through the dust cloud left behind by the rider already past.

"Look to the right, over by the tree line. Soldiers are leading their horses toward that pond by the forest." Mrs. Carrington peered toward a break in the tall, mature trees about fifty yards away. "Watering them in this heat, no doubt."

"Look there." Meg stifled a gasp. Five cannons were nearly hidden amidst a field of thigh-high cornstalks surrounded by at least two hundred Confederates. Some studied their muskets. Some counted the ammunition in their cartridge boxes. Others watched the women riding by. This was information she could pass on to her Union contacts. Unfortunately, there was no indication of the regiment or division. How many others remained out of sight in the woods beyond the field?

"Isn't it thrilling?" Elizabeth whispered. "Perhaps we'll see a battle this afternoon."

A shiver traveled up Meg's back. It was one thing to view battle smoke from a distant hilltop, as she had done the day before in Richmond. It was quite another to drive beside the soldiers in the field doing the shooting.

Cade Yancey, her new boss at the bakery where she worked, had tried to warn her of the danger, but the opportunity to acquire first-hand knowledge to pass on to her fellow spies in Washington City had proved irresistible.

Beyond that, she needed something to occupy her thoughts on this, the second anniversary of her husband's death.

Wiping sweat from his brow after drill practice in the sweltering heat, Cade Yancey stored his musket above the shelves on the hooks, which allowed it to rest horizontally. Most folks couldn't reach the weapon there without a chair, including his new baking assistant, Meg Brooks, yet Cade, a couple of inches above the six-foot mark, was taller than most folks he knew.

Floor boards rattled in his bakery. He sighed. Everyone in Richmond had become accustomed to the ground shaking, impacts from distant cannons. They all understood. Trouble was, recent battles had jaded their natural fear. Now, citizens watched nearby battles from hilltops and rooftops, ignoring the danger of having the Union army so near.

And Mrs. Brooks was out there in the thick of it, most likely. Cade blamed it all on Elizabeth Van Lew. She'd come by this morning and invited Meg—that was, Mrs. Brooks—to ride up the Mechanicsville Turnpike with her.

Cade had continued to knead his latest batch of bread as he'd listened unashamed to their whispered conversation in the front room, where all the baked goods were displayed for customers. His keen sense of hearing took in Miss Van Lew's excitement and Meg's less enthusiastic agreement.

At least one of them understood caution.

Still, she had agreed to go.

Worry gnawed at his gut. If fighting broke out in the widow's vicinity, she faced danger from stray bullets. If Confederate officers suspected her of being on a fact-finding mission, they'd arrest her as a spy.

For he knew that was her real purpose for living in Richmond.

His friend, Paul Lucas, had never told him Mrs. Brooks was a Union spy in so many words. No, the Unionists he knew in Richmond had learned to give such dangerous secrets indirectly. Hints. A certain look. A raised eyebrow in an individual's direction. Body language. So when Mrs. Brooks asked Cade for a job, Paul gave him a piercing look that said, "Trust her. She's one of us."

Cade might not completely trust Mrs. Brooks, but he did trust Paul. He had hired her nearly three weeks before. She had begun working in the bakery last week.

This morning, after Miss Van Lew left, he strode into the front room. "This isn't a good idea."

Meg's head jerked. "You heard?"

"Both armies are nearby." He propped his hand against the door jamb and leaned closer, searching her beautiful green eyes for some sign that sanity had returned.

"Yes, but three women should be safe enough traveling together." Her auburn curls, swept back with ivory combs, fell across her shoulders as she raised her chin. "Besides, we aren't heading in the direction as yesterday's battle."

"Armies move around." Cade shook his head. Her courageous determination sparked a twinge of admiration.

"I know, but Miss Elizabeth is set on going. " Her brow wrinkled as she studied him. "I'm looking forward to a drive. For weeks, I've done little beyond..." Her cheeks blotched bright red. "Please don't tell my cousin where I went if she comes by the bakery looking for me. She'll worry."

"Never." She didn't completely trust him either, though Miss Van Lew must have vouched for his loyalty. Meg never gave details of her previous activities. That was good. He knew nothing about them. There was plenty she didn't know about him, and he planned to keep it that way. The less she knew, the less danger she faced. "We must protect one another."

They stared at each other. Meg's glance dropped first. "Yes, well, Miss Elizabeth will bring a buggy by for me. Is it all right if I leave early?"

Nice of her to finally ask. Businesses closed in Richmond at two o'clock for the time being to allow the home guard to drill. "I'll not stop you, if your mind is set on it. I'd accompany you if not for drilling practice."

Meg's eyes had widened. "I never thought… It's good of you to…" She looked down at her clenched hands. "We'll return by evening, so I will be here in the morning."

What was she not saying? That she hadn't expected him to be concerned for her safety? He had watched her go, wishing he had the authority to stop her. Yet didn't they all take dangerous chances?

Now, he strode to the big window and stared at the northwestern horizon. Puffs of gray smoke showed the direction of battle. Deserted streets told him that many watched the battle from hilltops surrounding Richmond. Since nothing was in the oven this hot afternoon, he'd join them. Maybe he'd be able to figure out if Meg was in danger.

He strode outside. Childish laughter snagged his attention. That might have been his son, had God willed differently.

Cade shuttered his mind against the pain. He was almost thankful that Meg gave him something else to think about. *Be careful, Mrs. Brooks.* He didn't voice the words as he locked the door. He'd learned to remain silent.

Too dangerous to do otherwise in the Confederate capital.

Meg huddled near the window of the Botts's family farm with her companions. Sounds of the cannons roaring initially robbed them of a need for conversation.

The Richmond ladies had been invited into the Congressman's home, where they sat in the parlor with his wife and adult daughters. They all watched smoke billowing on the horizon. The gray-haired former Congressman Botts had been arrested in March for no greater crime than supporting the Union. That he had spent two months in solitary confinement both angered and troubled Meg. Such a fate might happen to any Unionist.

Artillery continued to thunder its murderous intent. Meg gripped the cushion of her chair and riveted her attention toward the sky, ready to bolt should a cannon rip toward them. The battle was within a mile or two of the farm—far too close for any sense of safety.

Yet the information Meg had gleaned might help the Union in upcoming battles, a sacrifice worth the danger for a childless widow. She kept a sharp eye on the horizon for soldiers in retreat, a bad sign for those watching at the window no matter the side running for shelter at the home. Thankfully, no one ran toward them.

Finally, the thunderous rumble slowed. Meg sat on the edge of her high-backed chair, watching the field for movement. Nothing.

No way to know which side was winning, yet the diminishing noise of battle released some of the fear palpitating in the room.

They spoke in hushed tones of what they'd heard, though all eyes were riveted toward the battle smoke creeping toward them.

"How thrilling to be so close to the fighting." Elizabeth's eyes gleamed.

Her excitement to be so near the fighting wasn't shared by everyone in the former representative's family. One of the girls, who all wore their brown hair gathered at the nape of their necks, jolted every time the window rattled from a shell's impact in the distance.

"I expect I could do with a little less excitement." The former representative patted his wife's hands, which were squeezed together in a prayerful pose so tight that her knuckles showed white.

"No doubt your family had enough worries this spring. How were you treated in prison?" Elizabeth scooted to the edge of her seat.

"They came without warning in the middle of the night." Sighing, he glanced at his wife, whose face tightened. "I was held at McDaniel's Negro Jail."

Meg, guessing that the Congressman was near sixty, shook her head at the indignity of the unwarranted arrest. Several other citizens were arrested without warrants around the same time, for no greater crime than being a Union supporter.

"The jail is now called 'Castle Godwin' after the prison's commander." Elizabeth stared at the gray smoke cloud billowing over the tree line. "I despaired of your release. How did it come about?"

"Captain Alexander told me he'd release me in exchange for my service as a brigadier general in the Confederate army." He waved his hand in disgust. "I'd not go against my own principles in such a manner. Finally, I agreed not to publish any more letters against the Confederacy in exchange for my release. It's good to be back with my family." He smiled at his daughters.

Mrs. Botts sandwiched his hand in hers.

Meg's heart constricted. Mrs. Botts still had her husband. While Meg... No, she wouldn't allow her thoughts to go there. It was the anniversary bringing her grief to the surface.

"The battle appears to be in the vicinity of Beaver Dam Creek." Congressman Botts turned his attention to the northeast.

"Think we're winning this one?" His wife scooted her chair closer to her husband. Whether she sought comfort or gave it was unclear.

"I asked one of the pickets who stopped us how the battle was going." A look of derision crossed Elizabeth's face. "In his opinion, the Confederates are whipping up on us."

"Perhaps, in this instance, they are." Meg spoke in a soothing tone. "Yet I believe events will turn in our favor eventually."

"Is it my imagination"—Mrs. Carrington's brow furrowed as she stared out the window—"or is the fighting becoming sporadic?"

Meg realized she was right. The floor didn't shake. Nor did the window rattle.

"I believe you're right." Elizabeth's eyes widened.

"Ladies, if you are determined to return today, I believe you must take advantage of this lull." Their host rose to his feet. "Confederate soldiers are near, but the battle is not coming from the Mechanicsville Turnpike."

"Yes, let's do leave now." Meg pushed the drawstrings of her reticule further up her wrist. There had been no need for a shawl in this heat. "We'll be back in the city well before sundown."

"A wise suggestion." Mrs. Carrington touched Elizabeth's sleeve. "I don't feel comfortable remaining this close to the musketry."

Meg was ready to return to Richmond—now that she had information to pass on. She stared at Elizabeth, who had secured the vehicle for the day's travel, hoping she agreed.

"It's such a thrill to be close to the thick of things. I feel there's more to be seen." Elizabeth sighed. "Since you both want to leave, we will go."

Meg gave a crisp nod, fearing if she showed any sign of faltering they'd be there overnight. She must be at work shortly after dawn.

They were on the road back within a quarter hour.

Canteens, bedrolls, and knapsacks lay in trodden-down fields where Meg remembered seeing soldiers a few hours earlier. The men might have advanced toward the battle, or they might be lined up, awaiting orders.

Lone riders on horseback cantered through the fields and along the turnpike at various points. A picket in high spirits checked their passes at an intersection. Was he happy to be near the battle? Or had the battle gone well for the Confederacy?

As they neared Richmond, she began to compose a letter in her mind.

Elizabeth turned onto Eighteenth Street, where Meg's boarding house was located. "Why, I do believe that landau belongs to Trudy Weston. I recognize her driver."

Meg craned her neck. Her cousin, Bea Swanson, stepped from the open carriage, her face tense and worried as she grasped her fiancé's hand. It was only then that Meg remembered an aunt of Bea's lived near Mechanicsville.

Get all the books in the Spies of the Civil War Series!

Book 1: Avenue of Betrayal

Book 2: Boulevard of Confusion

Book 3: Byway to Danger

ABOUT THE AUTHOR

Sandra Merville Hart, award-winning and Amazon bestselling author of inspirational historical romances, loves to discover little-known yet fascinating facts from American history to include in her stories. Her desire is to transport her readers back in time. She is also a blogger, speaker, and conference teacher. Connect with Sandra on her blog, https://sandramervillehart.wordpress.com/.

ACKNOWLEDGMENTS

Thanks to my agent, Joyce Hart, for her perseverance, guidance, and friendship for the past several years. Thank you, Joyce, for your persistent determination to get this Civil War book series in front of a publisher who is excited to bring it to publication.

I'd also like to thank Misty Beller, Robin Patchen, and the team at Wild Heart Books for helping to make this book the best it can be. Everyone at Wild Heart Books has been both professional and gracious to me. I look forward to working with them on the next book in the series!

As always, historical novels require much careful study to add authenticity. My research trips to Richmond were amazing. When I told Chuck Taylor and Ned Krack of the Richmond Railroad Museum that I was researching travel from Washington DC to Richmond in 1862, they immediately began searching their resources. I appreciated their help.

The staff at the American Civil War Museum was especially helpful. I had done much research by the time of my visit. They answered some specific questions that I hadn't been able to find. Thanks to all of them for their help.

The Historic St. John's Church where Patrick Henry gave his famous "Give me liberty or give me death" speech is part of my story. I had a wonderful and educational visit to this Richmond church. The staff there answered my questions and pointed out helpful charts and information. My husband and I attended a special service there as well as a church tour. It was inspiring to be in a location steeped in history. Thanks for the warm welcome by the entire staff.

Thanks to family and friends for their continued support.

Thank you, Lord, for giving me the story.

AUTHOR'S NOTE

When the time came to write a new Civil War novel series, I wanted to focus on an aspect of those turbulent years beyond the battles. History reports that a surprising amount of spying happened in the capital cities of Washington DC (largely known then as Washington City) and Richmond, Virginia, which was the Confederate capital.

Much has been written about Allan Pinkerton and his agents. Pinkerton's agents were loyal to the Union and were active in several southern cities, including Richmond. Pinkerton moved his headquarters from Chicago to Washington DC early in the war. His influence was greater early in the war and those connections touch this series.

Miss Elizabeth Van Lew was a wealthy Richmond resident and Union spy during the Civil War. Her mansion was located across from St. John's Church, which she attended. She and her mother sacrificed much to support Union soldiers. It was dangerous to publicly support the Union when in Richmond. Elizabeth's spy activities impact our characters.

Mrs. Rose Greenhow, a widow living in Washington DC at

the start of the war, was arrested for being a Confederate spy in *Avenue of Betrayal.* This historical figure built up a network of spies while living within blocks of President Abraham Lincoln at the White House. Rose's real-life story impacts the fictitious Swanson family in our series.

Confederate President Jefferson Davis made his home in the Confederate capital of Richmond, Virginia. He was inaugurated for a six-year term on February 22, 1862, an event attended by my fictional family.

General Clayton in my story was loosely inspired by General John Henry Winder, the man tasked with enforcing martial law in Richmond. History records him as a stern, gruff officer.

I found a wonderful book written by a Confederate soldier in the Twenty-first Virginia Infantry, *One of Jackson's Foot Cavalry* by John H. Worsham. This well-written book, originally published in 1912, provided details about marches, camps, and battles that Richmond soldiers in that regiment encountered. The hero of our book has a friend (fictitious name) in the regiment who keeps him informed of his regiment's activities.

I visited the impressive Fort Monroe in Virginia as part of my research. Constructed from 1819 – 1836, its rich history inspired me, leading me to include it in two books of this series. This important fort on the Chesapeake Bay was under Union control throughout the Civil War.

St. John's Church in Richmond where Patrick Henry gave his famous "Give me liberty or give me death" speech is another historic location in this series. The church's history and its current staff inspired me during a research trip. Some characters in *Boulevard of Confusion* (Book 2) and *Byway to Danger* (Book 3) attend this church.

While I have focused on what happened in the capital cities, spying took place in other important locations. It required greater courage and daring to spy behind enemy lines.

I hope you enjoyed this story set in Richmond in the first half of 1862. I invite you to read the whole series. Turmoil and danger await our characters in *Byway to Danger,* the next book in the series set in Richmond in the second half of 1862.

Sandra Merville Hart

Want more?

If you love historical romance, check out the other Wild Heart books!

Marisol ~ Spanish Rose by Elva Cobb Martin

Escaping to the New World is her only option...Rescuing her will wrap the chains of the Inquisition around his neck.

Marisol Valentin flees Spain after murdering the nobleman who molested her. She ends up for sale on the indentured servants' block at Charles Town harbor—dirty, angry, and with child. Her hopes are shattered, but she must find a refuge for herself and the child she carries. Can this new land offer her the grace, love, and security she craves? Or must she escape again to her only living relative in Cartagena?

Captain Ethan Becket, once a Charles Town minister, now sails the seas as a privateer, grieving his deceased wife. But when he takes captive a ship full of indentured servants, he's intrigued by the woman whose manners seem much more refined than the average Spanish serving girl. Perfect to become governess for his young son. But when he sets out on a quest to find his captured sister, said to be in Cartagena, little does he expect his new Spanish governess to stow away on his ship with her six-month-old son. Yet her offer of help to free his sister is too tempting to pass up. And her beauty, both inside and out, is too attractive for his heart to protect itself against—until he learns she is a wanted murderess.

As their paths intertwine on a journey filled with danger, intrigue, and romance, only love and the grace of God can overcome the past and ignite a new beginning for Marisol and Ethan.

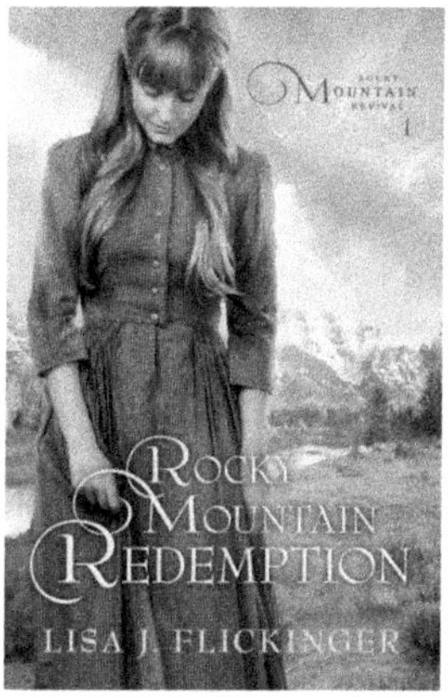

Rocky Mountain Redemption by Lisa J. Flickinger

A Rocky Mountain logging camp may be just the place to find herself.

To escape the devastation caused by the breaking of her wedding engagement, Isabelle Franklin joins her aunt in the Rocky Mountains to feed a camp of lumberjacks cutting on the slopes of Cougar Ridge. If only she could out run the lingering nightmares.

Charles Bailey, camp foreman and Stony Creek's itinerant pastor, develops a reputation to match his new nickname — Preach. However, an inner battle ensues when the details of his rough history threaten to overcome the beliefs of his young faith.

Amid the hazards of camp life, the unlikely friendship growing between the two surprises Isabelle. She's drawn to Preach's brute strength and gentle nature as he leads the ragtag crew toiling for Pollitt's Lumber. But when the ghosts from her past return to haunt her, the choices she will make change the course of her life forever—and that of the man she's come to love.

Lone Star Ranger by Renae Brumbaugh Green

Elizabeth Covington will get her man.

And she has just a week to prove her brother isn't the murderer Texas Ranger Rett Smith accuses him of being. She'll show the good-looking lawman he's wrong, even if it means setting out on a risky race across Texas to catch the real killer.

Rett doesn't want to convict an innocent man. But he can't let the Boston beauty sway his senses to set a guilty man free. When Elizabeth follows him on a dangerous trek, the Ranger vows to keep her safe. But who will protect him from the woman whose conviction and courage leave him doubting everything—even his heart?

CPSIA information can be obtained
at www.ICGtesting.com
Printed in the USA
LVHW081349200422
716260LV00021B/162

9 781942 265580